PRAISE FOR
THE ICON THIEF

"Alec Nevala-Lee comes roaring out of the gate with a novel that's as thrilling as it is thought-provoking, as unexpected as it is erudite. *The Icon Thief* is a wild ride through a fascinating and morally complex world, a puzzle Duchamp himself would have applauded. Bravo."
— national bestselling author Jesse Kellerman

"Alec Nevala-Lee is no debut author; he must have been a thriller writer in some past life. This one has everything: great writing, great characters, great story, great bad guy, and a religious conspiracy to boot. *The Icon Thief* is smart, sophisticated, and has enough fast-paced action to keep anyone up past midnight. I'm jealous."
— *New York Times* bestselling author
Paul Christopher

"Twists and turns aplenty lift this thriller above the rest. From the brutal thugs of the Russian mafia to the affected inhabitants of the American art world, this book introduces a cast of believable and intriguing characters. Add a story line where almost nothing is as it first appears, and where the plot turns around on itself to reveal startling contradictions, and the result is a book that grips and holds the reader like a vise. I devoured it in a single sitting."
— national bestselling author James Becker

THE
ICON
THIEF

✠

ALEC NEVALA-LEE

A SIGNET BOOK

SIGNET
Published by New American Library, a division of
Penguin Group (USA) Inc., 375 Hudson Street,
New York, New York 10014, USA
Penguin Group (Canada), 90 Eglinton Avenue East, Suite 700, Toronto,
Ontario M4P 2Y3, Canada (a division of Pearson Penguin Canada Inc.)
Penguin Books Ltd., 80 Strand, London WC2R 0RL, England
Penguin Ireland, 25 St. Stephen's Green, Dublin 2,
Ireland (a division of Penguin Books Ltd.)
Penguin Group (Australia), 250 Camberwell Road, Camberwell, Victoria 3124,
Australia (a division of Pearson Australia Group Pty. Ltd.)
Penguin Books India Pvt. Ltd., 11 Community Centre, Panchsheel Park,
New Delhi - 110 017, India
Penguin Group (NZ), 67 Apollo Drive, Rosedale, Auckland 0632,
New Zealand (a division of Pearson New Zealand Ltd.)
Penguin Books (South Africa) (Pty.) Ltd., 24 Sturdee Avenue,
Rosebank, Johannesburg 2196, South Africa

Penguin Books Ltd., Registered Offices:
80 Strand, London WC2R 0RL, England

First published by Signet, an imprint of New American Library,
a division of Penguin Group (USA) Inc.

First Printing, March 2012
10 9 8 7 6 5 4 3 2 1

PUBLISHER'S NOTE
This is a work of fiction. Names, characters, places, and incidents either are the
product of the author's imagination or are used fictitiously, and any resemblance to actual persons, living or dead, business establishments, events, or lo-
cales is entirely coincidental.
    The publisher does not have any control over and does not assume any re-
sponsibility for author or third-party Web sites or their content.

CONTENTS

There is no solution because there is no problem.
—Marcel Duchamp

PROLOGUE

In Russia, the outlaw is the only true revolutionary. . . .
The outlaws of the forests, towns, and villages . . .
together with the outlaws confined in the innumerable
prisons of the empire . . . constitute a single, indivisible,
tight-knit world. . . . In this world, and in it alone, there
has always been revolutionary conspiracy. Anyone in
Russia who seriously wants to conspire, anyone who
wants a people's revolution, must go into this world.

—Mikhail Bakunin

Andrey was nearly at the border when he ran into the thieves. By then, he had been on the road for three days. As a rule, he was a careful driver, but at some point in the past hour, his mind had wandered, and as he was coming over a low rise, he almost collided with two cars that were parked in the road ahead.

He braked sharply. The cars were set bumper to bumper, blocking the way. One was empty; the other had been steamed up by the heat of the men inside, who were no more than shadows on the glass. A yellow field stretched to either side of the asphalt, flecked with mounds of debris.

Andrey waited for what he knew was coming, barely aware of the music still pouring from his cassette deck. As he watched, the door of one car opened, disclosing a figure in a fur cap and greatcoat. It was a boy of twelve or so. His rifle, with its wooden buttstock, seemed at least twice as old as he was.

As the boy approached, Andrey reached into a bag on the floor of the van, removing a fifth of vodka and a carton of Bond Street Specials. He rolled down his window, allowing a knife's edge of cold to squeeze through the gap. As he handed over the tribute, something in the boy's eyes, which were liquescent and widely spaced, made him think of his own son.

The boy accepted the offering without a word. He was about to turn away, rifle slung across one shoulder, when he seemed to notice the music. With the neck of the bottle, he gestured at the cassette deck. "What band?"

Andrey did his best to smile, painfully aware of the time he was losing. "*Dip Pepl.*"

The boy nodded gravely. Andrey watched as he carried the vodka and cigarettes over to the other car, speaking inaudibly with the man inside. Then the boy turned and headed back to the van again.

Andrey slid a hand into his pocket, already dreading what the thieves might do if they asked to search the vehicle. Withdrawing a wad of bills, he peeled off a pair of twenties and held them out the window. When the boy returned, however, he waved the cash away and pointed to the stereo, which was singing of a fire on the shore of Lake Geneva: *We all came out to Montreux*—

"Cassette tape," the boy said with a grin. "*Dip Pepl.* You give it to me, okay?"

Andrey's face grew warm, but in the end, he knew that he had no choice. Smiling as gamely as he could, he ejected the cassette, silencing the music, and handed it to the boy, who pocketed the tape and went back to his own car. A second later, the thieves pulled over to the road's scalloped edge, clearing a space just wide enough for Andrey's van to slip through.

Easing the van forward, Andrey drove through the gap, keeping an eye on the thieves as he passed. Once they were out of sight, he exhaled and took his hands from the wheel, flexing them against the cold. Reaching up, he lowered the sun visor, glancing at the picture of the woman and child that had been taped to the inside. After a moment, he raised the visor again and turned his eyes back to the road.

The following morning, unwashed and weary, he arrived at a town on the river Tisza. Studying the ranks of buses preparing to cross over to Hungary, he saw a familiar face. The driver seemed pleased to see him, and was especially glad to load a cardboard box from Andrey's van into the back of his bus.

Andrey followed the bus across the border. At the customs checkpoint, he said that he was a businessman looking for deals in Hungary, which was true enough. Sometimes the officers wanted to chat, but today, after a cursory search, they waved him through without a second glance.

Driving slowly through the countryside, he caught sight of the bus parked at a roadside restaurant. The driver was leaning against the wheel well, smoking a cigar, which he ground out at the van's approach. The package in the rear was untouched. Handing the driver a carton of cigarettes, Andrey loaded the box into the van again. Back on the road, his mood brightened, and it grew positively sunny when, in the distance, he saw the city of Budapest.

He drove to a hotel on Rákóczi Road. In his room, he locked the door and set the box on the bed. The lid was secured with tape, which he sliced open. On top, there lay a loaded pistol, which he set aside, and ten rectangular objects wrapped in newspaper. Nine were icons taken from churches and monasteries throughout Russia, depicting the saints of a tradition in which he no longer believed.

The last painting was different. Andrey unwrapped it gently. It was no larger than the icons, perhaps twelve by eighteen inches, but it was painted on canvas, not wood. It depicted a nude woman lying in a field, her head gone, as if the artist had left it deliberately unfinished. Her legs were spread wide, displaying a hairless gash. In one hand, upraised, she held a lamp of tapered glass.

Andrey studied the painting for a long moment, stirred by feelings that he could not fully explain, then wrapped it up again. Casting about for a hiding place, he finally slid it under the bed, in the narrow gap behind the frame, which was just wide enough to accommodate the slender package. He put the gun back in the box, along with the icons, and went, at last, into the bathroom.

The shower stall was no larger than a phone booth, and the water took three minutes to grow warm, but by the time he climbed beneath the spray, it was steaming. Closing his eyes, he allowed his thoughts to wander. After the exchange, he would replace his lost cassette and buy ten kilos of the best coffee, five to sell, the rest to bring home. Even his son could have a taste.

He was still thinking about coffee when he emerged

from the shower, naked except for the towel cinched around his waist, and saw the man who was waiting for him in the next room.

Andrey froze in the doorway, drops of water falling onto the rug. The man, a stranger in a corduroy suit, was seated before the louvered window. He was very thin. Although his age was hard to determine, he seemed to be in his early thirties. Behind his glasses, which gave him a bureaucratic air, his eyes were black, like those of a nomad from a cold and arid land.

"My name is Ilya Severin," the stranger said, not rising from his chair. His legs were crossed, the tip of one polished shoe pointing in Andrey's direction. "Vasylenko wants to know why you're here so early."

Andrey felt beads of condensation rolling down his back. "How did you find me?"

"We have eyes on the road." Ilya hummed a few bars of music. *Smoke on the water, fire in the sky—*

Andrey thought of the gun in the cardboard box, which lay on a table across the room. "I was going to make the delivery. But—"

"But someone else wanted to see the icons." It was not a question, but a statement.

"Only to look. Not to buy. I was told that I could bring them to you as arranged." As he spoke, Andrey was intensely aware of his heart, which felt exposed in his bare chest. "He's from New York. I was never told his name."

Ilya's expression remained fixed. If this information was new to him, he did not show it. "All right," Ilya said, his voice affectless, as if he were reading off a column of figures. "Show it to me."

Unable to believe his luck, Andrey crossed the room,

the grit of the carpet adhering to the damp soles of his feet. As he approached the box, he forced himself to concentrate. He had never shot a man in his life, but had no doubt that he could do it. He only had to think of how much he had to lose.

He reached the table. Deliberately blocking it from view, he undid the flaps. The gun was at the top of the carton. Andrey reached inside, picking up an icon with one hand and the pistol with the other.

With his back to Ilya, Andrey said, "If you see Vasylenko, tell him that I am sorry." He turned around, the icon hiding the pistol from sight. "I meant no disrespect to the brotherhood—"

There was a muffled pop, as if a truck had backfired in the street. Andrey felt something heavy strike his chest. At first, he thought that the stranger had punched him, which made no sense, because Ilya was still seated. Then he saw the gun in the other man's hand. Looking down, he observed that a hole the size of a small coin had been drilled into the icon that he was holding.

Andrey fell to the floor, the towel around his waist coming loose. He tried to raise his pistol. When he found that he could no longer move, it seemed deeply unfair. He made an effort to picture his son, feeling dimly that it was only right, but could think of nothing but the painting under the bed, the headless woman lying in the grass. It was the last thing that he remembered.

As soon as Andrey was dead, Ilya, whose other name was the Scythian, rose from the chair by the window. Kneeling, he pried the icon out of the courier's hands, looking with displeasure at the damage to the wood. He put the icon back into the box, then left his gun next to the body.

Ilya sealed the carton and tucked it under his arm. He glanced around the room, asking himself if he had forgotten anything, and concluded that he had not. Leaving through the door, he was gone at once. Under the bed, the headless woman lay, unseen, at the level of the dead man's eyes.

I

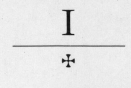

JUNE 19–28, 2008

The most intelligent man of the twentieth century.

—André Breton, on Marcel Duchamp

The strangest work of art in any museum.

—Jasper Johns, on *Étant Donnés*

1

The voice in her earpiece, with its soothing drone of encouragement, reminded Maddy of nothing so much as the sound of her own conscience. "Talk to me," Reynard said. "What do you see?"

"It's packed," Maddy Blume said, seating herself in the last row of the salesroom. Across the open floor, which was half the length of a soccer field, a temporary wall had been erected, with fifty rows of chairs set before the auctioneer's rostrum. The seat that she had been assigned was less prestigious than those in front, but it offered the best view of the crowd. "Our friends from Gagosian are here. And that girl who works for Steve Cohen."

"How about the skybox?" John Reynard asked through the earpiece. "Who's there?"

Maddy looked up at the balcony. "The curtain is drawn aside. Someone's there, but I can't see who."

She turned back to the crowd on the seventh floor of Sotheby's, where the chairs were rapidly filling. At the rear of the room, specialists from Christie's, the other great auction house in New York, were standing to observe the proceedings, while in a far corner, roped off from the rest of the audience, news crews trained their lenses on the ranks of attendees.

Across from her sat a trim Israeli, a cord running from one ear to the cell phone in his hands. She knew that he was buying on behalf of an investor in Tel Aviv, but at the moment, he seemed more interested in her legs. Maddy, who had blossomed only in her late twenties and, at thirty, sometimes feared that her face had been marked by recent disappointments, took a certain pleasure in this. She was a tall young woman with striking, almost sibylline features, and she always dressed carefully for these events, knowing that she was here to represent the fund.

As Maddy scanned the crowd, her eye was caught by a man in a navy blazer who was seated near the back of the room. His hair was short, emphasizing the blocky lines of his face, and his build was that of a boxer. "There's one guy who seems out of place. Cheap suit, bad shoes. He's on the phone. Maybe it's nothing, but it sounds like he's talking in Russian—"

"I'll make a note of it," Reynard said. As she watched the auctioneer mount the rostrum, Maddy knew that there was no need to spell out the rest. Russian money had been a primary driver of the art market for years, so any attendee with a Slavic appearance was automatically a person of interest.

"Good evening, ladies and gentlemen," the auctioneer said, dapper as always, placing a cup of water next to his hourglass gavel. "Welcome to the final auction of the summer season. Before we begin—"

As the auctioneer ran smoothly through the conditions of sale, Maddy wound up her call with Reynard.

"They're about to get started. I'll call you back as soon as our lot is announced."

"Fine," Reynard said. "I'll have Ethan standing by in case there are any surprises."

He hung up. Maddy removed the earpiece and turned to a fresh page in her notepad, checking to make sure that her phone was charged. Only then did she look at the canvas hanging at the front of the room. It was a painting of a headless woman lying in a field of grass, a glowing lamp in one raised hand.

A slide of the first lot of the evening, a nocturnal street scene by Magritte, appeared on a pair of screens. "Lot number one," the auctioneer said. "And I can start here with the absentee bidders. Two hundred and eighty thousand, two hundred and ninety, three hundred thousand. Do I have three hundred and ten?"

One of the clerks seated behind the counter raised his hand. He was one of only a few men stationed by the phones, with the rest consisting of the young women known as auction babes. Maddy, who had spent an uneasy year working these phones herself, knew the type well.

"The bid is with Julian at three hundred and ten," the auctioneer said, calling the clerk by name. "Do I have three hundred and twenty?"

A woman in the front row gave a slight nod. Bidding continued for another minute, with the woman, a buyer for a major corporate collection, prevailing for five hundred thousand. Maddy took notes on the bidding structure, using the shorthand that she and Reynard had developed. For the next forty minutes, as one lot followed the next, she wrote down paddle numbers and kept an eye on the faces around her, which, with their varying degrees of excitement or indifference, gave her an intuitive sense of each work's true value.

When her own lot drew near, she knew that countless eyes were watching her as well. Without particular haste, Maddy donned her earpiece and called Reynard. The fund manager answered at once. "Are we up?"

"In a minute," Maddy said, doing her best to sound calm. As she spoke, the previous slide vanished and another took its place, reproducing, on a greater scale, the image of the headless nude hanging at the front of the room.

"Lot fifty," the auctioneer said, pausing to take a swallow of water. "*Study for Étant Donnés,* or *Given,* by Marcel Duchamp, showing at my left. And I have outside interest here. Nine hundred thousand, one million, one million one hundred thousand, one million two hundred thousand. With the order at one million two hundred. Do I have one million three hundred?"

An auction babe raised her hand, rising from her chair in her eagerness. "Bidding!"

"Bid is at one million three hundred thousand. I have one million four hundred." The auctioneer said this without pausing, indicating that they had not yet reached the absentee bidder's limit. "Against you, Vicky."

The clerk whispered the new bid into the phone, listened to the response, then nodded. Her bidder would go higher.

"One million five hundred thousand," the auctioneer said. "I have one million six."

The process repeated itself several times. As had been previously arranged, Maddy, with Reynard on the phone, did nothing. She kept an eye on the Israeli seated across from her. His client was rumored to be a likely bidder, but he had yet to signal, which implied that either his price point had been exceeded or he was waiting for the right moment to jump in.

Maddy held back as the price climbed toward three million dollars, nearly twice the record for a Duchamp. Presale estimates had the study selling for between two and three million, but privately, the fund had calculated that the price might go much higher, given the mystery surrounding the work's reappearance. Finally, at three million one hundred thousand, the phone bidder exceeded the absentee bid. The auctioneer scanned the floor. "Do I have three million two hundred?"

Maddy looked over at the Israeli, whose paddle remained in his lap. "Tel Aviv isn't budging. I think he's been outbid."

"Duly noted," Reynard said. "This doesn't change our assumptions. Go for it."

Maddy raised her paddle, feeling a slight but pleasurable rush. The auctioneer smiled. "Bid is on my left at three million two hundred thousand. Do I have three million three hundred?"

The phone clerk checked with her bidder, then nodded. Turning back to Maddy, the auctioneer invited her to raise her bid. Although Maddy was more than ready, she forced herself to count off three seconds before nodding back. It was best to maintain a constant pace. By taking her time now, she would buy herself a few seconds to think as the bidding became more intense.

For a full minute, Maddy alternated nods with the clerk at the telephone. After every bid, she whispered the current price to Reynard, who did not reply. There was no need for him to issue instructions, at least not yet. According to their pricing model, she was free to go as high as five million dollars.

The bids reached four million and continued to rise. At four million two hundred thousand, Maddy sensed hesitation in her opponent. The clerk spoke into the phone, then waited. Finally, after a pause in which the crowd maintained an absolute silence, the clerk nodded.

"With Vicky at four million three hundred," the auctioneer said. "Against the lady at four million three hundred thousand dollars." He turned to Maddy, waiting politely for her response.

Maddy dutifully counted off three seconds, but knew that they were almost done. She was about to nod one last time, raising the bid to the final price, when the Russian at the rear of the room, who had been seated in silence since the auction began, raised his paddle into the air.

There was a murmur of excitement. The auctioneer was momentarily thrown off his rhythm, but quickly recomposed himself. "On my right at four million four hundred," the auctioneer said, moving slightly away from the rostrum. He glanced between Maddy and the phone clerk, extending his hands like a symphony conductor. "Do I have four million five?"

Maddy, flustered in spite of herself, whispered: "The Russian just made a bid."

"It doesn't matter," Reynard said, although he sounded surprised as well. "Take it to five million. We'll regroup from there."

"Okay," Maddy said, nodding at the auctioneer. Four million five hundred thousand.

Without hesitation, the Russian waved his paddle. Four million six hundred thousand.

The auctioneer, along with the rest of the room, was waiting for her response. Maddy counted to three. Before she could nod, however, the phone clerk raised her hand. Four million seven hundred thousand.

The Russian bid again. Four million eight hundred thousand. By now, the attendees were craning their necks to get a better look at the bidder, who was waving his paddle as if trying to swat a fly, his phone nowhere in sight.

"This guy won't stop at five million," Maddy whispered, watching as the phone bidder took it up to four million nine hundred thousand, only to have the Russian bid again. "What do you say?"

When Reynard failed to respond at once, Maddy knew that he was updating the pricing model with the latest information. At last, the fund manager said, "Okay. We can go up to seven million."

As soon as she heard this, Maddy caught the auctioneer's eye. The auctioneer gave her a smile, as if she had paid him a personal compliment. "Five million one hundred thousand," the auctioneer said, drawing out the syllables. "With the lady at five million one hundred. Do I have five million two hundred?"

The Russian, implacable, bid again. As Maddy studied his face, it seemed to her that he was bored, as if he felt that they were drawing out a process that had only one possible conclusion. Before she knew it, the price had blown past six million five hundred, more than twice the presale estimate. For the first time, she began to consider the possibility that she might lose.

She watched as the Russian bid seven million. As the auction babe conferred with her client, the room fell silent. Maddy sat still, heart thumping, waiting for Reynard to update the model.

Finally, after a long pause, Reynard sighed into the earpiece. "Too high. Let it go."

Maddy found herself blushing with shame, keenly aware of the news crews clustered in the far corner. She wondered if coverage of the auction would mention her by name. "All right."

"Don't let it get to you," Reynard said. "He doesn't understand the winner's curse."

But the lot wasn't over yet. As the auctioneer continued to play for time, repeating the current bid, drawing out the words for as long as possible, the clerk finally nodded. Seven million one hundred thousand.

Without a pause, the Russian raised his paddle in the air. Seven million two hundred.

Maddy, reduced to the status of a spectator, watched as the Russian and the clerk took the price even higher. As the bidding passed ten million and headed for eleven, the Russian raised his paddle and held it there, a lighthouse bid, signaling that he was willing to buy the painting at any price. It was a strange gesture, since the rival it was designed to intimidate wasn't even in the room, but it seemed to work. With the bid at eleven million, the clerk spoke into the phone, listened, and spoke again. The silence deepened, the room watching and waiting.

Finally, after a hush that seemed endless, although it could have lasted no more than a few seconds, the clerk shook her head.

"Eleven million dollars with the gentleman on my

right," the auctioneer said, relishing the moment. "At eleven million, are we all through? Fair warning at eleven million. Last chance, fair warning—"

The auctioneer rapped his gavel against its block. "Yours, sir, at eleven million. And your paddle number is?"

Before the Russian could read off his number, his voice was drowned out by a burst of applause. Maddy watched, drained, as the Russian was surrounded by members of the Sotheby's staff, who formed a protective circle as the news crews charged forward for a picture.

There was a camera in her purse, a piece of paper taped across the bulb to soften the flash. Switching it on, she took a picture of the Russian, who was handing his paddle to a representative of the auction house. It caught him with his face turned toward hers, arm extended, revealing a length of sleeve. When the flash went off, he glanced briefly in her direction. Their eyes locked. Then he looked away.

As the murmur of the crowd rose to a roar, Reynard shouted into her earpiece. "We need to fix our pricing model. And we need this guy's name." The fund manager's voice, normally so controlled, was cracking with emotion: "Find out who the buyer is. If he's as big as he looks, he's going to move the entire market, and we need to be ready for it. You understand?"

Maddy nodded, knees weak. She slid the camera back into her purse, then raised her eyes to the balcony. Behind the glass of the skybox, outlined against the light, a darkened figure was looking down at the salesroom. Before she could make out his face, he turned aside, drawing the curtain, and was gone.

2

Even before the patrolman said a word, Alan Powell knew what was coming. The officer, a swell of belly spilling over the belt of his uniform, studied Powell's badge with an air of amusement, then handed it back. "Who are you supposed to be?" the patrolman asked. "One of the Thundercats?"

Powell smiled at this quip, which had been popular among the Americans he had met so far. Not for the first time, he quietly cursed the man who had designed this badge, with its emblem of a snarling panther leaping across the globe. "No. Serious Organised Crime Agency. You know it?"

At the sound of his accent, which was incontestably out of place in Brighton Beach, the patrolman grinned broadly. Looking at himself through the officer's eyes, Powell saw himself for precisely what he was, an Englishman, nearing forty, with thick glasses and an alarmingly high forehead, who seemed stranded on the wrong side of the ocean, if not on the wrong planet altogether.

He was steeling himself for a second try when he saw Rachel Wolfe coming his way. Wolfe held up her own badge, which hung from a fine chain around her neck. "It's okay. He's with me."

The grin lingering on his face, the patrolman stood aside, allowing Powell to ascend the ramp to the boardwalk. As they approached the section that had been cordoned off, he turned to Wolfe. "Thanks. But this had better be important. I'm being deposed tomorrow, and I'm knackered enough as it is—"

"It takes a day to adjust for every hour of time change," Wolfe said. "You still have a day or two to go. Or is it nerves?"

"Something like that." Powell did not mention that when the phone at the hotel rang, he had been standing before his bathroom mirror, rehearsing the deposition that he was scheduled to give the following morning.

"Trust me, you'll be glad you came," Wolfe said. She was young, cute, and Mormon, a recent Quantico graduate, so new to the job that her pistol and package of bullets were still locked in a safe in her supervisor's office. In the days since his arrival, Powell had come to know her well, and she struck him as competent and tough, if exhaustingly straitlaced.

He looked down the boardwalk, which extended for two miles along the beach. It was an hour before dusk. From where he stood, he could see into the covered pavilions where old Russian men were playing backgammon in the dying light. To his left stretched a row of restaurants and clubs, their outdoor tables facing the ocean. Without surprise, he recognized the patio of the Club Marat.

A few steps ahead, yellow barrier tape had been strung on sawhorses, blocking off an area of the boardwalk twenty feet square. A crowd of onlookers had gathered around the uniforms who were guarding the scene. The golf carts used by boardwalk police were parked nearby.

Powell followed Wolfe to the sawhorses. "Any sign of our man from overseas?"

"Not yet. I've been watching the club all day. I haven't seen anyone we don't know." She lifted the tape, allowing Powell to duck inside. "Kandinsky and I were parked across the street when we noticed the crowd. When we saw what was going on, I figured you ought to see it."

Powell nodded absently as they neared the heart of the scene. A section of the boardwalk had been torn up, leaving a hole the size of a coffin lid. Standing around the opening were more uniforms and a hefty figure in plain clothes. Judging from his blue nitrate gloves and territorial air, Powell guessed that he was the detective who had caught the case.

Kneeling by the opening, Powell looked with detachment at what had been revealed. With the planks gone, the boardwalk's concrete supports had been exposed, along with the sand that came up nearly to the rim of the hole. As he regarded what was underneath, he understood why Wolfe had wanted him to see it, although he sensed that it would be nothing but a distraction.

A woman's headless body lay beneath the boardwalk, partly buried by drifts of sand. She was mummified. Dry heat had hardened her skin into something with the consistency of dehydrated beef, the flesh shriveled into a leathery toughness. Except for her panties and bra, once white but now a dirty yellow, she was naked. Her limbs, shrunken to the bone, seemed as fragile as a bat's folded wings.

Lowering his eyes, Powell felt another flicker of interest. The woman's hands were missing as well. Her arms were crossed over her chest, a pair of bloodless stumps where the hands should have been. The head had been removed at the jawline, leaving only the truncated cylinder of her neck, like a stout branch that had been pruned away. "Who found her?"

"A maintenance crew," Wolfe said. "One of the long boards was warping. When they pulled it up, this is what they saw." Turning aside, she led Powell to a spot several steps away. "Now do you see why I called?"

"I do," Powell said. He took a moment to clarify the situation in his own mind. Removal of the head and hands, while far from conclusive, was typical of *mafiya* killings. "You think that Sharkovsky was involved?"

"We know that he sometimes runs prostitutes," Wolfe said, glancing at the club behind them. "A lot of girls come through here. If one of them died, it wouldn't surprise me if he hid her under the boards."

"Maybe." Removing his glasses, Powell took out his handkerchief and polished the lenses one at a time. "We need to tread carefully. If the police go after Sharkovsky, he'll change his routine."

"If you're worried about this, you should talk to Barlow. He's the only one who can put a homicide investigation on hold."

Powell, putting his glasses back on, was about to reply when it occurred to him that there was another point that deserved further examination. Ducking beneath the tape, he headed for the officer who had met him on his arrival. The patrolman did not seem particularly receptive to his approach, but his manner thawed slightly at the sight of Wolfe. "Something I can do for you?"

"The sand," Powell said. "It comes up to the boards. Is it the same everywhere?"

"Under the boards?" In the patrolman's mouth, the word *boards* sounded like *bawds*. "Depends. On this stretch, sure, the sand comes all the way up. Eight foot deep, in some cases."

"So you can't walk under the boards," Wolfe said, understanding the problem at once. If the sand went all the way to the top, it would have been impossible to carry the body to where it had been found.

"Nope, no room," the patrolman said. "Of course, there used to be. When I first got on this beat, you could walk under the boards for miles. That was before the Army Corps of Engineers extended the beach. To keep out the homeless, we fenced off the rear of the boardwalk. And then the sand took it back." He paused. "But if you've got an open fence, like a chain link, the sand on the wind just blows through, instead of piling up under the boards. So in those places—"

Before the officer had finished, Powell was heading down the ramp to the parking lot, which gave him a view of the space beneath the boards. The boardwalk here was eight feet off the ground, sealed off by a wire fence that would allow blown sand to escape. As the others followed, he observed that the ground under the boards was clear, with a good seven feet of headspace.

To his right, there was a newer section of fence, with dense green mesh hung across the wire links. Beyond it, a concrete wall formed one edge of the parking lot. Here, where the fence and the wall created a solid barrier, the sand had accumulated in increasingly larger drifts. A few yards later, it was up to the boards. And it was there,

Powell saw, that the body had been found. "Can you open this gate?"

The patrolman glanced nervously at Wolfe, clearly thinking of the homicide detective standing above their heads. As a matter of professional courtesy, a detective owned his crime scene. "Normally, I'd say fine, but—"

"It's all right," Wolfe said, touching her badge. "Just a quick look, and we'll be out of your hair." Her tone was polite but persuasive, and Powell wondered, in passing, if she had learned it as a missionary.

"Well, okay," the patrolman said doubtfully. Taking out his key ring, he unlocked the gate, which keened on rusted hinges. As they went under the boards, Powell could barely make out the concrete supports, where drifts of sand, no higher than a few inches, had gathered against the pillars. Through the gaps between the planks, regular lines of light fell against the uneven ground.

Pulling the flashlight from his belt, the patrolman handed it to Wolfe, who switched it on, casting its beam against the wall of sand to their right. Examining it, Powell saw that a considerable problem remained. "It's impossible. We're ten feet from where the girl was found, but the sand is already above our heads. So how did our guy bring the body as far as he did?"

Wolfe studied the sand blocking their way. "Maybe the sand wasn't here at the time."

"Exactly." Powell went back to the fence. He noticed again that part of it was newer than the rest, with green plastic mesh covering the links. Because this section was less permeable to windblown particles, drifts of sand had piled up there until the area was impassable.

"When the body was dumped, this part of the fence

hadn't been installed yet," Powell said. "It was probably just a chain link that would leave the ground clear. If we can figure out when this section of fence was installed, we can narrow down the window of opportunity."

Powell turned away from the wall of sand and headed in the other direction. He found that he could walk without difficulty for a hundred yards. After another few steps, the sand reclaimed the space under the boards. Just before it became completely blocked, he came upon a second gate.

"This is where he came in," Powell said. "The entrance at the parking lot is exposed, but this is sheltered from the street. From here, he could drag the body to where we found it." He turned to the patrolman. "Can you open this?"

"Sure." Reaching through the fence, the patrolman opened the padlock and undid the chain. Emerging into the open air, which was sweet compared to the stink of the boards, they found themselves at the rear of a building set below the level of the boardwalk. An empty Dumpster sat nearby.

"So he brought the body here," Powell said. "Either he had a key for the padlock, or he cut through it with bolt cutters. He dragged the body inside and took it as far down the boardwalk as he could. But why didn't he just bury it here? Maybe he thought that if the body were found close to the gate—"

"—it would be connected to him," Wolfe said flatly. "Because look at where we are."

Powell followed her gaze. Ahead of him, a service door was stenciled with the name of a restaurant. "The Club Marat."

Wolfe switched off her flashlight. "If this is where the body was taken, our man went under the boards ten feet from Sharkovsky's back door. I don't know how they did things at the Met, but that's good enough for me." She handed the light back to the patrolman. "So what do we do now?"

"We talk to homicide," Powell said. "Find the fellow in the blue gloves and tell him what we've found. Try to be tactful."

"It's the only way I know how to be." Wolfe headed for the steps. "You coming?"

"In a moment," Powell said. He watched as Wolfe and the patrolman ascended the ramp to the boardwalk. Then he turned back to the club. Above the service entrance, a single light was burning.

Powell leaned against the metal railing of the steps, his arms folded. In the darkness, which was broken only by the row of lamps overhead, he was little more than a shadow. He continued to look at the Club Marat for a long time. Faintly, from inside the club, he could hear the low pulse of music.

3

Maddy arrived ten minutes early. As she waited at the bar, nursing a club soda and lime, she studied her face in the mirror. It was long and angular, like her body, the hair gathered back with a tortoiseshell clip. A stork's face. Growing up, she had always felt four inches too tall, and in the absence of a more attentive mother, it had taken her years to learn to dress in ways that complemented, rather than concealed, her natural length of bone.

A second later, the mirror disclosed another face. Turning, she saw a familiar figure sailing serenely across the restaurant floor, dressed in a peasant skirt and floral thrift store cardigan. Tanya was a librarian at the Frick, not yet thirty, her blue eyes blinking behind raven bangs. At school, they had not been particularly close, but Maddy had long since learned how useful this young woman could be.

Maddy rose, drink in hand. As she was approaching Tanya, she saw the final member of their party enter the room. He was handsome in a harmless sort of way, with a neat fauxhawk and an easy smile, and when Maddy went over to meet him, the warmth in her greeting was entirely genuine. Although he wasn't exactly her type, he was eager, ambitious, and a phone clerk at Sotheby's.

"I went to see the installation last year," Tanya was saying a quarter of an hour later. "It's in its own room at the Philadelphia Museum of Art. When you go inside, you see an antique wooden door set into a brick archway. At first, it looks like there's nothing else there. But if you go closer to the door, you see light coming through a pair of eyeholes. And if you look inside—"

"—you see a headless woman on a bed of dry grass," Maddy said. They were seated together at a table in the garden, among the wisteria and tin deer. "She's nude, and her face is missing or obscured. In one hand, she's holding a lamp. There's a forest with a moving waterfall in the background. Duchamp built the figure himself and covered it in calfskin. The illusion is perfect."

Tanya took a reddened sip of cranberry vodka. "And it felt like a betrayal. Duchamp's entire career had been devoted to conceptual art. He appropriated existing icons or objects and used them for his own purposes. The readymades. The urinal. The shovel on the ceiling. But his final work was grindingly representational. It made people wonder if he'd been toying with them all along."

The phone clerk leaned back in his café chair. He was wearing a pale pink shirt with a semi-spread collar, the lapels of his suit as peaked as a devil's ears. "So what's it supposed to mean?"

"Nobody knows," Maddy said. "Duchamp worked on it in secret for at least twenty years, claiming all the while that he'd given up art for chess. It was revealed only after his death, when it was installed at the museum without a word of explanation. And this new study upsets the established chronology. Previously, the earliest known study for *Étant Donnés* dated from the late forties, but the evidence suggests that this picture was painted more than thirty years earlier."

"Although it's hard to be sure," Tanya said. "It was found in Budapest, wasn't it?"

The clerk hesitated, martini in hand. "Yes. I can't give you the name of the seller, of course, but he's a legitimate dealer with a long history with the firm. Apparently he was browsing in an antique store, looking for nothing in particular, when he saw the painting hanging by a rack of samovars. The owner said it had been part of a larger consignment, but he didn't know where it was from—"

"And nobody knows where it went." Maddy glanced at the clerk. "Or almost no one."

The clerk smiled at her over the rim of his glass. "Even if I wanted to tell you, I don't have access to that information."

"Come on," Maddy said, suppressing an urge to strangle the clerk with his own pin-dot tie. "I know how the system works. There must be a copy of his passport or driver's license on file."

The clerk shook his head. "No more than two people know the buyer's identity. It isn't even something that the auctioneer would need to be told. You know how it is. Nobody wants to be responsible for leaking the name—"

"Of course." Maddy paused. She sensed that the clerk wanted to tell her something, but there was no need to force the issue. A year ago, the failure of her gallery in Chelsea had been avidly dissected at Sotheby's, creating a peculiar, illusory intimacy. It left perfect strangers with the impression that they knew her, which made them more likely to reveal something of themselves.

Finally, the clerk lowered his voice. "Listen. I've seen the bidder before. A few weeks ago, I was pulling a file at client services when I saw him talking to a girl at the front desk. He took a huge stack of Russian art catalogs, and before he left, he *tipped* her fifty bucks. Typical Russian."

"At least they tip well." Maddy studied the slush in her glass. "Who was the girl?"

"Look, I've said too much already." The clerk drained his martini. "Why do you care, anyway? If you're hoping to cut a deal with the buyer—"

"That isn't what we want," Maddy said. "At this price, we have no further interest."

Tanya finished her drink. "Quality counts, price doesn't. Isn't that what Ruskin said?"

"Ruskin also hyped Turner canvases while selling them on the side. In the financial world, he'd be guilty of insider trading." Maddy smiled. "It isn't hard to see why this painting set a record. Duchamp is the most influential artist of the twentieth century, so any unknown work would have caused a sensation. But if I've learned nothing else in this business, it's that price counts. Most buyers overpay. And masterpieces tend to underperform."

This was a line from an investor meeting that she had seamlessly appropriated as her own. As the table fell into silence, she remained aware of the clerk's curiosity about herself and the fund. Looking into his face, she saw that he was, in fact, rather attractive. A year ago, she might have been tempted to pursue this inclination, but these days, her solitude felt like the only thing that was entirely hers.

When the check came, she paid it, implying that the fund would be glad to pick up the tab. Outside the restaurant, they stood in an awkward circle until the clerk, taking a hint, headed off alone. "He likes you," Tanya said as soon as the clerk was out of earshot. "If I were you, I'd go for it—"

"Never date a man who uses more product than you do." Maddy watched the back of the clerk's fauxhawk wander up the block, feeling an odd twinge of regret, then turned to Tanya. "I have a job for you."

Tanya went to the curb, scanning the street for a cab. "What do you have in mind?"

"I'm going to send you a picture of the Russian from last night's auction. There's a symbol on his cufflink. A red circle. I was hoping you could tell me what it means. I'd do it myself, but I don't have the time. And you're the only person in New York who is better at this sort of thing than I am."

"I'll do what I can," Tanya said. Because her salary at the Frick did not come close to covering her student loans, she was usually open to whatever arcane assignments Maddy threw her way. "When do you need it?"

"Tomorrow morning. I have a meeting with Reynard, and I'd like to have something to show him." Maddy took a sealed envelope from her purse. "Your consulting fee. Courtesy of the fund."

Tanya took the honorarium, which, in reality, had come out of Maddy's own pocket, then slid into the cab that had pulled up at the restaurant. She looked back at Maddy, who had remained at the curb. "We didn't have a chance to talk tonight. You sure you're all right?"

"Nothing that a lifetime of therapy won't cure," Maddy

said. She smiled and waved at the departing cab, then continued on her way. Farther up the street, the clerk was walking alone. For a second, she toyed with the idea of catching up with him, but finally decided against it.

In her years in Chelsea, she would have taken a cab herself, but those days were gone for good. She glanced at her watch, the band of which had been invisibly repaired with a strip of electrical tape, and exhaled. As she headed for the subway, she felt drained but satisfied, her heels clicking rapidly against the sidewalk. It would be a long ride home to Brooklyn.

4

Ilya Severin, who sometimes still thought of himself as the Scythian, moved through the terminal without any sense of haste, surrounded by a cloud of other arrivals from London. In his slim brown suit, he might have been just another foreign tourist, although his luggage consisted of nothing but a suitcase barely large enough for three changes of clothes, along with a shoulder bag containing his hardbound copies of the *Midrash Rabbah* and *Sefer Yetzirah*.

He passed through an automatic door to the meeting area. At the edge of the crowd, a man in his early twenties leaned against one of the pillars that supported the terminal ceiling. He wore a tight shirt emblazoned with a double eagle, a medallion of the Virgin dangling from his neck. A bracelet and ponytail completed the picture. As Ilya drew closer, the man saw him at once, although his expression of mild boredom remained unchanged. "Severin?"

"Yes." Ilya inclined his head, but did not extend a hand. "And you must be Zhenya."

With his arms still folded, the man used his back to push himself away from the wall, then headed for the elevator bay at the rear of the terminal. He did not offer to take Ilya's suitcase. "Come with me."

Ilya fell into step beside Zhenya. The cool reception had confirmed his misgivings. Once, he would have been welcomed with respect, but ever since Budapest, he had been dealt another hand entirely.

They descended to the garage, where a sport utility vehicle was parked among the orange piers. Ilya lifted his suitcase into the rear compartment, keeping the shoulder bag. Zhenya slid behind the wheel and started the ignition. At once, the dashboard lit up like the console of a spaceship, and *blatnie pesni*, songs of the criminal underworld, began to pour from the speakers.

Merging onto the expressway, they followed a route that Ilya had studied beforehand. It was twelve wordless miles to Brighton Beach. When they left the parkway, it was early afternoon, the sun beating down on the ranks of row houses. Through his window, Ilya could see the same tradesmen and babushkas he had known as a boy, pushing carts along the sidewalk like the ghosts of his childhood.

They parked a block away from the club. As Ilya got out, his eye was drawn to the other man's ponytail, which would be a good place to grab in a fight. Ilya, his own hair cut short, had learned this lesson the hard way.

His suitcase rolled loudly across the pavement as they walked to the entrance of the Club Marat, which was marked by a faded awning. Inside, he found himself in a cheaply carpeted hallway lined with fake lampposts. The walls were draped in green nylon fabric, with tendrils of plastic ivy strung along the ceiling.

Rounding the corner, they reached a closed door. As

Zhenya knocked, Ilya saw that the walls were covered in countless photos of a man with a silver mustache, either standing beside local politicians or seated in massive trophy trucks that had been stripped and rebuilt for racing.

From inside the office, an unexpectedly soft voice responded in Russian: "Come in."

Zhenya opened the door. Inside, the office was spacious and dark, the walls covered with more pictures of trucks. In one corner stood a stack of unopened vodka cartons. The shelves were crammed with toys, dolls, and other tchotchkes, giving the room the atmosphere of a junk shop.

Behind the desk, his face illuminated by a computer screen, sat Valentin Sharkovsky. He was a compact man with the build of a former wrestler, which was exactly what he had been many years ago. His shirt, unfastened at the throat, displayed a tuft of gray chest hair and a chunky crucifix.

Sharkovsky rose gingerly from his chair. Watching his careful movements, Ilya saw the usual ailments of an aging athlete. The hand that the old man extended was all knuckles, but its grip was strong. "Flight was good?"

"Same as ever," Ilya said, ending the handshake first. As they moved to sit down, a tall man in his thirties, his hair dirty blond, limped into the room. His name, Ilya knew, was Misha. He, too, wore his hair in a ponytail, but unlike Zhenya's, it was gathered securely at the nape of his neck. The two younger men remained standing as Ilya spoke again. "Vasylenko sends his regards."

Sharkovsky sat heavily behind his desk. "It is good to hear of him. How is London?"

"Damp," Ilya said. He disliked small talk, and the men

standing behind his chair put him on his guard. He found that he could keep an eye on them in the glass of the largest picture, which displayed a line of the club's dancing girls. The two men were watching him closely as well, less out of hostility, it seemed, than curiosity, as if he were a member of some exotic species.

Sharkovsky straightened out the drift of papers on the desk, squaring the invoices and pay slips into neater piles. "Excuse the mess. It never ends. You know the restaurant business?"

"I've worked with Vasylenko at his club," Ilya said. "But he runs most of it himself."

"As he should. It teaches you something about the world. The most constant thing in life, I find, is loss of inventory. Shrinkage. Each month, it costs me five percent. A bartender sells shots out of his own bottle. A line cook leaves with two steaks in his pocket. You know what a night porter is?"

Another man might have thought that Sharkovsky was rambling, but Ilya knew that a *vor* never spoke without good reason. "He mops the floor, takes out the garbage, scrubs the ovens—"

"And he does it all alone." Sharkovsky stuffed the invoices into the top drawer of his desk, which he left open. "He stays for hours after the club is closed, and because he is by himself, he can do what he likes. If he finds a purse that a woman has dropped, he keeps it. Perhaps he even steals. And I overlook these things. Why? Because he does work that no other man would do. Like you."

The old man's eyes fell on Ilya's face. "When such a man does his job well, he is left alone. But if something goes wrong, it becomes harder for us to look the other way." He paused. "You came here to recover something. Yet you were the one who lost it in the first place. Why?"

Ilya, who had been expecting the question, was quick with his reply. "I was careless."

"I see. Which makes some of us wonder what happened in Budapest. The only other man who knows, it seems, is dead. And it would have been easy for you to return with empty hands, saying that the item you were sent to find was gone, when in fact you cut a deal of your own."

Sharkovsky reached into the open drawer. When his hand reappeared, it was holding a gun. Seeing it, Ilya's first impulse was to glance at the floor, which was carpeted. If it had been tile, he would have been more concerned.

The old man leveled the pistol at Ilya. "Carelessness may be an accident, but it may also be intentional. The Chekists have eyes in many places. It would not surprise me if they, too, had a hand in this. And it is not only because you are a *zhid*. Though I have never found it easy to trust such men, knowing that their loyalties were divided from the beginning—"

Ilya did not drop his eyes, but the word echoed through his brain, with all of its hateful associations. For a moment, he was no longer the Scythian, but a Jewish boy brawling in a schoolyard, books and papers spilled across the ground. "If you think I'm a Chekist, you should kill me now."

"But there is something that I want from you first," Sharkovsky said. "Something that you need to show me. I won't tell you what it is. You have one chance. And if you guess wrong—"

Sharkovsky struck the pistol once against the surface of the desk, making a hard rap.

Ilya allowed a second to pass. He was aware that this was nothing but theater, but reminded himself not to underestimate this man, who had cleared a space for business in this city through the force of his personality alone.

Undoing the clasps of his satchel, he removed a sheet of paper and set it on the desk. On the page was the image of a man's face, downloaded twelve hours ago from an art world website. The man held an auction paddle in one hand, his arm extended, exposing two inches of shirtsleeve.

"I came here for this man," Ilya said. "And I know that you can tell me where he is."

Sharkovsky regarded the picture for a wordless moment. Then he spoke quietly to the others. "Leave us alone, please."

Zhenya and Misha exchanged looks, then filed out of the office. As soon as they were gone, Sharkovsky lowered the pistol. Both it and the photo went into the open drawer of his desk. Taking a bottle from the same drawer, he poured a glass for himself. He did not offer any to Ilya. "When I implied that you were a Chekist, you grew angry. Do you hate them?"

Ilya knew that the reference to state intelligence was far from an accident. To call a thief a Chekist, even in passing, was to accuse him of the lowest kind of treachery, and it served only as a reminder of how far he had fallen. "Any man who values his freedom must hate the secret services."

"Spoken like a true thief." Sharkovsky stood and went

to the corner where the boxes of vodka were stacked. He turned back the rug, revealing a safe, which he opened with a twist of the handle.

Ilya studied the safe's contents. Most of the weapons were expensive pistols, plated in nickel and chrome, but he knew better than to trust a pistol that he had not maintained himself. As he examined the guns, he remembered their earlier exchange. *Zhid.* It had left him with a germ of anger, a seed that might grow unchecked if neglected for too long. He was careful to seem harmless, but he was not. He did not forget. And he did not easily forgive.

He picked out a revolver. A working gun. He held it up so that Sharkovsky could see.

"A careful man's choice," Sharkovsky said, closing the safe. His eyes flicked again across Ilya's face, their scrutiny cool and detached. "Good. But we'll soon find out how careful you really are—"

5

"We aren't trying to beat the market," Reynard said, his voice audible in the hallway outside the conference room. "If there's any confusion on that point, we can end this meeting right now."

Hearing these words, Maddy smiled as she headed inside, waving at the receptionist in the fund's pristine lobby. In contrast to the rest of the Fuller Building, which was a monument to Art Deco, the Reynard Art Fund had decorated its leased space in a style meant to evoke the white cube of contemporary galleries, resulting, at least to her eyes, in a sense of timeless sterility.

Inside the conference room, Reynard was seated at the head of a long steel table, next to Ethan Usher, one of the fund's quantitative research associates. Reynard's tieless collar bloomed from his sweater like a hothouse flower, his clothing studiously rumpled, while Ethan was decked out in quant casual, his math camp shirt tucked neatly into a pair of khakis. At the other end of the table sat two pension fund investors in identical pin-striped suits. As Maddy drew closer, something in their wary faces told her that the meeting was not going well.

When she reached the conference table, Reynard

broke off, favoring her with one of his celebrated smiles. "Glad you could join us. Gentlemen, this is Maddy Blume, our associate head of gallery relations."

Maddy shook hands with the visitors. "Don't worry about the title. I'm not sure what it means, either—"

She sat next to Ethan, who acknowledged her presence with a nod. Although he had been at the fund longer than she had, Ethan was a year younger, with a smooth forehead, green eyes, and sandy hair that always seemed two inches too long. Under the math shirt, his body was fit and trim, but there was a studied quality to his physique, as if it were the product of much solitary exercise. With his pale, impassive face, he struck her as something of an android, as if he were nothing but an extension of the machines that he understood so well.

Maddy turned her attention to Reynard, who offered a more interesting view. He was an improbably attractive man in his early forties, casually outfitted in sneakers and jeans, as if he were so used to wealth that he no longer felt the need to dress up in its presence. For all its informality, his appearance was carefully calibrated. Because it would be years before the fund could show any returns, its greatest asset, in the meantime, was his ability to sell himself. And at the moment, she thought, he was doing a rather indifferent job of it.

"Art lags behind other investments because of one fatal flaw," Reynard was saying. "It's beautiful. People buy art for reasons that are entirely irrational from the perspective of a disinterested investor. As a result, they're willing to pay a premium, which reduces their financial return by an average, we've found, of one percent per year. So why invest? It isn't because art provides outsized returns. It's because it can diversify and reduce risk in a larger portfolio."

"But we assume," the older of the two visitors said, "that you're looking for ways to increase returns as well."

"Of course. When I entered this business, I was an options trader. I didn't know the first thing about art, but I saw an opportunity to make the market more transparent. Our original intention was to track art transactions, which are notoriously opaque, and sell the data. Along the way, we discovered two things. First, the database was useful only if it was collaborative and free, so instead of keeping it private, we opened it up to the world. Second, we had information here that would give us an edge if we ever wanted to invest for ourselves. The size curve, for example—"

"It's a simplified illustration, but it gives you a sense of how we think," Ethan said. Taking a brochure, he opened it to a diagram of a straight line rising smoothly across the page. "Large paintings are generally worth more than small paintings by the same artist. Size equals prestige. A large Picasso sells for more than a small Picasso, so if you plot a painting's area against its price, you get a smooth line, with value increasing steadily with size."

"Although it falls off," Reynard interjected, "once the area exceeds the dimensions of a Park Avenue elevator."

Ethan pointed to an outlier on the graph. "And sometimes you see kinks in the curve. A Picasso sells for less than its position on the curve would indicate. Why? Maybe it's a bad painting, or damaged, or a forgery. Maybe the information is faulty. Or maybe it's a genuine bargain. And that's where we come in."

As the investors studied the graph, Maddy saw that

they seemed unconvinced. Glancing again at their pin-stripes, which reminded her that these were not imaginative men, she tried to redirect the conversation. "The approach is new, but the principle isn't. Pension funds have been investing in art for years. Instead of depending on the opinions of critics, though, we prefer to take a more systematic approach."

Reynard, seeing where she was going, quickly took up the thread. "Which only means that we're applying modern portfolio theory to the oldest asset class of all. Every sale is a source of information. We can identify drivers of investor behavior that no one else has ever noticed. If a painting is stolen, for example, prices for the artist's other works tend to increase—"

"Although it's the opposite, we've found, when the artist dies," Maddy said. "People assume that prices will go up after an artist's death, but that isn't true. Death locks in the oeuvre, making it impossible for new works to raise the estimation of existing pieces. As long as an artist is still alive, he has a chance to shape the story. Once he dies, though, the chance is gone."

"Except," Ethan said, deadpan as his eyes briefly lit on her own, "for Duchamp."

Maddy smiled, although she knew that the joke had been at her expense. After a few more questions, the visitors stood, saying that they would be in touch before the end of the month. As they walked the investors to the elevator bay, Maddy had trouble reading their expressions, which were more cordial than before, but remote. Reynard, by contrast, seemed assured that the meeting had been a success, and beamed broadly as he sent the visitors downstairs.

The smile lasted until the elevator doors closed. As soon as they were alone, Reynard turned to the others. "I'll update the tracker. We can lower the chance of an investment to thirty percent."

"Thirty percent," Ethan said glumly. "That puts us under our target for the quarter."

"A year from now, we'll be turning money away." Reynard headed for his private office. "As for the Russian, I'm making him a top priority. There are only twenty major buyers in the market at any time. If we can find out who he is and forecast his tastes, we can buy up the art he wants before he even knows it himself. And just so you take it seriously, there's a bonus involved. Ten thousand in deferred comp to whoever gets me his name first. Spread the word."

Maddy's face did not move, but on the inside, she felt a subtle tectonic shift. A year ago, after the failure of her gallery, a wave of debt had entered her life. Ten thousand dollars, while not enough to cancel her liabilities entirely, would buy her the time she needed to pay them off for good. "I'm on it."

Reynard paused at his office door. "One last thing. We need to fix our pricing model. We went in with a maximum of five million, and it sold for eleven. That's way outside the margin of error."

"I thought we agreed," Ethan said. "The buyer overpaid. It isn't the model's fault."

"It takes two to overpay. If he paid eleven, someone else bid ten million nine hundred. The model is wrong. I want to know why."

Reynard disappeared into the office. Parting ways with Ethan, who drifted off without a word, Maddy headed back to her own desk. As she sat down at her computer, she was tempted to open her personal balance sheet, but instead, she called up the picture that she had taken of the Russian. Enlarging it, she focused on the symbol on his cufflink, which had caught her eye earlier as a possible clue. According to Tanya, however, a red circle could mean anything or nothing.

Closing the file, it occurred to her that there was one possible source whom she had yet to call. After a moment's hesitation, she picked up the phone and dialed a number from memory. At the sixth digit, she paused, knowing that this amounted to a confession that she had run out of options.

In the end, she replaced the receiver in its cradle and got back to work. She would not call Lermontov yet. Later, if the situation became more desperate, she could swallow her pride. But not today.

6

Looking out at the hedge, Ilya was astonished. The hedge was eight feet tall and perfectly maintained, its sides so smooth that they seemed permanent, like a geographical feature that had been sculpted by the elements. When he thought of the effort required to grow this infinite hedge and keep it from wandering even an inch out of line, he was awed and angered by the wealth it implied.

Ilya glanced at Zhenya, who was slumped in the driver's seat, a toothpick wedged in the corner of his mouth. He had exchanged the tight shirt and silver medallion of the day before for a velvet tracksuit. Beneath the show of thug fashion, Ilya sensed that Zhenya was deeply uncomfortable in this Southampton neighborhood, ninety miles and a world away from Brighton Beach.

During the drive, he had been less subdued. "We all know about Budapest," Zhenya had said, shouting to be heard over the music. "Tonight, when we meet the Armenians, I'll have my eye on you, *keelyer*—"

Ilya had said nothing, knowing that any response would only be turned against him. Now, without warning, he got out of the parked car. "I'm going for a walk. Go around the house once and meet me at the beach."

Closing the door, he headed for the wall of green. Out of the corner of his eye, he saw Zhenya toss his toothpick aside and pull away from the curb. He waited as the station wagon, a concession to a low profile, eased itself into the deserted street. A moment later, it rounded the bend and was gone.

Once he was alone, Ilya went up to the hedge. Looking at the ground, he could see a flattened strip where the sidewalk had been. At some point, however, it had been torn up, allowing the lawn to run to the edge of the road. When he looked up, examining the places where the hedge grew less thickly, he found that he could make out what lay beyond. Aside from a few clumps of topiary and the white hexagon of a gazebo, he saw nothing but acre after acre of perfect grass.

Ilya headed for the main entrance, passing a sign that said *GIN LANE*. There was no gate, only a gravel driveway that curved sharply past the hedge, blocking his line of sight. He crossed to the other side of the street, hoping to get a better sense of the layout. As he reached the opposite curb, there was a splash of gravel, and a yellow jeep appeared on the driveway. Two men sat inside, wearing white polo shirts with red roundels embroidered on the left breast.

As the guards drove past, Ilya moved on. After thirty yards, the road curved and the shade trees vanished. To his left, the hedge continued as before. On his right, the houses disappeared, replaced by a pond trimmed with reeds and pitch pines. Ospreys floated on the calm surface of the water.

He arrived at the beach. At the end of the road, there was a small parking lot, but no sign of the station wagon.

Up ahead, the ocean was a pale expanse merging with the sky. The estate continued to the edge of the beach, and it was only here, he saw, that the hedge came to an end.

Ilya removed his shoes and stepped onto the sand, the grains warm between his toes. The sensation reminded him vaguely of something from his boyhood, a time when he had gone with his family to a place by the sea. He tried to cling to the memory, but it ran like water between his fingers and was lost.

Walking down the beach, he turned to regard the estate from the ocean side. Here, for the first time, he could see the house, which was twenty thousand square feet, its roof and siding shingled in cedar. It rambled as if its construction had been a huge improvisation, with many levels of gables and eaves.

He sat down in the sand, angling himself so that he could continue to observe the mansion. With the hedge gone, a dune planted with beach grass was all that separated the main house from the rest of the world. Across the dune ran a snow fence, its slats tilted at awkward angles, less for protection than to keep the sand from drifting. Otherwise, the house was completely exposed.

Waffled tire tracks were visible in the sand by his feet. In the distance, he saw a couple of teenagers in a luxury shooting brake. They had paused half a mile away, the hatch raised, their torsos muscular and brown. As he watched them drive farther up the beach, a plan began to form in his mind.

He heard the crunch of footsteps behind him on the sand. "So what do you think?"

As Zhenya sat down, Ilya said, "In my opinion, it probably can't be done. It's easier to steal from a museum than from a house like this. Museums don't pay for the art themselves, so they don't keep track of it. Private collectors are more careful, because they understand the cost of capital."

Zhenya seemed confused, as if he didn't understand the cost of capital, either. "So you're having second thoughts?"

Ilya overheard a sneer in his voice. Working with this man, he thought, was like sharing a bed with a wolf cub. Zhenya, like all enforcers, wanted to become a *vor*, without understanding what such a life truly entailed. When Ilya tried to imagine him growing into a man like Vasylenko, it seemed impossible.

A second later, it occurred to him that wisdom came from a lifetime of mistakes, and that Vasylenko, as a young man, might have been no less of a fool. Looking at Zhenya's pockmarked face, Ilya reminded himself that the material here was not entirely unpromising. Zhenya had spent a year in jail without turning state's evidence, an American jail, to be sure, but nothing to be dismissed out of hand. Which was to say that there was more to him than his ponytail.

Ilya turned back to the mansion on the beach. "We're sure that the painting is here?"

Zhenya sifted a handful of sand between his fingers. "Our eye on the inside says yes. If it isn't here now, it will arrive in time for the party. One hundred and fifty guests. Easy for us to get inside."

Ilya pictured the party, the glamour and money bright in the moonlight. "Security?"

"Six men. They will be focusing on the lawn. The house will be wide open. Twenty cameras on the grounds outside the house, but inside, except one covering the vault, no cameras at all."

Ilya considered this. The sun had grown low in the sky. If they were going to make it back in time for the exchange, they had to leave soon, but he didn't want to go just yet. He mentally retraced the journey that the painting had taken since Budapest. Instead of traveling the usual road, it had vanished for more than a year, and now it had resurfaced here, behind the endless hedge. But not for long. Because for all its protection by land, it was exposed from the sea.

"All right," Ilya finally said. "I'll do it. But I'm going to need a few things—"

7

When Maddy entered Reynard's office, he was on the phone, the shades drawn. As she took a seat, her attention was caught by what he was saying: "Well, the rate of return for dishonesty should be the same everywhere—"

The door opened again as Ethan came inside, carrying a laptop and a quad pad. Closing the door, he sat down across from Maddy. He seemed tired, although the exhaustion betrayed itself only as an additional level of opacity in his eyes, as if an internal screensaver had engaged.

On the phone, Reynard's tone shifted slightly. "Well, yes, we have checks in place to catch bad data. If a gallery enters false information into our database, it'll stand out like a sore thumb. Our algorithms are designed to flag any anomalies in an artist's price history. Sometimes it's an investment opportunity. Sometimes it's an honest mistake. And sometimes, more rarely, it's deliberate fraud."

A few seconds later, he managed to end the call, thanking the investor effusively for his time. Hanging up, he raised the window shade, allowing a rectangle of sunlight to fall across the Cindy Sherman centerfold above his desk. The photo, which depicted the artist lying on a linoleum floor, a scrap of newspaper in one hand, had always troubled Maddy, although she would have found it hard to explain why. Reynard sat down again. "So what have you got for me?"

After exchanging looks with Ethan, Maddy took the lead. She had already decided to save her most promising item for last. "A tip from Tel Aviv. The phone bidder at the auction was the Philadelphia Museum of Art. They own the finished version of *Étant Donnés*, and are planning an anniversary show for next year. Obtaining the study would have been a major coup."

"Not bad," Reynard said. "But it still doesn't give me the Russian. What else?"

Ethan held up his laptop. "I've compiled a spreadsheet of oligarchs from Russia or its former satellites. Cutoff is a billion dollars. I've managed to eliminate roughly half of the names. For example, given the agent's evident inexperience, it's possible that the buyer is new to the market—"

Reynard shook his head. "The agent was clumsy, but that doesn't mean that the buyer is a virgin." He gestured at the laptop screen, on which the photo of the Russian was displayed in a smaller window. "Come on. The two of you were hired to make connections like this. Anything else?"

"There's another possibility that I should mention," Maddy said, deciding to show her hand. Her source had been a girl from the client services desk, the one whom the Russian had tipped fifty dollars. After prying her name from the phone clerk, Maddy had taken her out, and the girl had let something slip after her second martini: "I have a source who says he isn't Russian at all."

Reynard seemed struck by this. "Which means that all of our assumptions are wrong. That's always a useful point of departure—"

Ethan studied the spreadsheet. "Technically, it could mean that he isn't a Russian, but comes from a former satellite state. Which leaves Vagit Alekperov from Azerbaijan, German Khan from Ukraine—"

"—and Anzor Archvadze from Georgia," Maddy finished. "I've looked into them already. Each one is a distinct possibility."

"Three names," Reynard said. "All right, we're getting closer. But now what?"

The question was directed at Ethan, who didn't reply. Maddy saw that he was frowning at her snapshot of the bidder. Sensing an opening, she took it. "I think we need to approach them directly."

"We've been over this," Reynard replied. "We can't act without more information."

"Information will only take us so far." Maddy halfway expected Ethan to object, but instead, he began typing rapidly, as if his thoughts were elsewhere. She turned back to Reynard, determined not to let this opportunity slip away. "We need to leverage our contacts. I know that I've said this before, but this business isn't built on information alone. It's built on reputation."

As she spoke, she watched the fund manager closely, knowing that this argument cut to the heart of why he had entered the art game in the first place. Years of trading derivatives had left him craving something more fundamental, a satisfaction greater than money itself could provide, and she knew that he valued nothing, not even returns, above his own evolving legacy. "So what do you recommend?"

"Only what you've always told me," Maddy said. "Reputation leads to information, so we work the social angle. I don't care how private these guys are. You don't buy a painting like this without telling someone about it. I can get into the right events, the right benefits. With the fund's full support—"

"Actually, that won't be necessary," Ethan said abruptly. "I know who the buyer is."

The others turned to stare at him. "What are you talking about?" Reynard asked at last.

"Anzor Archvadze." Ethan swung his laptop around. "Georgian industrialist. Made a fortune in auto parts and aluminum. Lived in Moscow, but went into exile after the Rose Revolution. Owns a big estate in the Hamptons."

Maddy looked at the headshot that he had opened. It wasn't the man from the auction. Archvadze was older, a wiry figure with a graying crew cut, his eyes set far apart. "And what makes you so sure it was him?"

Ethan called up the picture of the bidder. "The symbol on his agent's cufflinks."

"I've checked this out already," Maddy said, assuming that Ethan was simply showing off. "A red circle can mean any number of things."

"Except that it isn't a red circle." With a tap of the keyboard, Ethan switched to an enhanced copy of the photo, sharpening and enlarging the design on the cufflink. At this level of resolution, it was clear that it was not, in fact, a circle. "It's a heptagram. A star with seven points."

"A heptagram." Reynard bent forward to study the image. "What does that mean?"

"Well, let's see." Ethan brought up a search engine query. "It's an occult symbol. It was the seal of the Ordo Templi Orientis, a society associated with Aleister Crowley. It appears on the Navajo flag, and—" He pointed at the screen. "And it's the roundel of the Georgian Air Force."

"Georgia." Reynard sat back, evidently impressed. "So let's say that Archvadze is our buyer. He sends an associate to bid in his place, a former member of the air force with a thing for military nostalgia. It's possible. A little neat, maybe, but possible. Has he been a player in the market before?"

"Not as far as I know. Now that I have a name, though, I can dig more deeply."

"Good." Reynard picked up his phone. "I want a profile on my desk by tomorrow. Maddy, feel free to run the name by your contacts as well. Ethan, nice job. If it pans out, the bonus is yours."

This speech was delivered at a rapid pace. Before Maddy knew it, she and Ethan were standing outside the office door, as Reynard prepared for another investor call. Maddy looked at her colleague. "Congratulations."

"Thanks," Ethan said mildly. "I couldn't have done it without you. Or that picture."

She smiled. "Don't be so sure of yourself. For all we know, he could be a Navajo."

Turning aside, she headed back to her desk, feeling something alarmingly close to hatred as she pondered her next move. With her sources in the galleries, which were better than anything Ethan could find online, she could learn about Archvadze's holdings, his tastes, his intentions—

Even as she envisioned this, though, she found herself wondering what she was doing here at all. She had joined the firm for mercenary reasons, hoping to emerge with money and insight, but after taxes, her salary was barely enough to meet her repayment schedule, while finance was still a mystery, guarded by Reynard, Ethan, and other devotees of the cult of information.

But there was one place, she knew, where their expertise did not extend. To them, the fund's holdings were an abstraction, a series of lines in a balance sheet, but behind each piece of the portfolio stood something real, the visible evidence of an artist's life and work.

She rose from her desk. It was already late in the afternoon, but there was still time, she hoped, for the pilgrimage she had in mind. Gathering her things, she headed up the corridor to ask Reynard for the key.

8

"The autopsy will be difficult," the deputy medical examiner said. He was a South Asian pathologist with a tolerant regard for the British, and although the homicide detective assigned to the case stood only a few feet away, he had latched at once onto Powell. "If we cut her open without treating her first, she will break in half. So we use multislice computed tomography instead."

Through the glass of the observation room, the body of the headless woman resembled a strange sort of cocoon, swathed in yards of tissue and plastic. As Powell watched, a pair of orderlies in white gloves and masks undid the ties that secured the body to the gurney and lifted it gently, foam backboard and all, onto the table of the scanner. "What do we know about her so far?"

"Based on a preliminary examination?" The medical examiner gave a sideways shrug. "Not much. Young, less than thirty, although it's hard to say. Judging from her pubis and underarms, she had brown hair. Head and hands were removed after death with a sharp, serrated blade. And although this is only a guess, I would say that more than one person was involved."

"More than one?" The homicide detective, a large

man in his fifties, had a pink face and a good haircut, his jacket cut to accommodate the sidearm in its hard plastic holster. "What makes you say that?"

"Varying degrees of skill with the knife. When you examine the right wrist, the removal of the hand is clumsy and ragged, as if the man doing the cutting were elderly or hesitant. The head and left hand, by contrast, were removed more decisively. The cuts are uniform and professional."

"Or maybe one guy made all of the cuts, but got better at it as he went along."

"Perhaps. But to my eyes, it looks like two different men." The medical examiner turned back to the observation window. "As for trace evidence, there is a small bandage on her ankle, a possible source of hairs and fibers. We have already found shreds of what appear to be lamb's wool."

As Powell considered this, he watched the orderlies undo the clips that held the outer layers of plastic in place. He and the other observers were crowded before a rack of computer monitors. On the other side of the glass lay an examination room with a scanner at its far end. The scanner resembled a massive doughnut balanced on its side, with an aperture in the center like the door of a washing machine.

The orderlies removed the rest of the Aclar film and began to peel away the second layer. As the paper was rolled up to either side of the body, Powell got a good look at the mummy for the first time. The flesh of the arms and legs had collapsed against the bone, to the point where his thumb and finger could have encircled any one of them with ease, and the crests of the pelvis stood out like wings.

The detective leaned forward for a closer look. "What about the date of death?"

"Difficult to say," the medical examiner said. "She might have been there for a year, or ten years, or much longer."

"It had to be at least two," the detective said. He glanced at Powell. "We followed up on your idea about the gate. It looks like the newest section of fence, the one that would have kept our killer from dumping the body, was installed two years ago. So that's our cutoff date."

Powell watched through the glass as a warning light came on and the adjoining room was cleared. "And if you can't identify her?"

"Morgue keeps her for two weeks. After that, she goes to Hart Island. You ever been there? Potter's field gets two thousand coffins a year. Not a good place for anyone to end up—"

As the orderlies filed into the observation room, the scan began, with a radiologist at the computer overseeing the process. The table crept forward, bringing the body through the target ring a fraction of an inch at a time, as a series of discrete slices appeared on the nearest screen. Powell and the detective moved to the back of the room, clearing a gap for the others. "Seen one of these before?"

The detective kept his eye on the scan. "Not from here. Two years ago, I was the one on that table." Powell noted the telltale flush on his neck, the sign of a nitro-glycerin pill, as the detective leaned back against the countertop. "So what brings a guy like you out here?"

Powell considered the range of possible replies to this question. An image of his father's face, once angular, now fat and leonine, appeared unexpectedly in his mind's

eye. In the end, he contented himself with the usual exchange of information: "A man named Vasylenko. London *vor*. Brotherhood of Russian thieves. A member of
the same network as Sharkovsky."

The detective grunted. "I've heard that story before.
With all due respect, there are a lot of ways for a gangster to
make money in Brighton Beach without connections to
London."

"Fair enough," Powell said. "What do you know
about Sharkovsky's background?"

"A champion wrestler in Moscow," the detective said
without hesitation. "Started as a roof in the black market,
then took over the business himself. Came out here fifteen years ago. As far as the rest of the world is concerned, he runs a nightclub, owns a steam room in
Sheepshead Bay, and races trucks on the side. No record.
But he's the number one *vor* in Brighton Beach."

Powell, noting the detective's intelligence, adjusted
himself accordingly. "But there's more to it than that. He
spent eight years in Vladimir Prison in Russia, but was
freed after serving less than half his sentence. It's my understanding that he was sent here to organize criminal
activities throughout the city, with the unspoken support
of Russian intelligence. Of course, the mob claims to be
opposed to the secret services, but at the highest level,
there's no distinction between the two."

The detective, smiling, shook his head. "Listen,
you're new in town, so let me give you a word of advice.
The feds love to push the international angle internally.
It helps them get warrants, wires, funding. But when a
case actually goes to trial, their interest in the foreign
connection dries up real quick. They don't like to get

other agencies involved. Believe me, I've seen it before."

Powell sensed the detective testing his reactions, wondering if he had struck a nerve, which, in fact, he had. The day before, Powell had been deposed in the application for a federal wiretap, his statement taken by a lawyer who had seemed interested solely in the mob's ties to terrorism. Although Powell privately believed that the terrorism angle was a dead end, he had gone along with the charade, knowing that it was the only way to move forward on the overseas connection. A few days earlier, a confidential informant had told them to be on the lookout for an arrival from London. He had turned out to be a modest figure with an accountant's face, unmarked by a *vor*'s tattoos, but Powell knew you could never trust a man who clearly had nothing to hide.

In the other room, the scan came to an end. Powell and the detective watched as the radiologist scrolled through the images, then pointed to a shadowy region in one of the cross sections. "Some foreign material here."

Powell, going forward for a better look, recognized it immediately. "Breast implants."

"That's something," the detective said. "If the serial numbers are intact, we can trace her from patient records. What else?"

"Take a look at her feet." The medical examiner asked the radiologist to call up the relevant scan, then pointed at the screen. "My eye was caught by this. The metatarsals are widened and flattened. She spent much of her time standing. A waitress, perhaps. Or she ran marathons—"

As he studied the image, something clicked in Powell's head, leaving him with a sudden impression of light and music. "The bandage on her ankle. You said you found traces of wool?"

"Yes," the medical examiner said, his dark eyes brightening. "Lamb's wool—"

"Which is used to make ballet shoes fit securely." Powell looked into the examination room, where the dead girl was emerging from the aperture, as if she were being reborn. Then he turned to the others. "It might be too soon to know either way, but I believe that your girl was a dancer."

9

As Maddy entered the storeroom, a row of fluorescent lights stuttered into brightness, illuminating the area one row at a time. This storage space occupied the fourteenth floor of a warehouse on Third Avenue, a fireproof tower of limestone and brick. On both sides of a central aisle stood twenty mesh racks, each of which could be rolled out to reveal the strange portfolio of the Reynard Art Fund.

She moved down the aisle, her skin prickling as she passed into a constant climate of sixty degrees. It struck her again that this was a portfolio no human collector would have assembled. On one rack, for example, a synchromist canvas by Mark Russell had been set alongside pastoral scenes by Millet and Greuze. Across the aisle hung a mythological study by Van Loo, not far from a crate that contained eight bronzes from the Momoyama period, still unpacked after a year in storage.

The next few racks were empty, with bar codes indicating that they were reserved for absent works. Here, for example, was the space for an early Monet, currently pledged as security for a collateralized loan. Some paint- . ings were out for restoration or provenance analysis, while others had been lent to museums to augment their public profile, or were hanging in corporate lobbies for a monthly fee.

There was nothing new about any of this, except, perhaps, the fund's intention to manage the art historical process in the most deliberate way possible. As Maddy regarded the works in the storeroom, she found herself wishing, as she often did, that a similar model existed to guide her own life. She was closing in on a painful anniversary. It was nearly a year since the failure of her gallery, which had closed, like most such businesses, in the dead months of summer.

And it had fallen apart so quickly. Only five years had passed since she had left the phone bank at Sotheby's to accept a job from Alexey Lermontov. Even today, she wasn't sure how, precisely, she had caught the gallerist's eye, unless he had glimpsed a hunger in her youthful face that had reminded him of himself. Whatever the reason, she had been encouraged enough to ultimately spend a year at his gallery, where she had occupied its most visible and least understood position.

Maddy smiled at the memory. A gallerina was a sort of mythical creature, a modern incarnation of the sphinxes who had once guarded ancient temples and necropolises. She superficially resembled a receptionist, but her true role was entirely decorative. It was, in fact, the longest-running work of performance art in history, and as such, it was invaluable training for a life in the art world, in which one had to maintain a perfect exterior, regardless of what was happening on the inside.

A year later, then, she had traded Lermontov's gilded space for an empty storefront in Greenpoint. At first, it had been a nonprofit, with works by herself and her friends hanging from its sheetrock walls. She had covered the startup costs with a credit card advance and furnished it with chairs scrounged from the curbside. It had lacked a convenient subway stop, so she had driven visitors in an hourly van from Bedford Avenue. At night, she had slept on a futon unrolled across the concrete floor.

As her business slowly grew, the time she spent on her own art had diminished, then ceased altogether. After studying the numbers, she had moved the gallery to Williamsburg, converting it to a purely commercial enterprise, but had been there only six months before heading to Chelsea, operating on the principle that the art world rewarded nothing so handsomely as excess.

Later, as the market slowed, she hadn't been sure what was happening. In the end, she had been destroyed by her own overhead. Rent had been ten thousand dollars a month, with overall expenses five times that amount. As sales for emerging artists declined, she had fired staff, scaled back advertising, withdrawn from fairs and exhibitions. But even after selling her own modest collection and relocating to a smaller apartment, the day had finally come when she had been forced to close.

She looked around the silent storeroom, surrounded by art that a computer had chosen. It was unclear, even now, what the lessons had been. If she had held on for another two months, she might have pulled through. Instead, she found herself avoiding the block where her gallery had stood, even as it lived on in her debts, its outline faintly visible, as the soul's image might survive after death.

After another moment, she locked up the storeroom

and headed downstairs, still torn over whether to call Lermontov. Asking him for help felt like an admission of her own defeat, but the gallerist still understood investors in a way that she, or Reynard, did not. In a market that was shaped by a handful of invisible forces, pure logic took you only so far.

A quarter of an hour later, Maddy was back at the Fuller Building. When the elevator doors opened, she headed at once for her office, only to run into Ethan, who was walking quickly up the corridor. She saw at a glance that he had found something big. "What is it?"

"A new lead," Ethan said. They stood together in the hallway, close enough to touch. "What do you know about Archvadze's girlfriend?"

"Natalia Onegina," Maddy said without hesitation. "She's a distant niece or cousin of German Khan, the oligarch, and much younger than Archvadze. She's glamorous. I've seen her in the gossip columns."

"Yes, she's quite the socialite. But did you know she's opening a gallery in London?"

This news was enough to drive everything else from her mind. "How serious is she?"

"Serious enough to file articles of association." Ethan held up a sheaf of papers. "I've got the documents here. Archvadze is listed as a director. My guess is that he's financing the whole thing."

She tried to process this information. "You think he bought the painting for her?"

"I doubt it. From what I've been able to find, her taste runs more to the Wilson twins. But we need to keep an eye on what she's doing. I've already spoken to Reynard. He wants you to work with me on this. You've opened a gallery before, so—" He broke off. "Are you okay?"

"I'm fine. A little tired, maybe." Maddy smiled. "I need to make a few calls. Send me what you've got and we'll talk later."

She continued up the corridor, feeling Ethan's eyes on the back of her head. Going into her office, she closed the door, then collapsed into a chair. She couldn't believe that she had heard nothing about this gallery.

As she looked into the dead eye of her computer screen, feeling useless, she allowed herself to envision a different way of life. Advising a private collector, for instance, who was new to the art market and needed a guide. A collector, perhaps, like Archvadze himself.

If she wanted to get close to a man like this, there was only one person left to call. Taking a breath, she picked up her phone, and this time, she dialed the number without hesitation.

10

Sharkovsky rang the bell of the furniture store, which stood across from the fairgrounds, below the rusting track of the elevated train. All the shutters had been lowered except for one, over the entrance, where an old man with glasses presently appeared. Opening the door a crack, he considered the four figures on the sidewalk. "Three only," the owner said at last. "Arshak says so."

Sharkovsky turned to the others, who were huddled together beneath the yellow awning, taking shelter from the rain. Ilya stood aside, expecting to be told to wait, and was mildly surprised when Sharkovsky looked at Zhenya instead. "Stay here. Give the bag to Misha."

Zhenya blinked at this, but said nothing. He unslung his duffel bag and handed it to Misha, the limping enforcer whom Ilya had observed briefly at the club. Turning away, Zhenya fished a soft pack of cigarettes from his inside pocket, lighting one as the others filed into the store. In the orange spark of the lighter, Ilya saw something like resentment on his face.

Inside, the showroom was vast and dark, a labyrinth of couches and dining room sets. Strings of holiday lights hung from the ceiling, illuminating the gold tinsel twined around the columns. At the center of the room, the only area that was lit, couches and loveseats were arranged around a burgundy rug. A wardrobe stood to one side, flanked by a pair of lamps. Three men were seated on the nearest sofa. One had a knapsack resting across his knees.

"Turn up the lights," Sharkovsky said suddenly. "I want to see the rest of the floor."

The owner went over to an electrical panel. As he threw the switches one by one, hidden quadrants of the store came into view, revealing row after row of beds, desks, tables. Ilya surveyed the showroom. Aside from the three men on the couch, the sales floor was deserted.

As they approached the Armenians, Ilya saw that the two on either side were barely out of high school, while the third seemed in his late twenties. When the two groups were close enough, Sharkovsky came forward, met by the man in the middle, and they shook hands twice, first the right, then the left. Standing back, Sharkovsky studied the younger man. "How is your grandfather, Arshak?"

Arshak made a noncommittal gesture. "Are we here to talk, or to do business?"

Sharkovsky did not seem troubled by this show of impatience. "Business, if you like. We can start with the toys."

At his signal, Misha came forward with the duffel bag, which clanked softly as he set it on the ground. One of the younger Armenians, a boy with a cleft palate scar, knelt and unzipped it. After confirming that the contents were in order, Arshak tossed a sealed plastic bag to Misha. "And the fliers?"

Sharkovsky handed him a digital camera. Before turning it on, Arshak checked the camera's serial number against a slip of paper that he produced from his pocket, then examined its memory card. Reinserting the card, he turned the camera on and scrutinized the images on its preview screen. In the silence, Ilya heard a train rumble across the track overhead.

Arshak seemed pleased by what he saw. "These are the kind with wooden handles?"

"Yes," Sharkovsky said. "They are in Leninakan. As soon as we give the word, they will be sent."

"Good." Arshak nodded at the boy with the knapsack, who set it at Misha's feet. "As agreed. Half now, half on delivery—"

Misha opened the pack. It was stuffed with bundles of cash. Observing the exchange, Ilya reflected that Sharkovsky would not have agreed to this deal ten years ago, when conflicts across the globe had offered a more reliable stream of income. Even at the best of times, though, this was a dangerous moment, with so much money changing hands, and Ilya was watching the Armenians with even more than his usual intensity when an unexpected movement caught his eye.

Across from Ilya stood a vanity with an oval mirror, its silver surface reflecting the wardrobe behind him. The wardrobe was ample and wide, with a double door of pressed wood.

As he watched the reflection, one of the doors drifted open a fraction of an inch.

He turned. Before he could draw his gun, the wardrobe's door was kicked open from the inside, revealing a fourth man in its darkened interior. A leveled shotgun was in his hands.

Behind him, more guns were drawn. Arshak spoke softly. "Weapons on the floor."

Ilya turned back, keeping an eye on the man with the shotgun, who was emerging from the wardrobe. Guns had appeared in the hands of the other Armenians. Misha, who had been caught in a low crouch, looked furious, but Sharkovsky's face was stony. "This is really what you want?"

"Weapons," Arshak said, sticking his pistol in the old man's face. "I'm not joking."

After a beat, Sharkovsky gave an almost imperceptible nod. Ilya pulled the gun from his waistband and set it on the ground, never taking his eyes from the Armenians. Misha and Sharkovsky did the same, then, as ordered, set their clasped hands on the crowns of their heads.

The boy with the cleft palate scar frisked them one at a time. As Sharkovsky endured this latest indignity, he regarded Arshak with an air of scientific detachment. "So what is this?"

"A way to cut costs," Arshak said, lowering his pistol. "These days, money is tight."

The boy with the scar sneered, deepening the crease on his upper lip. "And which of you will stop us? The *zhid*?"

With the snout of his pistol, he poked Ilya roughly in the chest. Ilya lowered his gaze. On the table by the sofa stood a single lamp, its shade wrapped in cellophane. Before the gun could prod him a second time, Ilya turned, twisting his body, and locked his fingers around the boy's wrist.

The boy's eyes met his own. Without looking away, Ilya took the lamp in his other hand, his actions unfolding with an underwater slowness, and smashed it across the boy's face. He heard teeth shatter, then saw a blur of movement in the corner of one eye as the man with the shotgun raised it, shouting. Misha grabbed for the barrel, deflecting the gun an instant before it went off, and the chest of the second teen disappeared behind a cloud of blood.

Ilya, ears ringing, dropped to one knee, wrenching the pistol from the boy's hands. He felt his fingers close around the grip, then swung it up and around, vision red except for a single glowing tunnel centered on Arshak's face. When the world cleared, the boy was on the ground, crying, his scar obscured by blood. A second man lay dead on the floor. Misha was holding the shotgun. Arshak, gun raised but pointing at nothing, found himself face-to-face with two armed men. "Okay—"

"On the floor," Sharkovsky said. "Nose to the rug. Don't make me ask you twice."

Arshak and the surviving gunman lowered themselves to the ground. It took a while to get the boy with the scar to pay attention, but a few kicks persuaded him to lie flat as well. Ilya picked up his own revolver. As he covered the Armenians with a gun in each hand, Sharkovsky told Misha to bring in Zhenya, then turned to the owner. "Were you a part of this?"

"No," the owner said, his face pale. "I saw only three men. This one must have snuck in when I wasn't looking—"

As his voice began to quaver, Sharkovsky cut him off. "Enough. Get me some rope."

Misha returned with Zhenya, who was trembling with excitement. They bound the Armenians with cord from the storage room, then took stock of the situation. The cash in the knapsack consisted of *kukly*, rolls of plain paper with real bills on the outside. Taking one of the bundles, Sharkovsky showed it to Arshak, who was still on the floor. "So what was the rest of your plan?"

When Arshak did not respond, Sharkovsky threw the bundle in his face, then turned to the owner. "The rug is ruined. How much for it?"

The owner pondered this for a moment. "For you? Let's call it three hundred."

"Three hundred?" The *vor* seemed incredulous. "For this piece of shit? It's worth two fifty at the most—"

"But it's wool," the owner said, kneeling to turn over the label. "Tufted by hand."

Sharkovsky grunted, then signaled to Zhenya, who, after a sharp nudge, dug a bankroll from his back pocket and peeled off three bills. The owner accepted the money without speaking.

Turning back to the others, the *vor* took a cushion from the nearest sofa. Without being asked, Misha came forward and pressed his foot against the neck of the boy with the cleft palate scar.

With the air of a man who had been given a tiresome but necessary task, Sharkovsky placed the cushion against the boy's head, wrapping it around his gun. When he fired, the shot was muffled, like that of a damp noise-maker. Moving on to the man from the wardrobe, he fired again. Two dark pools began to spread slowly across the rug, leaving a feathery outline around each body.

When they arrived at Arshak, he did not say a word. His eyes were open and dry, and he flinched only slightly when he felt the pressure of the foot against the back of his neck. Sharkovsky took the cushion, which was leaking wisps of stuffing, and placed it against Arshak's head.

Resting the gun against the cushion, he pulled the trigger. Nothing happened. He tried again. The gun refused to fire. At the level of the floor, Arshak's one visible eye looked up uncertainly.

"Fucking thing is jammed," Sharkovsky said. He turned to Ilya. "Give me your gun."

Ilya handed him the revolver, grip first, and took the pistol in exchange. Without a pause, Sharkovsky pressed the gun against the cushion and fired. Rising, he gave the gun back to Ilya, then turned to the owner, allowing the cushion to fall from his hands. "You can see after this?"

The owner's eyes were fixed on the four bodies. "Yes. I will take care of it."

"Good." Sharkovsky told Zhenya to bring the guns. He had to repeat the order twice before Zhenya, face ashen, picked up the duffel bag. The shotgun and pistols went into the bag as well, along with the digital camera. With a handkerchief, Misha scooped up the shell that the shotgun had ejected, slipping it into his pocket. They left the phony cash where it was.

Outside the store, it was still raining. The shutter fell behind them, sliding down with a coarse whine. As they headed up the sidewalk, Ilya could make out the Wonder Wheel in the distance. It was, he saw, a wheel within a wheel.

"A waste of time," Sharkovsky said. He extended one hand, allowing the rain to wash the blood from his fingers. "It was hard to put that deal together. But not all is lost. We can always find another buyer—"

11

When the gallerina opened the door of the Lermontov Gallery, Maddy recognized her at once as a classic type, willowy and Eurasian, with a glossy ponytail and a touch of brown lipstick. She looked, in fact, a great deal like Maddy herself, which was not so surprising. Lermontov, while discreetly gay, understood his obligation to surround himself with polished young women. "Good afternoon," the gallerina said coolly. "Do you have an appointment?"

Maddy, feeling the girl's eyes on her face, sensed that the gallerina recognized her as one of her own species, a domestic animal that had escaped from captivity. "I'm here to see Alexey."

After sizing her up for another moment, the gallerina motioned her inside and disappeared down the hall. Left alone, Maddy looked around the foyer of the gallery, which had been furnished to resemble a parlor from early in the last century. A late Picasso held pride of place at the front of the room, displayed in a magnificent frame from the House of Heydenryk.

As she was studying the painting, which seemed more a concession to the public than to Lermontov's own tastes, a voice came from over her shoulder. "My dear girl. It's good to see you again."

When she turned, she found herself looking into Lermontov's gray eyes. She had not seen him in over a year, and he seemed older, his features sharper and more pronounced. Leaning forward, he kissed her lightly on both cheeks, encircling her with the scent of his cologne. The continental greeting was something of an affectation. For all his evident refinement, he had been born in Washington Heights.

Releasing her from his embrace, Lermontov studied her with a critical air. "You look reasonably well."

"So do you," Maddy said. As always, Lermontov was impeccably turned out, a coral pocket square peeking out from the breast of his suit. To a stranger's eyes, he might have seemed born to the bespoke way of life, but she saw more than a hint of Gatsby in such elegance. "I hope this isn't a bad time."

"Not at all." Lermontov went to the front desk, where the gallerina had resumed her station. "Shall we go for a walk?"

"A walk would be fine." Maddy watched as he left instructions with the gallerina. For a man of seventy, he was in admirable shape. In his younger days, she recalled, he had been a champion squash player. After the death of his father, who had owned a chain of drugstores throughout the city, he had gone hunting for masterpieces overseas. And, like her, he had never looked back.

Outside, as soon as the gallery was out of sight, Lermontov asked, "Why do you want to know about Archvadze?"

Maddy fell into step beside the gallerist. "First you

need to promise that you won't act on this information. I'm taking a risk by coming to you."

"I'm aware of that. I promise that everything you say will remain confidential."

"Okay." Maddy took the plunge. "We think he bought *Study for Étant Donnés*." She quickly outlined how they had reached that conclusion, explaining the meaning of the red heptagram. "We're assembling a dossier. I need to know his background, his habits, his tastes."

"He's an oligarch," Lermontov said, as if this were information enough. "I've never met him, but I'm sure that he only wants what is large and expensive. His woman seems more cultivated, but as for Archvadze himself—"

"But that's what seems strange. An oligarch who bought this painting would have advertised it to the world. Why pay eleven million dollars for something if nobody knows it's yours?"

"An excellent question. As you say, oligarchs are not known for their aversion to publicity. He must have a good reason for keeping a low profile. What do you know about his politics?"

"He's Georgian, so he can't be fond of Russia. He bankrolled the Rose Revolution, which put him on bad terms with Putin's crowd. They were going to indict him for financial fraud, so he left for New York. Ever since, he's used his wealth to undermine Russian policy in Georgia and sponsor opposition to the Kremlin, but he's still one of the richest men in the world. If we can figure out what he's buying next, it would be good for the fund."

"Is that all?" They entered the park, taking a path running parallel to Columbus Avenue. "I was wondering if you might be interested for personal reasons. He's a wealthy man, unfamiliar with the art world, with expensive tastes. Has it occurred to you that he might be in the market for an adviser?"

Maddy blushed at how easily he had read her mind. "I'm here because of Reynard."

"Of course. And I'm sure that he had no objection to your sharing such sensitive information with a former employer." Lermontov paused beneath the trees. "Are you satisfied with him?"

"Very satisfied," Maddy said. It was an automatic response, and she was glad that she had not hesitated. "I like my job. I'm learning the business of art, and how buyers think, which is what I didn't understand before."

"It's still a waste of talent. As much as you try to hide it, you know as much about art as anyone I've ever seen, and you have an eye for something elusive that the bankers will never appreciate. Art is nothing like finance. The sooner you accept this, the better." The gallerist looked out at the park. "People buy art for many reasons, not all of them rational. Let's assume that you're right, and Archvadze was the buyer. Have you wondered why he chose that particular painting?"

"It isn't hard to figure out. It's one of the most desirable works to emerge at auction in years—"

"Which doesn't explain why he was so eager to obtain it." Lermontov sat down on a vacant bench, carefully adjusting the crease of his trousers. "The study is a striking piece, but it wouldn't be easy to live with. A man buying art to impress others, which is what most oligarchs are doing, might prefer something less grotesque. It makes me wonder if there might not be another reason. This painting is a singular work, after all, and its reappearance raises questions of its own. Doesn't it seem strange that such an important study could have been lost for so long?"

Maddy sat beside him, the slats of the bench pressing through the back of her blouse. "It may have been displayed before. Early in his career, Duchamp exhibited a series of works in Paris, at a show called the Section d'Or. One of them is listed without a title. Nobody knows what this painting was, but there's a strong possibility that it was this study."

"That's a very important point," Lermontov said. "If I were you, I would look closely at the circumstances surrounding this exhibition. Do you know what Section d'Or itself means?"

Maddy knew enough French, and art history, to reply at once. "The golden section."

"But there's more to it than that. The show was named by Jacques Villon, Duchamp's brother, who came across the concept in a book by Joséphin Péladan. You probably don't recognize his name, but at the time, Péladan was one of the leading occultists in France. Among other things, he was the founder of the French order of the Rosicrucians. Another prominent member was Erik Satie, the composer, who became one of Duchamp's closest friends. You've heard of these circles, of course—"

"You've mentioned them to me before," Maddy said. "But I only know that they were some kind of secret society."

"Sometimes not so secret," Lermontov said. "You've always been an exceptional student of history. I don't need to tell you that the Rosicrucians were a key influence on the Symbolist movement, which led, in turn, to Dadaism. And they remain active up to the present day, often in surprising forms. Think of the Rose Revolution, which Archvadze claims to have financed. Supporters of the opposition party in Georgia invaded parliament with roses in their hands. Where did they get the idea? These things do not happen by accident."

As she listened, Maddy recalled that the Rosicrucians had long been one of Lermontov's private obsessions. Perhaps, being gay, and therefore a member of a group that extended across all social classes, high and low, with its own codes and secret knowledge, he was especially receptive to the idea of similar forces operating in history itself. "I'm not sure what you're trying to tell me."

"I'm only saying that there are currents in the art world, then and now, of which you may not be aware. Some of them influence schools of art, while others may influence a man's decision to buy a particular painting. In any case, there were probably more pressing reasons for Archvadze to take an interest in this study. His girl, for example. What do you know about her?"

Maddy thought that he was changing the subject too quickly, as if worried that he had been indiscreet. "I know that she's opening a gallery in London. Although I don't know how seriously to take it."

"She has certainly been serious about promoting herself to those who matter. Some of us even wonder if she might be the driving force behind Archvadze's acquisitions. Who knows? She may have asked him for this painting. Her birthday is coming up, I believe. He'll want to celebrate it in style."

It took her less than a second to draw the obvious conclusion. "Will there be a party?"

"If you were an aging oligarch with a pliant young girlfriend, wouldn't you jump at the chance to express your love? I hear that his house is quite marvelous. I imagine that he will do his best to fill it."

Maddy clutched the bench's iron armrest, no longer seeing the other faces in the park. Then, relaxing, she smiled sweetly at Lermontov. Reaching out, she gently straightened the knot of the gallerist's tie, which was slightly askew. "You don't suppose you could get me an invitation?"

"The art world helps those who hype themselves." Lermontov waited for her to finish smoothing his tie, then rose, motioning for her to remain seated. "If you want my advice, you'll look at the Rosicrucians. I'm not the first to draw a connection between them and Duchamp. And if you understand them intimately, when you do meet Archvadze, you may find that you have something to talk about."

He offered her a neat bow of farewell, a gesture as polished as the tips of his shoes, then headed back to the gallery. Maddy remained where she was. If there was a party, she would attend it. The Rosicrucians were one thing, but there was another society, remote but not so secret, that wielded substantial power in its own right. The art world had its own rituals, its own ceremonies and passwords, and as far as she knew, she was still a member.

12

On a sleepy block in Sheepshead Bay, a woman in scrubs and white clogs emerged from a brick row house, her hair tied back in a graying bun. Her house, like the others lining the street, was shaped like an antique cash register, its red metal awning peering out over a narrow porch. Locking the door behind her, she went down the steps, then headed up the sidewalk to the train.

Powell was parked at the corner. As he watched the woman ascend the platform to the elevated track, he scraped a blank key across a triangular file, like a chef running a knife along a sharpening steel. He had already filed it down until nothing remained but a row of five notches, cut to their deepest setting, and now took additional shavings from the key's tip and shoulder.

He waited until the train had come and gone. Then he blew on the key, slid it into his pocket, and emerged from the sedan, tucking the file up his sleeve. Although the day was warm, he had gloves on both hands. Crossing the street, he made for the row house, glancing up and down the deserted block.

When he reached the house, instead of going up to the porch, he headed around to the side, where a set of concrete steps led to a second door. Through a dusty pane of glass, he could see into the kitchen beyond. He took the bump key from his pocket, inserted it all the way into the lock, then withdrew it one notch. Straightening his arm, he let the file up his sleeve slide into his hand.

A sharp tap against the key was all it took. Going inside, he closed the door behind him, then paused to listen. The kitchen was silent. Dishes had been stacked in the drying rack by the sink, the fixtures old but clean. The refrigerator droned quietly. Opening it, he saw cubes of raw meat, probably lamb, marinating on the top shelf.

He went into the darkened parlor, the boards creaking softly beneath his feet. Thick rug, heavy furniture. A Siroun cross above the television. Against the far wall, a curio was filled with decorative plates and photographs.

Powell took a closer look at the pictures. The first was of a baby with a wide fissure on its upper lip. The next picture showed the same child at the age of three or so, his cleft palate repaired, leaving a faint scar. Other photos depicted the same boy at various ages. The last shot was of him as a teenager, standing beside his grandmother, his shoulders in an adolescent slump.

Turning away from the photos, Powell checked the rest of the floor, then went downstairs. At the foot of the steps, a rock poster had been taped to a closed door. *System of a Down.*

Entering the bedroom, he saw that more posters covered the walls, along with cutouts of pinups and action stars. A stereo was surrounded by stacks of pirated discs. There was a pile of textbooks on the floor. The bed had been made, its sheets black, its pillowcases clean but faded. It seemed far too tidy for a teenager's room, which meant that the boy's grandmother had accessed it freely.

In any case, there was no harm in checking the obvious places. Powell looked under the mattress, then searched the dresser, feeling under the drawers and beneath the sheets of contact paper. He was about to try the closet when his eye was caught by the heap of textbooks, which struck him as out of place. The boy in this room had not been especially studious.

Examining the books, he found that the thickest volume had been hollowed out. Inside, a rectangular compartment disclosed a disposable lighter, two joints in a plastic bag, and a folded piece of paper. Removing these, he observed that the inside of the compartment bore a number of dark scratches, as if it had formerly contained something that had rubbed against the pages. He put the book to his nose. Inhaling, he caught a whiff of old gunmetal and grease.

He turned his attention to the piece of paper, which had been torn from a racing magazine. When he unfolded it, he found that it was a photo of a pickup truck the color of a fire engine, a double eagle emblazoned on its ample hood. An old man was leaning against the truck. It was Sharkovsky.

Powell studied the photo for a moment, then refolded the page and put it back into the compartment, along with the lighter and plastic bag. Satisfied, he returned the textbook to its former place, then headed for the door.

As he was about to leave, he paused and looked back at the bedroom. In the yard outside, the weeds had grown above the level of the basement window, staining the sunlight the color of grass. Something in the green quality of the light reminded him of a room on the other side of the ocean, in another house where the lawn had long gone untended. He lingered there for a second longer, allowing himself, for once, to think of home. Then he turned and went softly upstairs.

Outside, the day had grown cooler. Powell left the house through the kitchen, locking the door behind him, and went down the concrete steps. As he headed back to the car, he dropped the triangular file into some bushes by the curb and tossed the bump key into the street. Then he removed his gloves.

He was about to unlock his driver's side door when he heard the low sound of footsteps behind him. Before he could react, someone pressed a hard metal object against his spine. "Don't move."

Powell froze. Then he recognized the voice. "Hello, Wolfe. How did you find me?"

He turned around. Rachel Wolfe was standing there, a pocket flashlight in one hand. She looked pissed. "Your transponder. Most of the new vehicles have one. Mind telling me what you're doing here?"

Unlocking the car, Powell motioned her into the passenger seat. There was a folded newspaper lying on the dashboard, which he handed to her as they sat down. "Take a look at this."

Wolfe studied the paper. It was a local Armenian weekly, opened to a headshot of a boy in his teens. A gold chain encircled his neck. On his upper lip was a cleft palate scar. "So what?"

"I keep an eye on the Russian and Armenian papers," Powell said. "Usually, all I read are the obituaries. If there's a picture of a young guy wearing a flashy chain, odds are it was a hit. This one is slightly different. Missing persons case. His grandmother says he's been gone for days. I don't know what happened, but Sharkovsky had something to do with it."

He told her what he had found. When he was done, Wolfe only shook her head. "Why didn't you come to us?"

"I didn't think you'd take it seriously," Powell said. "And don't tell me I was wrong."

Wolfe sighed. "You know, this is exactly the sort of thing that got you in trouble back home. Breaking and entering aside, you aren't supposed to be conducting investigations on your own. The terms of the exchange program are clear. You're here to advise, to consult on cases involving global organized crime—"

Powell broke in. "I'm here to get you a warrant. That's the only reason the Bureau agreed to embed me at all. They knew it would be easier to get a wire through FISA, so they flew me in to make the case for the foreign connection. Now that they've got their wiretap sorted, they're throwing me away."

He knew it would be hard for her to refute what he was saying. The day before, a federal court had approved their warrant application. Phones in the names of Sharkovsky and four others would be placed under electronic surveillance, along with landlines and pay phones at the club. Because privacy guidelines discouraged the sharing of wiretaps with foreign agencies, however, it had been decided that Powell would have no access to the wire that his own testimony had secured.

At last, Wolfe spoke again. "They aren't throwing you away. They want you to work with the police on the dead

girl. That's why I came looking for you. The autopsy results are in."

Although the dead girl was far from the first thing on
his mind, he still felt a trace of reflexive curiosity. "What
do they say?"

Wolfe reached into her purse, taking out a notebook,
and opened it to the most recent page. "It looks like she
was strangled. There's bruising and discoloration below
the left breast, and two of her ribs are cracked. As I see it,
she was lying on the floor, faceup. The killer wrapped his
hands around her neck, nearly straddling her, and pressed
a knee against her chest to pin her down—"

"Yes, that's one possibility," Powell said. "What about
the date of death?"

"Based on the condition of the body, she had to have
been dumped during a hot, dry season. And they found
fragments of green almonds in her stomach. You don't
see them in most stores, but they're available at Russian
markets for three weeks each year, usually from late April
to early May."

She turned to another page. "The scan also revealed
that she had breast implants. The police were hoping that
the serial numbers would let them trace her through patient records, but when they excavated the chest, they
found nothing but a yellow compound the consistency of
bread dough. It's an injectable alloplastic, formerly used in
breast implants of a particularly unsafe kind. Illegal in this
part of the world, but available, until recently, in Russia
and Eastern Europe."

Powell weighed this information. "So let's say she was
a dancer and prostitute at the Club Marat. She was killed

by one of her clients, maybe in the rooms above the club, and Sharkovsky's men hid her body under the boards."

"That's my guess as well," Wolfe said. "But we need to tread carefully. If the police start sniffing around the club, Sharkovsky will alter his pattern, so we need to make sure that they don't jump the gun. Barlow says he'll feel better with a liaison in place. That means you and me."

"A liaison." He looked out the windshield at the hot, drowsy street. Louis Barlow, the assistant special agent in charge of the criminal division, was a veteran agent with a reputation as a shrewd investigator, but he had shown limited enthusiasm for the foreign angle now that its purpose had been served. Powell, who knew exactly how it felt to see an investigation stall and die, sensed that he was being sidelined, but was also aware that there was nothing to be done.

In any case, the dead girl gave him an opening. It wasn't much, but it would do. "All right," Powell said. "If Barlow wants me to stick with the dead girl, I will. And I'll keep the police in line."

Wolfe opened her door. "Fine. And I'll see what I can find on the Armenian kid. But we're doing it my way, not yours."

She got out of the car. Just before heading over to where her own sedan was parked, she bent down to look at Powell. For an instant, he caught a glimpse of something steely behind her habitual reserve.

"It isn't the police I'm worried about," Wolfe said. "I'll be keeping an eye on you."

Turning away, she closed the door in Powell's face. A second later, she was gone.

13

"So I have considered the plan, and have decided to make one change," Sharkovsky said. "Misha, as you know, has a bad leg. Better to go with a younger man. Zhenya, not Misha, will accompany you to the party."

Ilya, the sweat falling in pearls from his face, was surprised by this. They had been seated in the *banya*, eyes closed, for nearly an hour. Beside them, Zhenya, who had just poured more water onto the stones, returned to the bench. Taking a damp bundle of birch branches, he lashed himself with the switch, which made a soft whack each time it struck his shoulders, the leaves flying to either side.

Looking down at the wooden floor, Ilya exhaled. Changing the plan now was asking for trouble, but he knew that he had no choice. It was not the first time he had remained silent. Killing the Armenians had been a mistake. With four men dead so close to home, it would not be long before the police came calling. But this was not something that he could ever say aloud.

He brushed the fragments of leaves from his skin. "It makes no difference to me."

"Good," Sharkovsky said. A moment later, as if he had only been waiting for the outcome of this exchange,

Zhenya tossed his switch aside and slid off the bench, leaving his towel behind. The door opened and closed with a flash of white. Through the rectangle of glass that looked onto the main bathhouse, Ilya saw the young enforcer plunge into the pool without bothering to shower off first.

He turned back to the old man. Naked except for a towel and hat of felt, his shoulders standing out like pinions, Sharkovsky was a poor forked thing, a pair of stars etched below his collarbone, a rose over his heart. Now he spoke without opening his eyes: "There is something I have wanted to ask you for some time. You were in prison. You have been with Vasylenko for years. So where are your tattoos?"

Ilya looked away. "I had tattoos once. Vasylenko arranged to have them removed."

"I see." Sharkovsky coughed. "I was wondering if it was because you were a Jew. I have known such men, brave ones, who refused to get tattoos because they said that the body was a gift from God—"

"Some don't get tattoos," Ilya said. "Others don't pierce their ears. Like my mother."

Sharkovsky's eyes opened. "I didn't know that Scythians had mothers. I thought they were raised on mare's milk. She is alive?"

Ilya shook his head, dislodging a cascade of drops. "Both are dead. Many years now."

The old man gave him a look of what might have been sympathy. "Your parents died when you were in Vladimir?"

Ilya saw that he was being tested, although the terms of the examination remained obscure. There was a cult of motherhood within the *bratva*, and many of its men bore tattoos testifying to a mother's love, in both the subjective and objective genitive, but it was an abstract devotion to the mother of thieves. Ilya had never known a thief who would give his own mother so much as a kopek.

He decided to avoid the question. "When I met Vasylenko, he became my family."

Sharkovsky only grunted. Ilya looked at the floor again, fighting a wave of unwanted memories. Even if his words had been on the rhetorical side, they were close to the truth. During his first year in prison, Vasylenko had been nothing but a scarecrow at the edge of the exercise yard, wearing loose coveralls and a cross of pounded aluminum. Then, one morning, the *vor* had cornered him at the fence. Before Ilya could speak, Vasylenko had turned over his crucifix, revealing what was on the other side. Scratched into the metal had been a star made of two linked triangles.

"For my mother," Vasylenko had said, turning it over again. "You understand?"

Ilya, astonished, had been about to reply, but the old man had silenced him. Later that night, a guard had brought him to Vasylenko's cell, where the *vor*, hands tucked into his robe, had spoken softly:

"I know about your parents. The snowfall, I hear, was heavy that day. When they lit the fire, they had no way of knowing that the flue was blocked. If it is any consolation, they would have died in their sleep, which is more than most of us are granted." The old man had paused. "I imagine that you blame yourself."

Ilya had said nothing. He had not spoken of the circumstances of his parents' death to anyone in the prison, and was not pleased to learn that Vasylenko had been looking into his past.

"But it wasn't your fault that you weren't there,"

Vasylenko had continued. "I know how it begins. You make a few deals on the black market to feed your family. Then, one day, some shit of a cop is killed when a deal goes wrong. The Chekists arrest you, decide that you are the perfect one to take the fall, and with that, your life is over. So much wasted potential—"

Ilya, thinking of the star scratched into the cross, had found his voice at last. "How do you know this?"

Vasylenko had smiled. "Do you know the story of the tzaddikim? They are the thirty-six righteous men for whose sake God permits the world to endure. They live in poverty, unknown, unhonored—"

"Yes, I know," Ilya had said sharply. "Some even sin, to avoid the charge of vanity."

"Or, perhaps, to secure a greater good. You see, there are many kinds of oppression. The oligarchs are as bad as the Chekists. They would replace wolves with foxes. They fail to see that the idea of order itself is to blame, which is why the righteous men have always labored in secret."

"But none of the tzaddikim knows who he is. And you still say you're one of them?"

"No. But they do exist, under other names. Men like us have been victims for far too long. I am offering you a chance to restore the balance." Vasylenko had studied his face. "I see promise in you. You have the eyes of a Scythian. A wanderer of the steppes. But even he needs a home—"

Ilya's head jerked upward. For a second, he had felt himself in Vladimir again, and was surprised to find himself in the *banya*, years removed from prison, with another old man watching him from across the bench.

Sharkovsky was regarding him with evident curiosity. "Come. Let's talk outside."

They rose, the sweat pouring down their bodies. Outside, the bathhouse was clean and bright. Framed hockey jerseys hung on the walls, along with admonitions not to run by the pool. A handful of bathers lounged in plastic chairs, paging through newspapers or watching the plasma screens mounted to the ceiling. Zhenya had left a few leaves on the water, but was nowhere to be seen.

A whisper of cool air caused Ilya's flesh to prickle. At his side, Sharkovsky stretched, his ligaments creaking. "You seem displeased that Zhenya will be playing a larger role. Does it bother you?"

Ilya's eyes fell on the leaves drifting on the mirror of the pool. "He's inexperienced."

"Yes. And he's no genius. But every wise man was once a young fool. And I have an old friend who says that even you, once upon a time, were not so different." Sharkovsky finished his stretch, then padded over to the cold plunge. "But you still haven't told me why you removed your tattoos."

Thinking of Vasylenko, Ilya reminded himself that these two men, for all their visible differences, were not so dissimilar after all. "For my work. The man who stands out gets killed."

"Which is something that not everyone understands." Sharkovsky's eyes flicked toward the nearest television. "You see?"

Ilya followed his gaze. On a news broadcast, a man was being interviewed about the rumors of war in South Ossetia. Although the volume was turned down, Ilya recognized the speaker at once, and experienced a moment of almost tender recognition, as if it were a dear friend. He felt the past fall blessedly away, replaced by the necessity of what was to come. It was Anzor Archvadze.

14

"Never trust anything you read online," Tanya said, pushing up her shutter shades. "I'm not just talking about the web, either. A scanned book is easy to search, but you lose crucial information. When you see a book in a library, you can tell if it's been read to pieces or never been touched. You can see which pages have been thumbed the most. And you can see other things, too. Here, smell this."

Taking a folder from her purse, Tanya withdrew a yellowed sheet of paper, which she thrust into Maddy's hands. They were seated together at a café table in Bryant Park. The lawn itself was closed for reseeding, so they had claimed a spot at the edge of the grass, among the flocks of office workers.

Maddy glanced doubtfully at the page, which was covered in faded copperplate. At her friend's urging, she raised it to her nose. Beneath the odor of old dust, she caught a whiff of something acidic. "Vinegar?"

Tanya took the letter back. "Exactly. In the eighteenth century, in towns where there were cases of cholera, vinegar was used to disinfect correspondence. A graduate student I know is assembling a map of outbreaks using letters at the Frick. He goes through our archives and smells the pages one by one. You can't get that kind of information from a scanned file."

"I'll keep that in mind," Maddy said. "So what exactly do you have for me?"

Tanya handed her a sheaf of photocopies. "A lot of the material is vague or contradictory, but as far as I can tell, the Rosicrucians first appear in two pamphlets printed in Germany in the early seventeenth century."

Maddy found the title pages. "The *Fama Fraternitatis* and *Confessio Fraternitatis.*"

"That's right. They tell the story of Christian Rosencreutz, who, two centuries earlier, had traveled through the Middle East to study alchemy and magic. When he returned to Europe, he founded a secret brotherhood of learned men. At first, there were eight members, all bachelors who took an oath of celibacy. Later, their numbers increased to thirty-six. They were called the college of invisibles."

"Okay. So we're talking about a secret society. But what were they trying to do?"

"Nobody knows. The manifestoes hint at a great secret, but they don't say what it is. The usual explanation is that they wanted to reform the state using alchemical methods. The goal of the alchemist isn't to transmute base metals into gold, but to transmute himself into a higher level of being. That's one possible meaning of the rose and the cross—life arising from lifelessness. The Rosicrucians, if they existed, may have been trying to do something similar for all of Europe."

"So it's a political organization," Maddy said. "They're trying to start a revolution."

"But not in the usual sense. Remember, this is only a century after Luther, whose coat of arms, incidentally, was a rose and a cross. People are disillusioned by wars of politics and religion, so the Rosicrucians propose an alternative reformation. A secret one. Which is ultimately the only kind that works. Revolutions, like Saturn, tend to devour their own children."

Maddy saw this quotation scrawled in the margin. "Let me see if I understand. Most revolutions end up repeating the mistakes of the regime they try to bring down. But a secret revolution—"

"—is harder to corrupt. Yes, that's one possibility. And there are precedents for this. There was a real vigilante group, the Vehmgericht, that operated in Germany in the years before the manifestoes appeared, conducting secret tribunals and executions. It was based on the premise that underground justice is the only kind that won't become compromised. And its symbol was a red cross."

"But that's what I don't get. If secrecy was so important, why did they go public?"

Tanya slid closer, the metal legs of her chair leaving grooves in the gravel. "I agree. It's strange. And no one knows why the manifestoes, if they were real, were published in the first place. Some think that they were meant to introduce certain ideas into public discourse. If so, it worked. Rosicrucian fraternities were founded in every country. And they had a real influence on the history of art."

"This is what I'm especially curious about," Maddy said, recalling her conversation with Lermontov. "I know that Joséphin Péladan, the founder of the Rosicrucians in Paris, commissioned paintings with mystical themes—"

"Which isn't even the most interesting part. André Breton, the founder of Surrealism, repeatedly mentions what he calls the great invisibles, a secret society that has shaped the course of history while hiding in plain sight. The Surrealists, it seems, required an existing grammar of myths for their paintings and poetry, and these stories offered exactly the kind of system they needed."

"And what about Duchamp?" Maddy asked. "Where does he fit into all of this?"

"He's right in the middle of it. We already know that he was friends with Erik Satie, the chapel master of the Rosicrucians in Paris, but his connection with these movements goes back even further. Look here."

Tanya turned to a reproduction of *The Large Glass*, Duchamp's first mature work, which looked like a freestanding window that had acquired a web of cracks and ominous encrustations. "You have two vertical panes of glass, one above the other. In the upper pane, there's the bride, like an angelic insect, and in the lower pane, the bachelors, nine cylindrical forms surrounded by alchemical pumps, grinders, and tubes. Remind you of anything?"

"The original members of the Rosicrucians. But weren't there eight bachelors?"

"Duchamp's original proposal had eight. He added the ninth later, to represent himself. Some critics even believe that the readymades are alchemical symbols. The urinal, the bicycle wheel, and the hanging shovel stand for the alembic, the wheel of life, and the pendulum. Duchamp was also fascinated by the alchemical concept of the androgyne. He posed in drag for his friend Man Ray, and signed his works with the name of a female alter ego. You know what that name was?"

"Rrose Sélavy," Maddy said, struck by the coincidence. "What about *Étant Donnés*?"

"This is the strangest part. According to the manifestoes, when Christian Rosencreutz died, the location of his tomb was lost. A hundred and twenty years later, the Rosicrucians were renovating their palace when they uncovered a secret door behind a wall. Inside, they found a vault lit by an artificial sun, as well as Rosencreutz's miraculously preserved body."

"So you're saying that the installation is a reference to the tomb of Christian Rosencreutz." Maddy weighed this for a moment. "But it doesn't fit Duchamp's personality. He was a skeptic. He wasn't part of any movement. He's the last person who would buy into any form of mysticism."

"I know. And his own statements on the subject are inconsistent. Sometimes, in passing, he seems to admit an interest in alchemy, but when the topic is raised in more formal interviews, he denies it. Which, of course, is exactly what you'd expect a real Rosicrucian to say."

Maddy flipped through the rest of the file. "What about the stuff involving Russia?"

"Here, for once, we're dealing with verifiable facts," Tanya said. "Russia has always been mad for secret societies. The Rosicrucian order in Moscow was the first such group to use code names and systems of confession, which were later imitated by the Bolsheviks. In the end, they were crushed by the Soviets, although there are rumors that they only went underground. And the rose remained a symbol of revolution." In the margin of the page, Tanya quickly sketched a fist with a rose. "You know what happened in Georgia, right?"

"So what are you saying? The Rose Revolution was influenced by the Rosicrucians?"

"I don't know. But if I wanted to start a revolution in that part of the world, I'd take a long hard look at what had been tried before." Tanya glanced at her watch. "Listen, I'm going to be late. Are we good?"

"Very good." Maddy handed her an envelope. It contained a hundred dollars in cash, leaving her with something less than seventy in her checking account. "For your trouble. Buy yourself a real bike."

Tanya accepted the honorarium with a smile. They parted ways at the corner, where Tanya climbed onto a fixed gear bicycle and Maddy took the train back to work. As she rode, she turned her friend's argument over in her head, concluding that it was highly unlikely. Collectors didn't buy art for political reasons. They bought it out of vanity, greed, and, occasionally, genuine aesthetic pleasure. The idea that anyone would pay eleven million dollars for a painting because of a secret revolutionary tradition struck her as inherently absurd.

Back at the office, she turned to a more promising line of research. A few phone calls had established that Archvadze was indeed throwing a party for his girlfriend's birthday. As she dialed the first number on her list of possible guests, she reminded herself that she was acting for the fund. She would see Archvadze and take a few photos of his collection. That was all. If she had yet to tell Reynard, it was only because she didn't want to oversell herself. Or so, at least, she tried to believe.

Her first two conversations were dead ends. The third was with the editor of an art journal in which the fund occasionally planted stories to influence the value of its portfolio. In response to a leading question and a few tidbits about an upcoming sale, the editor revealed that Griffin Wainwright, one of the journal's senior critics, was attending the party at Archvadze's mansion that weekend.

Maddy pumped a fist in the air. Griffin was unfailingly savage in his opinions, single, and painfully shy. Hanging up, she checked a few details on her computer, then dialed the critic's direct line.

Griffin seemed pleased to hear her voice. "How's life among the money changers?"

"Same job, better view," Maddy said, one eye out her office window. "In fact, there's something I'd like to talk to you about. The fund is looking into some pieces at the Vered Gallery in East Hampton, but we need an expert's opinion, and so of course I thought of you. I know that you're going to be up there this week, and was wondering if you'd like to have a drink on Saturday."

She paused, knowing that Griffin, like all art critics, had a somewhat inflated impression of his own usefulness. While critics could influence attendance at galleries, they rarely had any impact on the market, but it was still necessary to flatter their sense of importance from time to time.

When Griffin spoke again, a slight stammer had appeared in his voice. "I'm damned sorry, but I'm attending an important event that night. Natalia Onegina is opening a gallery in London, and her oligarch boyfriend is bankrolling the entire thing. I don't know if you're going to be there—"

"Oh, is that this weekend?" Maddy said carefully. "It completely slipped my mind."

"It's a bore, I know, but I don't have a choice. We could meet up earlier, if you like. How does six sound?"

"I'm afraid I'm booked through nine. It's really all right. I can bring in someone from *Artforum* instead—"

This was a low blow, but it had the necessary effect. Griffin was silent for a moment. At last, he said, speaking slowly, "You know, if you'd be willing to come out to Gin Lane, I suppose that I could add you to the list. The only trouble is that I've already responded for—"

He broke off. *For one*, he had been about to say. Sensing a moment of vulnerability, Maddy went in for the kill. "Well, it's out of my way, and I wouldn't want to impose. But it's been too long since we've talked, and I'd love to see you again. If it isn't any trouble, I could drop by the house."

"Not at all," Griffin said gallantly. "I have the number right here. I'll call them now."

"Wonderful," Maddy said, putting rather more honey into her voice than necessary. Outside her window, it was growing dark. In the glass, she could see herself suspended in midair, as if she were floating high above the city. Turning from the view, she smiled into the phone. "I promise to make it worth your while."

15

Louis Barlow, the assistant special agent in charge of the criminal division, had the build of a quarterback who had succumbed to a desk job, his heaviness not quite concealing the fact that he had once been a man of wicked handsomeness. As his office door opened, he glanced up. "What the fuck do you want?"

"We've narrowed down the window for the dead girl," Powell said, tossing a printout onto the conference table. "Weather records suggest she was buried just over two years ago, probably in early May." He sensed a distinct lack of interest in this information. "You want to tell me what the matter is?"

It was Friday afternoon. At the conference table, Barlow was seated with Mark Kandinsky, an agent from the wire room. Kandinsky was a pale slip of a redhead whose job, until recently, had consisted primarily of moving Barlow's car from one parking space to another, and although he was clearly pleased to have been assigned to such an important case, the strain was already showing.

Kandinsky removed his headphones, which were plugged into his laptop. "The good news is that we have hours of calls on Sharkovsky's phone. The bad news is that when he calls Misha, Zhenya, or a third phone belonging to our guy from overseas, half the time it's in a language that none of our linguists can understand. And these are pertinent communications. He'll start in Russian, then switch over to this other language, and rarely talks for more than thirty seconds."

Powell considered this in silence. An idea began to form at the back of his mind, knocking faintly against something that he had heard before. "Can you give me one of the audio files?"

Barlow turned slowly to face him. "Why? You know something that we don't?"

"I don't know anything," Powell said, not yet ready to show his hand. "I'm not even on the wire. So if you just want me to piss off—"

Barlow broke in. "Kandinsky, send him a file. Twenty seconds should be enough."

"Thanks," Powell said, already out the door. When he arrived at his desk, a message in his email account included the file as an attachment. He opened it. Two voices. Twenty seconds. He played it twice, then picked up his phone and dialed the switchboard operator.

An hour later, as afternoon was shading into evening, Powell led a stranger into Barlow's office at the Javits Building. He was a slender kid in loafers and jeans, a visitor's pass stuck to the front of his shirt. As they approached, Barlow looked up from the stack of line sheets on his desk. The wall behind him was covered in scores of his children's crayoned drawings. "Who the hell is this?"

The stranger stuck out his hand. "Eric George. I'm a graduate student at Columbia."

Barlow studied the hand, as if unsure what it was, then gave it a perfunctory shake. "A pleasure. What do you want?"

"It's the recording," the student said, glancing at Powell. "I know what language they were speaking. It's Assyrian."

When Barlow heard this, he went to the door and shouted down the hallway. A minute later, Kandinsky reappeared, along with Wolfe. Once they were all in the office, Barlow turned back to the student. "All right. Assyrian. But don't tell me they're discussing the *Epic of Gilgamesh*—"

"Not exactly," the student said, blinking rapidly at the sudden attention. "It's a form of Syriac spoken by the Assyrian diaspora. There are fewer than two hundred thousand speakers worldwide. The recording I was given is a conversation between two men. One of them asks if a package is ready. The other says it will be finished in time for the party—"

"For the party." Barlow did not speak again for a few seconds. When he did, his tone was decisive. "Listen up. You're about to get the world's fastest background check. Then you're coming to work for us. Congratulations."

Before the student could reply, he was hustled out of the office by the agent from the wire room. As they settled in to wait, Powell and Wolfe returned to their desks, where he explained how he had made the connection. "Does the name Vyacheslav Ivankov mean anything to you?"

"Sure, I've heard of him," Wolfe said. They were seated in her cubicle, nursing cups of cocoa, the only hot beverage that she would allow herself to drink. "They called him Yaponchik, right? The Bureau got him back in the nineties. He was deported a few years ago—"

"But before that, he spent some time in Lewisburg. While he was in jail, he continued to run criminal operations in his old neighborhood, speaking in dialects that the guards couldn't understand. I read his file. According to the report, one of the languages he used was Assyrian."

Wolfe looked at Powell as if he were an interesting freak of nature. "How did you remember that?"

"It's a gift, I suppose." Powell tried for an offhand tone, but he was glad to have made the connection. For much of the past year, he had been watching his thought processes with more than usual attentiveness, wary of the forgotten facts or misremembered names that might signal a mental decline. So far, he had noticed no loss of acuity, but each moment of insight was still a cause for relief.

"Well, I'm impressed," Wolfe said, draining her cocoa. "But it doesn't mean that Barlow will let you on the wire."

"It doesn't matter what he does. From now on, I've got a source in the wire room."

Powell grinned at her over the rim of his mug. Wolfe only stared at him. A hour later, after the student had finished a provisional translation, the agents filed into the office and listened to what he had found:

"There are four men on these calls," the student said. "One is called by two names, which confused me at first. When he's on the phone, he's called Ilya. But in his absence, the others refer to him as the Scythian."

This nickname got Powell's attention. In Russian literature, the Scythian was an archetypal wanderer, caught halfway between civilization and savagery. "But what are they actually talking about?"

The student checked his notes. "The calls fall into a few different categories. In some, which go primarily to Misha, Sharkovsky wants to discuss a shipment from Leninakan, although I'm not quite sure what that means. In another call, Sharkovsky asks Zhenya about their weekend plans, which have something to do with a house by the sea. Later, they talk about a man they're supposed to meet there. They call him a mutual friend. At one point, Zhenya lets a name slip, but Sharkovsky shuts him up right away. The name is Archvadze."

Something clicked in Powell's head, as sweetly as the last pin of a combination lock. As soon as the student had been dismissed with the promise of more work to come, Powell absently began to clean his glasses. "I know who he is. Anzor Archvadze. An oligarch with a place in the Hamptons."

Kandinsky wrote the name down. "You think he's working with these guys? They called him a friend—"

"It could be a code," Wolfe said. "Maybe they're planning a robbery. Or extortion."

Barlow leaned back in his chair, his neatly combed head brushing a child's drawing behind his desk, where an oily spot was already visible. "If that's all they're doing, forget it. I'm not going to shut these guys down over a fucking extortion case. What about this party?"

Powell felt the pieces fall into place. He put on his glasses, then looked at the others. "A party this weekend. At a house by the sea—"

16

On the day of his arrival, Ilya had been given the keys to a row house in Brighton Beach. A green pickup was parked by the rear garage, out of sight of the street. Its bed was long and capacious, big enough to carry cordwood or scrap metal, and its hood was the size of a double bed. Unlike most of Sharkovsky's trophy trucks, it looked street legal, although it was decidedly not.

Kneeling by the truck, Ilya used several strips of masking tape to secure a stencil to the driver's side door. The revolver holstered inside his waistband made it awkward to bend down, but he did not remove it. Around the stencil, he taped sheets of newspaper to protect the paint. Then he went around to the passenger side and affixed a second stencil, identical to the first.

An air compressor rested on the ground nearby, next to a spray gun. Ilya switched on the compressor, then inserted a rubber hose into a matching socket in the gun's base. A quick hiss of air escaped from the nozzle in the split second before he secured it. Once the hose was in place, he tied a respirator mask around his nose and mouth and got to work.

When he was done, he stowed the equipment in the

garage, then went into the basement. The workbench in the corner was covered with odds and ends. Two sheets of vinyl wallpaper were unrolled in the center. He set the wallpaper aside, placing the sheets on a pile of other materials, which included a photograph of an alarm system, its serial number clearly visible.

A computer's optical drive sat nearby, still in its original packaging. Ilya sliced open the box and withdrew the disc burner, which was a rectangular object the size of a trade paperback. Removing the screws, he took the case apart, lifting off the cover like the lid to a casket of secrets.

Inside the case lay a plastic drawer with a circular depression in which a disc could be placed. He removed the drawer, exposing the carriage assembly, a dense mosaic of gears and transistors. At the center of the assembly, like a blue jewel, was the diode used to inscribe data on the surface of the disc.

He took out the laser assembly, sliding it off the metal rails on which it was threaded. With a smaller screwdriver, he removed the fine screws in the assembly to get at the laser diode at its heart. When he was done, the diode lay in the palm of his hand, no larger than the nail of his little finger.

Ilya set the diode aside, mindful of how fragile it was. From another package, he took a laser housing, a silver cylinder the size of a lipstick tube. Taking it apart, he tapped out the existing diode with a ballpoint pen, then installed the diode from the optical drive into the housing, soldering two pins onto the terminals.

The final step was the easiest one. The day before, he had dismantled an aluminum penlight, removing the ring, the reflector, and the bulb. He had also drilled out the reflector so that the laser housing would fit comfortably inside. Now he inserted the housing into the reflector, put all of the pieces back together again, and loaded the batteries into the flashlight.

When he was finished, he checked the assembled device, then switched it on, careful to point it away from his face. A red dot appeared on the far wall, a tight amoeba of light no larger than a pencil eraser. He held the beam in place for a few seconds, then turned it off. The dot disappeared.

Ilya rose from his chair and approached the spot where he had aimed the laser. Where the dot had been, there was a tiny scorched circle, no more than a few millimeters across, where the laser had burned through the paint.

Satisfied by the sight, he cleared the materials from the worktable, tossing the rest of the optical drive into the wastebasket. The flashlight went into his pocket, where it made a reassuring bulge as he went upstairs.

He was a few steps away from the closed basement door when he heard the creak of a floorboard overhead. Instantly, he flattened himself against the stairwell and drew his gun. Someone was moving from the kitchen into the living room. As he listened, another series of creaks came from above.

Ilya reached out with his left hand. Moving very deliberately, he turned the knob. The latch clicked softly as it slid out of the strike plate, so that the door was held shut only by the tension of the jamb.

He counted to three, pulse rising, then kicked the door open. It flew backward and hit the wall as he moved into the kitchen in a combat stance, the gun pointed toward the next room.

A man was there, his back turned, examining something on the table by the foyer. At the sound of the door striking the kitchen wall, he spun around, then broke into a sheepish smile. It was Zhenya.

Ilya, disgusted, slid the revolver back into its holster. As his pulse returned to its normal rate, he noticed two things. The first was that Zhenya had cut his hair, his ponytail replaced by a neat professional cut identical to Ilya's own. The other realization was that the younger man had been toying with the camera on the hall table. He entered the living room. "What have you been doing?"

"Since we're going through all this fucking trouble, I wanted to practice." Zhenya grinned harmlessly. "I've been wondering if we shouldn't just shoot the *suka*. It would be easier—"

Ilya slid the camera back into its shoulder bag. "We aren't here to do things the easy way. We're here to send a message."

Even as he spoke, he knew that there was no way that Zhenya could appreciate the elegance of what they had in mind. For a second, he found himself thinking of the man from Yekaterinburg, a scientist whose hair had been bleached blond, in patches, by the peroxide sprayed from the ceiling of his lab. Years of research had destroyed his immune system, leaving him prone to colds, and he claimed to have lost his sense of smell entirely.

At the exchange, the scientist had not remembered him, but Ilya had known his face. At Vladimir, there had been a research ward, a row of cells facing a long hallway. In each door, a peephole of thick glass had been installed. The holes, no larger than a letterbox, had allowed men in the corridor to look into the cells, which were bare except for a mattress and toilet. The toilets had not been connected to the central plumbing system, allowing the waste to accumulate.

In their hotel room, the scientist had given Ilya a toiletries case. Opening it, Ilya had seen two small containers in separate plastic bags. "As promised," the scientist had said, applying lotion to his skin. "And the money?"

Ilya had handed over the bag. Opening it, the scientist had riffled through a bundle of currency with his raw fingers. Just as he had time to see that only the first few bills were real, Ilya had been behind him with the knife.

On that night, if only for a moment, he had felt like one of the righteous men. For most of his life, a war had raged between the tzaddik and the Scythian, and only rarely did the two halves fall into line. Tomorrow, he hoped, it would happen again. "We'll practice later," Ilya said now. "Is there anything else?"

"Yes," Zhenya said. "I have a present for you. We want to be sure of something."

They went outside, where a station wagon was parked at the curb. In the cargo area, inside a carrier, a mongrel puppy was sleeping. It was an ugly dog with chewed ears, its fur patchy and coarse. When Zhenya lifted the rear door, it raised its head and began to whine.

As he considered the dog, Ilya felt a flicker of pity, which he was careful to put out at once. Thinking again of the tzaddikim, he reminded himself that a just man was sometimes required to do unjust things.

"All right," Ilya said, regarding the dog with deliberate coldness. "Let's bring him inside—"

17

When Maddy emerged from the train at Southampton, she was one of the only passengers to disembark. She had traveled for more than three hours, passing towns with names like Massapequa, Babylon, and Hampton Bays, in order to reach this ramshackle station, where a girl in a sundress and with an orange chemical tan was waiting for her in the parking lot. Opening the door of the hybrid, Maddy slid inside. "Thanks for picking me up. I haven't seen you in so long—"

"I know," the girl said, backing uncertainly out of her parking space. She had been one of Maddy's classmates at art school, and currently worked for a firm that specialized in creating Pop Art canvases from photos of grandchildren and beloved pets. "I want to hear all about this new job of yours."

"What about the share?" Maddy asked. "Did everything work out like we wanted?"

"It's all set." The girl pulled noiselessly into the street. "To be honest, I'm glad you're here. This isn't as fun as it used to be—"

Maddy saw what she meant as soon as they arrived at the share house, an imitation saltbox girded by a low hedge. Ten cars were parked in the driveway, which was asking for trouble. If the police caught wind of the share, which was unambiguously illegal, they wouldn't hesitate to shut it down.

Around back, a dozen shapely bodies were lounging by the pool. The house manager was drinking a beer nearby. With his sheriff's sunglasses, he might have been a suburban weed dealer, although his actual profession was far more lucrative. He shook hands with Maddy, his palm cooled by the beer can. "Glad you could make it. Let me show you around."

Maddy followed him through the sliding glass door, sidestepping a pile of empty bottles. "How many people are here?"

"It's been a pretty good weekend," the manager said. "Maybe forty or so. Last week we had more than sixty—"

Inside the house, backpacks and jackets were heaped in the corners, and every surface was covered with cans and cigarette butts. They went upstairs to one of the bedrooms, in which five beds were wedged side by side. A male guest was passed out, snoring. The air smelled faintly of amyl nitrate.

"You're lucky," the manager said. "You've got a space of your own." Stepping over a mound of dirty laundry, he slid open the closet door. "Plenty of privacy. You even have your own light."

Maddy peered inside. An inflatable mattress was rolled up in one corner. "Perfect."

From her purse, she took two hundred dollars, a cash advance from her credit card, which she handed over with a touch of regret. The manager smiled. "I'll let you get settled, then. Any questions, I'll be outside."

He left the room. As soon as she was by herself, Maddy entered the closet and slid the door shut. She hung up the garment bag containing her dress, a Nicole Miller obtained at great cost from a Nolita rental boutique, then opened her pack, removing a sleeping bag wrapped around a large mirror. She knew from experience that it was important to bring a mirror of her own.

As evening fell, the women lined up for the bathroom, preparing for the shuttle buses that would ferry them to nearby clubs. After changing into her dress, Maddy arranged for a ride with another guest, a banker in boat shoes who had persistently sought her attention. She had been worried that he would make a pass, but as they drove toward Archvadze's estate, he seemed much more interested in peppering her with questions: "So you know this guy personally?"

Maddy sensed a barely concealed hunger in his casual tone. "Nope, just on the guest list. Looking forward to meeting him, though—"

"Yeah, I've heard some great stories. He's stepped on quite a few toes around here. I don't know how much he paid for that mansion, but these guys will shell out a lot for the right area code."

"I'm not surprised," Maddy said. "You say he isn't popular with the neighbors?"

"He's too Coney Island for this crowd. In the old days, you'd never see him south of the Montauk Highway."

They turned onto Gin Lane, where a pair of lamps marked the oligarch's driveway. The hedge was huge and monolithic, the wall of an ostentatious recluse, both discouraging and inviting the eyes of the world. As the car slowed, Maddy turned to the banker. "You can drop me off here."

The banker seemed visibly disappointed. "Well, maybe I'll see you again tonight?"

Maddy favored him with a neutral smile. When she got out, the banker did not drive off at once, as if waiting to see if she would make it inside. Maddy, who was wondering the same thing, approached the security guard at the entrance. "Hi there. The last name is Blume—"

The guard passed his flashlight beam across the clipboard in his hands. "Madeline?"

"That's right." The guard crossed her name off the list and stood aside. Looking over her shoulder, she waved at the banker, who gave her a mock salute and pulled into the road, the gravel crackling beneath his tires.

Overhead, an unaccustomed density of stars had appeared, as if the rich also qualified for a more impressive sky. As she rounded the arc of the driveway, which was curved to hide itself from the street, she entered a garden populated with copper beeches and oaks, trophy trees with their own provenances, each lit splendidly from underneath. A free-span tent had been erected at the center of the grounds, surrounded by countless pots of white flowers that repeated its shape in miniature.

As she picked her way across the lawn, the hem of her dress brushing the grass, she saw a hundred guests scattered across the garden, which was lit by glass votives and citronella torches in terra-cotta pots. Servers in tight golden vests were circulating with flutes of champagne. Pausing at the edge of the crowd, she plucked two glasses from a passing tray, more as a prop than anything else, but when she raised one of the flutes to her lips, she surprised herself by taking a long swallow.

Before venturing any farther, she fell back on an old trick, and imagined that there was a camera before her eyes. When she had first arrived in New York, she had carried a camera to parties, treating it as a protective shield. On most nights, it hadn't even been loaded, but it had been a useful symbol, allowing her to observe from a distance. From such a perspective, every party seemed lovely and doomed, as if it were already peopled by ghosts.

Through this imaginary lens, she scanned the crowd. Guests were clustered in loose handfuls across the lawn, the dark shapes of society photographers scuttling quickly from group to group. The women were dressed in that season's chiffon or satin sheaths, while the males ranged from older men in navy blazers, their buttons made of real mother-of-pearl, to younger figures with smartphones and cabala bracelets, sleeves rolled up in the Italian style.

Feeling the indifferent pressure of the crowd's eyes, she took a moment to savor her solitude. A second later, she saw a face that she was obliged to approach. Griffin, the critic who had added her name to the guest list, was standing near one of the tent's upright supports, his long white hand clutching a gin and tonic. She was about to head in his direction, still bearing two flutes of champagne, when she felt something like a vulture's claw close tightly around her upper arm.

She turned. Standing before her was a gaunt figure in a trapeze dress, the neckline cut to show off a fashionably prominent clavicle. The apparition gave her an alabaster smile and released her grip. "Haven't seen *you* here in a while. I was beginning to wonder if you'd given up on us—"

Maddy leaned in for an air kiss, the feminine movements brisk and precise, as if the two of them were crossing sabers. For a second, she was unable to place her assailant's face, but after mentally restoring a few wrinkles to that unnaturally perfect forehead, she recognized the wife of a distressed asset manager who had been one of her gallery's most reliable clients, and who had just as reliably withdrawn his business at the worst possible time. "Lovely to see you. Is Max here?"

A line of white teeth appeared, straining the tendons on the throat below. "Oh, you'll never find him at one of these things. Ever since the Blue Parrot closed, I can't get him out of the house—"

"A shame," Maddy said. Over the woman's shoulder, she could see Griffin shifting awkwardly in place, and sensed that she had to move quickly. "So how is he doing these days?"

The woman made a dismissive gesture. "Oh, don't ask me to explain what goes on at the office. Although he tells me that this is a fine time for distressed." She fixed her glittering eyes on Maddy's face. "And you? I read somewhere that you were working for one of those new art funds—"

"You can't believe everything you read." Looking at the woman's heightened brows, which had frozen her face into an expression of perpetual surprise, Maddy had an uncomfortable glimpse of her own future. She raised the two champagne flutes in her hands. "In any case, I'd love to catch up, but I should probably be off. My friend will be wondering where his drink is."

"Of course," the woman said, blinking at the glasses. "Delightful to see you again."

Maddy smiled brightly, then continued on her way. As soon as the woman had turned aside, her eyes resuming their scan of the crowd, Maddy discreetly tossed the contents of one of the flutes onto the grass at her feet. She deposited the empty glass with a passing server, then closed in on her target.

Griffin, fortunately, was still alone. When she tapped him on the shoulder, he turned, his face, already reddened into a beacon, lighting up even further. "*Maddy*. So glad you could make it. You look lovely—"

She found herself encircled in a sticky hug, which she did her best to return. "Thanks so much for the invitation."

"My pleasure." Griffin released her and stood back, swirling the ice in his glass. In his nearly shapeless linen suit, he looked to her like a creature from a Tenniel illustration. "I despise these things, but it's a critic's obligation."

"What about our host?" Maddy asked, relieved to have made it this far. "Is he here?"

"Yes, he's right there." Griffin motioned, his glass sloshing, toward a circle of guests standing near the string quartet. "I spoke with him a minute ago. Would you like to meet him?"

Maddy studied the group, which consisted mostly of older couples, the local royalty whom Archvadze clearly wanted to impress. Standing among them was a strikingly beautiful woman in a lilac dress with a brocade belt, her long dark hair gathered up in a flawless chignon. It was Natalia Onegina. A man in a sharkskin suit stood beside her, his back turned.

"That's Archvadze," Griffin said. "Come on, I'll introduce you. Follow me."

He set off into the thick of the crowd. Maddy followed, leaving her remaining glass on a serpentine serving table. As they approached, the clever things that she had planned to say flew out of her head. Her invisible camera had disappeared, and it was only with an effort that she managed to smile as the man in the suit turned around, bringing her face-to-face, for the first time, with Anzor Archvadze.

18

A few moments earlier, on the other side of the estate, a green pickup truck had pulled up at the service entrance. This second driveway, less ostentatious than its counterpart on Gin Lane, was manned by a pair of security guards who had spent most of the evening waving through catering staff, and who now were seated in a parked jeep, sharing a plate of sirloin and piri piri prawns.

The pickup truck slowed to a stop. Biting off most of a prawn, the older guard set its keratinous tail on his plate, wiped his fingers, and got out of the jeep. A heavy flashlight was secured to his belt. He unholstered it, directing its beam toward the truck. On both sides, a logo and phone number had been stenciled in white: SOUTH-AMPTON WASTE REMOVAL.

The guard approached the cab of the pickup, angling the flashlight so that it would not shine into the driver's eyes. Except for a pair of gloves on the seat, the passenger side was empty. "Evening," the guard said.

"Evening," the driver replied. He was an older man with graying hair and a mustache, his coveralls faded with use. Despite his age, he seemed wiry and strong. "Here for trash pickup."

The guard glanced at his watch. "A little early, aren't you? It's only nine o'clock."

"I was told to come now," the driver said. He had a slight accent, perhaps Russian or Eastern European. "Get stuff from caterers first, then come back at midnight for second load."

"Okay, let me check." Lowering his flashlight, the guard took the phone from his belt, pressing the button to talk. As he called the main house for confirmation, he shone his flashlight across the bed of the pickup, which was bare except for a folded tarpaulin. Checking under the canvas, he found nothing. Then he knelt and directed his light under the chassis, which was clean as well. Finally, he went back to the cab of the truck, shining the flashlight onto the empty passenger seat.

"Seems like a big job for one guy," the guard said. "You working alone tonight?"

The driver shrugged. "They paid for one man. If they pay for more, I bring more. Not a problem. I'll be out of here soon."

"Don't hurt yourself doing it," the guard said, thinking privately that there was something strange about the arrangement. Normally, these contractors would toss in a couple of undocumented workers for free, but instead, they'd sent an old guy, perhaps the owner, who had to be pushing sixty.

Before he could ask about this, his phone beeped. "Roger," the command post said. "They're on the list."

"Copy that." The guard stood aside. "You're good to go. Just follow the driveway."

"Thank you," the driver said. Touching the bill of his cap, he eased the truck through the service entrance, heading up the gravel drive. The mansion glowed in the distance, its windows lit brightly from within.

The pickup continued along the driveway until the service entrance was out of sight, then cut its lights and halted. At this point, halfway between the road and the main house, there was no outdoor lighting, and the pickup, which had been painted dark green for this very reason, was all but invisible.

It remained there, idling, for a few seconds. There was a click as the driver pulled the handle of the release cable on the dashboard, popping the hood. Then the hood swung up, rising like the cover of an antique phonograph, and two shadowy figures climbed out of the hood compartment.

Lowering himself to the ground, Ilya helped Zhenya out of the hood, the truck bouncing slightly on its springs. The two men were dressed in identical dark brown suits, black plastic glasses, and shoes with crepe soles. Each had a camera bag slung over one shoulder.

Ilya closed the hood and went over to the driver's side, where Sharkovsky was waiting behind the wheel. The old man's eyes glittered in the darkness. "Thirty minutes. No more. *Udachi.*"

"*Udachi,*" Ilya said. He turned away, moving quickly across the lawn, with Zhenya falling into step beside him. His glasses had steamed up, so he took them off and wiped them on the front of his suit. Behind him, the truck continued on toward the house, as if it had only paused to get its bearings.

Although it had not been his idea, Ilya was pleased by the ruse. The truck was a mid-engine pickup, its engine mounted at the center of the vehicle, beneath the seats.

For racing, the design provided favorable weight distribution, reducing the vehicle's moment of inertia and making it easier to turn. More importantly, it left the hood compartment empty, except for the battery, tank, and radiator. And no one ever thought to check under the hood.

The two men walked together across the grass, mirroring each other stride for stride. Before reaching the circle of light cast by the house, they separated. As he turned to go, Ilya caught the other man's eye. "*Udachi.*"

"*Udachi,*" Zhenya said, grinning broadly enough to push the glasses up his cheeks. Then he headed for the tent, the camera bag slung over his shoulder. Within seconds, he had disappeared into the crowd.

Ilya turned to face the mansion, which glowed like a winter palace. It was a labyrinth, but he knew all of its secrets. As he crossed the lawn, he undid the clasps of his bag, giving him easier access to his gun.

Keeping an eye out for security, he made it to the porch. The front doors were wide open. A bay window overlooked the lawn, illuminating a patch of manicured grass. When he looked inside, through the entrance hall, he could see guests in the living room, seated in tub chairs.

He went quickly inside, as if he were coming home. It was five minutes past nine.

19

"Anzor Archvadze, meet Maddy Blume," Griffin said, his shyness falling away as he assumed the role of art world insider. "Maddy works for the Reynard Art Fund. Perhaps you've heard of it?"

"Pleased to meet you," Archvadze said, taking her hand in a warm grip. Up close, he was not nearly as intimidating as his reputation had suggested. His voice was soft, with only the trace of an accent, and his demeanor retained something of the engineer he had once been. "We are very glad you could come."

"Thank you," Maddy said, her heart racing. "It's been a really wonderful party."

As she spoke, she saw a flicker of boredom in Archvadze's expression, and knew that she had said the wrong thing. Before the oligarch could turn away, she added quickly, "I was admiring your trees. The conifers remind me of plantings I've seen at Alfonso Ossorio's home. Have you been there?"

At the mention of trees, a light appeared in Archvadze's eyes. "Yes, I have," the oligarch said. "One of the saplings comes from Ossorio's garden at the Creeks. You're interested in trees?"

"I'm interested in Ossorio," Maddy said. "My fund owns several of his paintings."

"I've found that many artists are drawn to gardening, especially in such a town as this. The Japanese maple by the gazebo comes from a tree in the garden of Robert Dash, or so my gardener tells me. Of course, the provenance of older trees can be hard to establish—"

Maddy was about to respond when she saw something that drove all other thoughts away. Standing to one side was the bidder from the auction. Tonight, he was more fashionably dressed, but his neck still strained against his shirt collar, and when he raised his glass, she saw that his cufflinks were red heptagrams.

Archvadze followed her gaze. "If you admire the trees, you should thank my assistant, Zakaria Kostava. He is the one who arranges for their care. I have less time than I would like for such things."

Kostava inclined his head politely, then turned aside. It wasn't clear if he recognized her or not. "You seem to know your artists," Maddy said to Archvadze. "I hear you've got quite a collection."

Archvadze turned to his girlfriend. "Whatever she wants, I buy. That is all I know."

Natalia smiled at this. She was two inches taller than Maddy, with violet eyes and a Persian profile. "Nonsense. You have excellent taste."

"I have the taste of an old man," Archvadze replied. "If you look at revolutionists, you see that they always have the most bourgeois tastes in art. Even Lenin was afraid of the avant-garde."

"Lenin didn't have your money," Maddy said. "So what are you buying these days?"

Archvadze glanced at his assistant before responding. "Oh, I prefer something with a history. Art must be allowed to age before its quality can be known. It is the same way with trees, and, perhaps, with men. Natalia, of course, doesn't agree with me. She only wants the latest thing—"

Natalia turned to Maddy, who felt the woman's scrutiny as an almost physical tickling across her face, the cool appraisal of one alpha female toward another. "You know a great deal about this area. Were you born here?"

"No, I'm not a native," Maddy said. For an uneasy second, in the oily light of the citronella, she wondered if the other woman could sense her underlying desperation. "I live in the city, but I'm really from Athens, Georgia."

Natalia only pursed her lips, her interest snuffed out at once, but the oligarch seemed amused. "I'm Georgian, too," Archvadze said, laughing quietly at his own joke. "I only hope your Georgia is as beautiful as mine—"

Before Maddy could respond, a woman in a scalloped blouse plucked Archvadze's sleeve, saying that there was someone here he absolutely had to meet. Archvadze smiled distractedly at Maddy, saying that he was pleased to have made her acquaintance, and drifted off into the crowd. The others followed. Before Maddy knew it, the circle of guests had dissolved.

"He's an intriguing character," Griffin was saying. "Not nearly as rough as some of these other oligarchs. I suspect that he knows more about art than he claims. Or perhaps he only sees it as an investment."

Watching as their host approached another group of attendees, Maddy felt as if an opportunity had been lost.

Fighting off her dissatisfaction, she told herself that she had really come for the good of the fund, and that a look at the art collection would mean that the night had not been wasted.

"I need to run to the ladies' room," Maddy said to Griffin. "You'll wait for me?"

Griffin drained his glass. "Actually, I'll walk you there. It's a vulgar impulse, I know, but I'd like to get a look at this man's house. Afterward, we can talk about the Vered Gallery—"

Maddy stared blankly into the critic's face, then remembered her cover story. Leaning forward, she kissed him on the cheek. "Business can wait for now. Why don't you get me a drink and save me a place by the music? That way, when I get back, we'll be able to talk in private."

"Of course," Griffin stammered, a blush flooding across his face. "I'll be here."

He gave her a smile and drifted off toward the bar. Maddy waited until he was gone, then turned and all but ran for the mansion. After hightailing it for a second, she glanced back at Archvadze, who was enduring another round of small talk. A man in a brown suit and glasses had approached the circle, a camera in one hand. He said something inaudible to the guests, who lined up obediently, with the oligarch standing in the middle. The flash left a green smudge on her retinas.

Passing through the main door of the house, Maddy found herself in an entrance hall that smelled sweetly of cedar. It had been furnished in a patrician grandfather style, with a richly patterned carpet. In the living room, a few guests were seated near the bay window. As they glanced at her idly, wondering if she was anyone worth knowing, Maddy moved onward, keeping one eye on the walls.

What she found was disappointing. Above the mantelpiece hung a massive cityscape of Venice, which she recognized as one of thousands of identical oil paintings produced every year by factory cities in China. Reaching into her handbag, Maddy withdrew a digital camera and took a picture. The real collection, she told herself, had to be somewhere else.

She wandered into the dining room. The furniture was heavy and expensive, but the walls, again, were covered in postcard art, not far removed from Thomas Kinkade. Frustrated, she took another picture and moved into the sitting room, its hardwood floor covered in checked rugs, which shifted slightly beneath her feet. The art here was even worse. Without a trace of surprise, she saw that a Jack Vettriano had been given pride of place above the mantelpiece.

Feeling vaguely dissatisfied, Maddy did not notice, at first, that there was someone else in the room. Finally, she saw a man in a dark blue suit standing with his back to her. He was studying the painting above the fireplace with an almost humorous intensity. As she watched, he slid a camera from his pocket, took a step backward, and snapped a picture. When he turned around, Maddy saw who it was, and was unable to speak for a long moment.

"Hello, Maddy," Ethan said, his face brightening. "What are you doing here?"

20

"This is ridiculous," Powell said, looking out at the hedge wall. "How are we supposed to watch a house like this?"

They were parked on Gin Lane, within sight of the main entrance, observing the estate from an unmarked sedan. Through his window, which was rolled down, Powell could hear music from an unseen string quartet, rendered unreal by the distance, like fairy song. Above the hedge, there was a palpable glow, like the light flung onto an overcast sky by a city at night.

"I don't know what you expected," Wolfe said. There was an edge of irritation in her voice, perhaps because they had driven two hours to stare at a hedge. "All of these houses are like this."

"I still can't believe it." Powell ran his eyes along the hedge, which reminded him of the defensive wall, a thousand years old, that encircled the town of his boyhood. "What does he have to hide?"

"It makes you wonder how much of this wealth is real," Wolfe said. "Most of these mansions are mortgaged to the hilt. When the bottom falls out of the market, this will turn into a ghost town."

It wasn't the first time that Powell had heard her express these sentiments. "You think there will be a crash?"

"Read the signs. Too much debt, not enough capital investment. If I were you, I'd get ready for seven lean years." Wolfe reached for a cup of lime gelatin. "I say we go inside. Tell security. We aren't doing any good here."

"We can't," Powell said. "If Sharkovsky learns that we've contacted Archvadze—"

"He'll suspect that we have a wire. I know. But so far, this is all flipping pointless."

Powell didn't have a good response to this. They had been parked here for hours, dutifully noting each arrival, but had seen only the town cars and sport utility vehicles of the Hamptons elite.

Watching the guests from a distance, feeling disheveled from hours in the car, Powell had experienced a curious twinge of English guilt. It was easier to stake out a building in Brighton Beach, where domestic life often spilled out onto the streets. Here, the hedge formed a stark boundary between public and private space, as if the lives inside had nothing to do with the world beyond.

He watched as a jeep rolled down the driveway and signaled for a turn. As it passed, he caught a glimpse of the men inside, a pair of guards in white polo shirts. He wondered if Archvadze imported any of his muscle from home. In Russia, an entrepreneur needed protection to survive, usually in the form of corrupt cops and roofs from the local gangs. Even in his adopted country, the oligarch would not have been likely to change his ways, at least not entirely.

"I'm not even sure we can trust Archvadze," Powell said now, keeping his eye on the jeep. "You can't make a fortune in the Russian auto industry without reaching an understanding with organized crime. Privatization has always been funded by the underworld. So has politics."

Wolfe peeled back the lid from her cup of gelatin. "With all due respect, I'm not sure that I buy the government connection. These gangs hate the Chekists. They swear never to cooperate with the military or police, and if a gangster is revealed as a traitor or informant, he's exiled or put to death—"

"Which doesn't mean that they can't serve the state's interests in other ways," Powell said. "Take another example. Until a few years ago, a Delta jet flew from New York to Moscow five times a week with a hundred million dollars in its cargo hold. No one tried to steal it, because it was going to the mob. They would steal oil from Siberia, sell it on the spot market, then place a currency order in New York. When the cash arrived, it was used to pay off members of the Duma."

Wolfe popped a green spoonful into her mouth. "So what's your point, exactly?"

"My point is that it wasn't just the Russians who decided to look the other way. The bank earned a commission on every transaction. The Treasury Department earned ninety-six cents from every dollar that left the country. They'll only take action if we can prove that it's in their best interests to do so. The connection between money laundering and terrorism is what finally shut down the money plane. And another way to bring down the system—"

"—is to connect it to domestic crime," Wolfe said. "All right. But what makes you so sure that Sharkovsky is involved?"

"Experience. No *vor* works in isolation. If the money plane is out of commission, they'll find something else to take its place. The connections are there. It's only a matter of seeing them."

"It's also a matter of funding. And at the moment, it's a hard sell." Finishing the gelatin, Wolfe tossed the empty cup into the backseat, where it joined several others. "Why are you so interested in the foreign angle, anyway?"

"My father's influence, I suppose," Powell said. "He was a member of the civil service, a diplomat, with the most orderly mind I've ever seen. He spent most of his life chasing these connections."

He expected her to ask him what his father had done, but she only took a sip of cocoa. "He sounds like a remarkable man."

Powell looked through the windshield at the estate. "Yes. You might say he was."

"I'm sorry," Wolfe said, with what sounded like genuine sympathy. "I didn't know he had passed away."

"He hasn't." Powell turned aside. "Not exactly. But he hasn't been entirely well."

In the silence that followed, he had time to remember how insidious his father's decline had been, passing invisibly from harmless, even comical mistakes, like neglecting to turn off the cold water tap, to aimless wandering far into the night, opening drawers and rummaging in closets. In the end, a man exquisitely attuned to ideas had disintegrated to the point where he would repeatedly grope at patterns on the carpet, thinking that there was something on the floor.

Powell was still brooding over this when a pickup truck emerged from the service entrance, loaded with plump bags of garbage. It pulled into the road, then turned left, moving away from where the sedan was parked. Something about it caught his eye, but before he could reach for his binoculars, his phone rang.

It was Barlow. "There's a fax for you on my desk. They've identified your dead girl."

Even before the agent had finished speaking, Powell had his notepad out, glad for the distraction. "What do we know?"

There was a theatrical rustle of papers. "Her name is Karina Baranova. She was born in Kargopol and emigrated to the city ten years ago. Unmarried. No record. According to her file, she taught ballet in Brooklyn Heights. And guess where she worked on the weekends?"

Powell knew that this flood of information would make it impossible for the police to ignore the case any longer. "The Club Marat."

"You're one smart Indian—you know that? She danced in their floor show. When she vanished two years ago, she was reported missing by the ballet academy. Your analysis of the weather records was what narrowed it down. I suppose I should congratulate you for that—"

"What about Sharkovsky? Was he questioned in connection with her disappearance?"

"It looks like they interviewed someone at the club, but it wasn't him. There wasn't enough evidence to dig further, so they let it die. Now, of course, they're breathing down my neck. I need you and Wolfe to keep them in line."

Powell pushed his glasses up the bridge of his nose. "I'm not sure if that's the best use of my time. Or Wolfe's, for that matter—"

"You know why Hoover loved the Mormons? They respect authority. Wolfe understands how the system works. If you're smart, you'll take a page from her book. I'll see both of you in the morning."

Barlow hung up. Powell pocketed his own phone. "How much of that did you hear?"

"Enough," Wolfe said, her face in shadow. "Now that the police have a name, they aren't going to hold off on the investigation."

"We'll give them something discreet to do in the meantime. Something that will keep them happy, but won't blow our cover. If they want to put a tracker on Sharkovsky's car, say—"

A second later, he remembered what he had seen in the instant before Barlow called. "Oh, fuck me," Powell said. "I can't believe this—"

The car's tires sprayed gravel as he pulled into the street. Wolfe was flung sideways by the sudden movement, which sent empty gelatin cups flying. "What do you think you're doing?"

"*The truck.*" Powell slammed a hand against the dashboard, hard enough to hurt. "The one with the garbage. Did you see it?"

"Yes, but—" Wolfe broke off, struck by the same realization. "Are you sure?"

"I'm sure," Powell said. They reached the intersection at the end of the road. Even as he tried to decide which way to go, he feared that he had waited too long. The image of a truck danced before his eyes, the one that he had seen in the Assyrian boy's bedroom, in a photo taken when the hood had still been adorned with the crest of the Russian empire. Sharkovsky, or one of his men, was here.

21

Ilya moved silently through the mansion. Lights had been left on throughout the house, a luminous backdrop for the party outside, but he had no fear of being seen. Security cameras had been installed on the mansion's eaves, but the rooms themselves were unmonitored, allowing Archvadze to live in privacy. Only one door, the one that counted, was covered by a camera.

He passed a pair of women moving unsteadily across the carpeted floor, their bracelets softly clinking. Feeling their eyes glide across his suit and camera bag, pointedly ignoring him, he knew that they would not remember, or even register, his face. As indispensible as photographers were to the ecology of this world, it was in poor taste to even imply that you wanted your picture taken.

Once the women had gone, he took a flight of servants' stairs to the second floor. Going to the end of the corridor, he entered the master bedroom. It was an airy room with a Palladian window, the tieback curtains drawn. A third of the floor was dominated by the bed, its posts nearly touching the ceiling. An antique vanity was flanked by two doors. One led to a bathroom; the other, to the study.

Ilya shut the door behind him, leaving it slightly ajar.

Heading for the bathroom, he passed the vanity, which testified to a woman's presence. A second later, seeing the room reversed in the mirror, he noticed the night-stand. He turned. On the table by the bed, there was a hardcover novel, a lamp, and a cell phone plugged into its charger. He recognized it at once.

Placing his bag on the carpet, Ilya unzipped its main compartment and removed a pair of gloves and a surgical mask. He slipped the gloves onto both hands, his fingers groping in their cocoon of latex, and tied the mask around his face, keeping one ear tuned to sounds from outside.

From his inside pocket, he took a sealed plastic bag containing a cotton swab. Opening the bag, he fished out the swab and brushed it lightly across the surface of the phone. The residue dried instantly, leaving no visible trace. When he was done, he slid the swab back into its bag, which he resealed tightly and pocketed again. He replaced his gloves with a fresh pair, stuffing the used gloves and mask into a separate bag. The phone went back on the bedside table.

He headed for the study. Inside, all four walls were lined with books, leather-bound volumes that had been bought by the foot. A desk with a rolling Aeron chair stood in the middle of the room.

To his left, between two bookcases, there was a plain wooden door. Above the frame, a camera had been mounted to the wall, its convex lens trained on the area immediately before the doorway. Next to the doorknob, which locked with an ordinary key, there was a numeric keypad.

Ilya remained where he was. At this angle, he could not be seen. Opening his camera case, he removed the penlight that he had assembled the day before. He unscrewed the base of the flashlight, allowing one of the batteries to slide out, and reversed it. Earlier, he had inverted the battery out of concern that the light would accidentally switch on in his bag.

Screwing the base back on, he entered the study. He took one step, then another, until he could see the black hemisphere of the camera's lens, while keeping his body out of its viewing range. Then he extended his arm, aiming the penlight toward the camera, and pressed the switch.

A red dot, not quite as focused as the beam from a commercial laser, appeared on the lens. He knew that the camera's sensor, which was at least as sensitive as the retina of the human eye, would be burned out at once. At most, the camera would have registered a fleeting image of his hand with the flashlight, creeping into the frame a second before it went dark.

To be on the safe side, he continued to burn out the sensor until a thin wisp of smoke drifted up from the camera's housing. Then he switched off the flashlight. Now that the camera had been disabled, he estimated that several minutes would pass before a guard came to inspect it.

Ilya closed and locked the door of the study. Kneeling, he opened his camera case and removed the items inside. He slipped the penlight into his pocket, while the revolver went into the holster inside his waistband. Everything else he laid out on the carpet: a combination drill and jigsaw, a compass, a roll of tape, a magnet, a pair of pliers, and a large envelope made of vinyl wallpaper.

He looked up at the door of the vault, which was featureless and smooth, and allowed himself to picture what lay beyond it. Taking the compass in one hand and the drill in the other, he got to work.

22

"After Christian Rosencreutz died, the location of his tomb was lost," Maddy said, a sip of champagne going pleasantly to her head. "A hundred and twenty years later, the Rosicrucians found a secret door in the wall of their ancestral castle. Inside, there was a room lit by an artificial sun, along with an inscription that read: *While living, I made this compact copy of the universe, my grave.*"

"Too bad it's only an allegory," Ethan said. "There's no evidence that Rosencreutz ever existed, much less built a tomb for himself—"

"That isn't the point," Maddy said, feigning indignation. For all her own doubts about this line of reasoning, she wanted him to play along. "The Rosicrucians believed it. And it influenced Duchamp."

Ethan set aside a vodka and tonic. They were seated together on a living room sofa, across from another couple by the bay window, the woman's legs crossed to show off the red soles of her shoes. "Duchamp inspires all kinds of wild notions. If all you've done is turn him into a Rosicrucian, you aren't trying hard enough. Have you heard of his connection to the Black Dahlia?"

Maddy regarded him with amusement. She had been hoping to entertain him with her theory about the Rosicrucians, but now it seemed that he had done her one better. "I can't say that I have."

"If you read enough about Duchamp, especially online, it's bound to come up eventually. You know the story, right? A woman named Elizabeth Short was found dead in a field in Los Angeles, cut in half at the waist. The two halves of her body were ten inches apart, and her hands were bent over her head, like this—" Ethan arched his arms like a ballet dancer in the fifth position. "The killer was never found. But more than one critic has noticed that the crime scene photographs, with a naked body lying in the grass, look surprisingly similar to a certain work of art."

Maddy finished her champagne. "So Marcel Duchamp killed the Black Dahlia?"

"Unfortunately, he was out of the country at the time. But several enterprising critics have speculated that he knew the killer's identity. The prime suspect in the case is a doctor named George Hodel, an art collector and friend of Man Ray, Duchamp's closest collaborator. And the first study for the installation was once thought to have been executed only a few months after the murder."

"Or so everyone used to believe. But the new study pushes the date back at least three decades, when it was displayed at the Section d'Or. Which is more than thirty years too soon."

"But for the true paranoid, there's a deeper order at work. Section d'Or is the golden section, the ratio of the height of the body to the height of the navel. Which is precisely where Elizabeth Short was cut in half."

Although his voice was grave, she saw a playful gleam in his eye. "Are you serious?"

"Not really. But it's no more far-fetched than any other theory. Duchamp's art doesn't have a hidden message. It's about process, like a game of chess. He was a chess master, you know, and in chess, dogmatists get slaughtered. His critics would do well to keep this in mind."

She was surprised to hear him speak so passionately. "I didn't know you were a fan."

"For me, it's less about the art than about the man. Duchamp belonged to no school or movement, lived in poverty for years, and spent his life trying to meet his own standards of intellectual purity. A movement of one. I admire that. Which is why I can't buy any of these theories."

"But isn't that what you do for a living?" Maddy asked teasingly. "You reduce art to parameters in a pricing model. How is that different from what these conspiracy theorists have done?"

"It's completely different," Ethan said, his tone light and undefensive. "I deal in verifiable facts. If I enter bad data, the model will break. But if I want to connect Duchamp to the Rosicrucians or the Black Dahlia, as long as I'm clever enough, I can prove anything. It isn't fair to him, that's all."

As Ethan spoke, Maddy studied him, her gaze slowed and prolonged by the wine. In his suit and tie, he was oddly attractive. His face was as smooth as a doll's, but his eyes were quick, and they seemed to catch on her own. "So how did you get in here, anyway? Did you sneak past security?"

Ethan seemed genuinely surprised by the suggestion.

"Why would I do that? I called Natalia Onegina's publicist, dropped the name of the fund, and asked to be put on the guest list. It wasn't so hard. Of course, it would have been easier if I'd been an attractive woman—"

Maddy blushed, although she wasn't sure if it was because of the implied compliment or because this approach had failed to occur to her. "But how did you find out about the party?"

"I had my ear to the ground," Ethan said. "You aren't the only one with connections."

She saw again that she had underestimated him. "Does Reynard know you're here?"

"Not yet." Ethan gave her what was evidently meant as a cryptic smile. "I'm not sure he would approve, at least not before the fact. Later, if I bring him something useful, I'm sure he'll agree that it was necessary."

"But we may not have anything to show him. You've seen the art here. There's nothing you couldn't buy on a Carnival Cruise. For all we know, the real collection could be in storage. Or in a free port—"

"Or maybe it's in a part of the house we haven't seen yet." Ethan leaned forward, as if to confide a secret. "A few days ago, I found a profile of this house in an architectural journal. I was hoping to find pictures of the art on the walls, but it didn't have anything useful—"

"Where did you find a profile? I looked everywhere, and couldn't find a thing."

"Archvadze wasn't mentioned by name. I did a search for the previous owner, and found a profile that ran two months after the house was sold, probably just after Archvadze redecorated. But here's the important part. All the photos in the article were taken on the ground floor."

Maddy saw where this was going. "And there was nothing from the second floor?"

"Nope." There was something amused and provocative in his eyes. "Are you thinking what I'm thinking?"

Maddy, studying his face, realized that she was thinking of something that had nothing do with the art collection. An unmistakable feeling had been gathering over the past few minutes, in the part of her brain where bad ideas arose, and as she looked at Ethan, it only grew stronger.

An instant before the feeling was fully formed, she pushed it away. It was absurd. But the only way to remove it entirely was to replace it with another reckless idea, as one peg might be driven out by another.

"Come on," Maddy said, rising from the sofa. "Let's see what we can find upstairs."

23

Standing before the door in the study, Ilya ran his compass along the frame, watching the needle closely. When it passed across a point one foot above the knob, the needle trembled. He ran it over the spot a second time to make sure, and saw the same fluctuation. To be safe, he swept the compass all around the door, checking for a backup switch, and found nothing.

The camera case that had contained his equipment lay at his feet, empty. Picking up the bag, he slipped it over his right hand, which was clutching the cordless drill. The bag was large enough to cover both his hand and the drill itself, forming a sort of shapeless mitt. Squeezing the trigger, he activated the drill, boring a tiny hole in the base of the bag, which allowed the tip of the bit to emerge. Then he zipped the mouth of the bag over his wrist.

With the makeshift silencer snugly enveloping his hand, Ilya drilled a pilot hole in the door, next to where the compass had fluctuated. It took only a few seconds before the tip of the drill penetrated to the other side of the wood, allowing the bit to turn freely. Ilya withdrew it and removed his hand from the camera case, replacing the bit with a jigsaw attachment. Then he pulled the bag over the drill again, poking the tip of the saw through the hole that he had cut in the base.

Going back to the door, he inserted the blade into the pilot hole and began to cut through the dense wood, guiding the saw upward and to the left. Although it was tedious work, he was careful not to rush, afraid of dulling the reciprocating blade. He eased it up and around, sawing a circular opening in the door that was just big enough to accommodate his arm up to the elbow. His glasses doubled as goggles, protecting his eyes from stray chips.

When he was finished curving the incision back to where he had started, he was left with an amoeboid hole, sealed with a plug of wood. With his free hand, he pushed out the plug, hearing it fall to the floor in the other room. He put his eye to the opening that he had made, but saw nothing but darkness.

Two minutes had passed since he had disabled the camera. He estimated that he had another three minutes before he would need to worry about security. Although time was running out, he forced himself to move deliberately, knowing that a hasty mistake would cost him more than anything else.

From the equipment on the floor, he took a neodymium magnet, the size of a sardine tin, that he had procured from a hobbyist's kit. He applied several lengths of double-sided tape to the flat side of the magnet. Then he stuck his hand into the hole in the door and taped the magnet to the inside jamb.

Based on photographs of the system, provided by the same source as the floor plans, he had determined that it consisted of a simple reed switch. If the door was opened without deactivating the switch, its movement would remove a magnetic field, opening the contacts and triggering an alarm. Taping a second magnet to the jamb would circumvent the system. Or so he hoped.

In any case, it was too late to worry about this now. Reaching through the opening he had made, Ilya unlocked the door from the inside, turned the inner knob, and pushed the door open.

No alarm sounded. He entered the room, leaving the lights off. The space was windowless, the size of a prison cell. Inside, there were five racks of paintings, mounted on casters that allowed them to be rolled out one at a time. He took the handle of the nearest rack, yanking it in his direction. Two canvases slid into view, neither the one he wanted. He did not give them a second glance, although one was a Braque and the other was a Bonnard.

Ilya slid out the next rack. There, mounted securely to the mesh, was *Study for Étant Donnés*. In the darkness of the vault, illuminated only by the light from the room outside, the headless woman on the grass seemed furtive, concealed, as if she were the bearer of a secret message.

With a pair of pliers, he removed the fasteners that held the painting to the mesh and took it into his arms. In his hands, it seemed very light, a delicate armature of canvas and wood. Then he opened the envelope that he had made out of patterned wallpaper and slid the painting inside. It fit perfectly.

There was a flap at the mouth of the envelope, which he folded over and sealed with a length of tape. The finishing touch, of which he was inordinately proud, was a bow of red ribbon, which he removed from its adhesive backing and slapped onto one side of the envelope.

Moving quickly now, he stuffed the rest of his equipment, including the drill with the saw attachment, back into the camera bag. The flashlight remained in his pocket, next to the revolver inside his waistband.

He left the vault and returned to the study. Looking for a place to dispose of the bag, he saw that a gap of several inches separated the rear panel of the bookcase from the wall. He squeezed the bag into this space, shoving hard to push it inside. When he stood back, he could barely see the bag wedged between the wall and the shelf. It wasn't perfect, but it would do.

Ilya tucked the painting, disguised as a birthday present, under his right arm, carrying nothing else in his hands. Pausing for a moment, as he had in Budapest, he asked himself if there was anything that he had overlooked. This time, he decided, he was safe. He had outgrown his phase of carelessness.

With this reassuring thought, Ilya went to the study door, unlocked it, and reemerged into the master bedroom, still carrying the painting. It was only then that he realized that he was not alone.

24

Maddy and Ethan had left the living room a few minutes earlier, looking for a way to the second floor. The grand staircase had seemed too obvious; climbing it would be an act of blatant trespass. Although she didn't know where she was going, Maddy led the way, not wanting Ethan to assume control.

As they headed for the rear of the house, searching for a way up, she glanced back at Ethan, who was following close behind. Her feelings toward him were shifting rapidly, and she wasn't sure what form they would ultimately take. She was surprised by the possibility that she was attracted to someone so cerebral and detached, qualities that she had pointedly avoided in men, until now.

At the moment, Ethan seemed inseparable from his usual rational self. "If there's a servants' staircase, it's probably near the kitchen. Or the dining room. Didn't we pass one earlier?"

Maddy remembered the table flanked by Windsor chairs. "You're right." She pivoted, turning back the way she had come. "If you knew it was there, why didn't you say anything?"

Ethan grinned. "I was following you. You seemed to know what you were doing."

They retraced their steps to the dining room. As Ethan had guessed, a door beside a china cabinet led to a flight of stairs. Ascending, Maddy found herself in an empty corridor. "Now what?"

"He'll want to keep his art close," Ethan said. "Near the master bedroom, maybe."

Maddy saw the same challenging look in his eyes as before. "You're sure you want to do this?"

"If I were alone, I'd have turned back by now. With two of us, it's less suspicious."

Maddy saw his point. A man or woman wandering alone through the mansion would look strange, but a couple had a convenient motivation. Smiling at the unspoken implication, she advanced down the corridor so that Ethan would not see her face. She had picked the direction at random, and was surprised to find herself, a few seconds later, at an actual bedroom door. It was ajar. Turning back, she looked at Ethan, who was one step behind her. "You really want to keep going?"

Instead of responding, Ethan reached forward and pushed the door open. "Why not?"

Maddy's smile, already halfway formed, faltered at the thought that they were testing one another, trying to see how far the other would go. So far, it had been amusing, but she wasn't sure where it would end. If they found the art collection, the escalation would stop there. But if they failed, she had a feeling that the evening would conclude in some other way.

She entered the bedroom. At her side, Maddy felt

Ethan go quiet, as if he, too, sensed that the mood had changed. Five minutes ago, they had been embedded in the party, talking within earshot of the other guests, but now they were alone. Something about the bedroom it-self, with its visible signs of a couple's private life, made the situation seem even more charged.

Maddy, feeling pressed up against the awkwardness of the moment, decided to push straight through it. She went farther into the room, acting more boldly than she felt. A few steps ahead, a door led to the bathroom, while an adjacent door was closed. She was moving to-ward the second door, wondering if she was reckless enough to open it, when her attention was caught by something on the nightstand. Going to the bedside table, she picked it up. It was a cell phone.

Ethan came closer. The amusement was gone from his face. "What are you doing?"

As she looked at the phone, not listening, Maddy was struck by another thought. If this was Archvadze's phone, it would contain his address book, as well as a record of his calls. This was information that the fund would love to know, and it would only take a second to retrieve it.

Maddy slid a finger across the touchpad of the phone. The interface was sleek and intuitive, allowing her to find the call history with ease. "Give me a second. I want to check something."

"Wait," Ethan said. "Searching the house is one thing, but this is crossing the line—"

Ignoring him, she scrolled through the list of incom-ing calls. The first few were to contacts with Georgian names, a blur of consonants and patronyms. Failing to see anyone she recognized, she was about to switch to outgoing calls when Ethan, tired of being ignored, plucked the phone from her hands. He closed the call history, his finger moving swiftly across the touchpad, and put the phone back on the nightstand. "We need to get out of here."

She was about to tell him to mind his own business when she heard a door open behind her. When she turned, she saw a stranger emerging from the door of the study. He was slender, dressed in a brown suit, his face framed by a pair of black plastic glasses. A present wrapped in gift paper was tucked under his right arm. The paper, she saw, was covered in roses.

When the man in the brown suit saw Ethan and Maddy, his eyes widened briefly, then narrowed. Before either of them could speak or react, the man reached down and drew a revolver.

"On the floor," the man said, his words touched by a Slavic accent. "Both of you."

Ethan seemed caught off guard by the unreality of the situation. "Are you kidding?"

The man pointed the revolver at Maddy's head. "On the floor now. Nose to the rug."

Maddy knelt, her eyes on the gun. Even as she lowered herself to the ground, she was overwhelmed by a sense of the absurd. Through her dress, the pile of the rug pressed up against her knees.

"Lie down on your faces." The man moved forward into the bedroom. "Quickly."

Maddy obeyed, resting her face on the clean nap of the carpet. Ethan lay down next to her. He seemed on the verge of laughter, as if he couldn't believe it either, but there was a grain of real fear in his eyes. Then she felt the pressure of five cool fingers, and realized that he had taken her by the hand.

The man in the brown suit seemed to hesitate, as if weighing what to do next. At last, he headed for the door. "Count to one hundred. If you move before then, I'll be waiting for you—"

He left the bedroom, closing the door behind him. Maddy remained on the floor, her heart thudding against the carpet. She knew exactly what had been inside that package. Part of her wanted to share this insight with Ethan, whose face was only a few inches from her own, but in the end, she said nothing. Before long, she knew, they would need to confront what had happened, and both of their lives would change, but for now, she could think of nothing else but his hand in hers.

25

In the corridor outside the bedroom, Ilya dropped his glasses into a vase on the hallway table, hearing them ring softly as they struck the porcelain. His gloves went into the vase as well. He reached a second set of stairs, bypassing the one that led to the dining room. Descending to an empty corridor, he headed for the rear of the house, the package tucked securely under one arm.

As he was approaching the sun porch, through the open door, he saw the ember of a cigarette and the curve of a broad shoulder in a white knit shirt. At the sound of his footsteps, the guard began to turn. Without breaking stride, Ilya reversed himself and went in the opposite direction.

Now the only way out was through the front door. He went back through the house, moving unhurriedly past groups of guests, and headed for the foyer. A second later, he was outside. Ten yards away stood a cluster of shrubs, an island of refuge on the grass. On his way there, he passed a second guard, one close to his own age, who glanced at him momentarily before looking away.

In the distance rose the luminous pavilion of the tent, the sounds of laughter and conversation still drifting across the lawn. He walked past it at a brisk pace, the grass springy beneath his shoes, until he arrived at the topiary spheres. As soon as he was behind the shrubs, he took off at a run, moving parallel to the mansion. Up ahead, he could see the crest of the dune that led to the beach.

He reached the edge of the grass. The porch was to his left, illuminated by a single lamp. The guard who had been smoking a cigarette was nowhere to be seen. Beneath his feet, the lawn came to an end, replaced by the boards of the deck. Then he was on the sand itself.

The dune was steeper than he had expected, sloping toward the beach fifteen feet below. Grass had been planted here to keep the sand from drifting, but as he landed on the dune, the loose grains shifted beneath his heels, and he realized that he was going to fall. He tried to correct himself, failed, and found himself tumbling down the hillside. Before he slipped, he had the presence of mind to toss the painting aside, so that he would not crush it with his body.

Ilya slid down the dune, turning a somersault, and skidded to a stop at the base of the hill, near the slats of the snow fence. He got to his feet, brushing the sand from the front of his suit, and looked around for the painting. It was lying, apparently unharmed, a few feet away.

Holding the painting above his head, he climbed over the snow fence, its slats tilted at haphazard angles, and saw that he was only five steps from the beach. It was then that he noticed that his gun was missing.

He touched the holster inside his waistband. It was empty. Looking down, he found that the gun had slipped out of the holster when he had tumbled down the dune, and now it was nowhere in sight. The grass, though sparse, was six inches high, and the gun's dull finish made it impossible to see.

Fifteen yards up the beach, the truck's parking lights blinked twice. Ilya looked at the pickup, wondering if he should take the time to retrieve his gun, then decided to leave it. From his own examination earlier that week, he knew that the gun's serial numbers, both the one on the frame and the one that could be found only by taking it apart, had been carefully erased.

He crossed the sand to where the pickup was waiting. As he approached the truck, Ilya saw that Sharkovsky had disposed of the garbage and painted over the logo on both sides.

Ilya opened the passenger door. Behind the wheel, Sharkovsky had changed out of his coveralls. Zhenya, in the passenger seat, grinned at the sand on Ilya's shirtfront. "Looks like you took a tumble."

"No harm done," Ilya said, climbing into the pickup. Zhenya slid to the middle, allowing Ilya to take the passenger's side, the vinyl package still in his hands. "But I lost my gun—"

Sharkovsky started the engine. "Let it go. A true thief always leaves his gun behind."

He reversed the truck, backing up along the compacted sand of his own tracks, then went forward, driving smoothly down the beach with his wheels pointed straight ahead. As the truck planed along the sand, headlamps off, the lights of the mansion receded into the distance.

When they neared the parking lot that led to the main road, Sharkovsky depressed the clutch, allowing the truck to coast, and made a wide turn toward the asphalt. With his experience as a driver, he timed it just right, and the wheels of the truck bounced over the edge of the curb. He floored the gas, accelerating, and a few seconds later, they were on the street.

It was only a short drive to the staging area, a vineyard carved out of what had once been a potato field. Fifty acres of chardonnay and pinot noir vines surrounded a fake château, its gravel parking lot sheltered from the road. When they pulled into the lot, the château's lights were dead. Only one other car was in sight, a hatchback that they had rented under a false name.

Sharkovsky parked and turned off the engine. Climbing out of the truck, Ilya felt cool fingers of mist on his face. Next to him, Zhenya slid out of the pickup, visibly glowing with triumph. Ilya, for his part, found that he was exhausted. At the end of an assignment, he always felt drained, the energy devoted to a single goal abruptly depleted and dispersed. He had been hoping that this time would be different, but instead, he felt a strange emptiness, as if he had gained nothing but the canvas that would remain only briefly in his hands.

They were nearly at the car, which was parked three spaces away, when Ilya saw a flash of movement in the windshield of the hatchback, a gleam of bright metal in the darkness.

He fell to his knees, hearing the pop of a gunshot as a bullet passed through the space where his head had been an instant before. There was another shot, and something hit the ground beside him. He turned just in time to see Zhenya's bloodstained face, still smiling, strike the gravel with a hollow smack.

Ilya rolled. Under his back, gravel gave way to earth as he found himself in the field, away from the lights. Rising halfway, he plowed into the darkness, the painting wedged under one arm. Trellises toppled as he pushed himself through. He heard another gunshot, but felt nothing.

After ten yards, he halted, a stitch tightening in his side, behind a trellis draped with mesh to keep away the birds. Looking back, he saw a dark figure standing by the truck, a gun in his hand. As he watched, Sharkovsky reached into the pickup and switched on the high beams. At once, the field was illuminated, the trellises casting harsh shadows along the ground.

The old man looked out into the field, shielding his eyes with one hand from the glare of the headlamps. After a moment, he lowered his pistol, as if he had grown weary of its weight.

"I know you're there, *zhid*," Sharkovsky said. "And I know you can't hide forever."

Ilya did not move. Looking at the old man, who was outlined like a cutout against the lights, he groped for his own revolver, but his fingers closed on nothing. Only then did he remember that he had lost his gun.

Moving very slowly, he set the painting down so it leaned against the trellis, one hand resting on its upper edge. The trellis was two feet wide. If he shifted even a few inches in either direction, he would give himself away. Peering through the vines, he felt his pulse ticking warmly around his ears, the world around him growing soft and red. All his attention should have been riveted on what to do next, but his mind persisted, perversely, in searching for reasons.

As if the old man had overheard his thoughts, Sharkovsky said, "You must be confused. I can only say that the Chekists value discretion. Vasylenko was quite clear on this point. He was very insistent that I kill you both—"

Ilya's eyes fell on the coarse weave of the net. Although he knew that the next few seconds might mean the difference between life and death, he found himself distracted by a memory. For a moment, he could think of nothing but the star that had been scratched into the back of Vasylenko's cross.

Then his vision cleared, the weave of the mesh locking back into reality, and he saw that Sharkovsky was almost at the edge of the field. This jolted him into full awareness. If he allowed himself to be goaded, he would make a mistake. He was forcing himself to focus, knowing that otherwise he would die once the sun rose, when he became aware of a cylindrical object pressing against his thigh.

Ilya withdrew the penlight from his pocket, its brushed metal casing cold in his hand. He regarded it for a moment, then looked up again. Through the wooden slats, he could see the shadowy figure standing ten yards away.

Despite the adrenaline flooding his body, his hands did not tremble. He chose his target carefully, centering it on the circle of the old man's face. He thought again of the star on the cross, of snow singing underfoot in the prison yard, of the white scars that tattoos had left on his skin. Then he pressed the switch.

Sharkovsky swore, his head jerking back, as the laser struck him in the right eye. Ilya turned and scooped the canvas up from the ground. Fifty yards ahead, away from the lot, there stood a stone wall. He ran for it, trellises snapping and breaking as he fought his way through.

Behind him, the old man squeezed off a pair of shots, firing blindly. Ilya vaulted over the wall, landing in a tangle of vines. Bent over in a crouch, he moved along the sheltered side. The painting was slowing him down. He thought about throwing it away, but in the end, he did not.

Off in the fields, there was the cry of a bird, perhaps a raven, that had been caught in one of the nets. As Ilya ran, the old man's words boomed in his mind. If Vasylenko had betrayed him, he would not run forever. Even as he plunged into the fields, crushing the vines underfoot, he sensed that something inside him had changed. It was only then that he realized that the most human part of himself had already been burned away, and that nothing remained but the Scythian.

II

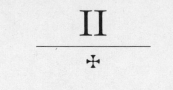

June 28–July 6, 2008

[In 1915,] Arts and Decoration *gives him "red hair, blue eyes, freckles . . ." while the* Tribune *reporter calls him "quite handsome, with blond, curly hair . . ." (The U.S. Immigration and Naturalization Service records for 1915 list Duchamp as five feet ten inches tall, with a fair complexion, brown hair, and "chestnut" eyes.)*

—Calvin Tomkins, *Duchamp*

The Pantheon should be cut in half vertically, and the two halves set fifty centimeters apart.

—Tristan Tzara

26

From a distance, when darkness still made it difficult to see things in their proper scale, it seemed as if a single sooty torch had been kindled in the vineyard parking lot. Powell slowed the car to a crawl. As he drew closer, a pattern of colored lights resolved itself into a fire engine and rescue unit. A third car, a hatchback, sat at the lot's edge, not far from where the fields began. It was on fire.

He parked at a safe remove from the blaze and got out, followed closely by Wolfe. A fire investigator stood at the entrance to the lot, clipboard in hand. As they advanced, badges raised, he blocked the way. "Stand back, please," the investigator said. "I'll tell you when it's all clear."

Wolfe looked over the investigator's shoulder at the flames. "Is it going to explode?"

The investigator grinned. "No, that only happens in the movies. But the pressurized struts in the trunk and hood can pop right out of the vehicle. You don't want to get one of those between the eyes—"

Powell watched as the fire crew sprayed the car with foam. "How long has it been burning?"

"Maybe twenty minutes. The fire started on the driver's side and spread back to the trunk. It hasn't burned through the firewall to the engine, though, so it can't have been going long."

"This was the only car you found?" Wolfe asked. "You didn't see a green pickup?"

The investigator shook his head. As the flames grew less intense, Powell could make out the figure in the driver's seat for the first time. There was something wrong with the body behind the wheel, a strangeness, like an optical illusion, that had nothing to do with the fire.

Finally, when the blaze had gone out and the fire crew, following the usual procedure, had disconnected the battery, Powell and Wolfe got the nod to move forward. They approached the hatchback cautiously, breathing in the smell of scorched metal and hydrocarbons. Powell could see white goo on the dashboard where the air bags had deployed and melted in the heat.

Then he realized that the man behind the wheel was headless. Looking through the windshield, he saw the cylinder of the dead man's neck poking up through the remains of his collar. His clothing had been badly burned, but the outlines of a suit were still visible. Peering into the side window, Powell looked at the dead man's arms. Both of his hands were gone.

Wolfe stared at the stumps. "Don't know about you, but I think I've seen this before."

Powell only nodded. As Wolfe relayed the car's description and license number over her phone, he bent down to study the gravel. Near the car, the uniform gray pebbles had been blackened with soot, but a few yards away, he saw traces of something dark and wet.

"They killed him here," Powell said to Wolfe, who was

closing her phone. "At least one gunshot wound to the head. Then they stuck him behind the wheel and took the trouble of cutting off his head and hands."

Wolfe crouched to examine the bloodstained gravel. "Looks like a rush job to me."

"Me too. Normally, a body like this gets dumped in the harbor. They must have been in a hurry—"

Powell went to the edge of the parking lot. Kneeling where the gravel gave way to the field, he noticed that some of the trellises were knocked over, their struts uprooted and flattened against the ground.

"A double cross," Wolfe said from over his shoulder. "The thief brought the painting here, and somebody killed him for it."

"It's possible," Powell said, although he found it hard to believe that the thief behind this heist could have ended up dead so soon. Fewer than ninety minutes had passed since they had lost the truck in the darkened streets, returning to the estate in time to see police cruisers pulling up at the entrance.

They drove back to the mansion, where guests were still gathered in uncertain groups on the lawn. Upstairs, the master bedroom was packed. Archvadze stood in one corner, a cell phone to his ear, next to Kostava, his assistant. A few steps away, Natalia Onegina was speaking rapidly to the chief of police, whose crew cut was so precise that it seemed as if part of his skull had been lopped off. Although Powell was unable to make out her words, he sensed that she was less concerned by the theft of the painting than she was by her party's failure.

As Powell approached, Archvadze pocketed his phone.

"Natalia, please calm down," the oligarch said in Russian. Turning to the police chief, he said in English, "I apologize. She is very upset."

Powell, his badge out, reached the circle. "Excuse me, but I was wondering if I could ask a few questions—"

To his surprise, Archvadze recognized his badge at once. "You're based in London. What are you doing in this part of the world?"

"We've been keeping an eye on your house," Powell said. "We had reason to believe that a crime would take place, but not a burglary."

Archvadze's eyes narrowed. "So what, exactly, did you think was going to happen?"

"We thought that there might be an extortion attempt," Wolfe said, showing her own badge. "Who else knew that the painting was here?"

"No one," Archvadze said. Then, correcting himself, he added, "Well, a few people did, of course. Natalia and myself. Kostava and a few members of my security team. My investment manager and my lawyer."

Powell wrote this down in his spiral notebook. "And the painting was insured?"

"It was insured from the moment it left the auction house." Archvadze made a gesture of impatience. "Please, this isn't about the money. I can afford the loss. But this painting is irreplaceable."

"Yes, I can imagine." As Powell looked at his notepad, his eye was caught by something that he had written earlier that evening. "What about the witnesses who saw the thief? Did you know them?"

"I believe that we met the girl briefly," Archvadze said. "I had never seen her before tonight. As for the other one, I don't think that I met him at all. Natalia, do you remember him?"

Natalia, who had been following the conversation, shook her head. "No. But I do remember the girl. She struck me as too clever by half. I don't know what she was doing here."

Kostava spoke for the first time, his accent considerably thicker than that of his employer. "She was on the list. A guest of another invitee. The other one called us himself. He said that he was working for a major art investor. We checked his story and said yes." By the end of this uncharacteristically long speech, his voice was shaking. "Were they a part of this?"

"We aren't sure," Powell said. "But we know that the getaway vehicle was disguised as a waste removal truck. How did it get inside?"

Kostava launched into a rambling explanation, from which Powell gathered that he had not hired the truck, but had allowed it onto the grounds on the assumption that the caterer had requested it. By the time he realized that no one had approved the pickup, the truck was already gone.

As the assistant finished his account, Archvadze broke in. "If you don't mind, I would prefer to answer the rest of your questions another time. If you require further assistance, you can get in touch with my lawyer." He wrote a name and number on the back of an ivory business card. "Please—"

Archvadze gave Wolfe his card, then led the others into a far corner. Powell let them go, then entered the study, where technicians were dusting every surface for prints. As he examined the hole in the closet door, something else occurred to him. "According to the girl's state-ment, the thief was holding a package that was exactly the size of the missing painting. No bag, nothing else in his hands."

"That's right," Wolfe said, coming up to his side. "Nothing except the revolver."

"Which means that he left some tools behind." Powell turned away, his eyes passing across the desk, the chair, the shelves. Donning gloves, he looked inside the waste-basket, sifting through the wads of paper.

Finally, he went up to the bookcases. He checked be-hind each of the volumes, pulling them away from the shelf five or six at a time. Then, going around to one side, he saw a gap of several inches between the shelf and the wall. Reaching inside, he felt his fingers close around a leather strap.

He pulled the parcel out from behind the shelf. As the others gathered around, he set the bag on the desk and opened it. Inside, as he had expected, lay a portable drill with a saw blade, along with the rest of the thief's tools, which he set on the desktop one by one. As he poked a finger through the hole in the bottom of the bag, it struck him that the thief had brought nothing except what he intended to use.

Powell noticed the police chief standing nearby. "The witnesses. Are they still here?"

"For now." The police chief picked up the drill, heft-ing it in his hands. "We're keeping them apart until we decide what to do with them. Technically, they're guilty of criminal trespass. If you want to talk to them—"

"I do," Powell said. Turning aside from the desk, he consulted his notes, reviewing what the witnesses had said. There were aspects of their accounts that didn't make sense, and if he was going to figure out what had happened here, he would need to sort through their stories while he still could. He closed his notepad and turned back to the others. "All right. I'll talk to the girl first."

27

When the door of the guest room opened, Maddy had been waiting for over an hour. Instead of the intimidating figure that she had been dreading, however, the man who appeared was unassuming, even tweedy, with a pair of blinking blue eyes. His air of harmlessness was only increased by the badge that he gave her for inspection, along with a worn business card that read *ALAN POWELL*.

Maddy glanced up from the badge. "It looks like you're one of the Thundercats."

Powell smiled. As he sat down, she caught a whiff of acrid smoke. "No, just a copper from London. I know you've already given a statement, but I'd like to clarify a few points." He looked at his notes. "When you saw the thief emerge from the study, he was carrying nothing but a package?"

"That's right," Maddy said. She expected him to ask what she and Ethan had been doing in the bedroom, but instead, he asked her to tell him about the man she had seen. As she replied, describing the thief in the same terms that she had used with the police, her apprehension began to slip away.

"You also say that you saw a photographer take a picture of Archvadze," Powell said. "You're sure that this was the same man?"

"Fairly sure," Maddy said. "I didn't get a good look at the photographer, but he was wearing a brown suit and black plastic glasses."

Powell noted this down. "Did the man in the bedroom have any tattoos?"

The specificity of the question made her wonder if the agent had someone particular in mind. "Not that I noticed."

"All right." Powell closed his notebook with the air of a man who was winding down a conversation. "I've been told that you live in the city. You must have spent almost three hours on the train to get here."

"I thought it would be worth it. A friend put me on the guest list. It's important for me to attend as many of these events as I can."

"Because of your job, I take it. According to your statement, you work for an art fund, along with the other witness. Did your firm take an interest in the painting that was stolen tonight?"

There was no point in denying this, since her presence at the auction had been widely reported. "Yes, we bid on the painting. But—"

"But you weren't willing to pay eleven million for it. What was your final bid?"

"Seven million," Maddy said. "We felt that the winner significantly overpaid."

"Yes, it seems that way, doesn't it? Especially now that the painting is gone." Powell pointed toward her purse. "I notice that you have a camera. Can I take a look at the pictures?"

Maddy saw that her camera was visible through the purse's open mouth. "Don't you need a warrant for that?"

"Under most circumstances, you'd be right," Powell said. He lowered his eyes, as if studying a flaw in the tabletop. "American law is not my strong suit. However, I believe that in a search incident to arrest, an arresting officer may search the arrestee, as well as any containers in his or her possession. According to the courts, these containers may include digital devices."

It took Maddy a second to understand. "You're threatening to arrest me? For what?"

"Criminal trespass. Even if you were invited to this party, the scope of permission did not extend to private rooms in the house. If we decide to place you under arrest, we can take a look at your camera. Of course, if you choose to cooperate, we may not be inclined to go so far."

After a tense pause, Maddy reached into her purse and pulled out the camera. "Here."

Taking it, Powell switched it on and went through the photos on the preview screen. "You were taking pictures of the art on the walls. You must have been interested in Archvadze's collection."

"I'm interested in anyone who buys art," Maddy said. "Nothing wrong with that."

"Not at all." Powell set the camera down. "Did you know that Archvadze had bought this painting?"

Maddy felt the beginnings of a headache gathering behind her eyes. "Yes, I did."

"But that fact was never made public. I hear that the buyer's identity was something of a mystery. So how did you know?"

"We narrowed it down," Maddy said, realizing that there was no point in holding anything back. "There aren't that many oligarchs who could have bid on the painting. When we looked at photos of the bidder at the auction, and saw the symbol of the Georgian Air Force on his cufflinks, the rest was easy."

"So you came here to see the rest of his collection. That's why you took the photos?"

"Yes. An undiscovered collection is always of interest. But the fund had nothing to do with this. No one knew that we were here. I didn't even know that Ethan was at the party until I saw him here tonight."

"In other words, the two of you decided, independently, to come out to Southampton, without telling anyone else what you were doing." Powell paused. "You can see why this interests me. Archvadze's purchase of this painting was a closely guarded secret. Only a few members of his inner circle were aware that it was here. Your firm seems to be the only other player in the market, besides the auction house, that knew he was the owner. Did you tell anyone?"

Maddy decided to sidestep the question. "We had no incentive to do so. Once we had the name, we were better off keeping it to ourselves."

"I can see why," Powell said. "If you know a collector's name and purchase history, you can establish a position in works that he might be interested in buying. I'll assume, then, that you might have had an interest in acquiring other works by Duchamp. Correct me if I'm wrong, but such pieces would be worth considerably more if this painting was stolen. Is that right?"

"Maybe," Maddy said defensively. "But it's only been

a week since the auction. We haven't had time to build up a meaningful position. If we were trying to influence prices with a theft, we would have waited."

"You know what? I believe you." Powell rose from his chair and headed for the door, where he paused. "There's one other thing I want to make clear. I expect it might be useful, for someone in your position, to know something that nobody else in the art world knows yet. There might even be an advantage in withholding information from the police. But if I find that you've been less than honest with me, I promise that you won't have the chance to profit from it."

Powell left the room. Once he was gone, Maddy realized that the back of her dress was soaked through with sweat. Sliding her camera back into her purse, she felt an unexpected mixture of anger and shame.

She waited there, alone, for another twenty minutes. Then, finally, the door opened. It was Ethan. He seemed tired, but when he looked at her, his eyes retained something of their old brightness.

"Come on," Ethan said. "Powell says that we can leave. I'll give you a ride back."

Outside, the sounds of the party still floated across the garden. Ethan went around to the rear of the house, where two parking attendants were sharing a cigarette. He handed a ticket to the nearest valet, who reappeared a moment later behind the wheel of his car, a white Honda Fit. "I can drop you off," Ethan said, sliding into the driver's seat. "Where are you staying?"

Opening the passenger's side door, Maddy was about to reply when she saw a figure in a linen suit wandering helplessly among the remaining guests. It was Griffin. Before she could slip out of sight, he noticed her, mouth falling open with surprise, and began to shuffle in her direction. "Maddy?"

She ducked into the car without a word. Closing the door, she gave Ethan the address of the share house, watching through the windshield as Griffin halted and stared. "Let's get the hell out of here."

They drove off. Maddy looked over her shoulder as Griffin's soft shape dwindled in the car's taillights, then turned back around in her seat. As they went through the main entrance, leaving the endless hedge behind, she felt as if she had contrived a miraculous escape. Then she heard herself say something that she had not intended to speak aloud: "I don't want to go back to the share house."

Ethan guided the car onto Gin Lane. He did not look in her direction. "Why not?"

"Because it's depressing." Maddy tried to catch his eye. "You're staying in town?"

"Not exactly. I found a room half an hour from here. If you want to stay with me—"

"I do. Otherwise, I'll end up on the floor of a closet. I can't handle that right now."

As they passed along a row of streetlamps, Ethan's face alternated between light and shadow. When he spoke again, his tone was neutral. "Okay. We'll swing by the house to pick up your stuff."

They drove in silence until they reached the share house. Although the driveway was still packed with cars, the windows were dark. Maddy slid out, saying that she would only be a moment, and ascended the front steps.

Going upstairs, she got her things, doing her best to ignore the muffled sound of intercourse in a nearby room, and was back in less than a minute.

For the rest of the ride, they said nothing. They drove for half an hour, midnight edging toward early morning, until they reached the inn, a sandstone cube north of the Montauk Highway.

Upstairs, the room had a bed, a sofa, and a desk with a laptop. Ethan's suitcase was on the coverlet, his street clothes laid across the arms of a chair. "I can take the couch, if you want to give me your sleeping bag. You can have the bathroom first. Sorry I can't be a better host—"

"That's all right," Maddy said. She went into the bathroom and closed the door. In the mirror, which gave back three walls of unforgiving whiteness, she saw a girl in an overpriced dress, now sweaty and rumpled. When she tried to recall what the point had been, she found that she couldn't remember.

She changed into pajamas, brushed her teeth, and scrubbed the makeup from her face. When she emerged from the bathroom, her dress over one arm, she saw that Ethan had unrolled her mummy bag and was lying on the couch, half inside the cocoon, his shirt and tie removed.

Without reflecting too much on what she was doing, Maddy draped her dress over the back of the chair, went over to the couch, and straddled Ethan's body, placing both hands on his chest. His eyes met hers, as if he were seeing her for the first time, and he smiled. The nylon of the sleeping bag was slippery between her thighs as she leaned down, her hair falling into his face, and kissed him.

He kissed her in response, his body radiating warmth and youth, although he was only a year younger than she was. After a few seconds of this, Maddy opened her eyes a crack, peeking through her lashes, and studied his face. Closeness had turned it into the face of a child, a cherub, a boy genius. She rested her chin on his perfect chest. "I think you're an alien being."

Ethan looked back at her, his eyes, as always, serene and opaque. "No. Only a robot." He paused. "So what does this mean?"

"I don't know," Maddy said. Running her fingers through the cornsilk of his hair, she slid off the sofa and led him by the hand to the bed. They undressed each other under the covers, not speaking. By some unstated understanding, they did not undress all the way. For now, sleep felt like the greater good.

They lay together in the dark for a long time. When Ethan spoke again, it was with a characteristic lack of self-awareness. "Did Powell ask you if the thief we saw had any tattoos?"

Maddy laughed, pressing her body against his. "Is that the only thing on your mind?"

"It just occurred to me. Powell works for an agency that investigates organized crime. And tattoos make me think of the Russian mob."

"It's possible." She rolled onto her side. "For all we know, it was the Rosicrucians—"

In response, he only draped an arm across her shoulders. Closing her eyes, she found herself being pulled swiftly into sleep, something she would have believed impossible even an hour ago. It was not an ending she could have foreseen, but unlike the rest of the evening's events, it seemed sweetly, organically right.

When she awoke, sunlight was seeping through the

curtains of the hotel room. Looking at the clock, she found that it was already morning, and realized that she was alone in bed. She straightened up, sheets gathered around her body, and saw that Ethan was seated at the desk, dressed in his undershirt and shorts. He was reading something on his laptop. "What are you doing?"

Ethan stirred, as if he had been deep in thought. "Nothing. It's something that struck me last night—"

Maddy slid out of bed, goose bumps rising, and padded over to the desk. Placing her hands on his shoulders, she saw that he was looking at an online copy of a scanned book. "What is it?"

"The Rosicrucians." Ethan took one of her hands absently in his own. "Your friend was right. When we were talking about Duchamp last night, something stuck in my head, but I wasn't sure what it was. Now I know." He looked up, his eyes gleaming. "There *is* a connection between Duchamp and the Rosicrucians. A real one. And his name is Walter Arensberg."

28

In the early morning, as a gray false dawn crept across the rooftops, Ilya moved quietly through the yards of an unfamiliar neighborhood. He was tired and sore, his legs aching from the effort of walking in the dark, which had made it hard to maintain a consistent rhythm. Although he did not know where he was, he estimated that he was no more than five or six miles from the vineyard.

Just before sunrise made it impossible for him to look any further, he found what he was searching for. At every home, he had sought out the gas meter, which was usually mounted to one side of the house. At last, in the backyard of a summer home with a garden and enclosed patio, he saw that a tag had been hung on the meter, indicating that the gas had been turned off.

It was simple matter to break through the rear door onto the patio, and to move from there into the dining room. On the wall by the door, the keypad for an alarm system had been installed, but its liquid crystal display was dead. A flick of a light switch confirmed that the electricity had been disconnected as well.

A winterized house did have its minor inconveniences. Going upstairs to the bathroom, he found that a cross of masking tape had been laid across the toilet. When he tried the sink, nothing came out of the tap. In the end, he stood in the shower and pissed down the drain.

Looking for a place to wash up, he removed the lid of the toilet tank. He was about to set it on the floor when he paused. Inside the tank, taped just above the filler valve, was a small waterproof bundle. He peeled away the package, shook off the adhering drops, and unwrapped it.

Inside, nestled within two layers of plastic, was a block of cash. Rifling through the bundle, he guessed that it contained upward of fifteen hundred dollars. For a moment, he weighed it in his hands, then stripped away the rest of the plastic and slid the money into his pocket.

As he washed up in the tank, his hands growing numb, he studied himself in the mirror. What he saw was not encouraging. His eyes had a wildness, a feral watchfulness, that he had not seen since prison, and the smooth, faceless surface that he had tried so hard to cultivate was gone.

Glancing down, he saw a spot of blood, no larger than a dime, on the tip of one shoe. It was Zhenya's. Two points of warmth bloomed on his cheekbones as he reached down and wiped away the smear. The smudge that it left on his finger filled him with renewed resolve.

He spent the following hour scavenging equipment from the house. In the kitchen, he drew a carbon steel knife from the block next to the oven, guarding its tip with a disc of cork from the bulletin board beside the refrigerator. It went into the holster inside his waistband, where it fit snugly. Even better, in the drawer of a nightstand in the upstairs bedroom, he found a rectangular device, no larger than a deck of cards, that lay cold and heavy in his hand. It was an electric stun gun.

As he continued his search, he tried to get a sense of his resources. He had next to nothing. His passports were in Brighton Beach. Without proper identification, it would be hard to travel or find a place to stay.

He needed information as well. If Vasylenko wanted him dead, then the entire *bratva* could be compromised. Before anything else, he had to find out how deep the poison went, and if there was anyone left to be trusted.

Ilya glanced at the package that he had propped against the bedroom wall. Here, at least, was a source of leverage. For a moment, he thought about stashing it nearby, perhaps in this very house. Then he decided that he would need to keep the painting close, and that he was not going to remain here for long.

From a set of luggage in the bedroom closet, he took a rolling suitcase that was large enough to hold the painting. He was about to leave when, passing through the kitchen, his eye happened to fall on the phone on the counter. On an impulse, he put it to his ear and heard a dial tone.

Ilya stood there for a moment, the suitcase in one hand, the phone in the other. He did not want to make this call, at least not yet. Before he could bring himself to put down the receiver, however, he had already dialed. After three rings, a fatherly voice answered the phone, roughened by vodka and cigarettes: "Yes?"

Ilya felt his heartbeat kick into a higher tempo. He set the suitcase down. "It's me."

There was a pause. "Ilya," Vasylenko finally said, his tone guarded. "I never expected to hear from you again."

"I know." Ilya groped forward one word at a time. "You wanted me dead. Why?"

"Because you failed me in Budapest. That painting was important in ways that you couldn't begin to imagine. There were other reasons, to be sure, but that one alone should suffice."

Ilya closed his eyes. "Sharkovsky told me that you're working for the Chekists. That you betrayed the oath you swore—"

"The only oath that counts is the one a man swears to himself," Vasylenko said. "I don't expect you to understand my reasons, but before you judge me too harshly, I would advise you to look closely at your own life. For all your talk of righteousness, you are still a man who can do nothing but kill."

Ilya, thinking of the dog in its plastic carrier, pushed the memory away. "Which gives you all the more reason to fear me."

"I have no doubt that you could hurt us. Given your nature, I would expect nothing less. But consider this. Not even a Scythian can survive on his own. These men will find you and kill you. Right now, I'm the only one you can trust, because you have something I want. Now tell me where you are."

Ilya saw the world go red, like the smudge that had been left on his forefinger. When it cleared, he spoke carefully. "This is the last time that you will ever hear my voice. Tell Sharkovsky that I'm coming."

Hanging up, he pulled the phone out of its jack. Sharkovsky, he reflected, might not know all the answers, but he would, at least, know some of them. From his pocket, Ilya withdrew the stun gun, his thoughts already turning to how it might be used. Then he slipped it into his suitcase and left the house.

29

"You know who Walter Arensberg was," Ethan said, angling his laptop so that she could see the screen. "A renowned art collector and the most important patron of Duchamp during his lifetime."

"I know," Maddy said, standing behind the chair in which Ethan was seated. "He bought most of Duchamp's major works, then left his collection to the Philadelphia Museum of Art. But I don't see why this matters."

"It matters because Arensberg was obsessed with the Rosicrucians." Ethan pointed to his browser. "He was convinced that Francis Bacon, the English philosopher, was the true author of the works of Shakespeare, and spent years looking for coded messages in the plays. He also claimed that Bacon was the founder of the Rosicrucians, and that his grave was the real tomb of Christian Rosencreutz."

Maddy wanted to wrap her arms around Ethan's smooth chest, but something held her back. "Was he crazy?"

Ethan scrolled to the next page. "Well, let's see. He claims to have discovered the location of the tomb, based on the shape of some gravel on the floor of Lichfield Cathedral. He notes that two of the pebbles look like a vulva, a symbol for the philosopher's stone. Later, he finds that the gravel has been removed, which he takes as evidence of a massive cover-up."

Maddy wasn't sure what to say. "And what does this have to do with Duchamp?"

"Everything. An artist is always influenced by his patron's obsessions. Look here."

Ethan opened a web page in his browser's recent history. On the screen, Maddy saw a photo of one of Duchamp's earliest readymades, a ball of twine sandwiched between two metal plates. "I've seen this work before," Maddy said. "Arensberg put something inside the ball without telling Duchamp what it was—"

"And here, on the plates, Duchamp inscribed a coded message with missing letters, a reference to Arensberg's interest in Shakespearian cryptography. But the most important thing about this piece is the day it was made."

Maddy read off the date in the caption under the photo. "April 23, 1916. Which is—"

"Easter Sunday. And three hundred years to the day after the death of Shakespeare."

Maddy was surprised by this sudden eagerness, which seemed even less explicable in light of his earlier skepticism. She was on the verge of asking him about this when a musical tone sounded from across the room. Going to her purse, Maddy took out her phone. "It's Reynard."

When he heard this, Ethan's enthusiasm seemed to wither. "You'd better take it."

The phone rang again. Maddy thought about letting it go to voicemail, but in the end, she answered it. When

Reynard spoke, there was a hollowness to his voice that she had never heard before. "Are you in Southampton?"

Maddy shut her eyes. She had been dreading this moment. "Yes. I'm with Ethan."

"I want both of you in the office right now," Reynard said. "I know it's the weekend, but I need you here anyway. I assume that you've seen the story that came out this morning—"

Maddy glanced at Ethan, who was watching her intently. "No, I haven't seen it."

Reynard read off the name of an influential art website. "It's bad, and it's only going to get worse. But I'm sure you knew that already."

He hung up. Maddy, feeling Ethan's eyes on her face, went to the laptop and typed in a web address. When the page loaded, the lead headline and the name of the author came as a blow to the gut. They read the story together. After they had reached the end, Maddy looked at Ethan. "We're fucked."

"Yeah, I know." He rose from the chair. "Come on. We've got a long drive home."

As they hurriedly dressed and checked out of the hotel, Maddy kept her distance. She did not speak again until they were driving west on the Montauk Highway. "This isn't going to end until they find that painting."

"If they ever do." Ethan looked out at the road. "I still can't see why the thief went for that particular work. I know something about these guys. Aivazovsky is more their style. Why the fuck would they care about Duchamp?"

"They care because it was worth eleven million dollars. It isn't so complicated."

"It might be more complicated than you think," Ethan said. "I'm not sure how much you know about our pricing system, but it's what you call a multifactor model. The price of a work of art is a function of a set of variables, including size, provenance, and sale history. Feed in the right variables, and it spits out a range of prices. For this painting, the range was between three and seven million."

Maddy's background in computational finance was less than extensive, but the underlying point was clear enough. "Which means that eleven million is way outside the expected range."

"Exactly. It's crazy. There's no good explanation, unless—" Ethan hesitated. "Unless we failed to account for some important variable. Ever since the auction, I've been trying to figure out what factor might be missing, and a strong possibility occurred to me this morning. It's the occult factor."

She searched his face for irony, but saw that he was serious. "That's hard to believe."

"But it isn't unprecedented. At the turn of the century, occult societies commissioned art based on Rosicrucian principles. These commissions were a source of demand, which drove prices. What if this demand still exists? Maybe it's underground, and collectors say they're buying art as an investment when, in fact, they're driven by other factors. And if this demand is strong enough for certain works, it might be enough to upset our pricing model."

Maddy recalled that Lermontov had said much the same thing. Collectors did not always base their investment choices on rational motivations. "How do you know so much about this?"

"It's my job," Ethan said simply. "And there's something else. If I'm right, and this painting has a secret significance to certain buyers, it may also explain why it was stolen. And if we can figure out why the painting was targeted, we can narrow down the list of suspects."

Maddy saw an unsettling light in his eyes. "That isn't part of your job description."

"Maybe not," Ethan replied. "But neither was looking at Archvadze's call history."

Something in his voice, which had the tone of an unintentional rebuke, shocked them into silence for the rest of the ride. An hour later, they were seated in Reynard's office, where the fund manager had been awaiting their arrival. With the blinds drawn against the morning glare, the only light came from his computer, its browser opened to the story that had appeared a few hours before.

Griffin's article was casually brutal. Citing anonymous sources, it disclosed that two employees of the fund had been present when the painting was stolen. It noted that the fund had bid on the study only a week before, and speculated that it was under suspicion for a role in the heist. Worst of all, it had unearthed an interview, given a year ago to a pension magazine, in which Reynard had cheerfully outlined the impact of a theft on demand for an artist's work.

Now, as Maddy and Ethan related what had happened, Reynard listened in silence. When he finally spoke, his words were for Ethan, and they were the last thing

Maddy had expected to hear: "Would you leave us alone, please?"

Ethan seemed surprised as well, but he rose quietly, his eyes touching briefly on hers as he left the office. As soon as he was gone, Reynard turned to Maddy. "There's something we need to discuss."

Maddy suddenly knew precisely what was coming. Her eyes strayed, of their own accord, to the picture above Reynard's desk, the woman on a kitchen floor with a scrap of newsprint in her hand. "What is it?"

"I know you're in debt," Reynard said. "We've never spoken about this before, but people are going to ask questions now, and we need to be ready. When your gallery went under, it put you in a difficult position. Am I right?"

Maddy felt the office walls pulling away from her in all directions. "I owed money to vendors and clients. I also had a lot of credit card debt. You knew all this when you hired me."

"Yes. There was talk of a lawsuit, if I remember correctly. Artists claimed you'd sold works without paying them—"

"It never went to court," Maddy said. "I was late paying a few artists, yes, but that was only because I needed money to keep the lights on. It was all settled a long time ago. I've been through debt restructuring and consolidation. Half of what was left has already been paid down—"

"But that leaves half still outstanding. Under the circumstances, your position at the fund must present you with certain temptations. As far as we can tell, nobody else knew where this painting was. You had a convenient motivation for selling this information. If you've done anything like this, I need to know."

Maddy shook her head, a region of numbness spreading throughout her body. "Listen, I know how bad this looks—"

"I'm not sure you do," Reynard said sadly. "This business is founded on reputation. A painting is only worth what the market believes. The same is true for dealers. Taste can't be proven either way, so the art world runs on trust. I've spent years building this fund's reputation. It's all I have. And if I don't make an example of you, everything I've tried to accomplish here will be lost."

His voice hardened. "As of now, you're suspended from all contact with our investors. Ethan, too. As far as the outside world is concerned, you no longer exist. I'm also revoking your bonus for the year. To get it back, you'll need to make yourself useful. We'll discuss the details later, but for now, you're an unperson. Now tell Ethan to come in."

Reynard turned away. Maddy wanted to speak, anything to ease the sting of these last few words, but she only stood in silence. Going outside, she felt something close around her wrist. Ethan, who was standing in the corridor, had taken her by the hand. "Hey, it's going to be all right. And about everything else—"

Maddy saw that he was trying to comfort her. It was only then, with complete clarity, that she realized what she had to say: "It was a mistake. We need to stay focused, and this will only complicate things."

She could tell that he was surprised. Before he could respond, she set her face into an expression she had mastered as a gallerina, cool, helpful, but utterly unavailable, even as her heart continued to pound.

"It can't happen again," Maddy said calmly. "But listen to me. You were right. This painting was stolen to order. If anyone can figure out who took it, we can. And I can't do it without you."

Watching his face, she saw him take this in, then nod. "All right," Ethan said. "I have an idea about where to look first. But I need some time to work it out. Maybe we can talk tomorrow?"

"That would be fine." Maddy said nothing more, hands at her sides, until he gave her a smile and went into the office. She stood where she was until the door had closed. Then she felt her legs almost give way.

As she returned to her desk, she reminded herself of something that Lermontov had often said. In the art world, buyers tended to follow the heart instead of the head, so her job was to be the one person in the room who kept her wits at all times. She accepted this without question. But when she looked down at her hands now, she saw that they were trembling.

Her cell phone rang for the second time that day, breaking into her thoughts. Maddy reached into her purse, wondering if it was the press or the police, and saw that the number was restricted. "Hello?"

Instead of a response, there was nothing but silence, a seashell emptiness on the other end. It was more than just the absence of noise. Someone was there, but would not speak. Before she could ask who it was, there was a gentle click. The caller, whoever it was, had hung up.

30

The boy in the cooler was looking rather the worse for wear. He had been shot at close range in the back of the head, and at some point after his death, his face had been lightly splashed with acid. In the places where it remained whole, his skin had turned a sickly green, but on his upper lip, which was miraculously intact, a cleft palate scar was faintly visible.

Looking at the yellow burns on the boy's cheeks and forehead, Powell reached into the body pouch and withdrew the right arm. He did this gently, aware that the loose skin of the hands could slip off altogether, like a latex glove. Taking it by the wrist, he examined the boy's hand. More acid had been applied to the tip of each digit, eating the fingerprints away.

He turned to regard the two other bodies lying nearby. Each had been subjected to similar treatment, their faces and fingertips also erased. One had been shot at the base of the skull, while the other bore a starfish wound in its decomposing chest, the mark of a shotgun blast.

Powell let the boy's hand drop, then left the cooler, emerging into the relative warmth of the decomp room. Glancing at Wolfe, he saw that she looked a little green herself. The morgue attendant seemed to notice this as well. "If you're going to be sick, do it in one of the sinks," the attendant said, closing the cooler door. "Don't forget to take off your mask first."

"I'll be fine," Wolfe said. They were standing in a small room off the main morgue. The walls and floor had been painted with gray acrylic that could be easily mopped and bleached. In the ceiling, next to the fluorescent lights, an exhaust fan was loudly at work, but the most distinctive part of the room, far more than its visible furnishings, remained its indescribable smell.

At the center of the room stood a single autopsy table, a rolling metal pan on swivel wheels. Its narrow end had been mounted to one of the sinks lining the far wall. On its steel surface, which was sloped to allow fluid to drain, a fourth body was in the process of being undressed by the deputy medical examiner whom Powell had encountered before. Next to him stood the detective he had last seen at the scan of the dead girl, his face as pink as always.

Powell and Wolfe approached the body. Beside the table stood a gurney draped in a white sheet. On it, the dead man's clothes were being laid one article at a time, along with the contents of his pockets.

As they drew close, the deputy medical examiner looked up. Behind his plastic safety glasses, his eyes crinkled. "Glad to see you again. You always manage to show up for the most interesting cases—"

Powell gave a nod of greeting, then turned to the body. "What do we know so far?"

The detective cleared his throat. There was a dab of mentholated ointment under his nose. "We found them at an industrial site in Gowanus, a few blocks from the canal. My guess is that someone planned to dump them in the water, then got cold feet. Each body was stuffed in a steel drum. The lids were sealed, but not very tightly. The smell drew the workers to the scene."

Wolfe looked down at the dead man. His face and fingerprints had also been erased. "Do we know who he is?"

"No identification or wallet on the body, so it's hard to say, but we're pretty sure that it's a gangster named Arshak Gasparyan. Armenian, late twenties, arrests for assault and firearms possession. Vanished last week. We're still waiting to identify two of the others through dental records. The youngest one was the easiest. His cleft palate scar narrowed it down pretty quick—"

Powell studied the remains of the dead man's face. The skin of his head and forearms had turned green, but the parts that had been covered with clothing were in better shape. "Do we know what kind of acid was used?"

The medical examiner spoke up. "Based on the yellowing of tissue, it looks like nitric acid. Not something that most people have lying around the house. It's used primarily in chemical fertilizers. And to stain wooden furniture."

Powell made a note of this as he went to examine the dead man's belongings, which had been laid on a clean sheet of paper. No wallet or keys. A few coins, a wad of tissue, and a paper scrap, which he picked up. On the slip, a string of numbers had been written in ballpoint pen, along with what looked like a manufacturer's code. "Any idea what this is?"

"We called it in already," the detective said. "Judging from the format, it's the serial number for a memory card, probably used for a digital camera. Not sure what it means, though."

Powell set the scrap of paper down. "Have you recovered any slugs from the bodies?"

"Two so far," the medical examiner said. "The younger one in the cooler had a nine-millimeter slug, too misshapen to eyeball. Our friend here has what looks like a .45 ACP with a clockwise twist. Why?"

"There's a comparison I want you to run. A revolver we found in Southampton. It's a Smith and Wesson Model 625, which fits your bullet."

"I'll have our ballistics unit follow up," the detective said. "Anything else you need?"

"No. We're good for now." Powell signaled to Wolfe, who seemed more than ready to move on. "Let's go."

They left the decomp room. A few minutes later, they were back in the car, the smell of the morgue still lingering. Powell slid into the passenger's seat as Wolfe got behind the wheel. "So what do you think?"

Wolfe took a bottle of perfume from her purse and misted the air before responding. "Honestly? I'm not convinced that Sharkovsky was a part of this. The modus operandi doesn't match up. Instead of losing their head and hands, these guys were splashed with acid. It doesn't fit."

"True," Powell said. "But it doesn't mean that Sharkovsky wasn't involved. Maybe he got someone else to take care of the bodies. Because what we're looking at here is a mob deal gone bad."

Wolfe started the car and pulled away from the curb. "What makes you say that?"

"The page in the dead guy's pocket. It's standard operating procedure for an overseas exchange. Say you have a shipment of weapons coming in. You give your supplier a camera of your choice. He mails it overseas to take pictures of the merchandise, then returns it. Before you look at the pictures, you check the serial number to verify that the memory card is the same."

They halted at a red light. "So what kind of merchandise are we talking about?"

"Guns," Powell said. "According to my guy in the wire room, we've been hearing rumors of a weapons deal. So we need to make sure that any warrant for the club includes camera equipment."

Wolfe turned onto Second Avenue. "I don't know about you, but I doubt we'll be seeing a warrant anytime soon."

"So do I," Powell said. For now, at least, they had hit a dead end. The hatchback at the vineyard had been rented with a stolen credit card. Since the heist, neither Zhenya nor Ilya had been seen, while Sharkovsky had gone to work as usual, sporting a bandage over one eye. In the absence of more conclusive evidence, however, the investigation had been left with no choice but to focus on side issues. One was the oligarch. The other was the art fund.

As Wolfe continued down the avenue, her thoughts seemed to be running along similar lines. "You know what I was thinking? If I were Maddy Blume, and I knew who stole the painting, I'd cut a deal with the thief. If you could buy the painting at a fifth of its legitimate value—"

"—it would be a real bargain." Powell rolled down his window, hoping to disperse the remaining stench. "And if I were the thief, I'd want a buyer lined up. Otherwise, the painting would be almost impossible to move."

"So maybe they made a deal with the fund, and the

girl was there to see it through. Or maybe she cut a deal of her own. Her background check says she's a true prodigy, but ran a gallery that went belly up last year, so she's loaded down with debt." Wolfe spoke with the disapproval of one convinced that debt was the worst of all possible evils. "So she might have been willing to work with Sharkovsky."

"I wouldn't rule it out," Powell said. "But even if the fund got its hands on the study, the underlying problem remains. How do you sell the most famous stolen painting in the world? A heist like this only makes sense if the recipient intended to keep it for himself. Not a dealer, but a collector. Sharkovsky doesn't qualify, but a man like Vasylenko, perhaps—"

"Maybe. But there's one other person involved who has the motive to fake a heist."

"I know," Powell said. There were reasons to be suspicious of Archvadze himself. A theft was a reasonably effective way to monetize a work of art. Even if Archvadze paid a generous fee to Sharkovsky, once he claimed the insurance, he would get the painting at a huge discount. As remote as the possibility seemed, it would be necessary to learn more about how the painting had been insured. "You still have the phone number for Archvadze's lawyer?"

"Yeah, hold on." At the next light, Wolfe checked her pockets and came up with the business card. "You want to arrange a meeting?"

"It can't hurt to try." Taking out his phone, Powell dialed the number, dimly recognizing the name of the lawyer, who had built a substantial practice for himself around a clientele of wealthy expatriates.

After being placed briefly on hold, he got through to a secretary, who transferred him to the lawyer's private line. The phone rang twice before the lawyer brusquely answered. "Yes?"

"Hi there," Powell said, giving his name and reaching for a notepad. "I'm a liaison officer with the Serious Organised Crime Agency in London. I'm calling about one of your clients, Anzor Archvadze—"

The lawyer broke in. "Anzor Archvadze is no longer a client of mine. We terminated our professional relationship this morning."

Powell, surprised, glanced over at Wolfe. "Do you know where I can reach him?"

"I'm afraid not." The lawyer's voice grew distant. "When we last spoke, he indicated that he was going to be unreachable for the foreseeable future. As far as I know, he's on his way back to Georgia."

The lawyer hung up. Powell closed his cell phone. He found that the smell of death was still in the car, even though the windows had been rolled down. It seemed to be in his clothes.

"I think," Powell said, looking out at the street, "that we have a bit of a problem."

31

Later that day, Maddy began an investigation of her own. She had spent the morning on the phone with a public relations representative, feeding her the names of gallery contacts who might be inclined to issue a statement of support. As the exercise wore on, however, one fact became increasingly clear. Nothing they did would make any difference until the stolen painting was recovered.

As soon as she had a moment, then, she turned to another plan of attack. Like Powell, she knew that there were a limited number of ways to dispose of a stolen painting. You could store it in a country, like Italy or Japan, that had a short period of repose, claiming it once the statute of limitations had expired. You could use it as collateral for a drug or weapons deal. Or, most likely, you could sell it to a buyer who had arranged for the heist in the first place.

If this last possibility was correct, then she had investigative resources at her disposal that were not readily available to the police. The fund had devoted thousands of hours to analyzing the motives of collectors, and the name of the heist's unknown beneficiary was almost certainly in its database. The hard part was knowing what to look for. Because the painting couldn't be resold or displayed, the familiar motives of greed or emulation didn't apply. Neither did the usual metrics of wealth. The collector behind the heist didn't need to be rich. He didn't need to be anything at all.

But there was another way to narrow down the search. Going to the major art world and society websites, she downloaded photos from the party, which were already beginning to appear online. It was nothing but a hunch, but as she studied the snapshots from the oligarch's mansion, she felt with sudden conviction that whoever had arranged the theft would have wanted to be there that night. And as she looked into one of the photographs, trying to see past a row of forced smiles, she noticed a blurred figure in the background.

She enlarged it. It was a man in a brown suit and black plastic glasses, a camera bag slung over his shoulder. His face was turned away from the lens, but she could remember it all too well.

Ethan, for his part, seemed to be moving in an entirely different direction. For most of the morning, his door remained closed, but from their occasional email exchanges, she sensed that he was working on something unusual. When lunchtime arrived, they met in front of the Fuller Building, where Ethan, somewhat to her surprise, hailed a cab at the corner. "Where are we going?"

"On a field trip," Ethan said, opening the taxi door. "Come on, you'll enjoy this."

After a beat, she entered the cab, and Ethan gave the driver a crosstown address. As they drove off, she studied his face. Aside from the circles under his eyes, he looked good, and he had resumed the professional tone of their relationship with an ease that she found vaguely depressing. "So what's this all about?"

Ethan glanced at the driver, who did not seem to be listening to their conversation, then lowered his voice. "So you remember what I said yesterday. You can gain insight into an artist by considering the interests of his patrons, who inevitably influence his work."

"You don't need to convince me of this," Maddy said, rolling down her window as they took the transverse road through the park. "Anyone who claims to be untouched by the market is lying."

"Well, Duchamp claimed it, and at first, it's hard to prove otherwise. For one thing, it's unclear where he got the money to live." Taking a rumpled sheet of notes from his pocket, Ethan glanced at their driver once more before continuing. "Look at the timeline. In 1913, Duchamp appears in his first major show, making him famous overnight. The following summer, Walter Pach, a prominent critic, meets with him in Paris, shortly after war is declared."

"I know who Pach was," Maddy said. "He was an important New York art adviser."

Ethan refolded his notes as they emerged from the park, heading a block north. "Then you probably know that one of his clients was a lawyer and art collector named John Quinn, who advised him to see Duchamp. We don't know what they talk about, but the following year, instead of joining the war effort, Duchamp goes to New York. When he arrives, Pach arranges for a place for him to stay. Which, as it happens, is where we are now."

They halted halfway up a street lined with shade trees. After paying the driver, Ethan slid out, followed by

Maddy, who saw that they were standing before a prewar apartment complex. "So where are we, exactly?"

"Walter Arensberg's apartment." Ethan pointed to a window two stories up the brick façade. "He and his wife lived on the second floor. Pach arranged for Duchamp to live here while the Arensbergs were gone."

Maddy leaned back, trying to see past the overhanging branches. "All right. So what's your point?"

"Well, you can't tell from here, but we're standing at the tip of a very interesting triangle." Ethan gestured toward the park. "Quinn's apartment was three hundred yards to the southeast. Duchamp went there every day, supporting himself by giving French lessons to Quinn, or so he claimed. But look here."

He pointed southwest. "Soon after Duchamp moved out of Arensberg's apartment, he took a room in a building on Broadway, also three hundred yards away. In the meantime, he briefly lived across the street from Walter Pach. Which means that in all the months he spent in New York, a city of five million people, he was never more than a block away from one of these three men. Now follow me."

As they headed up the street, moving toward the unseen vastness of Lincoln Center, Maddy felt obliged to assume a more skeptical tone. "None of this is so surprising. This whole neighborhood was an enclave for artists."

"Fair enough," Ethan said. "But look at what happens next. When Duchamp says that he's looking for a steady job, Quinn tells him to contact Belle Greene, the director of the Morgan Library. She finds him a position at the French consulate, but pays his salary herself. Even his biographers don't know why."

"It isn't so strange," Maddy said. "A lot of artists have messy financial lives."

"True. In fact, I can tell you a similar story. Around the same time, a British writer is hired as a purchasing agent in New York, a position for which he has no obvious qualifications. On his arrival, he meets with Quinn, who gives him financial assistance. The writer's name is Aleister Crowley."

Maddy recognized the name of the notorious occultist. "Quinn was friends with both Crowley and Duchamp?"

"More than just friends. It's generally believed that Crowley was working as an intelligence agent. Quinn was his paymaster, probably through Belle Greene, whom Crowley mentions in his diary. His mission was to investigate individuals believed to harbor sympathies toward Germany, notably Roger Casement, an Irish revolutionary who was negotiating for support from the Kaiser."

As they continued toward Columbus Avenue, Maddy began to see where this was going. "And Duchamp was doing the same thing?"

"Look at his profile. Crowley was recruited because, as an avowed sexual deviant, he could get close to Casement, who had a fondness for young boys. And Duchamp was chosen because he was a famous painter who could easily befriend a patron of the arts. I'm talking about Walter Arensberg."

"Why would the intelligence community care about what Arensberg was doing?"

"Because of his obsession with the Rosicrucians. Arensberg is openly interested in a secret society founded in Germany, which automatically makes him a target of suspicion. The proof is that Crowley, in his capacity as an intelligence agent, made a point of befriending the founder of the Rosicrucian order in New York. If Quinn ordered him to infiltrate the Rosicrucians, it isn't hard to believe that he told Duchamp to keep an eye on Arensberg for the same reason."

They arrived at the main square, where Ethan pointed toward the plaza. "Duchamp lived right here, at the old Lincoln Arcade. The building was torn down in the fifties, but at the time, it was a rat's nest of artists, fortune-tellers, and detective agencies, exactly the sort of place where an undercover agent would feel at home. And, as we've seen, it was only a block from Arensberg's apartment."

"But it must have been a waste of time," Maddy said. "Didn't we say that Arensberg was a lunatic?"

"Exactly. You've seen his book. It isn't the testimony of an insider. He's on the outside, looking in. Duchamp evidently concludes the same thing, which is why he goes to Buenos Aires, saying that he's bored by the Arensbergs. Once he's there, what does he do? He plays chess. He carves his own pieces and devotes himself entirely to the game. Or so he says."

"But you think that he kept working as an intelligence agent, even after the war."

"If he did, it explains his unknown source of income and his love of disguises, as well as some of the stranger episodes in his life. You see? He says that he has retired from art to focus on chess, but he's really playing a game of chess that spans the entire globe. And the proof is in the art itself."

Maddy, who had been looking out at the crowds in the plaza, was brought up short by this last statement. "Hold on. You're saying that his art was influenced by his intelligence work?"

"Well, after the war ends, he becomes a Grand Satrap of the Society of Pataphysics, a parody of Rosicrucianism. He poses nude at a ballet performance, using a rose as a fig leaf. Even the readymades are messages. Look at that ball of twine. It was made on the three hundredth anniversary of Shakespeare's death, but it was also the day of the Easter Rising in Ireland, a rebellion organized by Roger Casement, the man Crowley was watching in New York."

Maddy was struck by this connection, but still wanted to slow the conversation down. "How do you know all this?"

"It's what I do every day. We've gathered an enormous amount of information on the art world, not just price data, but articles, reviews, academic research. It's how we make money. And this isn't so different. Once you have the basic premise, the rest of it is obvious—"

Ethan trailed off. Following his gaze, Maddy saw that he was looking at a young man with a violin case standing a few yards away. "See that guy?" Ethan asked softly. "I think he's been following us."

Maddy frowned. "He's a music student. He's probably heading for Juilliard."

"Maybe." Ethan watched as the student continued toward a crosswalk, waiting for the light to change. "In any case, we need to be careful."

She was unsettled by the note of paranoia in his voice. "But what's the point? You said you were working on something that would help the fund. I don't see how any of this qualifies."

"Easy. We use it to figure out who ordered the heist." Ethan waited until the student had crossed the street, then turned to her again. "It's a trade model in reverse.

Normally, we look at an investor's behavior to forecast what he'll buy next, but I can also use sales records to create a portrait of a hypothetical collector. A man like Arensberg, say, who is looking for insight into the groups that Duchamp was watching. If he's been active in the market, we can track him through his purchases. It's like finding a black hole by observing its gravitational field."

"So we look at works by Duchamp, or other artists with Rosicrucian ties, and see who has bought them before," Maddy said, understanding his idea at last. "And if we can find our hypothetical collector—"

"We find the study," Ethan said, his eye straying back to the student, who had taken a seat near the fountain. "Simple as that."

He hailed another cab. As they returned to the office in silence, Maddy tried to work out the implications of what Ethan had said. She ultimately concluded that the approach might be worth pursuing, but only if they could narrow its scope. With so much data at their disposal, it would be easy to see connections that weren't really there. To refine the parameters, they needed a source who could help them sort through the noise. Which meant that she had to talk to Lermontov.

The rest of the afternoon passed quickly, although Maddy continued to wonder about the paranoid streak that Ethan had begun to display. Four hours later, she got off the train at Atlantic Avenue and walked the five blocks to her building. As she was ascending the brownstone steps, her eye was caught by a car across the street. Behind the wheel sat a man in a tracksuit, his blond ponytail gathered in a tight apostrophe at the nape of his neck.

Maddy turned away from the driver, then looked

back. She wasn't sure why her attention had been drawn to him, but as she went inside, she had the unmistakable feeling that she was being watched. When she glanced back over her shoulder, however, he was not looking in her direction, but through the windshield, as if waiting for someone to return from nearby.

After another moment, she closed the door behind her. There were a few bills in the mailbox, including an overdraft notice, which she tucked behind the others as she trudged up the stairs. When she entered her apartment, tossing the bills aside, she noticed that the hallway light was on. It annoyed her to think that it had been on all day, burning a soft hole in her utility costs. Unless—

Feeling suddenly uncertain, she looked more closely at the living room, which was small enough to take in at a glance. At first, it seemed untouched. The heap of papers on the table, including the report from Tanya, lay exactly where she had left it. Setting down her purse, she went down the short hallway to the bedroom. When she switched on the light, she saw that the laptop on her desk was open.

She regarded the laptop for a long moment. Usually, whenever she left the house, she made sure that it was closed. When she tried to remember if she had shut it that morning, she became increasingly sure that she had.

An instant later, she flashed on the car parked outside. Going back into the entryway, she found herself racing down the stairs to the ground floor. Her phone was in her hands, ready to call the police, but when she opened the door that led to the sidewalk, she halted, pulse high. The curb across the street was deserted, and she was alone. The man in the car had disappeared.

32

Standing before the counter of the hardware store, Ilya accepted a bag from the cashier. Inside were a pair of needle-nose pliers, a ball of nylon cord, and a roll of plastic sheeting, the kind used by painters to lay down drop cloths. In a second bag at his side, he already had a travel umbrella and a pair of shipping tubes, one two inches in diameter, the other slightly wider.

Outside, in Herald Square, the day was warm. He quickly covered the three blocks to his hotel, the bag thumping against one leg. Since returning to the city, he had cut and tinted his hair, and a pair of reading glasses from a drugstore display rack was pushed up on the bridge of his nose.

Passing through the revolving doors, he entered the lobby. Because of its location, the hotel drew throngs of tourists, making it a convenient place to disappear. All the same, his situation was far from secure. The day before, when he had asked if he could pay for his room in cash, the clerk had requested identification. When Ilya had handed over the driver's license, the clerk had barely glanced at it, taking it into the rear office for a photocopy before giving it back.

Obtaining this license had been the weekend's most

challenging task. On Sunday, he had taken a train into the city. Upon his arrival, he had immediately gone to Central Park. Positioning himself on a bench across from the boathouse, he had watched it for several hours, keeping a close eye on the station in the parking lot where tourists rented bicycles. When the station attendant had ducked out for a bathroom break, Ilya had forced the lock and slipped into the empty kiosk.

Forty bikes had been out, the renters required to leave a driver's license and credit card. The licenses had been filed in an expanding folder. Closing the door behind him, Ilya had swiftly rifled through the cards. Half of the renters had been women, while half of the remaining possibilities could be discarded at once for differences of race or age. Of the remaining ten licenses, Ilya had chosen one that was close to his own coloring and build. He had slipped it into his pocket and left the station, emerging only seconds before the attendant returned.

Looking back on this adventure, it seemed to him that he had taken considerable risk for a limited payoff. When he examined the license with a cooler head, its resemblance to him was less than impressive. The man's nose was longer, his eyes set farther apart, his stated height three inches shorter than Ilya's own. The haircut, tint, and reading glasses made the impersonation slightly more convincing, but Ilya knew that he could not rely on it for long.

When the elevator arrived at his floor, Ilya went down the hall, using a key card to enter his room. Inside, the cramped, dingy space was very warm. Before leaving, he had made sure to turn off the air-conditioning and close the windows, despite the heat of the day outside.

Ilya set the shopping bags on the bed and went over to the dresser. Reaching into the gap between the dresser and the wall, he felt his hand close around the upper edge of the painting, which he withdrew from its hiding place.

He studied the headless woman, looking for signs of craquelure. There were no visible cracks, which made things easier. Using the pliers, he extracted the painting from its frame and removed the staples that held the canvas to its stretcher. He worked slowly, aware that a mistake would cause irreparable damage.

When the staples were out, he unfolded the corners of the canvas and peeled it away from the stretcher. Time had stiffened the fabric, which bore an intricate pattern of creases where each corner had been folded over the wood. The image itself occupied the center of the canvas, with margins of raw fabric on all four sides. As for the stretcher, without the canvas, it was a plain wooden armature, covered with labels from galleries and shipping companies.

Taking the mailing tubes, he used his knife to trim them to the width of the painting. From the plastic sheet, he cut a rectangle that was the exact size of the canvas. He spread the plastic on the floor and laid the canvas on top, the painted side facing down. Working carefully, he rolled the canvas around the smaller tube, the painted surface on the outside, with the plastic serving as interleafing. So far, it all seemed pliable enough. It was fortunate, he thought, that the weather was warm.

When he was done, the painting was rolled snugly around the cardboard cylinder. He slid it into the larger of the two tubes, which was just wide enough for the painting to slip inside. Removing the collapsible umbrella from its nylon sleeve, which was the only part that he needed, he used the shears to punch four holes in the sleeve, one pair at the base, another at the mouth. Then he threaded two lengths of cord through the holes, tying them with slipknots.

Ilya inserted the rolled painting into the sleeve. He pulled the loops of cord across his shoulders so that the sleeve hung down his back, like an archer's quiver, then regarded himself in the mirror. It took a few minutes of tightening and loosening the straps before the package hung to his satisfaction. He took off the harness and replaced the slipknots with blood knots, each of which he hardened briefly in the flame of a match. Now he had a harness, customized for his body, that would be all but invisible under a loose shirt or jacket.

Gathering up the staples, he scattered them in the slots of the heating vent that ran along the baseboard, hearing them rain against the metal. Then he rolled the remaining scraps of debris into a loose ball, which he stuffed behind the dresser, along with the stretcher and frame.

Drained from an hour of focused activity, Ilya lowered himself into the chair by the window. On a table beside the chair lay a copy of that day's paper, which he had bought on an earlier excursion. It had been opened to an article on an inside page of the city section. Most of it consisted of an account of the heist, but there was also a sidebar about the Reynard Art Fund. Looking at it reminded him of the two guests he had encountered at the party. Especially, for some reason, the girl.

Ilya glanced at the article again, then put it down. What he needed, more than anything else, was information. At the moment, he had only one source, as unreliable as it might be.

From his pocket, he took a prepaid phone that he had bought at the same drugstore where he had found the reading glasses. He dialed. The phone rang twice before he heard the clank of the receiver. "Club Marat."

Ilya, picturing the *vor* seated in his downstairs office, spoke softly. "Sharkovsky."

There was a pause before the old man spoke again. "You took my eye. I should take yours in exchange."

"Then you won't get your package." Ilya felt as if he were skating along the grooves of a conversation that had been predetermined long before he had placed the call. "Has Vasylenko spoken to you?"

"He called last night. He says that you're willing to make a deal. What do you want?"

"I want money and protection," Ilya said. "In my bedroom in Brighton Beach, there's a shoulder bag with books and papers inside. I want the bag and everything inside it. And I want eighty thousand dollars."

"Eighty thousand dollars is a lot of money. I will need time to get that much cash—"

Ilya cut him off. "If you need cash, look to your left. You keep at least sixty thousand in change funds in the safe. Raid the *obshchak* for the rest. Considering what I'm giving you in return, I'd call it a bargain."

"A shame, I'm sure, that you can't sell it yourself. Where shall we meet? The club?"

"No." Ilya named the location that he had in mind. He had spent the morning looking at potential sites, and had decided that this one seemed the most promising. "I'll see you at noon tomorrow."

"Misha and I will be there. We will bring your cash and books. As for my eye—"

Before the *vor* could finish, Ilya switched off the phone. Trying to get a sense of his feelings, he found that he was pleased. As he set the phone down, he hoped that Sharkovsky would conclude that all he wanted was money. Greedy men, he knew, always assumed that others were driven by the same thing. If Sharkovsky believed this, he would underestimate him, which was all for the better.

It did not occur to Ilya, at least not then, that he might be underestimating Sharkovsky as well. Nor did he wonder, not even in passing, if their conversation might have been overheard.

Three miles south, at a fake pine desk at the heart of the cubicle farm, a man rose and removed his earphones. The computer on his desktop was running the internal system employed to collect information from cell phones and landlines under electronic surveillance. It could be used to copy recordings and route them to translators, but for now, no translation was necessary.

Leaving his cubicle, the agent approached an office at the far end of the floor. As he entered, Barlow looked up. "What is it?"

"It's Ilya," Kandinsky said. "They're meeting at the New York County Courthouse."

33

The following morning, a few blocks from the courthouse, Ilya watched flocks of children tossing basketballs and playing on swings. This park lay near the heart of the Five Points, where Swamp Angels and Daybreak Boys had once fought for control of the city, but today, the area was relatively tranquil, with the silence broken only by the quick snap of sneakers against concrete.

Ilya waited for a moment longer, then headed for the comfort station. The restroom was fashioned from rough limestone, as simple as a child's house of blocks. Inside, it was a mildewed cave with aluminum fixtures, a perpetual stream of water trickling from the sink. Under the window stood a heavy garbage bin. Behind it, he wedged a plastic bundle containing his stun gun, knife, and penlight.

Outside, he took in a lungful of fresh air and headed for the courthouse, approaching it from the rear. The building was stately and imposing, its hexagonal lines obscured by a severe Corinthian portico. As he mounted the steps, which took him a full story above the street, he noted that the federal courthouse next door was under construction, encircled on all sides by a sidewalk shed.

Past the revolving doors, he approached a security checkpoint where marshals in blue uniforms were waving visitors through. Without being asked, he unslung his shoulder bag and set it on the conveyer belt, where it was fed into a scanner. When he walked through the metal detector, it remained silent.

One of the marshals studied the cathode display. "Any electronics in the bag?"

"Cell phone," Ilya said. He had been asked the same question the day before. "And a radio."

The guard did not take his eyes from the screen. Aside from the cell phone and radio, he would see nothing but a Windbreaker and a mailing tube. "The phone have a camera? If it does, you have to declare it."

"No camera." Ilya wondered if they would ask him about the radio, but the guard said nothing more. When his bag came out the other end of the scanner, he picked it up and slung it over his shoulder.

As he was about to proceed into the courthouse, a second guard spoke. "What brings you here today?"

Ilya found that it was easiest to tell the simple truth. "I am here to get a passport."

Leaving the checkpoint, he entered the courthouse. It was floored with echoing marble, six wings radiating outward from a central rotunda. Above him hung mosaics of the great lawgivers of the past, giant enthroned figures of Moses, Blackmun, Hammurabi. To his right, set apart from the main entrance, stood an emergency exit. It was cordoned off by two stanchions linked with a retractable belt, but there was no guard, and the door itself was held shut with nothing but a panic bar.

The passport office, a drab hallway lined with three

wooden benches, occupied one of the rotunda's wings. On the first bench, a man in a suit, perhaps a lawyer, was speaking rapidly into a cell phone; on the second, a redhead in a greasy denim jacket was slumped against the wall, gazing down vacantly at the floor. Ilya sat on the third bench, which was otherwise empty.

A second later, the lawyer rose and moved away, still talking on his cell phone. This left only the redhead in the denim jacket, who did not seem altogether aware of his surroundings. Ilya was studying the vagrant, wondering if it might be better to find a different location, when he saw Sharkovsky and Misha walking across the polished floor of the rotunda.

Although he had come half an hour early, he had anticipated them by only a few minutes. As the two men drew closer, he observed that Sharkovsky was wearing an eye patch, and that Misha carried his satchel in one hand. When they reached the hallway outside the passport office, Sharkovsky lowered himself onto the bench. Misha sat gingerly beside him, careful of his bad leg.

A moment passed in silence. At last, Sharkovsky spoke. "I see no reason to draw out this transaction any longer than necessary, *keelyer*. Unless, of course, you have anything else on your mind."

As he looked into the old man's sole visible eye, Ilya was reminded of a crow peering sideways at its prey. "If Vasylenko is a Chekist, he will answer for it in the end. But what about the rest of the brotherhood?"

"What do you want me to say?" Sharkovsky said in Assyrian. "Chekist or thief makes no difference. Power is what counts. If you were told otherwise, it was because it was what you wanted to hear."

Ilya felt the truth of these words as another tightening of the noose. He thought again of the cross around Vasylenko's neck, and of the star scratched into its hidden side. "So why did he choose me?"

"He saw potential. Not every man can become what you are. It takes—" Sharkovsky paused to consider his words. "Detachment. Intelligence. And morality. There is nothing so dangerous as a deeply ethical man, once his life has been erased. And all it took was a word from him to leave you with nothing—"

Ilya's hands grew cold, as if all the blood had withdrawn to his heart. He found that he knew precisely what the old man was going to say, as if the realization had been lurking there, just outside his circle of awareness, ever since the night of the vineyard. "What are you talking about?"

"You mean you don't know?" Sharkovsky gave him a smile of monstrous tenderness. "You had to be on your own. Otherwise, you wouldn't be an effective instrument. So he did what he had to do. At least they were allowed to die in their sleep. Not everyone receives the same consideration."

Sharkovsky extended a hand for the satchel, which Misha gave to him at once. The old man turned back to Ilya, his good eye shining in its socket. "Now then. Are you ready to make the exchange?"

34

A few moments earlier, Powell and Wolfe had watched from across the street as Ilya entered the courthouse. Barlow's voice came over Powell's headpiece: "The marshals want to handle the security themselves. I've signed off on this. If our guy cased the site beforehand, we don't want to scare him away—"

Powell saw a door by the main entrance. "Do we have a man on the emergency exit?"

"One second." Barlow went silent for a moment, then returned. "All right, it's done. Kandinsky is in place. He knows the drill. We're going to let them talk for as long as possible. An interpreter is on the line. After they've left the courthouse, we put tails on all of them. Security says that our primary target isn't carrying the package. Once he leads us to it, we grab him."

As Barlow signed off, Powell kept an eye on the courthouse, wondering if they were underestimating the Scythian. It was clear now that Ilya had stolen the painting. Based on the security footage, there had been two different men at the mansion, dressed in identical clothes. The heist had gone off as planned, but there had been a double cross, leaving one thief, probably Zhenya, dead.

There was also the small matter of the ballistics results, received less than an hour ago, indicating that the gun recovered at the mansion had been used to fire a bullet into Arshak Gasparyan's brain.

And now Ilya had been heard on the wire, offering to trade a package for eighty thousand dollars. It wasn't hard to guess what might be inside. As Powell reflected on the situation, though, he doubted that the demand for cash was real. If Ilya had been betrayed, he would not be content to be bought off. Which meant that this meeting might be about something else entirely.

Powell was about to share these thoughts with Wolfe when he saw that she was motioning for him to lower the volume on his microphone. He muted the headpiece. "What is it?"

"I found out what happened with Archvadze's attorney," Wolfe said. It was their first chance to talk privately since the day before. "I got the story from a junior partner at the firm. He teaches criminal procedure at Quantico every other summer, and loves to sound off to his former students, especially the girls."

"I'm sure he had no trouble remembering you," Powell said. "So what did he say?"

Wolfe kept her eye on the courthouse. "Archvadze went nuts. The door was closed, but you could hear him shouting halfway across the floor. He accused his lawyer of working for the Chekists, of leaking information about his art collection, and generally of being in league with the powers of darkness. Then he stormed out of the office. They haven't heard a word from him since."

Powell studied the figures passing through the revolving doors. "Was he right?"

"As far as I can tell, the lawyer is clean. His client list includes some shady members of the expatriate community, but if there's a connection to Russian intelligence, I can't see it—"

She broke off. Following her eyes, Powell saw a familiar pair mount the courthouse steps. It was Sharkovsky, his eye patch distinctive from a distance, and Misha, a bag over one shoulder. "What about the art fund?"

Wolfe inserted her headpiece again. "I've looked into it. Reynard is clean as a whistle. No record of financial irregularity. And his business model depends on a sterling reputation. These days, he's more famous as a trader, but he also runs a public database of art transactions. It's the industry standard. For people to trust his numbers, he needs to keep his house in order."

Powell considered this point as his earpiece was flooded with the ambient din of the courthouse. A moment passed, the echo broken now and then by the thunderous rustling of fabric, before a voice came over the wire: "I see no reason to draw out this transaction any longer than necessary, *keelyer*."

When Powell heard these words, all his attention became fixed on the feed. It was the first time he had ever heard Sharkovsky speak. Based on the transcripts, he had expected something harder, and was struck by the quietly authoritative voice that came over his earpiece instead. When he heard the old man say the word *keelyer*, he felt another shiver of recognition. This was slang for a hired gun, twisted into something sinister by the Slavic pronunciation.

As the meeting began, Powell tried to tune out the interpreter's voice, focusing on the speakers themselves.

When the conversation shifted to Assyrian, he switched gears, listening to the translation instead. What he heard was astonishing. Ilya had been one of Vasylenko's men, but was now convinced that his mentor was a Chekist. Powell saw at once that this gave them an opening. If Ilya suspected the mob of working for the secret services, he would be completely on his own. And if they got to him now, when he was still vulnerable, he might be open to a deal.

Powell, his mind already working out the possibilities, forced himself to listen as the men prepared for the exchange. There was a pause as the interpreter searched for a word for an obscure phrase. "I'm not sure what they're talking about," the interpreter said. "It's something like—"

A commotion erupted on the other end of the line. Powell's earpiece filled with a wild thumping and scratching, as if something were striking the microphone itself. Then, with a whine, the wire went dead.

Barlow came back on the line, roaring. "What the fuck is going on? Did we blow it?"

Powell took a step forward, then another. Before he knew it, he was running. Fewer than fifty yards stood between him and the courthouse. Wolfe was sprinting at his side, shouting for pedestrians to get out of the way.

They were almost at the steps when the emergency exit flew open, clanging against the side of the building. A lone figure stumbled into the light, a bag clutched in one hand. As he stood against the portico, far above the street, his eyes caught briefly on Powell's own. It was Ilya.

35

Ilya had considered the bag in Sharkovsky's hands, which was within his reach at last. To disappear would require nothing but silence, exile, and cunning, but now he saw that such an escape was no longer possible. He looked into the *vor*'s one good eye. "Why are you telling me this?"

In response, Sharkovsky only lifted the patch, revealing the eye of a vulture, rheumy and unfocused. "Because you took this from me. Before we parted ways, I wanted to take something from you in return."

Ilya rose from the bench. Before he could make another move, Misha stood as well, their faces only a few inches apart. Sharkovsky, still seated, lowered his eye patch with a sigh. "Don't be a fool. Even if you could kill us now, it would not take back what has already been done."

Looking at Misha, Ilya found himself thinking, strangely, of how easy it must have been. Breaking the flue would have required only a few strokes of the hammer, and with such accidents common among the old, the police would not have been inclined to draw out their investigation.

For a second, an iris seemed to open on his past,

threatening to swallow him whole. Then his head cleared, and he saw that the old man was right. He would accomplish nothing this way. Even as he made his decision, he heard himself speak in a low voice. "How do I know there isn't a tracking device?"

Sharkovsky's smile broke his face into many discrete planes of flesh. "Once our business is concluded, I see no reason to follow you."

Ilya sat down again. His head was light, but his hands retained something of their old competence as he opened his own bag and removed a device the size of a transistor radio, with a liquid crystal display and a retractable antenna. It was a radio frequency counter that he had bought the day before, following a habit of caution that now seemed to belong to another lifetime.

He turned on the counter, forcing himself to focus. After the display had tested its segments, cycling through each mode in turn, he held the antenna against the satchel, sliding the range switch to its lowest setting.

Ilya examined the display. The counter was picking up waves of random noise, but it was weak, the result of other devices, such as cell phones, in the neighborhood of the rotunda. The bar graph that registered signal strength indicated that there was nothing in the bag itself. He switched the range to another setting and scanned it again. There was still nothing.

A second later, he paused. Looking at the counter, he saw that it had picked up a signal strong enough to fill eight of the ten bars. According to the display, its bandwidth was too low for a cell phone, but well within the range of a listening device. Then he saw that the antenna was no longer pointing toward the bag, but aimed at the vagrant on the opposite bench.

For the first time, he noticed that although the redhead's clothes were dirty, his nails were neatly trimmed. Beside him, Sharkovsky glanced between the display and the man in the denim jacket, his predatory mind making the connection at once. "Hey," the *vor* said. "Hey, you fuck—"

The man's head jerked up. A twitch of uncertainty crossed his face. "Excuse me?"

Sharkovsky rose, fists balled, radiating a joyous rage. "You like what you're hearing, *suka*?"

The man stood, startled, hands rising in an instinctive gesture of defense. "Wait—"

Before he could finish, an object that had been hooked on his waistband fell off and shattered against the floor, a pair of alkaline cells flying in opposite directions. It was the battery pack for a wire.

Ilya turned to the *vor*, warmth spreading across his face. "You brought the police."

Sharkovsky looked back, his one visible eye vibrating back and forth. "I did nothing. It must have been you—"

Ilya did not press the argument. Picking up his own bag, he headed for the rotunda, seeing that the satchel was already back in Misha's hands. He could feel his depth of field narrowing, contracting into tunnel vision, and fought it, knowing that he had to remain intensely aware of his surroundings.

It was fifteen quick steps to the rotunda. When he saw the emergency exit, he froze in midstride. A moment ago, it had been unguarded. Now a marshal in blue was blocking his best route to the outside world.

The marshal's eyes met his own. For a fraction of a second, Ilya took in isolated details of the scene: the guard's holstered gun, the silver in his hair, a spot of food on his tie. Then his attention locked onto the four yards of tiled floor that stood between him and the only way out.

He did not hesitate. Lowering his head, he plowed into the guard's center of gravity, knocking him off his feet. That should have been enough, but something took hold of him as he collided with the other man's body, a savage despair awakening after days on the run, and before he could stop himself, he lashed forward with the heel of his hand, breaking the guard's nose with a neat snap of cartilage.

There was a meaty thud as the marshal hit the ground, clutching his face. The courthouse boomed with screams. Without slowing, Ilya pushed aside the stanchions and flung himself against the panic bar. An instant later, he passed through a portal of white light and emerged on the other side.

Behind him, the door swung shut. For a heartbeat's pause, he stood on the edge of the terrace, high above the square. The guards would flood out of the courthouse soon. If he went down the steps, he would be in their line of fire.

A metal railing separated the terrace from the ground twelve feet below. Ilya couldn't remember what the ground was like on that side of the building, but it was too late to wonder about this now.

He jumped. A weightless moment and then he was rolling on grass, angling his bag to protect the canvas as he rose to a sprinter's crouch. Across the narrow street stood the federal courthouse, its lower half hidden behind blue plywood. He ran for it, clambering up the chain link fence, the wire rattling and quivering. As he threw himself over the top, he heard the seams of his jacket rip open.

Pain blossomed in his left ankle as he fell to all fours, eye to eye with the concrete. He forced himself to his feet. Around him, the construction site was deserted. He ran parallel to the courthouse, feet clocking against the pavement, heading for the sheltered side. Behind him, the fence rang. He glanced back just long enough to see a man in glasses hauling himself over the gate.

Rounding the corner, he saw a pyramid of tiles stacked against the plywood fence. He climbed it, tiles falling and shattering, and seized the upper edge of the barrier. Splinters bit into the palms of his hands as he pulled himself over, landing badly in an alley by a church.

When he saw where he was, he had no choice but to laugh, two muffled detonations blooming in his lungs. At One Police Plaza, a hundred yards away, officers were milling around the concrete block of police headquarters, an inverted ziggurat covered by a grid of windows. He did not think that anyone had noticed his sudden appearance, but knew that he could not remain here for long.

Ilya limped around the front of the church. A sign pointed him toward a gift shop in the basement, which could be reached by an outside set of stairs. Descending, he entered through a side door and found himself in an empty auditorium. Another sign pointed to the men's room.

Going into the bathroom, he locked the door, his

ankle sending out periodic calls of pain. His jacket and shirt, soaked with sweat, went onto the countertop. Opening his bag, he withdrew the tube with the painting and slung it across his shoulders. He put on his shirt and Windbreaker, checking to make sure that the harness was invisible, and stuffed everything else into the garbage.

As he worked, he thought of what Sharkovsky had said. It had never been his intention to run, only to bide his time until the right moment came, but now he saw that it was no longer possible to wait.

He watched himself in the mirror until he was satisfied that he no longer looked like a hunted animal. When his hands were steady again, he went out into the basement. Then he headed back to the Five Points.

36

When the gallerina unlocked the door of the Lermontov Gallery, Maddy brushed past her without a word, heading for the office at the rear. The gallerina followed close behind, heels clicking against the floor, protesting this invasion of her sacred space. Maddy tuned her out. She couldn't remember if the gallery had a security guard, but supposed that it probably did.

Lermontov was at his desk, going over a stack of index cards with a blue pencil. As she entered, he set the cards aside. "Yes, my dear?"

Maddy shut the door, stranding the gallerina in the hallway. "I need to talk to you."

After what seemed like the briefest of internal debates, Lermontov rose from his desk, went to the door, and opened it. The gallerina was waiting outside, a look of indignation on her perfect face. "It's all right," Lermontov said. "I've been expecting her. You can go back to work."

Closing the door, he turned to Maddy. "I was wondering when I might see you again. How can I help you?"

Maddy handed him the tabloid that she was carrying. The paper was turned to an inside article, which she had seen entirely by accident, about yesterday's altercation at the courthouse. Below the headline was a screen capture from a security video, showing the man who had assaulted a guard and fled the scene. The image was grainy and blurred, but she had recognized his face at once.

"This is the thief from the party," Maddy said, knowing that Lermontov would have heard the entire story by now. "The press hasn't made the connection yet, but I know what I saw. And if what happened at the courthouse is any indication, he's still trying to move the painting."

Lermontov studied the article, handling the tabloid gingerly, as if he had been given a baby to hold. "What makes you say that?"

"It's the only reason I can see for going to the courthouse at all. It's an ideal place for a meeting or exchange. There are metal detectors and security guards, so you know you aren't walking into an ambush. But it didn't end well. Which makes me think that he still has the study."

The gallery owner handed back the paper. "So what, exactly, do you need from me?"

"If I can learn why the painting was targeted, I can find out who ordered the theft. So far, the best theory I have is the one that you mentioned the other day." Maddy paused. "I don't know if you were serious about the Rosicrucians. But if this is real, you need to tell me."

Lermontov glanced away. Following his eyes, she saw that a velvet curtain had been draped across a wall of his office. When he spoke again, he seemed tired. "You mustn't overestimate my resources. I'm an old man with my own share of private notions. But if I've succeeded in this business at all, it's because I have an eye for market forces that no one else has observed. Look here, for example."

He went over to the curtain. With a gesture that struck her as more dramatic than was strictly necessary, he drew it aside.

"*The Origin of the World*," Lermontov said. "Not the original painting, of course, but a copy by René Magritte. This copy appeared in an obscure gynecological publication in the late sixties, and was believed lost, until I found it in a collection in Berlin. Based on what you've told me about Archvadze, it's the kind of thing he might find interesting. I tried to call him about it the other day, but haven't been able to reach him. It seems that he has disappeared entirely—"

Maddy looked at the canvas, trying to decide if any of this made sense. It was a replica of a painting by Gustave Courbet, which itself was one of the more notorious works in the history of art. It showed a woman with her legs spread, her genitals depicted with an almost pornographic attention to detail. Her body was draped in a white cloth, her face unseen, so that the eye was drawn inexorably to the thatch of her pubic hair and the slit of her labia. "So just because he bought the study, you thought he might be in the market for another headless nude?"

"There's more to it than that. It's generally agreed that Duchamp modeled the pose in *Étant Donnés* on this painting. And both works are visible manifestations of a secret current in art history."

"I'm tired of your secret currents," Maddy said. "Show me something real."

Lermontov drew the curtain, hiding the picture from view. "There's no real mystery. I have a theory about why Archvadze is buying, and I can give him what he wants. I'm not an occultist, but if a major buyer is collecting works for esoteric reasons, I see no reason why I shouldn't profit from it."

"But I still don't understand why a man like Archvadze would care about the occult."

Lermontov returned to his desk, waving her into a chair. "He's an oligarch. And what do oligarchs want? Power. I'm not talking about mystical power, you understand, but the most useful kind of political power. Secret power. The only kind that lasts." He glanced at the curtain again, as if he could see past its velvet veil. "I know it seems hard to believe. The evidence that anything like the Rosicrucians ever existed is extremely tenuous. For the most part, it rests on a few old rumors—"

Maddy sat down. "Like the manifestoes. Which could have been forgeries or hoaxes."

"Or wishful thinking. Yes. But there was another society in Germany, in the same region where the Rosicrucians later appeared, that really did exist. I'm talking about the Holy Vehm."

Maddy recalled that Tanya had mentioned this group in passing. "The Vehmgericht."

"So you've heard of them." Lermontov smiled faintly, as if recalling something from his own past. "Secret tribunals tried and executed criminals in the absence of more orderly systems of law. They met in the forest, under a hawthorn tree. The condemned man was either hung by the neck or cut in two, so that the air would pass between the halves of his body—"

The image of a woman lying in a field, cut in half at the waist, ran briefly through her mind. "So where do the Rosicrucians come in?"

"It's no coincidence that the Holy Vehm used a red

cross to mark the doors of their victims. When it became too dangerous for them to continue under the old dispensation, they resurfaced under a new name. And their legacy was of interest to many men. Do you know Proudhon? He was the first man to call himself an anarchist, and was obsessed with the Holy Vehm. For a time, he considered reviving it as a form of people's justice. These plans never came to pass, but it's likely that he discussed them with his closest confidant. It was, of course, Gustave Courbet."

Maddy's eyes returned to the drawn curtain. "Courbet and Proudhon were friends?"

"Is it so surprising? Courbet was a leading member of the radical scene in Paris. And it was their shared interest in these underground movements, as well as the occult, that inspired *The Origin of the World*. It's a curious fact that this painting, as well as its copies, has always been displayed behind a curtain or screen, like a parody of the Holy of Holies. What's the origin of the world? See for yourself. It isn't God. It's what an alchemist would call the bride."

Maddy thought of Walter Arensberg, who had seen a vulva in the gravel strewn on a cathedral floor. "That's your reading. But why should anyone else interpret it in the same way?"

"The best way to discover a painting's true meaning is to see who paid money for it. The original version passed through the hands of many collectors, and was even seized for a time by the Soviet army, but in the end, it was sold to Jacques Lacan, the psychoanalyst, who hid it behind a sliding panel. His wife, Sylvia, had previously been married to a charming fellow named Georges Bataille.

And if you want proof that Lacan bought the painting for esoteric reasons, you should look into what Bataille was doing before the war."

A flashbulb went off inside Maddy's head. "You're talking about Acéphale."

Lermontov smiled. "Very good. I always knew that you paid attention in class."

Maddy, thinking back to graduate school, wondered if the impulse that led Lermontov to indulge in these speculations was also the urge that had caused him to reshape his own life, transforming himself from a drugstore heir into a worldly dispenser of wisdom. "But I still don't understand why Archvadze would care, unless it has something to do with the Rose Revolution."

"The rose is only a symbol," Lermontov said. "I'm more concerned with what a man must do to effect change in that part of the world. One secret society is often built on the ruins of another, even if they have nothing else in common. And if I were trying to start a revolution in Georgia, I might find it useful to learn more about the forces that were already in place."

"But what could a collector learn from Duchamp that he couldn't learn elsewhere?"

"Great artists are sensitive instruments, tuned to the subtlest currents of their time. If Archvadze is as intelligent as he seems, he'll seek insight from them, not from more mediocre minds. There's a reason, you see, why his assistant wears red heptagrams on his cufflinks. They're an air force roundel, yes, but they're also the seal of the Ordo Templi Orientis."

Lermontov rose and led her to the entrance of the gallery. "Bataille was another such instrument. Once you've considered this carefully, come see me again. And if you need anything else—"

"I'll be all right," Maddy said quickly. "I've had some bad moments, but things are under control."

Lermontov smiled. "Control is the easy part. There's no shortage of ambitious young women with veins of ice." He glanced at the gallerina at the front desk, who was typing something with her headphones on. "The hard part, as Bataille knew, is knowing when to embrace the irrational. If we'd had more time together, I might have taught you this, too. There's always a place for you here, if you want it—"

A few seconds later, before she had a chance to say goodbye, Maddy found herself on the sidewalk. It struck her, belatedly, that Lermontov had been offering her a job. A week ago, she would have dismissed the idea at once, but these days, the prospect of returning to the gallery was disconcertingly seductive.

In any case, there were more important matters to consider. Lermontov had given her an idea. There were two forces at work here. One was the art market; the other, the occult. For the most part, these groups occupied separate worlds, but there were areas where they might intersect. And it was precisely on that common border, Maddy told herself as she pulled out her cell phone, that the collector she was seeking was most likely to appear.

Tanya, to her credit, seemed to know precisely what Maddy had in mind. "Acéphale is easy," Tanya said after Maddy had explained the idea. "I can pull together the material tonight."

"Good," Maddy said into her phone. As she went up

the block, the distant prospect of the park reminded her of another possibility. "One more thing. I'd like you to look into Monte Verità. Have you heard of it?"

"Sounds vaguely familiar. Some kind of health resort in Germany, wasn't it?"

"Actually, it's in Switzerland. It's only a hunch, but it might be useful. I'll give you a call later to tell you more."

After exchanging goodbyes, Maddy hung up. She was about to head for the subway, her mind already turning to this new plan of action, when she saw a familiar figure standing across the street.

She sucked in air at the sight. It was the man with the blond ponytail. She had nearly managed to convince herself that her stalker had been nothing but her imagination, and seeing him now, in daylight, seemed like an active act of defiance. Staring at his face, she felt, not fear, but an unexpected sense of anger.

Opening her purse, she removed her camera. Before the man across the street could react, she took his picture. He blinked, his brow creasing with dismay, and turned aside, limping rapidly up the sidewalk. She had intended to let him go, but instead, she found herself running after him, pushing aside the shoppers and tourists who were blocking her way.

"Hey," Maddy said, her voice rising. "Who are you? Why are you following me?"

The man glanced back, his face unreadable, but did not slow his pace. A second later, he rounded a corner onto Columbus Circle. She followed, impeded by a sea of bodies. When she reached the intersection, he had vanished.

37

The following day, a clerk at the hotel recognized Ilya's face on the news. An hour after the tip was called in, a tactical response team was assembled in the stairwell of the hotel's seventh floor, along with Powell and Wolfe, who felt hemmed in by agents in hardshell vests.

Propping the door open with a rubber wedge, the unit poured silently into the corridor. The agent at the head of the line swiped a card through the lock of the hotel room, swearing under his breath when the green bulb on the keypad did not light up at once. When he swiped it a second time, there was a low electronic tone, and the door finally unlocked.

At a shout from the commander, a swarm of tactical agents entered the room. Powell and Wolfe followed close behind, only to find the unit looking around, disappointed, at nothing. The room was empty.

As the agents continued their sweep, Powell, whose arms and knees still ached from climbing the fence two days before, tried to infer as much as he could about the room's absent occupant. In the bureau, there lay several neatly folded changes of clothes, their tags still attached. A receipt on the bedside table indicated that Ilya had paid in cash. "Looks like he has a lot of money to throw around."

"And he paid cash for the room," Wolfe said. "He wouldn't have been carrying this much at the mansion."

"Check for burglaries on the night of the heist. Look for houses within walking distance of the vineyard." As he spoke, Powell searched the rest of the bedroom. The wastebaskets were empty, but on the carpet, something had been missed by the cleaning staff. He picked it up. It was a sliver of cardboard, curved like a potsherd, as if sliced from a length of tubing.

Looking at the piece of cardboard, he thought back to the scene in the study, remembering the camera bag that he had found wedged behind the shelves. He went over to the bureau, pulling it away from the wall. In the space behind the bureau, along with some scraps of plastic and cord, a frame and wooden armature had been concealed. It was the stretcher from a painting.

"Here we go," Powell said quietly. "See what he did? He took the painting apart."

Wolfe picked up the stretcher, which was very light. "So what did he do with it?"

Powell showed her the scrap of tubing. "He rolled it up. Which means that he probably had it with him at the courthouse. We thought he'd stashed it elsewhere, but he was carrying it the entire time."

Feeling crowded by the tactical unit, they went into the hallway. "So he paid cash for the room, but used a stolen license, which means that he doesn't have a passport," Wolfe said. "Now that the license is blown, it'll be hard for him to travel. He's on his own. So he should be easy to flip."

"Maybe," Powell said, although he privately doubted that it would be so simple. "But he'll go after Sharkovsky first."

"Then he'll come right to us. We've got men posted at the club around the clock."

"I know." Powell headed for the stairwell, going past the elevator, which had been disabled by the tactical team. This was something else to keep in mind. Barlow wanted to move against the club soon. In the confused aftermath at the courthouse, Sharkovsky had slipped away, but there was no doubt that his suspicions had been aroused. The criminal division was already transcribing tapes to prepare a warrant for a raid, possibly within the next few days.

In the meantime, there was nothing to do but push forward with the murder case. An hour later, they were at the ballet studio where the dead girl had worked, speaking with the head instructor. A glass partition in her office looked into the studio itself, its sprung floor streaked with chalk, where ten children were doing exercises at the barre, their daypacks heaped against the mirrored walls.

"Yes, I remember Karina," the teacher said, removing the cotton gloves she had been wearing. She was tall and angular, her hair shot through with gray. "At the time, we had only seven principal dancers, so when she vanished, it hit us hard. We all hoped that she had gone home, but in my heart, I knew the truth."

"She danced at a club in Brighton Beach," Wolfe said. "Did she ever talk about this?"

"Only in passing. It wasn't something she liked to discuss. Maybe she was afraid that we would disapprove.

But I know very well what it takes to keep dancing." The teacher looked out at the class in the next room. "I kept some of her things when we cleaned out her locker. Would you like to see them?"

When Wolfe said that they would, the teacher produced a carton from under her desk, removing the lid to reveal a folded leotard and a roll of surgical tape. Underneath, there lay a bottle of mouthwash and a package of antacids, along with a stack of photos and a clay figurine. Powell picked up this last object, turning it over in his hands. "What's this?"

"It's a toy from her hometown," the teacher said. "Kargopol is famous for them. I believe it was made by her father—"

Powell examined it. The clay had been painted and fired into the image of a fairy with tangled green hair. For all its crudeness of execution, there was something uncanny about the figure. Its face had been shaped with nothing more than a few quick movements of the sculptor's fingers, but it had an expression of sly seductiveness, a cross between a succubus and a mermaid.

He turned his attention to the pictures. There were twelve photos in all, their corners marked with adhesive from where they had been taped to the locker. Most were pictures of students and dancers. Karina herself appeared in a few of the shots, brooding and blond, with attractive, faintly oversized features.

One of the photos was much older than the rest. It showed a family of four standing before a house by a river. In the faded snapshot, Karina was no more than fourteen, bundled in a sweater and wool cap. Her younger sister's hand was clasped in her own. Looming over the girls were their parents, the mother wearing a quilted jacket, the father in a flannel coat, his flushed face peering into the lens.

"It was taken in Kargopol," the teacher said. "That was their house by the river."

Powell checked the other side of the photo. It was blank. "Did she ever talk about her family?"

"Only occasionally. For the most part, she was very private, except—" The teacher hesitated, then said, "A few years ago, when she danced the lead in *Coppélia*, something in the role seemed to open her up. You know the story? An inventor builds a dancing doll, and a boy becomes obsessed with it, until his true love shows him what a fool he is by taking the doll's place—"

Wolfe reached out and took the photograph from Powell. "What did Karina say?"

"As I mentioned before, her father was a toymaker. The girls would dig clay out of the riverbed so he could make it into figurines. When I looked at that toy, and thought of the things she said about her father, I used to wonder if he had done anything to those girls. If he dressed them up, or—" The teacher hesitated again. "I can't prove any of this. But I always wondered."

Wolfe wrote out a receipt for the photos and figurine. "What about the sister?"

"She vanished years ago. According to Karina, she ran off when she was a teenager. The rumor was that she had gone to Moscow. I don't think Karina ever saw her after that."

Something about this fact lodged in Powell's mind as they wound up the interview. As they left the studio, Wolfe seemed thoughtful. "You know, there's something

I should probably mention. There were antacids and mouthwash in that box. You know what that says to me? She was bulimic. It's a shame that her head is gone. I'd need to look at her teeth to be sure—"

Powell was surprised to hear Wolfe speak so clinically. "You're serious about this?"

"It isn't so unusual. Dancers can be monsters about their weight. You've got men lifting you overhead all day, and that darned Balanchine ideal. Swanlike neck, long legs. But the perfect ballerina, by those standards, has a short torso and a flat chest, so I don't know why she got breast implants. Unless it was for her night job. You said yourself she was probably a prostitute—"

"I'm not so sure about that anymore," Powell said, removing his glasses. "I've been looking at the record of prostitution in Brighton Beach, and the Russians have had trouble entering the business. They'll import a few girls from overseas, and after a week, the local pimps tell the police, who shut it down."

"But if Karina was nothing but a dancer, then why did she get her breasts done?"

Powell finished cleaning his glasses, then pushed them back up the bridge of his nose. "Conflicted body image, perhaps."

As they neared the subway, Powell found himself thinking of the ways that a woman might try to reinvent herself. There was the body, yes, but there was also the mind. Karina had focused on transforming her body, much as a toy might shrink and harden in her father's oven, a process that had not concluded until long after her lonely burial in the sand. Her sister had run away at an even younger age. And perhaps she had tried to transform herself as well—

These thoughts ran through his brain, ramifying and evolving, until they were on the train. Then, as they were passing through a darkened tunnel at the heart of the city, something clicked in his head, and he knew.

He rummaged in his briefcase, finally emerging with a copy of the coroner's report. "Look here," Powell said, showing the page to Wolfe. "According to the report, based on her pubic area and underarms, the dead girl had brown hair. But in her photos, Karina is a peroxide blonde."

"So cuffs and collar didn't match," Wolfe said, looking at the report. "So what?"

"Let's see how she might have looked as a brunette." Powell took a headshot from the file, uncapped a marker with his teeth, and used it to color in the dead girl's hair and eyebrows. The changes subtly altered the character of her face, emphasizing its buried exoticism. "Remind you of anyone?"

Wolfe took the headshot from his hands. "Not really. What am I supposed to see?"

"The face of another woman tied up in this case," Powell said. "Natalia Onegina."

"Archvadze's girl?" Wolfe frowned and looked at the picture more closely. "Maybe. But I don't really see it."

"It isn't obvious. But it's there." From his briefcase, Powell removed the picture of Karina standing by the river with her family. He pointed to the younger sister. "I'm not entirely sure, but I think this is Natalia Onegina. She's the sister who went to Moscow. Which means that these two cases are connected."

The subway pulled into the City Hall station, disgorging its passengers onto the platform. Powell shoved the files back into the suitcase, keeping the family photo in one hand, and followed Wolfe to street level. "We need to delve more deeply into Natalia's background. Every profile repeats the claim that she's a niece of German Khan, but I don't know how seriously anyone has ever looked into this. And there's one more thing we need to check."

Wolfe climbed the stairs to the crowded sidewalk. "And what would that be?"

Powell handed her the snapshot. Now that the connection was so clear in his mind, he was troubled by how long it had taken him to understand the dead girl's importance, as if the lapse were a portent of a more permanent decline to come. "We need to find out the name of that river."

They reached the granite chessboard of the Javits Building, which was guarded by a row of iron posts, like pawns. Caught up in his thoughts, Powell was a few steps from the entrance when he heard someone call his name.

He turned. A young woman, who had been seated on one of the backless benches that lined the sidewalk, was walking in his direction. Although he had studied her image carefully on the mansion's outdoor security tapes, it took him a moment to recognize her in the light of day. It was Maddy Blume.

38

"They told me you'd be back soon," Maddy said, approaching Powell and the woman she had glimpsed briefly at the mansion. "They wouldn't let me wait in the lobby, so here I am."

Turning to his colleague, Powell said that he would be up in a minute. As the woman headed for the main entrance, he turned back to Maddy, looking as if there were something else on his mind. "If you're concerned about the investigation, I can assure you that you're no longer under suspicion."

"Then why is someone following me?" Maddy handed him a copy of the photo that she had taken yesterday. "Is he one of yours?"

Powell glanced at it. At once, his expression darkened. "Where did you take this?"

"On Sixth Avenue. I was running an errand and saw this man on the street. I also saw him outside my apartment a few days earlier. He was watching me." Maddy searched the agent's face. "Do you know who he is?"

"Maybe." Powell studied the photo. "Did you notice if he walked with a limp?"

"Yes. It was his left leg." As she spoke, Maddy felt a

244 / Alec Nevala-Lee

strange sense of relief, then decided to push it further. "Does this have anything to do with what happened at the courthouse?"

Powell's look of surprise was rather satisfying. "How did you know about that?"

"I saw the thief's photo in the paper. He was there to meet someone, wasn't he?"

Powell was silent for a moment. Finally, he said, "I need you to keep this to yourself. I don't know why this fellow is watching you, but he won't be on the street for long." He folded and pocketed the photo. "If you see him again, don't confront him. Just call me. In the meantime, I'll do what I can."

He went into the Javits Building. Watching him go, Maddy felt simultaneously terrified and exultant. Now that her suspicions had been confirmed, she felt vindicated, but no less exposed than before.

Forty minutes later, Maddy emerged from the train station at Atlantic Avenue, but did not take her usual route home. Instead of going to her building directly, she rounded the corner one street early, then circled the block, advancing on her brownstone from the opposite side. When she was twenty paces from her door, she halted, pausing in a convenient area of shade.

Three cars were parked across the street. As far as she could tell, they were empty. Aside from a solitary woman on the far corner, walking a dog on a retractable leash, the sidewalk was deserted. Maddy scanned the windows across from her house, looking for a raised blind or a gap in the drapes, but saw nothing out of the ordinary. Only then did she continue toward her own building.

When she entered her apartment, she closed the door,

then set her things down in the hallway. Taking a camera from her purse, she turned on the preview screen and scrolled to a series of pictures that she had taken that morning. The first shot was an image of her dining table, covered, as always, in a drift of junk mail and unpaid bills. Going up to the table, she studied it, then compared it to the shot on her camera. As far as she could tell, nothing had changed.

She advanced to the next picture, the first of several close-ups of the bookcases that lined her living room wall. Approaching the shelves, she checked them one by one. None of the books had been moved.

Finally, she went into the bedroom, where the surface of her desk was buried beneath the usual files and papers. Scrolling to the shot from that morning, she examined the picture, then compared it to the scene before her.

She paused. Although most of the desk looked the same as before, something about one of the stacks of paper caught her eye. Maddy scrutinized the photo again, then looked back at the desk. It was hard to be sure. The papers were from one of Tanya's reports, removed from their folder and carelessly piled, and as she looked at it now, it seemed to her that the cover page was slightly out of place.

Maddy stared at her desk for a full minute, trying to see if it had really been touched. Then she switched the camera off. It was more than possible, she thought wearily, that the pages, which she had stacked untidily on the desk, had resettled on their own. Or, more likely, that she was seeing things. With that unreassuring thought, she put the camera away, then went to prepare for her expected guest.

Two hours later, she was seated at her dining table with Ethan, who was pouring her a glass of wine. It had been his idea to cook dinner at her house, and after some initial reluctance, she had agreed. He, in turn, had layered the lasagna and garlicked the bread efficiently and respectfully, and if he had noticed how small her kitchen was, he had been too polite to mention it.

"We've been going about this the wrong way," Maddy said now, accepting the wine. She had already told him about her conversation with Lermontov, but something kept her from mentioning the man who had been following her, as if this would only give Ethan license to push deeper into her life.

Ethan handed her a plate of arugula and sliced avocado. "What do you mean?"

Maddy scooped up a forkful of salad greens. "We need to take a step back. If artists are driven by the interests of their patrons, collectors are driven by forces of their own. To find our unknown collector, we need to look at the context in which he might have arisen."

Ethan dug into his own salad. "So what kind of context are we talking about?"

"A place where occult movements have influenced art in a meaningful way. Let me give you an example."

She pushed her plate aside. Going into the bedroom, she returned with a large sheet of paper, which she unrolled across the table. It was a historical map of Europe during the First World War, the colors and contours of a ravaged continent spreading softly before her eyes.

"When you look at the history of Europe, you find that there are times and places in which art and the occult are especially close." She pointed to a spot on the map.

"Munich, for instance. Duchamp spent several weeks there shortly before the war began. Nobody knows why he went, but it was an occult center at the time, and when he returned, his art suddenly changed. Before, it was experimental and detached, but afterward, it was full of stylized images of ritual violence."

"As if he were following up on a clue." Ethan frowned at the map. "But about what?"

"I'm not sure. At least not yet. The point is that Munich was a center for both art and the occult. Zurich was as well. But the place I want to talk about is here, only a few hours away from both cities." Maddy pointed to a speck of blue. "Monte Verità. It was founded as a commune, following the principles of Rosicrucianism, and was home to a lodge of the Ordo Templi Orientis, the society headed by Aleister Crowley. But there was another group active in the region at the same time. I'm talking about the men from the Cabaret Voltaire."

Ethan set aside his salad, shifting his attention to the lasagna. "The Dadaists?"

"That's right. Tristan Tzara and Hugo Ball spent months at Monte Verità, side by side with occultists and aspiring Rosicrucians. I read about it in graduate school. Europe was at war, and they were looking for alternatives to the culture that had led to so much death. The occult was one. Dadaism was another."

Ethan studied the map. "So what you're saying is that these relationships could have survived, in other forms, to the present day. That's useful. But we still need to tie them to specific works of art."

"I know." Maddy took a generous sip of wine. "So far, I haven't spent much time on the visual evidence, but it's there. Tanya and I found a postcard, for example, that Tristan Tzara sent to Julius Evola, a mystic who later became tied up with Italian fascism. On the photo of a cross on a church spire, he drew a rose, along with a finger pointing toward the sky."

Ethan seemed to consider this. "And Duchamp was keeping an eye on these groups?"

"Yes, as an artist," Maddy said, rolling up the map again. "But he would have seen right away that the Dadaists weren't serious about the sort of revolution that the Rosicrucians wanted. For that, he would have to wait for another twenty years. Ever hear of Georges Bataille?"

Ethan's lack of recognition disappointed her. He refilled his wine glass. "Who?"

"A writer associated with the Surrealists, until he was excommunicated for his rather extreme opinions. Later, he founded a secret society of his own, influenced by the Marquis de Sade. He called it Acéphale."

"Headless," Ethan said, translating it easily. "Like the woman in *Étant Donnés.*"

"Or a society without a leader. They met under the full moon in a forest near Paris, around an oak tree that had been struck by lightning, with Bataille serving as high priest. There was even talk of inaugurating the society with a human sacrifice, although no one wanted to be the executioner. Their goal was to start a chain reaction that would destroy the capitalist state. Which sounds a lot like the alchemical reformation that the Rosicrucians had in mind. Look at this."

Maddy showed him a drawing, which she had photocopied from one of her old textbooks. It depicted a headless man standing with his arms spread wide, a flaming heart in one hand, a knife in the other. His genitals were covered by a skull, and a pair of stars were tattooed on his chest.

"This is the cover of the first issue of the journal associated with the society," Maddy said. "It was drawn by André Masson, who was married to the sister of Bataille's wife, who later divorced him and married Jacques Lacan. At the bottom of the drawing, there's a symbol that looks like a modified swastika. Both the swastika and knife are emblems of the Vehmgericht."

Ethan was clearly struck by this. "That's interesting. But was Duchamp involved?"

"He certainly knew Bataille, and it's likely that he was approached to join Acéphale, but declined. Later, years after the war, he designed and cowrote one of the group's manifestos."

"But we're left with the same problem as before. Acéphale is more organized than the Dadaists, but there's no proof of what they actually accomplished. For these groups to be of interest to Archvadze, or our unknown collector, we need to show that they had real power."

"I know," Maddy said. "We're missing something. The groups we've seen so far are pale reflections of the real thing, or deliberate artistic distortions. That's why I'm not quite convinced that anyone is buying these paintings for the information they contain. Even if it's there, it's hopelessly compromised."

Ethan chewed in silence for a moment. "Let's work backward, then. If there were a real society with the power to influence world events, what would it look like? It would be global. It would have the capacity to move men and resources from one country to another. It would have access to power at the national level, but its influence would be invisible and untraceable. You know what that sounds like to me? It sounds like organized crime."

Maddy drained her glass. Her head was starting to throb. "So you're saying—"

"What if the societies we've been discussing and global organized crime are two aspects of the same phenomenon? We know that the early revolutionists drew inspiration from the underworld. Look at Bakunin. Look at Stalin, who robbed banks to raise money for the revolution."

Ethan gestured at the picture of the headless man. "Look at this guy. There are a pair of stars on his chest. Even I know that's the sign of a gangster. And didn't Powell ask us if the thief had any tattoos?"

Maddy thought of her stalker. Then she remembered the man at the mansion. "But if that's true, then we've been going about this all wrong. We've been talking as if the study was stolen by someone like Arensberg. An outsider. But if you're right, then the heist was ordered by someone connected to the Rosicrucians themselves. They found out that Archvadze had the painting—"

"—and then they took it back." Ethan stood, eyes bright with excitement, and began to pace around the room. "You're right. This isn't about discovering a secret. It's about trying to cover it up."

"But there's no proof that organized crime has anything to do with the Rosicrucians. Except—" She broke off, remembering something that Tanya had said. The Rosicrucians in Moscow had been the first such group to use code names and systems of confession. In the end, they had been crushed by the Soviets, along with all such societies, but there were rumors that they had only gone underground—

She rose from the table. "Let me get my notes. There's something I need to check."

Maddy headed for the desk in her bedroom, a clear image in her mind of the page she wanted, on which Tanya had sketched a fist clutching a rose. Riffling through the papers, she kept an eye out for the sketch, then frowned. She had reached the bottom of the pile, but the page wasn't there.

A second later, she began to ransack her desk, tossing books and papers aside, looking frantically for the missing page. Even as she tore the room apart, heart pounding, she knew at last that this was not her imagination.

Ethan appeared in the doorway, a look of concern on his face. "Are you okay? Is—"

"*Someone was here.*" The words tore themselves from her lips. "Some of my notes are missing. They were here, and now they're gone." Shoving aside a stack of books, which tumbled in an avalanche to the floor, she looked into Ethan's eyes, which were wide and startled. "They went after my notes, but didn't touch anything else. They knew exactly where to go—"

Ethan came forward. Sensing that he wanted to put his arms around her, she took a step away, her face burning. She finally knew what to do next. The painting, she saw, had been stolen to protect a secret. Her home had been invaded for the same reason. And the only way to find the painting, and the men who had taken it, was to destroy whatever secret they were trying to hide.

39

Powell had seen his share of luxury over the past few days, but was still impressed by the view from the penthouse, which looked out onto the Metropolitan Museum of Art. When he complimented his hostess on this, Natalia Onegina smiled. "Yes, this is my favorite room in the apartment. It's the only place in New York where I can look down on the art world."

Wolfe took a seat. "We hear you've been having some issues with your gallery."

"No worse than you might expect." Natalia offered them tea from a pot on the coffee table, then poured a cup for herself. She was barefoot, dressed in jeans and a flattering cotton top, and even without makeup, she was still faintly ravishing. "Some people actually think that we staged the heist to generate publicity. Can you believe it? As if it were anything other than an embarrassment—"

Powell sensed Wolfe waiting for him to begin. They had decided on the way here that he would take the lead. "We've had trouble reaching Archvadze. Word is that he's gone back to Georgia."

"I don't know where he is," Natalia said. "I haven't spoken to him since the party. Sometimes he'll vanish without a word, as if he's afraid to tell me what he's doing. It's a habit he acquired in less happy times. Neither he nor Kostava will answer their phones. I can't even leave a message."

"But it's been almost a week since the heist," Wolfe said. "Aren't you worried?"

"Anzor knows how to take care of himself. I don't pry into his affairs, and he doesn't interfere with mine." Natalia looked between the two of them. "Is there anything else? I'm rather busy, and if you haven't found the painting, I'm not sure what else we have to discuss—"

"No, we haven't found the painting," Powell said. "But we'd like to ask you about something else."

Reaching into his pocket, he withdrew the clay figurine that they had found among Karina's possessions. He set it on the table without looking away from Natalia. When she saw it, a shadow of unease seemed to pass across her face, but she regained her composure at once. She picked up the figure. "What is it?"

"It's a toy from the town of Kargopol," Powell said. "Have you ever been there?"

"No. I'm not familiar with that area." Natalia put the toy down. "Why do you ask?"

"We're just trying to get our facts straight," Wolfe said. "Where were you born?"

Natalia took a sip from her cup, which was wreathed in wisps of steam. "In Moscow. But you already know this."

"And you're related to German Khan? We weren't sure what the connection was—"

"He's my uncle. I can't say we're especially close, although I've gone hunting with him a few times."

Powell studied Natalia, hoping to see a trace of nervousness, but her face was a mask. "Do you know a woman named Karina Baranova?"

Natalia shook her head, her eyes on Powell. "No. Should I recognize the name?"

Wolfe took a photo of the dead girl from her briefcase and handed it to Natalia. "She was murdered two years ago. Her body was found last week, buried under the boardwalk at Brighton Beach."

Natalia glanced briefly at the headshot. "I've never seen her before. Would you mind explaining why you're telling me this?"

"Because Karina was your sister," Powell said. "We've looked into your background. Your name isn't Natalia Onegina. It's Alisa Baranova. You ran away to Moscow, where you renamed yourself after the Onega River, which flowed by the house where you grew up. Isn't that right?"

Natalia's eyes hardened into flecks of ice. "I don't know what you're talking about."

"Let me remind you, then. You hadn't seen your sister for years. One day, after you moved to New York, she learned that you were here. Maybe she saw your picture in the paper. She gave you a call, and you agreed to meet her. I want you to tell me what happened next."

This speech was compounded of equal parts conjecture and speculation, but Powell hoped it would have the desired effect. Natalia regarded him for another moment, then rose from the couch. "This is absurd," Natalia said, heading for the door. "I'm not going to dignify this any longer—"

Powell watched her walk away, knowing that his window of opportunity was closing. "Wait. Before you go, look outside your balcony."

Natalia paused in the middle of the floor. She made no effort to conceal the hatred in her fine features. "Why?"

"Just look," Wolfe said, rising from the sofa as well. "Then we'll be on our way."

Natalia glared at her, then finally headed for the glass door that led outside. Drawing aside the curtain, she slid the door open, allowing a whisper of a breeze to penetrate the apartment's interior.

They went onto the balcony, which was ample enough to comfortably accommodate a table and chairs. Natalia approached the railing and looked down. Powell spoke quietly at her side. "You see?"

Natalia did not respond. Across the street, parked at the curb near the museum, was a squad car with a uniformed officer behind the wheel. Leaning against the hood was a detective in plain clothes.

"The police are downstairs," Wolfe said. "They agreed to let us go in first, but if we leave without you, they'll be here in ten seconds, and I promise that they won't be as understanding. They don't care about anything except closing a murder, but we're interested in Valentin Sharkovsky, the man who hid your sister's body. If you testify against him, we can make a deal."

Natalia said nothing. It was a hot day, and a sheen of sweat had already appeared on her face. Watching her closely, Powell held his breath. Because she was at home, and not in a custodial situation, it wasn't necessary to inform her of her rights, but she was still entitled to a lawyer. If she remained silent, the case would stall until they caught another break, which he knew might never come.

At last, Natalia turned away. Reaching up, she removed her barrette, allowing her hair to fall loosely across her shoulders, and sat down at the table on the balcony. Taking a fistful of hair in each hand, she lowered her head. When she looked up again, there was an Eastern wildness in her eyes.

"It's strange," Natalia said. "Ever since the party, I've been having nightmares. I knew you were coming. I just didn't know it would be like this." She looked into the next room, where the figurine still sat on the table. "That toy is a *rusalka*. You know what that is?"

Powell, feeling a tentative rush of relief, said, "It's a mermaid. Or is it a demon?"

"In a way. It's the spirit of a woman who drowned herself." Natalia turned back to the others. Her eyes had acquired a glassy shine. "I haven't seen one in years. You see, it was made by my father."

Wolfe sat down, the chair's legs scraping against the concrete. "Tell us about him."

"He—" Natalia raised a hand to her mouth. "He never touched us. I want to be clear about that. But his eyes on me were enough. I ran away before it was too late, but I don't know what happened to Karina. I asked her to come with me, but she didn't. So I left on my own."

"You went to Moscow," Wolfe said, prompting her gently. "What happened then?"

"I worked until I had enough money for new papers." As Natalia spoke, the color began to creep back into her face. "I had plenty of time to think about what to do next. All I needed was a sense of style and a famous name. I picked

German Khan because I thought he would be too reclusive to object, and told people that I was estranged from my family. Once I met Anzor, it was too late to stop. And by the time Karina called me, we hadn't spoken in years."

She looked away, as if a private film were unspooling behind her eyes. "When I got to her room above the club, she was wearing her costume from the show. Green ribbons in her hair, a white dress. We had a drink while I asked about her dancing. But when I told her about my own life, I saw her face change. She threatened to tell Anzor the truth. Then she said—" Natalia hesitated. "I won't tell you what it was. But it had to do with our father."

Powell pictured an exchange of whispers across a darkened room. "And she came after you."

Natalia paused, as if wondering if she should seize upon this excuse. "No. It was me. I took her by the shoulders. I shook her to make her stop talking, but she wouldn't. Then I put my hands around her throat. I only wanted to scare her. Before I knew what was happening, she was on the floor."

Wolfe glanced over at Powell. "On the floor? You mean she lost consciousness?"

"Her eyes rolled back and she fell to her knees. Then she stopped moving. I couldn't believe it. I tried to wake her up. I pounded her chest, though I didn't know how. But she was already dead—"

"Heart failure," Powell said. He saw that Wolfe was thinking the same thing. Bulimia, once it progressed beyond a certain point, could lead to an increased risk of cardiac arrest.

"So you called someone for help," Wolfe said, turning back to Natalia. "Who was it?"

"Kostava. I couldn't call Anzor, but I trusted his assistant, and I knew that he cared about me. He came to the club right away, and spoke with the owner in private. I don't know what kind of deal he made, but after he arrived, a man with blond hair took the body into the bathroom. The owner went in later. I never found out what they did to her, but the next morning, Kostava told me that everything was going to be fine. And that was all. Until last week."

Powell sensed that they had reached a turning point. "What happened last week?"

"He got a call. I don't know the details. But I know that Sharkovsky never let him off the hook. Now he was asking for a favor. There was a painting that he wanted from Anzor's collection, and Kostava would help him steal it. Otherwise, he said, he would tell the police everything he knew."

"Kostava must have given him details about the house's security system," Wolfe said. "And he arranged to let the truck into the mansion on the night of the party. Do you know if he did anything else?"

"I don't know. He wouldn't say. I only know that he was doing it to protect me." A tear rolled down Natalia's cheek. Although her sorrow was real, the tear seemed false, a mechanism that only happened to coincide with what she was actually feeling. "What else was I supposed to do? We knew that the police had found the body. If we didn't cooperate—"

"We understand. You didn't have a choice. But why was the painting so important?"

Natalia wiped the tear away. "I'm not sure. It meant a lot to Anzor. When I asked him about it, he said it would give him power over his enemies. I don't know what he meant by that. But then he told me about something that had happened in Budapest. Something about a courier being killed."

At the mention of a courier, Powell felt one more piece lock into place. As he considered what it might mean, he saw that Natalia was looking at the railing, and realized that its plunge of twelve stories might present a temptation. He tensed himself to go after her, but in the end, she turned away from the view.

Rising, she went back into the living room, followed by the others. When she reached the coffee table, she picked up the toy. For a moment, Powell thought that she was going to smash it, but she only took it gently into her hands. "I've pledged myself to Anzor. I don't want him to learn about this from the papers."

"I know," Powell said. "You still have a passport in your real name? Bring it here."

Natalia left the room, accompanied by Wolfe. Powell remained behind, feeling curiously empty. Taking out his phone, he dialed a number and spoke quietly to the man who answered. A minute later, after hearing a knock, Powell went to the door and opened it to the police.

When Natalia returned to the living room, passport in hand, she turned to Powell, her eyes burning. "You promised to protect me."

"I will," Powell said. "The police will book you as Alisa Baranova. Archvadze won't know about it until we have a chance to talk to him. The rest of it is out of my hands. But we'll be in touch soon."

Powell stood aside as the detective handcuffed Natalia and informed her of her rights. After exchanging a few words with the detective, he and Wolfe headed downstairs. They did not look at Natalia again.

"I think she's telling the truth," Wolfe said as they went outside. "It would be hard to find signs of cardiac arrest in a mummified body. And the bruising of the chest may have been caused when Natalia tried to revive her. If that's the case, we're looking at possible manslaughter and criminal conspiracy, but not murder. Which won't be enough for Barlow."

"I know." Across the street, vendors at the museum were selling postcards and prints. It reminded him of his encounter with Maddy, which had raised its own set of questions. He didn't know why Misha had been following her, but it bothered him. He had already asked that an agent be detailed to keep her under observation, but the request had yet to be approved.

As he was wondering what to do about this, Wolfe's cell phone rang. She answered it, offered a few terse replies to the caller, and hung up. "It looks like we're still behind the curve," Wolfe said, looking out at the museum. "Barlow got his warrant. We're raiding the club tonight."

40

When Maddy arrived at Ethan's building, a brownstone in Prospect Heights, she rang the bell, but there was no answer. She pressed it again. Nothing. She was about to leave, resolving to find him at the office the next day, when the front door finally unlocked with a low metallic drone.

She went inside. The apartment was built on two levels, with a narrow flight of steps connecting the living room and kitchen with a bedroom and study upstairs. On this level, the house was empty, but in the rectangular space formed by the upper stairwell, she saw a greenish glow.

Upstairs, in the study, Ethan was hunched over his laptop, which was the only source of light. Pop music blared from a stereo in the corner: *In every city and every nation from Lake Geneva to the Finland Station*—

As she entered the room, Ethan clicked through a series of web pages. She put a hand on his shoulder. "Are you okay?"

He looked up. For a second, seeing his haunted face, she felt an instinctive flinch of revulsion. Then, when he smiled, he looked almost like his old self. All the same, though, she could tell that he hadn't showered that day.

Looking around the study, she saw that it was a mess. Countless books lay on the rug, their pages marked with whatever oddments had been closest at hand. A snow shovel hung from the ceiling. Following her eyes, Ethan said, "I'm trying to figure out the true meaning of the readymades."

He pointed to a bottle rack that stood nearby, a conical iron structure with several tiers of hooks. "This is another readymade that caught my eye. Most bottle racks have an even distribution of hooks on each tier, but the one that Duchamp used has an odd number. I'm still trying to figure out why—"

"Ethan, wait." Hearing the note of obsession in his voice, she took it upon herself to project an air of calm. "You need to slow down."

"I understand." Without warning, Ethan bounded downstairs, leaving her alone in the study. A moment later, he returned with a bottle of wine and two glasses. "Have a drink with me."

"I don't know," Maddy said hesitantly. "I haven't had anything to eat today—"

"That's all right. Neither have I." Ethan poured the wine, handed her a glass, and sank into a chair in front of the fireplace. "Very well, then. What is it that you wanted to talk about?"

Maddy paused, wondering how to begin. "Tanya and I have been looking at Hugo Ball, one of the founders of Dadaism. He was obsessed with the occult. According to his diary, he staged rituals that were inspired by the Vehmgericht, complete with drummers in black cowls—"

"Interesting," Ethan said. "But you didn't come all the way out here to tell me this."

"No." Maddy took a swallow of the wine, which was unpleasantly skunky. "I've decided to go to Reynard."

Ethan only contemplated his own glass, as if he saw something in its dregs. "Go on."

"We need to go public. By keeping this a secret, we're just playing into the hands of whoever stole the study. And we can't keep doing this on our own. Our names were in the paper. The thief saw our faces. Someone broke into my house. And there's something else."

She described the man who had been following her, as well as her conversation with Powell. Ethan listened in silence, his expression unchanging. When she was done, Maddy said, "I've checked Reynard's schedule. He'll be in the office tomorrow. If we go to him, we can use the fund's resources to break the story—"

"No," Ethan said quietly. "Not yet. If we go public now, we'll be exposing ourselves too soon. You see, I know what these men are trying to protect. And they're even more dangerous than we imagined."

Raising her glass, Maddy found that it was already empty. "What do you mean?"

Ethan poured more wine before responding. "I've been thinking about Monte Verità. You said that it was a place where art and the occult could intersect, and you were right. But there were other forces at work as well. Who was the first man to settle there? Mikhail Bakunin, the Russian anarchist. You see, it wasn't just home to artists and occultists. It was home to revolutionaries. Like Lenin."

The wine began to expand in her head like a soft bullet. "Lenin was there, too?"

"We know that he and Trotsky spent time at Monte

Verità," Ethan said. "His house in Zurich was right across from the Cabaret Voltaire. He and the Dadaists passed each other in the street. He played chess with Tristan Tzara. And after the war, Tzara was questioned by the police for consorting with the Bolsheviks."

"All of these artists were infatuated with communism," Maddy said, trying to slow things down. "They were trying to start a revolution in the arts. It isn't surprising that they'd also be interested in politics."

"So what was in it for Lenin? Look at it from his perspective. He was an exile, without power, so he needed what every revolutionist needs. Organization. An infrastructure that can be used for conspiracy and subversion, a system that crosses national borders. As soon as he saw what these aspiring Rosicrucians had created, he knew it would be useful. So he sought them out."

Maddy remembered something that Lermontov had said. One secret society could be built on the foundations of another, even if they had nothing in common. "But how did he even know they existed?"

"He heard about them in prison," Ethan said. "Lenin spent years in Siberia, side by side with outlaws and thieves. The more I look at it, the more I'm convinced that these groups have been entwined from the very beginning. And without their help, Lenin never would have made it home."

Going through his notes, Ethan found a map covered in dates. "You know the story, right? Lenin is in Switzerland, stranded by the war, but he's allowed to travel through Germany to Russia on a sealed train. Germany hopes that he'll create political unrest, ending the war on the eastern front. The plan is carried out by the general staff without the knowledge of the Kaiser. And it works. A few months after Lenin comes to power, Russia withdraws from the war."

"Wait," Maddy said. "I'm not following you. You're saying that the *Rosicrucians* had something to do with this?"

Ethan lit a cigarette. In the past, he had been circumspect about his smoking, but now he didn't seem to care. "Look at the facts. Before his return is approved, Lenin is a minor revolutionist, a nonentity. Someone must have brought him to the attention of the general staff. Who was it? Nobody knows. But we do know that Aleister Crowley, who by now was deeply immersed in these groups, was in contact with Erich Ludendorff, the chief manager of the Kaiser's war effort."

"But this has nothing to do with the art world. Does anyone else even believe this?"

"Kaiser Wilhelm did. In his memoirs, he blames the war on a group called the Great Orient Lodge, and says that it held a conference in Switzerland in 1917. Well, the Ordo Templi Orientis arranged a conference that year at Monte Verità, where the communist problem was publicly debated. For the Rosicrucians, this was their big moment. They'd been hanging around the margins for decades, maybe centuries, and now they finally had a chance to change history."

As Ethan paused to take a breath, Maddy took the opportunity to speak. "Okay. But there's one problem. When they came to power, the Bolsheviks repressed all secret societies, including the Rosicrucians."

"Yes, but it didn't happen all at once. At first, there were hints of cooperation. Crowley even wrote a letter to

Trotsky, not long after the revolution, offering his help in ridding the earth of Christianity. But it didn't last. Lenin outlawed all secret societies, and he also went after artists, which always seemed strange to me. Why was he so afraid of poets and painters?"

"It happens in every totalitarian regime. Paranoia flourishes in those conditions—"

"It wasn't just paranoia. The Bolsheviks knew how powerful an alliance between artists and occultists could be, so they resolved to eliminate the Rosicrucians, first at home, then in the rest of the world."

Maddy had an uneasy premonition of where this was headed. "So what did they do?"

"In Eastern Europe, they could suppress the Rosicrucians directly, but on the other side of the Iron Curtain, they had to adopt more indirect methods. It was a war of subversion and implication. Rumors of human sacrifice had been swirling around these groups for years, so it was easy enough to make them real. All it took was one murder. And the victim was the Black Dahlia."

The wine was pulsing in her head. "I can't take much more of this. I feel sick—"

"Listen to me," Ethan said, speaking with a vehemence that startled her. "George Hodel, the doctor most sources agree was the Black Dahlia killer, was friends with Man Ray and other artists in the Arensberg Circle, but he also had connections with the Soviets. His parents were from Russia and Ukraine. He was a member of the Severance Club, a Bolshevik organization, and only a few months after the murder, he was in contact with the Soviet embassy in Washington."

Closing her eyes, Maddy rested her head on her knees. "You're making this up—"

"Hear me out. Hodel lived in Pasadena, which at the time was the headquarters of the Theosophical movement, the home of the sole remaining lodge of the Ordo Templi Orientis, and the center of the Arensberg Circle. If the Soviets wanted to strike at the heart of the Rosicrucian establishment, it had to be there."

"But why would the Black Dahlia murder cast suspicion on the Rosicrucians?"

Ethan rifled through a stack of crime scene photographs. "Look at the style of the killing. Elizabeth Short's body is posed after the fashion of the Vehmgericht, who cut their victims in half. It evokes the faceless woman in the grass that Duchamp had painted thirty years before. And it worked. The police focused on a possible occult connection from the earliest stages of the investigation. Within a year, the lodges were closed, and the circle of artists was dissolved."

In the darkened study, Maddy could not see Ethan's face. "So what happened to the Rosicrucians?"

Ethan inverted the bottle over his glass, draining the last few drops. "They've spread across the globe, mostly as a criminal enterprise, but maybe, in some strange way, they're trying to finish the revolution that their predecessors began. And that's why they went after Archvadze. He's an interloper, like Arensberg, except richer and better organized. He wanted to start a revolution in Georgia, so he decided to explore the roots of the one revolution that had already succeeded in that part of the world. And his best source was Duchamp, who had put the group's secrets in his art, including one message so important that it could only be revealed after his death."

"But why would this be useful to Archvadze? What could the study have to tell him?"

"Maybe it's the key to solving *Étant Donnés*. In his notes, Duchamp implies that the installation is a sort of chess problem, and that the viewer's task is to find the solution. Perhaps it's only fully visible in Philadelphia, when you're standing before the installation itself. And if Archvadze was close to an answer, it explains why the study was stolen. These men protect their secrets."

As she listened, her hands growing cold, Maddy found herself thinking of her failed gallery in Chelsea. She had always sensed that there was an order to the art world that she would never be allowed to understand, a door that would remain closed forever, and as she thought now of the thief at the mansion, she knew for the first time why his face had haunted her. It was the face of a man who had seen into that secret world. And now Ethan had the same look in his eyes.

But the image of her dead gallery refused to go away. She reminded herself that she had been wrong about these things before, and that to make the same mistake here would mean humiliation or worse. She took a breath. "Before we go further, we need to be sure. I can ask Lermontov—"

Even before she finished, Ethan was already shaking his head. "No. That's something else we need to talk about." He dug through his notes, emerging with a computer printout. "When you told me that Lermontov was trading in Rosicrucian art, I went through the database to look at transactions in which he had been involved, hoping to get a sense of which artists were relevant. I didn't find anything useful. But I noticed something strange."

He handed her the printout, which turned out to be a list of art deals. "There's a pattern in these transactions. For many of these works, the listed seller doesn't appear in any other transaction except the ones involving Lermontov. Often they're dead businessmen with no record of having invested elsewhere in art, or collectors for whom no independent evidence exists at all. You understand? The names are fake. He's covering up the real source of these paintings."

Maddy's forehead continued to pound. "But we've always said that provenance data is notoriously unreliable. The database isn't perfect."

"I know. And I might have dismissed this if it only applied to one or two transactions, but there are scores of them. The odds against this being a coincidence are astronomical. No. He's getting pieces from somewhere outside the traditional art market. I think it's a secret network of collectors, like Archvadze, who want to trade art with hidden meanings without there being a record of it. His involvement isn't just theoretical. He knows the names of these collectors."

Maddy shook her head. She was about to repeat her objections when, looking down, she saw a piece of paper that had been uncovered when Ethan removed the list of transactions.

She recognized it at once. It was a page from her notes. And in the margin was drawn a hand clutching a rose.

Maddy stared at the page. "Where did you get this? I told you it was missing."

Ethan looked away, his lips stained red by the wine. "I'm sorry. I took the spare key from your office. I didn't mean to worry you—"

Maddy rose slowly to her feet. "You're the one who broke into my house? But why?"

"I wanted to see if you were working for Lermontov. I wasn't sure if you were telling me the whole truth, so I looked at your notes to see if you were hiding something. I must have taken that page by accident." His voice was flat. "But I never meant for you to find out."

They looked at each other across the darkened room. A wordless anger was gathering in her body, mingled with something even worse, which was disappointment. She opened her mouth to speak, then stopped herself. In a flash, she understood that anything she said would only bind them closer together.

Turning aside, she went onto the landing, her footsteps loud on the stairs. She kept an ear tuned to the study, wondering what she would do if he called for her, but heard nothing. Sensing that it was too late to stop, she went into the entryway. A second later, she was on the street, walking away, if only to prove to herself that she still could. Her hands were shaking with rage.

Maddy went blindly up the sidewalk. For a moment, she expected to see the man who had been following her standing outside, but there was no one. There was only the street, one that she knew all too well, the street of missed opportunity, when the evening's fantasies had collapsed into the reality of a solitary walk home. No one was watching. She was alone.

41

"Gentlemen, we have a warrant," Barlow said. As Powell entered the briefing room, he found it packed with members of the tactical unit. Taking a handout from the stack by the door, he looked for a few square feet of space in which to stand, and finally squeezed into the corner next to Wolfe.

Barlow stood before a slideshow presentation, stripped down to a tie and shirtsleeves. "As most of you know, we've been building this case for weeks. Normally, we'd wait for the buyer to take delivery, but because one sorry fuck forgot how to sew a battery pack into his coat pocket, we're moving up the timeline."

There was mild laughter, most of it directed at Kandinsky, who sat in the far corner, his face red. "Until now, the details could not be revealed, except to a few of you," Barlow continued. "Now that you're being asked to execute this warrant, it's only fair that you hear the full story."

Touching a key on his laptop, he advanced the slideshow to the mug shot of an Armenian male. "This is Arshak Gasparyan, an aspiring gangster from Sheepshead Bay," Barlow said. "He was on the verge of a weapons deal with Sharkovsky when he vanished, along with three of his cronies. A few days later, they were found at a construction site in Gowanus, minus their faces and fingerprints. Which left our man with a shipment of guns and no buyer."

Barlow went to the next slide. "This is Garegin Solomonyan, a more experienced gun runner from Gravesend. In recent weeks, we've intercepted and recorded a series of conversations between him and Sharkovsky. The conversations are usually in code, so it's taken us a while to put together a picture of the deal. At this point, though, it looks like our *vor* is storing a crate of rocket launchers and something like a thousand grenades on the club's ground floor."

There was an appreciative murmur as Barlow advanced to a plan of the Club Marat. "The club stands in a line of restaurants on the boardwalk, with a row of housing projects to the rear. There are two floors and three entrances, one on the street, one on the alley, one on the boards. Teams of five men will cover each door. Sharkovsky will have watchers posted, so we'll keep well back until the signal is given. Powell and Wolfe will be our eyes on the inside."

Powell felt the room briefly scrutinize his face as Barlow brought up a list of names. "Once we're in, we grab Sharkovsky, secure the merchandise, and turn up the lights. It's the weekend, so the club will be packed. We lock down the doors, run every name, and scoop up the guys we need. You each have the list, so you know we're looking at twelve to fourteen extractions. Disarm them, cuff them, get them in the van. We're also looking for computers, paper files, and cameras."

Barlow paused like a preacher surveying his congregation at a particularly dramatic moment. "If we get our man, he's looking at a life sentence for arms trafficking conspiracy, interstate firearms trafficking, and illegal transfer and possession. I can't speak for all of you, but that's good enough for me. Direct any questions to your unit commander. We move in twenty."

The meeting broke up. Powell waited until the conference room was clear before approaching Barlow, who gave him a wolfish grin. "Good work on the dead girl. Your report just crossed my desk."

"Not that it mattered," Powell said. "We were moving against Sharkovsky anyway."

"Never tell anyone that your work is unnecessary. If you don't watch out, they'll start to believe you." Barlow headed for the door. "Either we have accessory after the fact for a death that isn't even in our jurisdiction, or we have a thousand grenades and a life sentence. Which would you prefer?"

"That's what I wanted to talk to you about." They went outside, with Wolfe following them down the hallway. "I know you want to move tonight, but I think we should push back the timeline."

Barlow headed for his office. "Don't waste my time with this shit. Those guns won't be there forever—"

"This is about more than weapons. You overheard the conversation at the courthouse. Russian intelligence is working with these groups. Sharkovsky will never talk about this, but the Scythian will. It's only a matter of time before he shows up. If we move too soon, we'll scare him off."

"So what are we looking at here?" Barlow asked. "Fraud? Money laundering?"

"Art smuggling," Wolfe said. "I just got off the phone with the Budapest police. A year ago, they found a courier's body in a hotel, shot once through the heart. There was paint and gold leaf embedded in the wound. He was bringing art from Russia, but someone else got to him first. Whoever killed him must have overlooked one painting. The Scythian came here to get it back."

Barlow halted at his office door. "What does that have to do with state intelligence?"

"I don't know," Powell said. "But it can't be a coincidence that the buyer was an oligarch who has been a thorn in the Kremlin's side for years. The heist was an intelligence operation. That's why one of the thieves ended up dead. It's standard operating procedure for the Chekists. Ilya is the only missing piece. If we wait long enough, he'll come after Sharkovsky. If you look at the big picture—"

"The big picture? Let me paint you a picture of my own." Barlow put a hand on Powell's shoulder. Powell braced himself for a viselike grip, but to his surprise, the big man's touch was almost reassuring. "Ilya has no passport. No resources. He'll turn up soon. When he does, he's yours."

Powell was unsettled by this show of reasonableness. "I've got your word on this?"

"No, but you don't have a choice. This is shaping up to be a major case. If we get Sharkovsky, this division will see increased funding for years to come. If we blow it, we get nothing. That isn't in your interest. And it certainly isn't in mine. Get your piece. We're leaving soon."

Barlow went into his office and shut the door. Wolfe looked at Powell. "He's right."

"I know." They headed for their cubicles. "But even if we interrogate Sharkovsky or Misha, they won't talk to us. We don't even know the right questions to ask. If we could track down Archvadze, and find out why this bloody painting is so important, we might stand a chance—"

"Well, I don't know what to tell you. As long as he's missing, it's a dead end."

As they reached their desks, Powell was struck by an idea, one that appeared so fully formed that it seemed as if it had only been biding its time, waiting to rise to the surface. "Maybe we can lure him out of hiding."

"How?" Wolfe answered her own question at once. "Natalia? But we promised—"

"I know. But I'm out of ideas. Is there anybody you trust on the police blotter?"

"I can think of someone," Wolfe said. He saw the wheels turning in her head. Leaking information about Natalia's arrest was a calculated risk. If Archvadze saw it, he might come forward, but if not, they would have broken a pledge to a key witness and received nothing in exchange.

Wolfe seemed to come to a decision. "All right. I'll make the flipping call."

"Do it, then." Powell watched as she headed for a far corner, dialing a number on her cell phone, as if she wanted to keep the call off the main switchboard. After a few seconds, as someone answered, she began to speak. Studying her face, he thought in passing of the body that had been buried under the boards, and of the two sisters standing together by the river Onega.

A minute later, Wolfe came back to the cubicle, her face unreadable. "It's done."

"Good," Powell said, glad that it was out of his hands. He glanced at the clock on his computer. "Time to go."

"One second." Wolfe unlocked her desk drawer and removed her gun. Only a week ago, it had been in a safe in Barlow's office, but now, for the first time, Wolfe had been entrusted with her own weapon. Following her lead, Powell got his jacket and pistol. Then they went downstairs to join the raid.

42

A t the playground by the ocean, the sun was going down. A solitary figure stood near the basketball courts, hands in his pockets, looking across the parking lot at the wooden ramp in the distance. From the ramp, which sloped up toward the boardwalk, it was a hundred paces to the Club Marat.

As he waited for the sun to set, his eye was caught by a spherical object bouncing across the ground in his direction. It turned out to be a tennis ball, closely followed by a tiny child, no more than three or four, racing after it with arms extended. Reflexively, the man reached down and scooped up the ball. He was pleased to discover that his ankle was no longer bothering him.

"Daniel!" the boy's mother shouted. At the sound of the name, Ilya's head gave an involuntary jerk. He released the tennis ball, which bounced twice and rolled to a stop at the boy's feet. The boy bent down awkwardly and retrieved the ball, clutching it in both hands, and ran away.

Watching the boy rejoin his mother, Ilya thought of the many transformations that he had undergone since he had last referred to himself by that name. He had only recently completed another metamorphosis. His hair was cropped short and tinted blond, his face rough with several days' growth of beard.

Now he headed for the parking lot at the edge of the playground, not far from his most recent home. With his description broadcast over the airwaves, he had no longer felt safe in hotels. After some thought, he had decided on a place to sleep, one that required only a pair of bolt cutters and a mummy bag.

Lying on the sand, he had felt like a body buried in the desert. His connections to the world had been severed one by one, leaving only a single spark of consciousness tethered to the pain in his ankle, which he had wrapped in an elastic bandage and elevated above the level of his heart.

For much of that lonely time, as he waited for his ankle to heal, he had thought of the breaking of the vessels. When God created the world, the cabalists said, the vessels meant to hold his glory had shattered, spilling gross matter throughout the universe, along with fragments of the divine being. These fragments had to be regathered, one piece at a time, by the cumulative efforts of all men.

Ilya, his own life broken, had once seen this as his task as well. According to the cabalists, the vessels had shattered because of an original impurity, a network of evil that undermined the order that God had put in place. Ilya, in turn, had traced his exile back to another system, the forces of the state, and had dedicated his life to bringing this system to its knees.

His mistake, he saw now, was to believe that the world's restoration required another system, the tzaddikim, which he had blindly identified with Vasylenko. The truth was that no system was required. It was the lonely work of each man, working in isolation, to restore the balance of the world.

The error did not lie in any particular system, but in the desire for a system itself.

As the last rays of sunlight disappeared, he crossed the parking lot. The time it had taken for his ankle to recover had also allowed him to consider what to do next. With the police watching Sharkovsky, he had to act soon. Aside from the roll of canvas strapped to his back, he had few resources. But he had enough.

When he reached the ramp that led to the boardwalk, he noticed a separate area for quarterly permit parking. In one of the spaces, a pickup truck was wedged, its wheelbase far too broad for the white lines. It had been cleaned and repainted since the night of the heist, its body red instead of green, but it was easy enough to recognize. He marked its location in his mind.

On the beach, the crowds had dwindled. When he was sure that no one was looking, Ilya ducked under the ramp, where a wire fence blocked off access to the area beneath the boards. Unlike most parts of the boardwalk, the gate allowed sand to blow through, so the space under the boards was clear.

Ilya hooked his fingers through the wire and pulled. A section of mesh came away from the posts, bending upward like a stiff curtain. He had been careful to make the cuts in an inconspicuous place.

A moment later, he was under the boardwalk. Ilya replaced the mesh, then moved into the darkness, walking between the dunes that had gathered against the columns. He had come to know this area well, especially the length of sand that stretched between the ramp and the rear of the club, only a few feet from the spot where a body had been found two weeks before.

As he made his way toward the club, he thought again of his role in the order of the world. Each act of justice, the cabalists taught, brought the universe one step closer to its original perfection. Reaching into his pocket, Ilya locked his fingers around what he carried there. He was no tzaddik. He knew that now. But he could restore the balance of the world in a small way. Tonight, he suspected, was the evening in which all debts would be repaid at last.

43

When Powell and Wolfe arrived at the club, a line of patrons was already standing at the door that faced the street. The crowd consisted mostly of Russians, both young and old, dressed for a night out in backless tops and gold lamé. Wolfe herself was wearing an attractive blouse of silky material, loose enough to conceal the belt of medical elastic that secured her pistol around her waist.

They went down a corridor lined with plastic foliage and streetlamps, then climbed a flight of stairs to the main dining room, a dimly lit space with mirrored pillars and brass railings. Their table was deep in Siberia. The dance floor was empty, the girls offstage for a costume change.

Once they were seated, Powell donned his earpiece. He saw that he was not the only man in the restaurant with such a device in his ear. As Wolfe ordered a bottle of wine, he spoke softly. "Command post, we're here."

"Copy that," Barlow said. "We'll be ready in five. You'll know when we're in place."

Powell looked around the club's darkened interior. His own service pistol was riding in a canted holster high up on his waistband, its weight undeniably comforting. "Any issues so far?"

"Negative. A few lamps on the boardwalk have gone out, probably a wiring problem. We can work around it."

Powell wanted to know more about this, but before he could ask, he saw Sharkovsky and Misha seated in the corner, backs to the wall, a carafe of vodka between them. As he watched, Misha drained his glass. Because of his bad knee, which had been shattered by a bullet a year before, Misha had a tendency to drink. Powell spoke low into his headpiece. "I've got eyes on primary and secondary targets."

Even as he said this, the lights went down, and the club was flooded with music. A spotlight flung a colored circle onto the stage. Through a curtain at the rear of the room, eight women filed into view, each wearing a headdress of leaves and vines. As they began to dance, their movements stiff and mechanical, Powell saw that they were always aware of Sharkovsky's eyes.

He glanced at Wolfe. On the way to the club, she had applied makeup, giving her face more color than usual. When their wine was poured, Powell was surprised to see her take a sip. "I thought you didn't drink."

"I don't," Wolfe said, blushing slightly. "But if we don't drink a little, we'll stand out. Besides, I'm worried."

Powell responded by taking a sip of his own. Looking around the room, he observed several other members of the *bratva*. In a low voice, he forwarded their positions to Barlow, who relayed the information to the tactical units that were assembling on all three doors. What he did not mention was that the crowd was making him uneasy. There were too many people here.

Wolfe, who had continued to take quick, nervous sips from her glass of wine, nudged him gently on the shoulder. "Check it out. Don't make a point of it, but our man's getting a call."

Powell turned to see Sharkovsky studying his cell phone. Frowning, the *vor* put it to his ear. There was a pause as he listened to whoever was on the other end, replied, then hung up. He said something to Misha. When Misha responded, the old man only shook his head.

Barlow's voice came over the earpiece. "The wire just picked up a call. It's Ilya."

Powell looked across the room at the two men, who continued their conversation beneath the deafening music. "What did he say?"

"He wants a meeting. He's waiting at the aquarium up the boardwalk, ready to make the exchange." Barlow paused, as if covering the microphone with his hand, then came back on the line. "I'm sending a team after him. Keep calm. Just tell me what the target is doing."

Out of the corner of his eye, Powell saw Sharkovsky and Misha rise from their table and make their way across the club. He noticed that Misha's arm swing was clipped on the right side, his forearm close to the body. "They're heading for the western end of the floor. Secondary target has a concealed weapon."

"Don't let them out of your sight," Barlow said. "Wolfe, stay in position. Keep tabs on the others. Powell, attach yourself to the primary target and feed us whatever he does. *Move.*"

Powell was already on his feet. As he rose, pulse accelerating, he felt the vast machine of the raid preparing to reconfigure itself, ready to move on his word. He whispered instructions to Wolfe, then crossed the dining room, his eye on the two men, who were heading for the stairs that led to the floor below. Powell stood aside for a waiter, who squeezed past with a tray of caviar and butterfish, and forced himself to wait. He counted to five, then went downstairs.

On the ground floor, a headless mannequin stood guard by a sofa. A corridor was set at right angles to the stairs. Powell peeked around the corner in time to see Sharkovsky and Misha disappear into a room at the end of the hallway, closing the door behind them. He tried to remember the plan of the club. "They're in the office on the north side of the ground floor. I can't see inside."

"Copy that," Barlow said after a pause. "Watch the door. We're on our way."

"Okay." Powell drew his gun. His mouth had gone dry. Listening to the dull thump of the music overhead, he wondered what the two men were doing. Ilya had called with the offer of an exchange, but the aquarium would not be as secure as the courthouse, so they would be sure to arm themselves accordingly—

Half a minute went by. He was about to speak into his headpiece again, asking what was taking the unit so fucking long, when a pair of muffled blasts exploded from behind the closed door.

"*Shit*," Powell said. "Command post, I have shots fired downstairs. Do you copy?"

Without waiting for a response, Powell forced himself to move toward the source of the shots. Halfway down the corridor, a second doorway opened into the hall. Leading with his gun, he swung inside and saw a disused kitchen piled high with rusty appliances. He ducked into it, crouching in the protective well of the doorway, only a few steps from the door of the office.

Leveling his gun at the closed door, Powell waited for it to open. He was terrified, but this fact seemed insignificant. He hoped that the momentum that had brought him this far would not abandon him yet.

44

Ten minutes earlier, a busboy had emerged from the service entrance of the club, which faced an alley below the level of the boardwalk. Propping the door open, he went down a concrete ramp to a shed with a corrugated metal roof. This shed adjoined the vacant space beneath the boardwalk, which provided a convenient home for the club's fleet of Dumpsters.

Unfastening a padlock, the busboy slid open the door of the shed and wheeled out the nearest Dumpster, which was empty. As he did, it seemed to him that the alley was darker than usual. Glancing up, he noticed that the streetlamps on the boardwalk overhead had gone out.

He was about to go back for the garbage when a shadow detached itself from the rear of the shed and pressed a small hard object against his side. Before he could react, he felt white lightning flow through all the nerves of his body, then slumped, twitching, to the ground.

Ilya held the stun gun against the busboy's side for five seconds. Although the victim was paralyzed, he was still conscious, his eyes looking reproachfully at his assailant as he was hauled into the depths of the shed.

Propping him up in a seated position, Ilya removed

the boy's apron and tied it around his own waist. Then he headed for the door of the club. A few minutes earlier, he had cut the electrical wire strung between the streetlamps, aiming with the laser penlight through a gap between the shed and the boardwalk.

He entered the club, leaving the door open. Through a brightly lit doorway in the hall, he could hear the voices of kitchen staff. He moved silently past this door, not pausing, and was not observed.

Rounding the corner, he found himself in a corridor on the ground floor. Up ahead was a disused kitchen. To his left, a flight of stairs led to the dining room. The office was to his right.

He knocked on the closed office door. "Open up. I need a case of Stolichnaya—"

There was the sound of a man rising from his desk. A few seconds later, the door opened. To his mild disappointment, it was not Sharkovsky, but the restaurant manager, a tough old crook who had run various clubs and restaurants in Brighton Beach for twenty years. When the manager saw his face, his eyes widened. Before he could close the door, Ilya reached through the gap, set the stun gun against the manager's sternum, and pressed the button.

A blue arc jumped between the electrodes at the business end of the gun. The manager convulsed, froth spraying from his lips, and fell to the ground. Ilya stepped over the body into the office and closed the door.

Taking the manager beneath the arms, Ilya stuffed him into the corner. The manager glared at him, eyes rolling in his frozen face, as Ilya bound him with a few twists of wire and sealed his mouth with tape.

Ilya took off the apron. Going to the other side of the office, he rolled back a corner of the rug, revealing the gun safe in the floor. He opened it and reached inside, pulling up the rack of weapons. It took him only a second to select a revolver, which he slid into the empty holster in his waistband.

After filling his pockets with moon clips, he sat down at the desk. He was about to reach for his phone when something else occurred to him. Looking at the computer, he saw an email inbox in one window. He scrolled through the most recent messages until one caught his eye. Although he had never seen the sender's name before, he knew exactly who it was from.

He closed the program and turned off the computer. Taking out his phone, he dialed a number. After a few rings, a familiar voice answered, disco pounding on the other end. "Yes?"

"It's me," Ilya said quietly. "Do you want to give it another try? Or are we done?"

After a long pause, Sharkovsky said, "You *suka*. You're working for the police."

"No. If they're watching you, it has nothing to do with me. But my offer still stands. Eighty thousand and my bag in exchange for the package. Meet me at the aquarium in ten minutes. If not, I'm coming after you."

Ilya switched off the phone. Then he rose, turned off the lights, and withdrew into the corner by the door. As he loaded the revolver, he could see the whites of the manager's eyes, which were rolled up to meet his own.

A minute passed. Another. Leaning against the wall, Ilya remained perfectly still, his breathing slow and even,

THE ICON THIEF / 289

and when he finally heard footsteps in the hallway out-side, his pulse quickened only slightly.

The door opened, casting a trapezoid of light. Ilya pressed himself against the wall, retreating before the door as it swung inward. The lights came on, revealing the manager on the floor, gesturing frantically with his eyes.

Sharkovsky's voice sounded low and bewildered. "What the fuck is all this?"

The door swung closed. As it shut, Ilya came out of the corner, handgun raised. When Sharkovsky turned, Ilya could feel the old man gathering his resources swiftly, like a fist. Misha, by contrast, radiated a diffuse, nebulous rage, and Ilya saw at a glance that he was drunk.

"Up against the wall," Ilya said, the revolver held in a combat stance. "Both of you."

The two men began to turn. Ilya took a step forward, the sequence of motions clear in his head. Disarm them, get them on their knees—

With startling speed, Misha went for the gun in his belt. Ilya had been applying two pounds of pressure to the trigger, but had not been expecting such a reckless move, and it was only reflexively that he fired.

The first gunshot caught Misha in the chest, while the second took away most of his lower jaw. He fell to his knees, dead before he hit the floor, and toppled sideways. One of the pictures on the wall, the framed photograph of a line of dancing girls, had been struck by the second blast. It hung askew, dangling from a single fastener, then fell off and shattered.

Sharkovsky looked down at Misha's body, shirt speckled with the other man's blood. "Stupid, going for his gun like that."

"I might have done the same." Ilya forced the old man against the wall and frisked him, the ringing in his ears beginning to diminish. "I want my bag and books. I know you have them here, so don't lie to me."

"Why would I lie?" Sharkovsky gestured toward the desk. "They're in the drawer on the right. As for the cash—"

"You can keep it." Ilya went to the desk and opened the drawer, keeping the revolver trained on Sharkovsky. As the old man had said, the bag with his books was there. Ilya slung it over his shoulder, where it hung beside the tube secured beneath his clothes. "It was never about the money—"

He broke off. A sound had come from the hallway outside. It had lasted for only an instant and had been cut off at once, but he recognized it. It had been the feedback from a police radio.

Sharkovsky turned to Ilya. "Looks like someone is here, *suka*. Friends of yours?"

"No," Ilya said, his mind working furiously. He could not leave the old man behind. To get the answers he needed, he had to walk out of here with Sharkovsky alive. "The truck in the parking lot. You have the keys?"

Sharkovsky's visible eye blinked once. In the corner of the office, the manager began to howl against his gag, flailing helplessly on the floor. The paralysis had worn off. "Yes, I do."

"Good." Keeping his eye on the door, Ilya motioned with the gun. "Let's go. You're coming with me."

45

Powell crouched on the threshold of the disused kitchen, his pistol raised, eyes on the office door. Thirty seconds had passed since he had heard the twin blasts of the revolver. At last, Barlow's voice came over his earpiece: "We're on the move. Wolfe, I want you downstairs."

"Already here," Wolfe said. Powell turned to see her standing two yards away. Her blouse had come untucked from when she had drawn her pistol from its concealed holster. Their eyes met as she spoke again into her headpiece. "I'm with Powell. We're covering the office door."

"Maintain your position," Barlow said. "We're taking the service entrance now."

Even as these words went over the air, there was a commotion in the kitchen. Within seconds, the corridor was filled with members of the assault team, four men in hardshell vests and web gear, shotguns loaded and racked. A fifth man had been left behind to secure the entrance. Barlow stood at the head of the group, his radio in a harness across his chest.

Powell fell back as the unit took up position in the

hallway, guns leveled at the closed door. "What about upstairs?"

"We're doing this in stages," Barlow said. "We secure the ground floor first. Then—"

Barlow broke off as a squawk of radio noise burst from the epaulet of the agent at his side. The agent silenced his mike at once, but all eyes went to the office door. Barlow, furious, whispered, "If anyone else makes the least fucking bit of noise, I'll send him straight to hell."

He turned to the unit commander. "We're going in. Take the fucking door down."

The commander nodded, then signaled to the team. Two members of the unit stacked themselves on the knob side of the door, while a third covered them from across the hall. The breacher, a sledgehammer in his hands, listened at the door, watching his commander for a signal.

A second later, before any of them could move, the door swung open on its own.

The unit pulled back, their guns trained on the opening. Powell raised his own pistol, watching as the door opened all the way, revealing two figures on the threshold. One was Sharkovsky, his features drawn tight against the bones of his face. The other was a man whom Powell had never seen at close range. He had changed his appearance since the day of the courthouse, his hair shaved and bleached. His left hand was looped around the strap of a bag over his shoulder. With his other hand, he was pressing a revolver against Sharkovsky's skull.

"Ilya," Powell said, unable to contain himself. "Or should I call you the Scythian?"

At the sound of his name, Ilya turned to face Powell,

his eyes taking in the situation. He spoke quietly in English. "Who are you?"

Powell raised his badge, which hung from a lanyard around his neck. As he did, he suddenly remembered the thousand grenades that were stored somewhere on this floor. It was unlikely, yes, but if a gunshot struck one of the crated rockets, each of which carried a booster charge, the ensuing string of explosions would blow them all to pieces. "Alan Powell. Serious Organised Crime Agency. You want revenge, I know, but if you cooperate, we can take it further—"

"Stand back," Ilya said flatly. "All of you. If you don't lower your guns, he dies."

Barlow kept his pistol raised. "How do we know that you won't kill him anyway?"

In response, Ilya only pushed the gun harder against the old man's head. Feeling the pressure, Sharkovsky took a gasping breath, saying, "You stupid fuck, give him what he wants. He's already killed one of my men."

Powell glanced into the office, but was unable to see past the doorway. "Misha?"

"He would have done the same to me." Ilya scanned the room. "I came here to kill this man, but if you do as I say, I will let him go. If not—" He shoved the old man a step forward.

"Okay," Barlow said, lowering his gun. "Standing down. Tell us what you want."

Ilya's eyes passed across the unit. Powell could see him working out the odds. "You have men on all the doors?"

"That's right," Barlow said. "I'm not going to lie to you. There's no way out of here."

"Tell them to fall back from the door leading to the

boardwalk. I'm walking out with Sharkovsky. If I suspect you're even thinking about taking me down, I put a bullet in his head."

Picturing the layout of the club, Powell understood his reasoning. There were three exits, one on the street, one on the alley, one on the boardwalk. The first two opened on blind zones, while the boardwalk stretched for miles in either direction, with nowhere to hide an ambush.

After a moment's hesitation, which might have been feigned, Barlow pressed the button on his radio. "South side team, stand down. Pull back from the door." He looked at Ilya. "Is that good?"

"Yes," Ilya said. "Now lower your weapons and fall back. Fifteen feet on all sides."

At a signal from their commander, the men in the tactical unit lowered their guns. Ilya pushed Sharkovsky into the hallway. Now that the door was no longer blocked, Powell could make out the outline of Misha's body on the floor. A second man was slumped in the corner.

Ilya and Sharkovsky moved along the hallway, the *vor* going first, Ilya's back to the wall. The unit stood aside, allowing the two men to pass. Once they had made it halfway down the corridor, Ilya forced Sharkovsky to execute a tight pivot, so that the old man continued to stand between him and the others. At the end of the hall, they rounded the corner and disappeared.

"Hold your position," Barlow whispered to the unit commander. "I don't want to start a riot. Powell and Wolfe, follow me."

They went for the stairs, guns holstered but cocked and locked. Ilya and Sharkovsky were already at the top of the steps, with only the old man's legs still visible. Upstairs, the club was packed and pounding with music. Everyone's eyes were on the dancers, so no one noticed the pair creeping sideways through the colored lights. Ilya's gun had been lowered to the small of Sharkovsky's back.

The two men reached the doors, which had been left open to the breeze, and emerged onto the terrace. Powell and the others followed close behind. Up ahead, the boardwalk was empty, swept clean by the tactical unit. The unit itself was nowhere in sight, although Powell knew that the agents were watching from their fallback positions. Farther off, he could see a white line of sand.

"Stay there," Ilya said, replacing the gun against Sharkovsky's head. The men inched backward toward the edge of the boardwalk. When they reached the steps that led to the beach, six feet below the boards, they turned sideways so that Sharkovsky could go first. Then they descended to the sand, each step taking them farther out of view, until both of them were gone.

As soon as they were out of sight, the three agents ran forward. "He's on the beach," Barlow barked into his radio. "Get a unit on the sand now. We'll pin him down until he sees that there's no way out—"

It took ten seconds to cross the boardwalk. Reaching the steps, they went down to the beach, then looked around in confusion. The shore was deserted, with nothing but sand stretching to either side. In the distance, the ocean was a dull mirror. Ilya and Sharkovsky had vanished.

"*What the fuck?*" Barlow looked up and down the beach. "*Where did they go?*"

Powell, heart thudding, looked more closely at the

stairs. A pair of drinking fountains stood on the level of the boardwalk. To allow maintenance crews to reach the plumbing, a snow fence had been installed nearby, keeping the area clear and leaving a gap beneath the boards.

He ran over to the opening. Without pausing, he slid onto his belly and squeezed himself through the gap, grains of sand skating beneath his weight. Part of him was expecting a trap, but instead, he found himself alone in the dark. In the distance, faintly, he could hear footsteps.

Barlow knelt by the gap, his face barely visible. "What the fuck are you doing?"

"Put men on the fences," Powell said, trying to remember what he had seen when he had last been under the boards. "There's a gate behind the club. Another at the parking lot. They'll come out one way or the other—"

Without bothering to reply, Barlow turned aside to radio the instructions to the rest of the unit. As he did, a shadow fell across the opening, and Wolfe slid down through the gap, landing on the sand next to Powell. From her inside pocket, she produced a penlight. Before he could say anything, she was already leading the way, heading farther into the darkness.

46

"I don't know what you have in mind, but it isn't going to work," Sharkovsky had whispered as they inched together across the restaurant floor. "There's only one way that this can end—"

Ilya said nothing. They reached the doors that opened on the boardwalk and stepped outside, moving past the tables on the terrace. Ilya kept his eye on the agents. Although the larger of the two men, the one with the radio harness, was clearly in charge, he found his attention drawn repeatedly to the other, the Englishman, who had spoken to him in the hallway.

"Stay there," Ilya said to them now. He replaced the gun against Sharkovsky's skull, his forearm aching from the effort of bracing it for so long, and began to creep backward across the boards. As soon as they were far enough away, Ilya whispered, "Listen closely. When we get to the steps, you'll see a gap between the boards and the sand. We're going underground. You first. The parking lot is one hundred paces west. Once we're through the fence, we go for the truck."

Although his voice was calm, he had no idea if the plan would work. His original intention had been to leave the way he came, but this was no longer possible. At least one unit would be covering the alley, and even with the streetlamps extinguished, there would be no chance of escape.

At the edge of the boards, Ilya told Sharkovsky to turn so that he reached the steps first. Glancing back, he saw that the agents, as instructed, were keeping their distance. Descending, the two men reached the sand. The gap in the boards lay directly in front of them.

"Move," Ilya said, pushing the old man forward. "You only get one chance at this."

Sharkovsky slid through the narrow opening. Ilya followed, gun aimed into the darkness, and landed on the ground beneath the boardwalk. It smelled faintly of salt and dry shit, and was covered in debris that had blown through the gap without being caught by the fence.

The two men marched forward, Sharkovsky staying one step ahead. Behind him, Ilya heard voices on the beach. It would not take them long, he knew, to discover where their quarry had gone.

They had crossed slightly less than half the distance when Sharkovsky threw a punch. Ilya, who had been expecting such a move, blocked it easily, and it was only when he felt the other man's foot slide softly next to his own that he understood that he had fallen for an old wrestler's trick.

Sharkovsky swept his foot forward, striking Ilya's ankle, then knocked him off his feet. Ilya fell, the sand rising to meet him, the moment endless until the ground clouted him awake. A hand closed around his throat. Ilya reached up, fingers going for the other man's eyes, but

Sharkovsky snapped his head away in time. The old man's breath was warm and stinking. "You like this, *zhid*?"

As the grip around his neck tightened, Ilya saw his night of retribution slipping away. He lifted the revolver, seeking a shot, then felt a set of fingers sink between the tendons of his wrist. His hand loosened for only an instant, but it was enough. A twist of his arm, and then his gun was gone.

Sharkovsky raised the revolver. In the second before he could squeeze off a shot, Ilya, groping in the sand, felt his hand close on a billet of wood. He lashed out randomly, striking the gun, which flew off into the shadows.

Without a pause, Sharkovsky drew something bright from a sheath around his ankle. Ilya was trying to remember if he had searched the old man's legs when he saw a flash of silver. A hot line opened on his cheek, just below his right eye, and warmth began to flow down his face.

Ilya drew his own knife, the one that he had taken from the kitchen in the Hamptons. There was no pain, at least not yet, but he knew that he had only a few seconds of clarity remaining. He was about to charge forward when he heard the sound of footfalls against sand. Someone else was here.

As if by mutual consent, the two men drew apart, ducking behind the nearest pair of concrete supports. Sharkovsky's voice was a hoarse whisper: "If I prick you, do you not bleed?"

Ilya, breathing hard, did not respond. Peering around the pillar, he saw the gleam of a flashlight. Two figures were coming his way. A moment later, the light winked out. The agents were using it sporadically, to avoid turning themselves into targets, but it was clear that they were closing fast.

It took him less than a second to conclude that he had no choice. Throwing himself out from behind the support, he began moving quickly across the dark drifts of sand, then broke into a run.

A rectangle of gray light appeared up ahead. He reached the gate and hooked his fingers through the diamonds of wire. When he pulled, a section of the fence lifted away. He squeezed through the opening he had made. As he did, a corner of the wire caught on his bag. He reached back, trying to free himself, but the strap was twisted. With his knife, he cut the strap, yanking the bag loose, then found himself under the ramp that led to the boardwalk.

The parking lot was deserted. Leaving the shelter of the ramp, he ran forward, weaving between the rows of cars. In a moment, he knew, the lot would be surrounded. Behind him, he heard the ring of metal as someone else pushed his way through the fence. He did not look back to see who it was.

Ilya reached the abandoned playground. He did not know if Sharkovsky had escaped, but hoped blindly that he had. With all he commanded in ruins, the *vor* had been left with only one way out. He would seek refuge with the Chekists. And it would be there, at the very end, even as he offered thanks for his safety, that he would find the Scythian waiting for him at last.

47

Ethan left his apartment just after sunrise. He had no destination in mind, only the urge to walk for hours, which he hoped would silence the noise in his head. As he went out onto the porch, a passing uncertainty made him feel the molding above the door to see if his spare key was still there. It was. He reached up to put it back, then reconsidered, and slid it into his pocket instead.

He crossed the Manhattan Bridge on foot, then passed into a secret city, one that was his alone. Above Houston, the grid became abruptly rational, short blocks going north, long blocks east and west. When he tried to envision the path he was tracing, he saw that it resembled a knight's tour. You began at a random position on the board, then visited each square once, only to end up, like his own tangled thoughts, at precisely the same place as before.

For the last twenty years of his life, he remembered, Duchamp claimed to have given up art for chess, while working all the while on a secret installation. This was usually interpreted as a massive deception, but perhaps it had been nothing but the simple truth. Duchamp had said, "I am retiring to play chess," and after his death, the world had been surprised by his final masterpiece, never suspecting that the two projects were one and the same.

As he walked past Washington Square, where chess hustlers would soon gather at their tables of stone, Ethan found himself imagining a game of chess that spanned the globe. Duchamp had not been the only player in those circles. Crowley had also been obsessed with chess. So had Lenin. Perhaps the real game had begun years before, at the Cabaret Voltaire, and had lasted beyond Lenin's death, when a chessboard had been entombed along with his body.

There was a chessboard in *Étant Donnés* as well. Beneath the installation, invisible to casual viewers, a linoleum floor bore a checkered pattern in black and white squares. The floor had been part of Duchamp's original plan, and had been faithfully transferred from his apartment to the museum, even though it formed no visible part of the tableau. It was repeatedly mentioned in the instructions for assembly, but no one knew why the artist had deemed it so essential. Unless, Ethan thought now, it was nothing less than a hint on how to read the work itself.

He reached Park Avenue and headed north. If the installation was a chess problem in disguise, the next step was to figure out the names of the players. It struck him again that there was one place where those names might have been found, but he had thrown his best chance away. The memory made his face hot. He had ruined things with Maddy. The only way to regain her trust was to show that his fears had been justified, but he had no chance of proving this without her.

Or almost no chance. There was, in fact, another possibility, a way to get the information on his own. It involved a certain amount of risk, and would force him to expose himself more than he might have liked, but as he thought about it now, it seemed to him that it was his only real option remaining.

He gradually became aware that he had wandered into a familiar neighborhood. His legs had taken him all the way to the office, which meant that he had walked almost seven miles. He stood before the building, wondering if he should go in, until his legs, which had brought him this far, made this decision as well. Using his key card, he let himself inside.

Five minutes later, he was on the street again. Feeling not entirely himself, he headed for his second destination, which was three long blocks away. When he arrived at the gallery's gilded doors, he rang the bell. Part of him knew that no one would be here so early, especially on the weekend, and he was already feeling his resolution falter when he heard the door unlock.

It opened. Ethan looked into the gray eyes of the man standing inside the threshold, then heard himself speak. "You don't know me, but my name is Ethan Usher. I work with Maddy Blume—"

"I know who you are," Lermontov said, his voice concerned. "Is Maddy all right?"

"That depends." Ethan paused, nearly retreated, but something in the other man's expression encouraged him to continue. "I know it must seem strange. But if you care about Maddy, you'll listen to what I have to say."

Lermontov regarded him for a second, as if deciding whether to let him in. At last, he stood aside. "Come. We'll talk in my office."

Ethan went into the gallery. Around them, the lights had been turned down, the gallerina's counter deserted, as if awaiting the return of its resident goddess. In the rear office, Lermontov sat down at his desk, on which a number of index cards were arranged. "What can I do for you?"

As Ethan took a seat, he noticed that a velvet curtain had been hung across one wall. The words began to come more easily. "It's about Maddy. Has she tried to contact you since last night?"

"No," Lermontov said. "She came to see me on Wednesday afternoon, but I haven't spoken to her since. What's this all about?"

"It's something that she and I are working on together. I'm not sure how much she's told you, but we've been looking into the study that was stolen from Archvadze. At this point, our theory is that the theft had something to do with the painting's connection to the Rosicrucians—"

"Yes, I know. Maddy explained this to me. I've already told her everything I can."

"I'm not sure if that's entirely true." Reaching into his pocket, Ethan removed the page that he had copied out at the office. "This is a list of clients who have done business with your gallery in the past. I can't be sure about all of them, but I believe that at least some of the names are fake. Either your clients have given you false information, or you're deliberately concealing their identities."

Lermontov studied the list. His face did not change. "And why would I do that?"

"To protect them," Ethan said. "If their real names were known, they'd be exposing themselves to the same risks as Archvadze. But there's something else going on. One of your clients isn't what he seems."

Ethan saw a flicker of doubt pass across Lermontov's eyes. If a name had occurred to him, however, the gallerist did his best to hide it. "I'm still not sure what you expect me to say."

"Let me help you, then. The man I'm looking for is probably Russian. He's wealthy, but the source of his income is unclear, and his tastes are selective and eccentric. At various points, he would have expressed interest in Duchamp and the Dadaists, especially those associated with Monte Verità. And he's very interested in *Étant Donnés*." Ethan looked across the desk at Lermontov. "I think you already know the man I have in mind. If you want to help Maddy, you'll tell me."

Lermontov put the list down. He seemed suddenly more frail than before. "What does Maddy think of all this?"

"She trusts you," Ethan said. "She doesn't believe that you would mislead her, even if you had a good reason for doing so. And she doesn't need to know that the name came from you. If he appears anywhere else in the public record, I can say that I found him on my own."

Lermontov was silent for a moment. Then, looking away, he said, "I do care about Maddy. You may have trouble understanding why. I thought that my silence would protect her, but—" He turned back to Ethan. "Perhaps I was wrong. Because I think I know the man you want."

Ethan saw that a great effort lay behind each of the gallerist's words. "Who is he?"

"A client. One with whom I have recently discussed

the sale of a certain painting." Lermontov glanced uneasily at the velvet curtain. "See for yourself. It will be easier to explain if I show you."

Ethan rose from his chair. As he went to the curtain, he found that his exhilaration had been touched with a strange sense of pity. For all his reassurances, he knew that it would be impossible to protect Lermontov entirely, so it was with a feeling of unexpected regret that he drew the curtain aside.

For a moment he looked, confused, at what had been revealed. There was no painting. The wall behind the curtain was blank.

Behind him, there was a short, sharp detonation, like the burst of a single firecracker. A handful of red pigment struck the wall at the level of his heart. Ethan regarded it with surprise, as if it were a hasty work of abstract expressionism. Then, looking down, he saw the ragged hole in his own chest.

He turned. Lermontov stood by the desk, a gun in his hand. Ethan tried to take a step forward, warmth gushing from between his fingers, then found that he was going to fall. Before he could hit the floor, Lermontov caught him in his arms, which were very strong, and lowered him to the ground.

Lermontov's voice was soothing and calm. "Gently, now. Let yourself go. It will only be a moment like any other—"

Ethan stared up at Lermontov. The moments of his life, which had once seemed infinite, had dwindled to fewer than ten. He tried to speak around the blood in his throat, but no words came. He felt the countdown continue, three seconds left, now two, and before he was ready, it was over.

Silence in the gallery. Lermontov waited until he was sure that Ethan was dead. Then he got to his feet.

There was blood on his hands. He shook out his pocket square and wiped them off.

Looking down at the body, he considered what to do next. One phone call would be enough to sink it into the river. Then he reflected that it might be possible to put it to better use.

He looked at the wall where the blood had splashed. At the height of the boy's chest, near the center of the starburst, the bullet, which had passed cleanly through the body, had left a perfect hole.

Reaching out, he put his hand over the mark, thinking. Then he drew the curtain shut.

48

When Maddy went to see Reynard later that morning, the fund manager was on the telephone, looking out his window at the city. "Yes, I understand," he said into the receiver. "I'm well aware of the situation—"

He motioned for her to come in. As Maddy sat down, she saw that Reynard seemed tired and drawn. For a moment, she thought about leaving, but forced herself to remain where she was.

She had made up her mind last night, after speaking to Tanya, who had informed her that she was leaving the project. "My manager saw my notes," Tanya had said over the phone. "When I told her what they were, she said it was a bad idea to get involved with your fund."

"But that's ridiculous," Maddy had said. "I know we've been having problems—"

"I'm sorry, but that's how it has to be. It could cost me my job." Tanya had paused. "You see, Archvadze is a client of ours."

"A client?" Maddy had tried to get her head around this. "What do you mean?"

But her friend had hung up without saying goodbye. The more Maddy thought about this conversation, the more convinced she became that she and Ethan could no longer push forward on their own, which had given her the resolve that she needed to open up to Reynard now.

A moment later, Reynard hung up the phone, a strange expression on his face. Maddy thought that he looked like a man who was contemplating his own ruin. "Is everything all right?"

Reynard stirred, as if awakening from a private reverie. "Another investor pulling out. The two pension guys from last week, remember? They say that they can't invest as long as our legal issues remain unresolved."

Maddy sensed that there was something he was holding back, but didn't know how to ask about this. "I'm sorry."

"It's all right. We all knew there would be days like this." He turned to her at last. "In any case, we'll manage. What is it?"

"We need to talk," Maddy said. "Ethan and I have been working on something of our own. We thought we'd hold off on telling you until we were ready, but I don't think we can wait any longer."

Reynard gave her a guarded nod, as if he had been expecting this. "I knew that you were working on your own project, but I didn't know what it was. What is it? Some kind of trading model?"

"Not exactly." Speaking slowly at first, then gradually picking up speed, Maddy described what they had uncovered, beginning with the hint to look into the Rosicrucians, although she did not mention Lermontov by name. Reynard listened patiently, breaking in with the occasional question. As she finished her account, Maddy said, "Even if some of the details are wrong, the overall picture is clear. And I still believe we can use it to track down the stolen painting."

Reynard seemed to consider this for a moment. "But how much of it can you prove?"

"I don't know. But I've noticed strange things in my own life. For one thing, I'm being followed." She told him about the man she had seen on the street, along with what Powell had said. "It frightens me. If we're right about this, these men would do anything to keep their existence a secret."

Reynard frowned. "If you think that someone is following you, you need to go to the police. Not Powell. He isn't interested in protecting you. I wish you'd told me about this earlier—"

"But there's something else. You know that before I joined the fund, I worked for Alexey Lermontov, who helped me get an interview here. He's the one who put us onto the Rosicrucians in the first place, but we've also been looking at his trade history, and we've found something unusual."

She related what Ethan had found in the database. "At first, I didn't want to believe it, but then I looked at the data myself. A few days ago, Lermontov showed me a painting that he claimed to have bought in Berlin. When I checked the transaction in our records, though, the seller's name didn't appear anywhere else. And it isn't the only one. There's no record of these collectors. They don't exist."

As he listened, Reynard seemed to grow increasingly disturbed. Rising from his chair, he went to the window. After a pause, he said, "Older records are inherently unreliable. Private sales, in particular, may go unrecorded for years. We looked into all this when we first put the database together—"

"But you wouldn't have been looking for systematic

THE ICON THIEF / 311

fraud, at least not on this scale. It's so vast that it's invisible. And this could just be the beginning. Our database and trading models could be fundamentally flawed."

Reynard glanced at the clock. Forty minutes had passed since Maddy had entered his office. "Look, I've got a conference call soon, so I can't give this the attention that it deserves. But I want to propose an alternative explanation for what you've found. If nothing else, if there's a simpler theory that fits all the facts, it deserves our consideration, too. Do you agree?"

Maddy nodded, although part of her resisted the possibility of another interpretation. "Go ahead."

Reynard sat down. "First of all, I know something about the history of art. There's no evidence that Lenin met any of the Dadaists. He lived near the Cabaret Voltaire, yes, but no one knows if they ever crossed paths."

"Tzara said that he played chess with Lenin," Maddy said. "After the war, he—"

"—would have had good reason to make that claim," Reynard interrupted. "You see the problem? Artists love to seem colorful. Tzara could say that he'd played chess with Lenin because there was no way to prove otherwise. Crowley is another example. He was a fabulist. A mythmaker. And even if he really was an intelligence agent, it doesn't prove anything. Men involved with the occult are often drawn to spycraft. They love codes and secret handshakes."

"But what about John Quinn?" Maddy asked. "He was an intelligence paymaster who gave money to both Duchamp and Crowley."

"Maybe he was just what he appeared to be, a patron of the arts who cultivated interesting friends. So far, you've shown that there are connections between artists, occultists, and spies, but that isn't surprising. They're all forms of nonconformism, so they tend to draw from a common pool of dreamers."

Maddy felt her convictions melting away. "So you think I'm paranoid. Is that it?"

"No," Reynard said. "But I think you've fallen victim to a common mistake. You're looking for patterns in a chaotic system. At worst, it leads to the cranks who see a Jewish or Bolshevik conspiracy behind every global crisis. Or analysts who try to explain every market movement in terms of oil prices or interest rates. I've been a trader for most of my life, and I can tell you that the market moves for reasons of its own. The same is true for history."

"But what about the man who was following me?" Maddy asked. "Or the burglary?"

"Based on what you've told me, there's no evidence that anyone but Ethan broke into your house. And the fact that someone is following you doesn't mean that the Rosicrucians are involved. Someone stole a painting, and you saw the thief's face. That's enough of a connection. Have you tried to tell the police?"

Maddy shook her head. "I haven't told anyone about this yet, except for Powell, and he doesn't know about the larger pattern we've uncovered. I don't think he'd believe me, anyway—"

"Tell you what," Reynard said. "It's the weekend. Go home. You need to deal with this stalker, which is the one thing we know is true. As for the rest—" He paused. "I'll look into Lermontov. But we need to be careful. If we go public too soon, the press will destroy us. We're staking our reputation on this. I can't take that risk until I know exactly what it is that we're saying."

Maddy managed to nod. "I understand. I know I haven't been making much sense."

"It's all right." Reynard walked her to the office door, laying a hand on her shoulder. "If you see Ethan, tell him that after all is said and done, I still want him here. And that goes for you, too."

"Thank you," Maddy said weakly. Excusing herself, she fled down the hallway. She had been sure that Reynard would believe her argument at once, but instead, he had made her see how fragile it really was. For a moment, she felt that fragility take hold, threatening to break her completely, but when she reached more deeply into herself, she was able to find a reassuring core of coldness.

The real question was what to do next. For all her anger at Ethan, she still wanted to talk to him, but whenever she tried his phone, there was no answer. Powell might listen, but the story she had to tell him sounded absurd, even to her own ears. And then, perhaps, there was Lermontov—

Maddy entered her office and sank down into her chair. She was staring blankly at her desk, wondering what to do now, when she saw that a folded piece of paper had been left on her keyboard.

She picked it up. After her arrival that morning, she had gone directly to Reynard, so she had not seen this note before.

Feeling warm and cold at the same time, her stomach lifting inside of her, Maddy unfolded the page. Inside, there was a key, not hers, and a handwritten message. It was from Ethan.

Philadelphia, it said. And below that, in smaller letters: *In case I never see you again.*

49

"Listen to me," the caller on the other end of the line said, his voice rough and accented. "We need to meet."

Powell, his desk buried in a snowdrift of arrest reports from last night's raid, wedged the receiver of the phone between his shoulder and ear as he accepted a fresh file from a passing secretary. "Who is this?"

"We met at the mansion a week ago," the caller said. "My name is Zakaria Kostava."

Powell sat up in his chair. He signaled to Wolfe, who was seated nearby, going over a mass of legal documents and initialing the corner of each page. "I was hoping that you'd call me sooner—"

"I know. Things have not been easy." Archvadze's assistant paused. "I read about Natalia in the paper."

"Yes, it's unfortunate," Powell said, careful not to say too much. He did not know if Kostava suspected that Natalia had implicated him as an accessory to her sister's death. "We're still trying to get the full story."

"I can give you some of the information you need," Kostava said. "I have nothing to hide. But I want to make sure that Natalia will be treated well. Can you come to meet me today?"

Powell fished a pen out of the mess on his desk. "That depends. Where are you?"

Kostava gave him the address of a hospital. "It is a private clinic in Glen Cove. I am here with Mr. Archvadze. When you get to the front desk, ask for a patient registered under the name of Kakutsa."

Powell wrote down the name, then underlined it. "You're at a clinic? Why?"

"It will be better if I explain in person. You need to see what they've done."

Kostava hung up. Powell set the receiver in its cradle and turned to Wolfe. "That was Kostava. He wants to meet at a hospital on Long Island. Archvadze is there. Can we get a vehicle?"

"I'll handle it," Wolfe said. She seemed aware of the urgency of the moment. With their workload snowballing in the aftermath of the raid, word was that the heist investigation would soon be turned over to Southampton. Once that happened, the case would be nothing but a memory.

Wolfe went into the next room. A moment later, she returned with the keys to a Bureau sedan. "I said that we were driving to Brighton Beach to take statements from the neighborhood. If we aren't back in a few hours, they'll suspect something. What was the address again?"

Powell handed her the slip of paper. "Glen Cove. Let's hope traffic is on our side."

After picking up the car, they headed for Long Island. Both were depressed by the results of the raid. Although a dozen men had been arrested and a cache of weapons seized, the tactical unit had failed to cover the parking lot in time, and both Ilya and Sharkovsky had escaped.

Forty minutes later, they left the expressway and went five miles north to the clinic. Instead of the vaguely menacing network of buildings that Powell had expected, the hospital campus turned out to be leafy and secluded, a wooded landscape that lacked only a hedge to embody the Hamptons ideal.

They parked at the end of the road, near the hospital itself, a converted mansion overlooking the sea. At the front desk, which was just inside a portico flanked with sun chairs, Powell showed his badge to the receptionist. "We're here to see a patient registered under the name Kakutsa."

The receptionist eyed the panther logo, but instead of making the usual wisecrack, she clicked through the records on her terminal. "We have a patient by that name in the burn ward on the fourth floor."

"The burn ward?" Wolfe leaned over the counter to look at the computer. "What happened? Was there an accident?"

"I don't have any information about that," the receptionist said, turning her monitor to hide the screen. "If you'd like to wait—"

"That won't be necessary," Powell said. They headed for the elevators, moving down a tastefully furnished hall. Except for the faint whiff of disinfectant and medical waste, it might have been a corridor in a private resort.

On the fourth floor, Kostava was seated in the hallway, a copy of that day's paper unfolded across his lap. When he saw them, he rose, the legs of his chair leaving marks on the tile. "I am glad to see you," Kostava said, holding the paper before him like a shield. "Where is Natalia?"

"At the Tombs," Wolfe said. "A bail hearing is scheduled for tomorrow. She didn't try to call you?"

"There was no way for her to reach us," Kostava said. "After the incident at the mansion, my employer decided to withdraw until he knew who his enemies were. He feared that his phone was tapped, or that members of his inner circle were working for the Chekists—"

"I know," Powell said. "He fired his own lawyer. And yet he trusted you. Why?"

"Because of all that we have been through together." Kostava's eyes grew damp, as if his emotions were seeping through the one available gap in his defenses. "He trusted me. And I betrayed him." With a sudden gesture, he crumpled the newspaper and threw it to the ground. "I was only trying to protect her."

Powell sensed that Kostava's feelings for Natalia went far beyond an assistant's natural regard for his employer's girlfriend. "Tell me what happened. I need to know everything."

Kostava looked at his hands, which were covered in smears of newsprint. "I will do whatever you ask, as long as you promise that these men will be punished. Come and see for yourself."

He headed down the corridor. Powell followed, noticing a peculiar bluish glow spilling across the tiles. Reaching the source of the light, they halted, looking through a glass panel into the room beyond. Kostava wiped his eyes. "He was the finest man I have ever known. Now look at what they have done to him."

Powell stared silently through the glass. It took a moment for him to recognize what he was seeing, and even longer to comprehend it. When, at last, he understood, the final piece fell into place, and it all seemed obvious. The heist had not been about the painting at all. At least not entirely.

Archvadze, his arms folded across his chest, lay in a hospital bed, doused in blue light from an ultraviolet lamp that had been mounted to the ceiling. Most of his skin was gone. So were his hair and eyebrows. Although much of his body was swathed in bandages, some silver, others filled with cooling gel, wherever his skin was exposed, it had peeled away in large fragments, exposing the raw pink underneath. His face was covered in clots of blood. His mustache had fallen out, leaving his mouth as featureless as that of a baby mouse.

Wolfe stared at the ruin in the other room. Her usual reserve fell away. "Holy shit."

Powell himself was unable to speak. He could not believe that this bleeding piece of earth was the same man he had seen at the mansion a week ago. At the party, the oligarch had struck him as sophisticated and capable, in full possession of his faculties. Now he had been reduced to the core of a man, like a mummy that was crumbling to pieces after exposure to the open air.

From up the hallway came the sound of efficient footsteps. A resident was walking in their direction, his feet clad in rubber sandals. "I was told that I would find you here," the doctor said, transferring his clipboard to the crook of his arm. "I see you've found our star patient."

Powell numbly shook the resident's hand. "Can you tell me what happened?"

The resident peered into the next room, his smooth face unruffled by the sight. "Toxic epidermal necrolysis, also known as Lyell's syndrome. The worst case I've ever seen. We've tried everything we can, but at this point, all we can do is treat the pain. Chances of survival are very low. I remember a case—"

"Toxic epidermal necrolysis," Wolfe said. "What does that mean? His skin is dying?"

The resident blinked at the interruption. "The upper layer of skin, the epidermis, has sloughed off across ninety percent of his body. It's being rejected, like a transplanted organ. That's why we have him under ultraviolet light, which slows down immune system response. We're also treating him with ciclosporin, but at this point, it doesn't seem to be making any difference."

"But how did it happen?" Powell asked. Out of the corner of his eye, he saw Kostava turn away, as if he had heard this all before.

"It's very mysterious," the resident said. "Our first theory was that it was an allergic reaction to medication. The immune system tries to force the drug out of the body by depositing it in the skin, which kills the tissue. We found traces of fluoroquinolone, a synthetic antibiotic, in his bloodstream, but not in sufficient quantities to cause a reaction this severe."

"So he was poisoned," Wolfe said. "There's no way that this could be an accident."

"Forensics isn't really my field, so I can't say. But severe reactions can be caused by interactions between multiple compounds. So far, if there is a second component, we haven't found it yet."

Powell turned back to the glass. The oligarch's eyes were open, but he did not seem aware of his surroundings. He was breathing, but his mind was gone. Powell had seen it before. "Is there any prospect of recovery?"

"There's always a chance of a miracle, but honestly—" The resident shook his head. "Even in the best of circumstances, the mortality rate is close to fifty percent, and this is no routine case. His airway is too badly damaged."

"Then I need to question him now," Powell said. "Before he dies, I need to find out how he was exposed."

"I'm afraid that's impossible," the resident said. "Even if he were awake, he's been suffering from acute paranoia and dementia. His skin loss and suppressed immune system leave him vulnerable to infection. It might be permissible with the right protective gear, but it would take a while to get the equipment together—"

"Do it, then," Wolfe said. "In the meantime, we need access to his clinical history."

"It's in my office," the resident said. "If you'll come with me, we can take a look."

"Fine. I'll need copies, too." Wolfe looked at Powell. "Can you get a statement from Kostava?"

Her eyes flashed a covert message, one that he decoded easily. "Yes, I can do that."

"Good. I'll be back in a few minutes." Wolfe followed the resident down the hallway and disappeared around the corner. Kostava was nowhere in sight. Powell stood there for a few seconds, waiting until he could no longer hear the squeak of rubber sandals against tile. Then he got to work.

Across the hall, there was an empty examination room. He ducked inside, scanning the rows of medical supplies on the shelves, and finally took a surgical mask and a pair of nitrate gloves. He tied the mask around his face and donned the gloves as he went back to the room where Archvadze was dying.

He opened the door. As he approached, Archvadze's

eyes widened. At the center of each pupil, Powell saw, there was a bright star of dementia, a fevered spark that he knew all too well.

Powell thought that the oligarch recognized him, but just to be sure, he took out his badge and held it up. Archvadze studied it, then lifted his head in an imitation of a nod, saying, "Powell." His enunciation had grown soft, like that of a man who had gone days without water. "From London."

"That's right," Powell said. He pulled up a chair and sat down. From the bed, a faintly sweet odor of antiseptic was underlined by something darker, the smell of the body glistening and exposed. Embarrassed by the proximity of death, he took out his notebook. "I'm here to learn who did this to you."

Archvadze said something inaudible. When Powell leaned closer, the oligarch licked his lips, his tongue emerging from his mouth like a worm in dead soil. "Cell phone. The Chekists—"

Powell felt the hairs rise on the back of his neck. "What about your cell phone?"

"Chekists put something on my phone," Archvadze said, breathing heavily. "I figured it out. That's why I threw it away. Don't know what else they've touched. Or who else is working for them. I should have known. I thought I had power, but all I had was money. Money is nothing. Money is shit. I smell it in me, this corruption, and I have no doubt. It's oozing out of me—"

"Why did the Chekists want to kill you?" Powell asked, raising his voice. Listening to the drone of the machines by the bedside, he knew that he was almost out of time. "What did you find out?"

"The trophy commission." For a second, the oligarch's eyes seemed to fill with light and lucidity. "The painting. You found it?"

"No," Powell said. "It's still missing. We'll find it, I promise, and get it back to you."

"Look closely," Archvadze managed to say. "Not the front. The back. That's where the truth lies. On the other side—"

He began to cough. A second later, Powell heard an alarm go off. When he looked at the monitor next to the bed, he saw the line weakening and flattening. Archvadze's lungs were failing.

Powell bent down, eye to eye with the dying man, and whispered, "Who killed you? Tell me. Give me a name—"

Archvadze stared at him, eyes bulging. "Camera," the oligarch hissed. "Camera."

The oligarch's eyes rolled back in his head. Powell heard the door bang open like a gunshot as the resident ran into the room, shouting for him to stand aside, a nurse and technician a few steps behind. Powell fell back, the oligarch's last words echoing in his brain. He looked down at his notes. In the ultraviolet light, the paper of his notebook was glowing.

50

The old man walked along the Avenue of the Americas, his hatred for the city deepening with every step. Back home, each face he passed granted him the proper deference, but here, as he gazed up at the towers of steel and glass, he could sense their mute dismissal of the life he had carved out for himself.

When he arrived at the gallery, he rang the bell, keeping his face turned away from the street. A second later, the door opened, revealing an elegant figure standing just inside. The two men regarded each other for a long moment. Sharkovsky did not look away from the other man's eyes.

At last, Lermontov stepped aside. "Be quick. You've kept me waiting long enough."

As Sharkovsky entered the gallery, he kept on his sunglasses, which he wore in place of an eye patch. His right eye ached all the time now, as if a grain of sand were embedded in the optic nerve, and the constant irritation had begun to affect his judgment. If he had been able to think more clearly in recent days, he reflected, he might have avoided some of the mistakes that had turned him into an exile.

He followed the gallerist into the back office. When

he closed his left eye and looked around the room, he saw only a vague blur of color. On the far edges of his field of vision, he could still sense movement and light, but the laser had burned out his fovea, making it impossible to see anything in detail. The room smelled faintly of soap, as if the floor had been recently washed.

Lermontov took a seat behind his desk. "Do you wish to make your confession?"

Sharkovsky lowered himself into the nearest chair. From most other men, the question would have made him laugh, but Lermontov was in a category all of his own. "You know what happened. My men were arrested. My club was raided. There must have been an informer—"

"Or your phone was tapped. Did that never occur to you? What about the guns?"

"All gone. We were storing them in the basement until we could figure out the timing of the exchange. I will repay the loss to you."

"The money isn't important. I can make up the shortfall. What matters more is trust. It makes us wonder how useful you really are." Lermontov paused. "Did you ever say my name over the phone?"

"Never on the phone," Sharkovsky said. "All over encrypted email, like you wanted."

As he spoke, he studied the gallery owner. There had been a time when he had seen Lermontov as little more than a revenue stream, a means of channeling art, which arrived in Brighton Beach along the same routes as guns and stolen merchandise, to collectors throughout the city. It had not taken him long, however, to figure out where the money went. Ever since, he had been unable to stifle a secret shudder, a protective tightening of his insides, whenever he saw this man.

"I have one piece of good news," Lermontov said. "Anzor Archvadze is dead."

Sharkovsky felt a faint sense of satisfaction. "The Scythian knew his business."

"But there are complications. Natalia Onegina has been arrested, along with Kostava. If the police listen to what they have to say, sooner or later, they will become interested in this painting. We need to tie up the loose ends. One is the Scythian. You've repeatedly failed to take care of him."

Sharkovsky tried to sound dismissive. "He doesn't know your name. He knows nothing of our arrangement. It's only a matter of time before he makes a mistake. When he does, the painting will be ours."

"That isn't good enough. We need to tighten the screws. Do you have the gun?"

Sharkovsky drew the revolver from his belt. After Ilya had lost it, he had retrieved it from under the boards. "Here it is."

"Good." Rising from his desk, Lermontov headed for the door. "Come with me."

They went down the hall, past a row of canvases in wooden racks. There were drying streaks of water on the floor. Going to a closed door at the end of the corridor, Lermontov opened it, then switched on the lights.

Sharkovsky looked over the gallerist's shoulder. Beyond the door lay a restroom with a toilet and sink. Lying on the floor was a young man's body. He had been shot once in the back, with the slug emerging cleanly through an exit wound in his chest, and his eyes, at the level of the tile, were halfway open. Sharkovsky had never seen him before, but knew at once who it was.

At his side, Lermontov had donned a pair of gray leather gloves. "Give me the gun."

After a moment's hesitation, Sharkovsky handed him the revolver. Lermontov took it, checked the cylinder, then aimed it carefully at the body. When he fired, there was a wet thump, and the bullet lodged in the dead man's shoulder, caught by the hard blade of the scapula.

Lermontov handed the gun back, then went over to the sink, on which a wallet, keys, and cell phone had been placed. He gave them to Sharkovsky. "The boy's address is in his wallet. Go to his house and destroy all his notes. Don't overthink it. Burn his papers and get his computer. Then I need you to take care of the girl. The same gun. You follow me?"

Sharkovsky nodded, understanding at once. Once the bodies had been found, ballistics would link them to the gun that killed Misha. Since both victims had witnessed the heist at the mansion, the police would assume that Ilya was simply cleaning house. "How do I find her?"

"I'll figure out when she's going to be home. She's been calling the boy all morning. Keep his phone in case she tries him again. If necessary, we can text her to set up a meeting. But don't use it to call me. Get a disposable phone, then contact me once you have the number."

Sharkovsky pocketed the cell phone and the remaining items. "And after that?"

"I can get you to London. What happens next isn't my concern. But you still need to prove that you deserve my protection." Lermontov looked down at the body. "Now get out of my sight. I have work to do."

Turning aside, Sharkovsky wanted to say something that would cause the gallerist to remember him, but in the end, he remained silent. He left by the front door, which locked automatically. Although nothing of his former life remained, he was comforted by the fact that he had a destination, a future, a chance to use his hands. It was almost enough to make him feel young again.

As he headed for where he had parked, he did not see the car at the curb halfway up the block, or the man watching him through the windshield. Ilya was about to follow on foot when he saw Sharkovsky enter the parking garage. Straightening up in his seat, he kept an eye on the ramp. He had been parked there for the past two hours. The car had been rented at the airport, using the identity documents and credit card that he had recovered from the binding of the *Sefer Yetzirah*.

He had known that Sharkovsky would appear sooner or later. The night before, when he had examined the computer at the club, the message from the gallery had stood out at once. Sharkovsky would need a paymaster. While pondering the purpose of the heist, and the larger system of which it was a part, Ilya had concluded that the paymaster could only be a member of the art world.

The pickup truck appeared at the ramp. As it rolled down to the curb, Ilya started his own engine. When the truck was half a block away, he pulled out into the street. He could see the back of Sharkovsky's head through the window as they turned onto Park Avenue, heading south. They were going downtown.

51

Maddy lay on the floor of the study, looking up at the ceiling, a scrap of paper clutched in one hand. A few days earlier, Ethan had hung a snow shovel from a cord next to the overhead light. Now it drifted in a slow circle, blade downward, the only whisper of movement in the otherwise deserted apartment. Maddy watched it. The shovel cast an expanding and contracting shadow across her face as it turned in the air. She watched it some more.

As the shovel described its perfect circle, it seemed to her that there was something obscene in its continued motion. She rose, back stiff, and took the shovel down. Looking for a place to put it, she finally leaned it against the inside of the closet. It was not the only readymade in the room. An antique bottle rack with five tiers of hooks stood at attention near the door.

A pack of cigarettes was lying on the windowsill. After cracking the window, she slid out a cigarette and lit it, using a coffee cup by the laptop as an ashtray. A crime scene photo of the Black Dahlia murder had been posted above the desk. Maddy stared at it. In the hour since she had entered the apartment, she had gone through everything, searching for whatever Ethan had meant her to see, but so far, she had found nothing resembling an answer.

What she had found, instead, were chess problems. Ethan had made copies of all Duchamp's writings on chess, including his one published book on the game, which Maddy now leafed through again. It described an extraordinarily rare endgame situation, never encountered in regular play, in which only the white and black kings remained on the board, along with a pawn or two. With the rest of the men eliminated, it came down to a duel between two pieces, the last ones standing. And the best possible outcome for black, it seemed, was a draw.

She put the book down. It wasn't hard to see why Ethan had become fixated on chess. The title *Étant Donnés*, or *Given*, came from the language of geometric proofs. Given a diagram and a set of assumptions, you made a series of deductions until you had proven a theorem. A chess problem was not so different. It was a diagram of a game in progress, paused before a decisive moment. The challenge was to figure out what came next. And Duchamp's last message, as embodied in the installation, seemed to depend on the same process of reasoning.

And that was the trouble. If *Étant Donnés* was a chess problem, as Ethan's notes implied, then her task was to figure out what the next move should be. But this brought her up against an insurmountable obstacle. She didn't know anything about chess. She barely knew how to move the pieces.

As Maddy looked around the room, she found herself wondering if Duchamp would really have played by the rules. His entire career had been devoted to undermining convention, so perhaps the answer lay outside the game itself. You could knock the pieces from the board with a sweep of the hand, or unplug the chess computer, or shoot your opponent in the heart. Like severing the Gordian Knot. Or like Solomon, ready to cut the baby in half—

She sat upright in her chair. For a moment, she felt as if the world had tilted sideways. Before her was the crime scene photo that Ethan had posted above his desk. It showed the murder victim, Elizabeth Short, lying dead in a field, cut in half at the waist. Maddy stared at the picture, concentrating on the insight that was hovering just out of reach, and finally managed to grasp it.

Duchamp, she saw, had left the tableau incomplete. He had known it would evoke the Black Dahlia murder, but had not taken his reconstruction to its logical conclusion. Elizabeth Short's body had been cut in half, but the body in the installation was whole. That was the next move. The scene had been paused before its climax. And to complete it, the body had to be cut in two.

She remembered the readymade that Duchamp had constructed with Walter Arensberg. A ball of twine had been sandwiched between two pieces of metal, but beforehand, Arensberg had inserted an object inside the ball without telling Duchamp what it was. To see what was inside, you had to cut it in half, like the Gordian Knot. And if Duchamp had done something similar with the installation, it wasn't hard to guess what kind of information it might contain.

As she looked at the Black Dahlia, the picture seemed to dissolve before her eyes, and then the world went away. When her vision cleared, she found that she was seated at Ethan's laptop, on which she had opened two windows. One displayed the hours for the Philadelphia Museum of Art. The other was a bus schedule. If she left soon, she could be there an hour before it closed. *Étant Donnés* had an alcove of its own, and it was usually deserted, so she would have it all to herself—

For the first time, Maddy clearly saw what she was contemplating. She closed the browser window as if slamming it shut, then looked at the photo again. "What am I thinking?" she whispered. "What am I really thinking?"

She was still trying to answer this question when she heard the door open downstairs.

Relief flooded her body. Rising from the desk, she went onto the landing. The apartment was on two levels, the bedroom and study upstairs, the living room on the ground floor. She was already on the stairwell, ready to tell Ethan that she was here, when she caught a glimpse of the man who had entered the apartment. His back was turned, and she saw him for only a moment, but it was more than enough time to see that it was not Ethan at all.

She backed up from the stairwell. When the foyer was out of sight, she paused, heart juddering, listening for steps on the stairs. Instead, she heard the door swing shut. Downstairs, floorboards creaked as the stranger moved into the living room. There was no sign that he had heard her. At least not yet.

Then she saw that there was no way out. The front door was within sight of the living room. The windows of the study were covered in bars. And the fire escape was at the other end of the house.

Even as she finished this train of thought, the stranger began to climb the stairs.

Maddy retreated into the study. As the footsteps drew closer, her eyes fell on the closet. There was no time to think. Going to the closet, she squeezed inside and pulled the door shut, one trembling hand on the knob.

She had hoped that the stranger would go into the bedroom, clearing her way to the stairs. Instead, he entered the study. Through the gap between door and jamb, she could see the desk by the window. A pencil line of smoke hung in the air. She had forgotten to put out her cigarette.

A man came into view. He was old, perhaps sixty, wearing a pair of wraparound sunglasses. He surveyed the room, eyes passing briefly across the closet, and finally went to the desk, riffling through the papers. Then he moved out of her field of vision. She heard a low squeak of metal and a soft click, then felt the air grow warm. He had turned on the gas fireplace.

Returning to the desk, he scooped up an armful of notes, then vanished from sight again. As he came back for more, Maddy smelled burning paper. She watched as he took another stack. Then another. And another.

Soon the room stank of smoke. The man went over to the window, then paused. From this angle, she couldn't see his face.

Then she saw him pick up the cup with her cigarette inside. It was still smoldering.

Putting the cup down, the stranger took a step forward, disappearing from her line of sight. Maddy, hands groping, felt something cool and heavy at her side. It was the handle of the shovel.

Her fingers had scarcely closed around the shovel when the closet door flew open.

The man stood in front of her, a hand on the knob,

close enough for her to see herself in his glasses. In his surprised face, she saw recognition. He knew her. For a single intake of breath, they stood eye to eye—

—and before he could come any closer, she smashed the shovel against his face.

He fell back. After a heartbeat, blood began to flood from his nose. Maddy emerged from the closet, the shovel in her hands. The man was clawing for something in his belt. She saw the taped handle of a revolver.

"*Fuck off!*" The words exploded from her lips as she struck him on the wrist, driving his hand away from the gun. She hit him on the head, denting the shovel's blade, a hot line of pain whipsawing up her right arm.

The man fell to his knees. Maddy swung at him again, connecting with the crown of his skull, then turned to run. Before she could take a step, a hand shot out and seized her ankle. She fell forward, fumbling the shovel, and knocked her head against the floor, an abyss stretching between her and the stairs.

The hand around her ankle tightened, the fingers sinking in savagely. She rolled over, forehead aching from where it had struck the floor. The bottle rack stood at eye level. Without thinking, she picked up the bottle rack with both hands, muscles shrieking, and swung it toward the stranger's left temple.

The man screamed as a hook caught him in the soft spot beneath one ear, knocking away his sunglasses. Maddy, gasping, yanked her ankle out of his loosened grip, tears leaving stinging tracks on her face. She got to her feet. On the floor, the man was breathing but unconscious. The top button of his shirt had come undone. And above his heart, there was the tattoo of a rose.

Keeping the bottle rack raised, ready to bring it down at the first sign of movement, she turned off the fireplace, then picked up her purse. When she went over to the desk, she saw that all of the notes were gone.

With shaking fingers, Maddy took out her cell phone and dialed Ethan's number, her eyes fixed on the man on the ground. "Come on," Maddy whispered, bringing the phone to her ear. "Pick up, Ethan, pick up—"

From inside the man's coat, a ringtone sounded. Lowering her phone, Maddy stared. She recognized it.

As the cell phone rang again, the man's eyes opened. His lips parted, forming a fine bubble of blood. Maddy screamed and fell backward. As the man tried to rise, she ran, nearly falling down the staircase. Without looking back, she threw herself against the front door, clutching at the knob. It wouldn't turn. She tried it again, fingers slick against metal, then finally remembered to undo the latch. Opening the door, she fell through to the other side.

A car was parked across the street. Behind the wheel, watching her, was the thief she had seen at the mansion.

For an instant, their eyes locked. Before he could come after her, she was running.

As she fled, the faces on the sidewalk regarding her with amusement or concern, she found that she understood everything. Ethan had been right, and had paid the price, but not before leaving her one final message. Maddy ran up the street, hoping that it would protect her, but knew that this city, for all its power, could not keep her safe. The answer was not in New York. It was in Philadelphia.

III

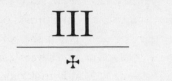

To revenge the misdeeds of the ruling class, there existed in the Middle Ages in Germany a secret tribunal called the Vehmgericht. If a red cross was seen marked on a house, people knew that its owner was doomed by the Vehm. All the houses of Europe are now marked with the mysterious red cross. History is the judge; its executioner, the proletariat.

—Karl Marx

Arensberg, some two years later, thought he discerned a pattern in Duchamp's work. "I get the impression," he wrote, "when I look at our paintings of yours from the point of view of their chronological sequence, of the successive moves in a game of chess." Duchamp readily agreed to the analogy and wondered, "But when will I administer checkmate or will I be mated?"

—Alice Goldfarb Marquis, *Marcel Duchamp*

52

Outside a diner in Herald Square, an express bus idled at the curb, a string of passengers waiting to board. Unlike the other travelers, who were shoving packs and suitcases into the cargo hold, Maddy carried nothing but a purse. As the line inched forward, she found herself standing before the driver, a massive figure in a crimson parka. Pointing to the bus, she asked, "Is this Philadelphia?"

"No, ma'am. This is New York. Don't you know where you are?" A flash of white teeth signaled that he was joking. "Sure, ma'am, this is Philadelphia. You got a ticket for me?"

"I don't have a ticket," Maddy said. "I'd like to buy one, please. One way only."

"Fifteen dollars." The driver waited as she fished the bills from her wallet, then gave her a slip of paper in exchange. "You doing okay?"

Maddy felt his gaze coming to rest on her right temple, where a large dark bruise had formed. "I'm fine."

Looking away, she mounted the steps of the bus, moving down the aisle to an empty row. As she took a seat, arms aching from swinging the shovel, it seemed to Maddy that the other passengers were staring at her.

The driver slid behind the wheel, the doors closing with a hydraulic hiss. As they turned onto Ninth Avenue, shouldering their way downtown, Maddy looked out the window and tried to tell herself what she knew for sure.

First, Ethan was dead. The man at the apartment had carried Ethan's phone, and had let himself into the building with his keys. Maddy could imagine all too clearly what had happened. After their argument, Ethan had gone looking for something, pausing only to leave her a note. Whatever he had been looking for, he had found it. Or, more likely, it had found him.

Which brought her to the second point. The Rosicrucians, or something close to them, were real. She didn't know if they were exactly what she and Ethan had conceived, but they had been watching her at least since the night of the heist. They were real enough to follow her. And they were real enough to kill.

This, then, was the crucial point. She could never go home. The man at the apartment had recognized her. She had seen it in his face. If he didn't come after her a second time, someone else would. Perhaps someone worse. Maddy had already taken out her phone to call Powell about this, but before she could dial, she had been brought up short by uncertainty over what she could possibly say.

Because this was about more than one man. Even if the police caught her attacker, they would only send her home again. And even if she walked away, turning her back on all Rosicrucians, real or imagined, the day would inevitably come when she would find the thief from the mansion waiting at her door. She had no doubt of this. And this meant that the only way out was to destroy their secret itself, to expose and explode it until there was nothing left to hide.

Which brought her to Philadelphia. For the moment, at least, she was safe. Nobody knew where she was. And it was only now, when she was free and unobserved, that she could follow her argument to its logical conclusion.

Duchamp's final secret was in the installation. To find out what Ethan had been killed to protect, she had to see it in person. Despite what she had concluded about its intended solution, she hoped that it was something she would see at once, now that her eyes were prepared. Once she had been to the installation, and was ready to reveal its secrets, she would call Powell, from the steps of the museum itself if necessary. But if she wasn't able to see it with her eyes alone—

Before she could finish this line of thought, which hinted at something monstrous, it was cut off by a vibration against her hip. Taking the phone from her purse, she looked at the display. It was Lermontov.

She answered it. On the other end of the line, Lermontov sounded troubled. "I'm glad I could reach you. Are you all right?"

Maddy took a deep breath. Her hands were shaking. "Yes, I'm fine. What is it?"

"There's something I need to show you. It involves our discussion from the other day. I've been reviewing my client list, and I've found something strange. You were right. The Rosicrucians are real—"

His words filled her with an almost painful sense of gratitude. Until now, she hadn't known how desperately she wanted to avoid facing this final outrage by herself. "What did you find?"

"I'd rather not discuss it over the phone," Lermontov said. "It might even be best if we met away from the gallery. Would it be possible for me to see you at home? I've spoken with Ethan, your colleague, and he indicated that he might be able to meet you there as well—"

Maddy opened her mouth, then closed it. A sudden flowering of paranoia made it impossible to speak. Up ahead, the entrance to the Holland Tunnel loomed like the maw of a whale.

"I'm going out to Boston for a few days," Maddy said, choosing her words carefully. "Don't worry about me. I just need time to think." She looked out at the street. "I'm going into a tunnel. I can't talk for much longer."

Without waiting for a reply, she hung up the phone. As she slid it back into her purse, the bus entered the tunnel, the sound of traffic deepening to a roar as they passed through the tube, which was lit by a strange fluorescence.

Carried along by the bus, she felt like a bullet in the barrel of a gun. It was two hours to Philadelphia. Maddy closed her eyes, searching for that part of herself that was unwavering and cold. Instead, she pressed her head against the window, feeling the glass vibrate against her skull, and cried. It was too late.

53

On the refrigerator in Ethan's kitchen, nestled among a skyline of other bottles, stood a fifth of vodka, halfway full, of a brand more famous for its typography than for the quality of its contents. At the moment, Sharkovsky was not inclined to be choosy. He seized the bottle's slippery neck in one hand and took it into the bathroom, closing the door behind him.

Unscrewing the cap, he sucked down some of the alcohol. Without swallowing, he swirled it around in his mouth, ignoring the ensuing pulses of pain, and spat it into the sink. A stream of pinkish liquid went down the drain, along with a few white fragments. He took another mouthful, rinsed again, and spat a second time. Less pink. A third time, and it was almost clear.

Satisfied, he set the bottle on the toilet tank and opened the medicine cabinet. A vial of prescription painkillers caught his eye. He shook out two pills and swallowed them. Pocketing the vial, he closed the cabinet, his face swinging into view on the hinged mirror.

What he saw was not reassuring. There were shallow cuts on his forehead and temples where the sunglasses had broken, and yellow bruises had formed on his jaw and the side of his face. Taking a wad of toilet tissue, he inserted it into his mouth and bit down. His good eye, which had been as glassy as that of a fish, grew watery, then regained some of its customary brightness.

Sharkovsky left the bathroom. He cursed his weakness and age, sensing that he had to counteract it with an act of sympathetic magic. It would require blood. And he knew exactly whose blood it should be.

A glance at the clock forced him to get moving. He had been unconscious for more than forty minutes. His nostrils were packed with blood and snot, making him whistle and wheeze as he looked around the room. The laptop went under his arm. After a moment's consideration, he took the vodka as well.

Outside, his truck was parked at the corner. Sharkovsky opened the driver's door and slid behind the wheel, tossing the laptop onto the seat beside him. He had just inserted the key into the ignition when his phone rang.

It was Lermontov. "The girl is leaving town. Have you been to her house yet?"

"No. She was here." Speaking as quickly as possible, he told the gallery owner what had happened. As he spoke, he saw that there was no way to describe the incident without looking like a fool.

Lermontov's voice hardened. "We need to find her. She said she was going to Boston, but that may have been a lie. Was there any indication at all of what she was doing at the apartment?"

"If there was, I burned it," Sharkovsky said. "Up in smoke, like you asked. Except—" He glanced at the laptop on the passenger's seat. "The computer. I have it here. Let me look."

He opened the laptop. With so many transactions occurring online, he had long since been obliged to learn something about computers. Going to the menu of recent files, he found nothing of interest. Without a wireless signal, he couldn't connect to the web, but was still able to view a list of recently visited pages. His attention was drawn at once to the two addresses at the top.

"Philadelphia," Sharkovsky said. "Bus schedule. The Philadelphia Museum of Art."

"To see *Étant Donnés.*" Lermontov fell briefly silent. "Fine. If you leave now, you can get there first. Sit on the museum until she appears. Don't show your face again until this is resolved."

"All right," Sharkovsky said. "It's done. I will call you again from Philadelphia."

He hung up and pulled away from the curb. Turning at the intersection, he headed south, performing a mental survey of his faculties, like a pilot checking his instruments before takeoff. The ache in his jaw was subsiding, but the pain in his eye was as maddening as ever.

In time, he came to a ramp that took him onto the expressway. For an instant, as he entered the stream of traffic, he contemplated turning around. There was a hint of insanity in following the girl all the way to Philadelphia. Even if he picked up her trail at the museum, it would not be easy to take care of her there. Far better, he thought, to turn back while he still could.

As he reached the bridge, however, he understood that he had to make her suffer. In London, he would be nothing but a name. If he wanted to be feared, he had to resolve this situation in a way that silenced any questions.

Caught up in these thoughts, he did not notice the car

that passed through the toll gate a second after he did, following him onto the bridge. It had tracked him faithfully from Brooklyn, keeping a block's distance at all times.

In the car, Ilya glanced at his fuel gauge. He had not expected the *vor* to travel so far. With every mile, the chances of his success, which had not been great in the first place, grew increasingly remote.

An hour ago, when Sharkovsky pulled over in Brooklyn, after making a brief stop at a convenience store, Ilya had been forced to keep going, since there were no other spaces available. Driving past with his head turned away, he had circled the block and doubled back. When he returned, the pickup had still been there, but Sharkovsky had been gone. Since none of the houses seemed more likely than any other, he had seen no choice but to park and wait, hoping that the old man would reappear.

A few minutes later, he had been startled by the appearance of another familiar face. From outside his line of sight, a girl had come running around the corner. For a second, their eyes had locked, and he had recognized her. Before he could approach, she had disappeared. And another hour had passed before Sharkovsky, freshly bruised, had returned to the truck.

Now the truck passed under the central tower of the bridge. As Ilya followed, ten lengths behind, he tried to make sense of what he had seen. The appearance of the girl from the mansion, whose face he remembered well, could not be a coincidence. Sharkovsky, he saw, had been ordered to silence her, but somehow she had escaped. Now the old man was tracking her again.

As they continued along the interstate, then merged onto the turnpike, he sensed that his moment of retribution was being postponed. If so, that was fine. Tzaddikim knew how to be patient. They could wait forever, if necessary. And he knew that his time was coming soon.

54

The voice emerging from the speakerphone, transformed by distance into a metallic rasp, was that of a forensic examiner in Fort Detrick, Maryland. He sounded worried. "You're sure that nobody else touched this thing?"

"Yes, we're sure," Powell said, leaning across the table to talk into the phone. "The agent acted in accordance with his training. As soon as he realized what he had, he sealed it off and alerted his unit commander."

The speakerphone rasped again. "And where's the agent who handled the device?"

"He's under observation," Barlow said. "Quarantined. Until we know what the fuck it is we're dealing with."

They were seated in Barlow's office, along with Wolfe. Spread before them was a series of photos depicting, from various angles, a single lens reflex camera that an agent had found in a drawer at the club. As the agent was examining it, the back of the camera had come off in his hands. Within the hour, it had been airlifted to the bioforensics lab for analysis.

"We've completed our preliminary evaluation," the forensic examiner said. "The inner workings were removed from the camera and replaced with new components. A heating element vaporizes a solution in the central chamber, and a pressurized cartridge propels the atomized substance across a limited area when the shutter release button is pressed."

Wolfe took notes on her copy of the pictures. "Any idea what this stuff could be?"

"It looks a lot like a drug called pravastatin. In large doses, it can cause adverse skin reactions, including toxic epidermal necrolysis, as well as psychological effects like anxiety and paranoia. In most cases, they aren't nearly as severe as the symptoms you've reported, but a weaponized version might be responsible for what you saw in Archvadze. And the dog."

Powell made a note of this. Following one of his hunches, agents had used a methane probe to uncover a dog that had been buried in the yard of the house where Ilya had been staying. The dog, though badly decomposed, had shown symptoms similar to what he had seen in Archvadze, with most of its fur and skin eaten away. "So this drug is some kind of lethal agent."

"That's how it looks. From what I can tell, it's perfect for assassination. The dosage is small, and it can be easily inhaled."

"One question," Wolfe said, looking up from the photos. "When the chemical was deployed, several guests at the party were standing nearby. Why haven't they shown any symptoms?"

"My best guess is that we're dealing with a binary weapon," the forensic examiner said. "Two separate substances are required, each one relatively harmless in itself. One component is inhaled as a vapor, while the other might be absorbed through the skin. It could be a gel rubbed onto the body, for example, or brushed onto a doorknob or steering wheel—"

Powell remembered what Archvadze had said at the hospital. "Or a cell phone?"

"It's possible. In the past, they've spread contact poisons, like cadmium, on telephone receivers. This wouldn't be so different."

"Let's be clear here," Barlow said. "When you say *they*, who are you talking about?"

"Russian intelligence," the forensic examiner said. He seemed surprised by the question. "This murder has their fingerprints all over it. We're looking at a textbook example of covert assassination."

"Great," Barlow said, although he did not seem at all happy about this. "We'll touch base with you again soon."

Barlow pressed a button on the phone, ending the call. He sat back in his chair with a peculiar expression, like a climber working his way across a difficult rock face. "So what do you think?"

"He's right," Wolfe said. "This was a political murder. Whoever was behind this assassination wanted to send a message. They made sure to kill him as slowly and agonizingly as possible."

Barlow looked pained. "Counterintelligence will be all over us. Compared to this, the guns are nothing."

Powell remained silent. If it turned out that they had overlooked an assassination plot in their haste to pursue the weapons angle, the assistant director would not hesitate to transfer the investigation to a separate division. In order to retain control of the case, they had to make it seem as if they had been following this lead from the beginning. And as Powell felt Barlow's eyes on his own, he found that he knew exactly what the other man was thinking.

"A FISA court approved our warrant for the wiretap of Sharkovsky's phone," Barlow said carefully. "The existence of our request demonstrates that we were concerned that he might be the agent of a foreign power. Powell, in your deposition, you made sure to mention this fact?"

"Yes," Powell said. "However, the emphasis of the warrant was on his possible ties to terrorist groups. I seem to remember that I was strongly encouraged to make that connection—"

Barlow dismissed this with a wave of his hand. "That's irrelevant. What matters is that we have you testifying, on the record, that the mob is a tool of foreign intelligence. When you come right down to it, that's how we got our warrant. Which means that we've been pursuing this angle all along." He picked up his phone. "I'll arrange for you to brief the executive assistant director."

"I thought that you saw me as a liability," Powell said. "Why do you want me there?"

"Why do I want you there?" Barlow looked genuinely surprised. "Because you're the agent in charge of this case."

As Barlow dialed, it occurred to Powell that he had won. For now, at least, the gradients of power, which had been turned against him for so long, were flowing in his direction. His first thought, strangely, was to call his father, although he knew that the old man would forget the conversation at once. A moment later, the impulse passed, caught up in the wave of work that remained to be done.

Powell rose. As he gathered up his notes, his eye was caught by a photo of the camera. He remembered the oligarch's last words, forced out of his dying lungs. Somehow he had understood that a camera had been used to kill him. Powell wondered how he had known this.

Looking at the photo, he saw a word in his mind's eye, in blurred Cyrillic characters, as it might have appeared to the dying man. It was then that he realized that the oligarch had not been talking about a camera at all.

Камера. In Russian, it meant *chamber.* A room, a cell. It made him think of the vault in which the painting had been kept, the hospital room in which Archvadze had died, and even of the installation itself. But beyond these obvious connotations lay something else, something deeper, darker—

Powell's fingertips grew cold, but as he picked up his notes, his hands did not tremble. He maintained an impassive expression until he had left the office, the skin tingling on his face, then turned to Wolfe. "Meet me in the kitchen in an hour. I need to make some calls."

Before she could ask him why, he had retrieved his jacket from its hook. Opening his cell phone, he checked to make sure that the numbers he needed were there, then headed for the elevator.

He spent most of the following hour in a café across the street, speaking first with a former colleague at the Met and then with a contact at the Security Service. After calling in a request to evidence control, he met Wolfe in the office kitchen, where he explained what he had found. "Archvadze knew who killed him. He told me before he died. Remember his last words?"

Wolfe, seated at the table, took a sip of cocoa from a stained ceramic mug. "*Camera.*"

"Right. But he wasn't trying to tell me that a camera was involved. He was telling me who made the poison. Kamera, or chamber, was a code name for Laboratory Twelve. The poison laboratory of the Soviet secret services."

"I've heard of these guys," Wolfe said. "Weren't they involved in the Markov case?"

"And others. The Soviets were always big on poisons. Kamera was their most ambitious project. Its mandate was to develop poisons that wouldn't appear in a conventional autopsy. They experimented with mustard gas, digitoxin, ricin. They conducted tests on convicts in prison. And they've been implicated in at least one murder, that of a journalist investigating an intelligence scandal, where the victim died of toxic epidermal necrolysis. So if they went after Archvadze, too—"

"—he might have been doing something similar," Wolfe said. "All right. Let's say he's conducting an investigation into something that would embarrass state intelligence. They get wind of it and arrange for him to be silenced. It wouldn't be worth the trouble unless he had found something big. But what?"

"I can think of one possibility. Let's say that state intelligence is trafficking in stolen art to raise money for covert operations. If they were working with organized crime to move art out of Russia, it's possible that Archvadze got his hands on evidence of this. Or almost did."

"You're talking about Budapest," Wolfe said. "The

courier was going to cut a deal with Archvadze, but someone else got to him first. Then they went after the oligarch himself, using a method that gave him dementia and paranoia, so that nobody would believe his story—"

"It's possible. And if we're right, I'll bet that Archvadze tried to get his hands on stolen art before. Hence his secret collection. He was buying art to investigate its origins and make the connection to state intelligence. And if that was his plan, maybe this painting was the smoking gun."

Wolfe stood. "So we need to look at the other paintings in his collection. If Archvadze bought them from someone he suspected was trafficking in stolen art, there has to be a record of it. His lawyer might be willing to talk. And we can access the provenance data online."

"Do it," Powell said. They left the kitchen together. "But keep it to yourself for now. I don't want to run it past Barlow until we're absolutely sure. If we go to him with a partial case—"

"—he'll think we're stalling," Wolfe said. "I know. Let's compare notes in an hour."

As she headed down the corridor, Powell returned to his cubicle, where he found the package that he had requested from evidence control. It was the stretcher from Ilya's hotel room. It still bore the manila tag used to mark evidence in storage, but otherwise, it seemed untouched.

Turning the stretcher over, he examined its other side, which would be hidden whenever the canvas was put on display. It was a simple wooden armature with a strut running across the middle, marked with exhibition stickers, gallery labels, and douane stamps. Looking at it, he remembered what the oligarch had said before he died. Not the front. The back.

His eye was drawn to the largest label, which ran across the central strut. It was made of thin paper and pasted directly to the wood. *Ch. Pottier / Emballeur / 14 Rue Gaillon / Paris.* Even with his bad French, he could tell that it was the label of a packing company that had crated the canvas at some point in its long history. And yet something about the label seemed strange.

Powell reached out and took the uppermost corner of the label in his fingers. When he pulled, it peeled away from the stretcher with surprising ease, revealing the wood underneath. Something had been written on the strut beneath the label, a row of letters painted hastily with a fine brush. He tugged at the label until the first four letters were exposed, then paused.

Underneath the label, there was a hidden message, and its first four letters said ROSE.

55

On Market Street in Philadelphia, beneath the old post office, vans were selling Jamaican food, the aroma of jerk chicken carving out pockets of spice in the air. Maddy emerged from the bus, following a line of passengers onto the sidewalk. As she passed the driver, she tried to give him a smile, something to show that she was all right, but was unable to do so.

Walking past the train station, she began to feel better, as if the indifferent industrial settings were surrounding and protecting her. Compared to the blind grandeur of industry, the Rosicrucians seemed almost insignificant. The world was run by bureaucrats and engineers, not an occult brotherhood. They were not as powerful as the banks. They were not as powerful as compound interest.

On the other side of the bridge, however, as she neared the string of museums that ran along the parkway, this argument seemed less tenable. She averted her eyes from the windows she passed, afraid that they would reveal that she had gone mad, and it was only belatedly that she noticed, waiting at a crosswalk for the light to change, that she was standing in front of a hardware store.

She went inside. Passing a glass display case, she saw,

to her surprise, that she didn't look half bad. The bruises on her face had faded, and her eyes no longer had that haunted look. If she had seen a hint of insanity, she might have turned back, but this glimpse of her old self was enough to keep her going.

Picking up a basket, she wandered through the store, pulling objects off the shelves at random. A canvas bag came first, followed by a hammer, a putty knife, a painter's apron, and a set of box cutters. As she drifted down the aisles, she told herself that she was buying these things only as a precaution, in case the installation did not give up its secrets at once. She was going to the museum only to look.

And in any case, she said silently to herself, there was no harm in being prepared.

The obvious way inside was through the wooden door itself. Duchamp had bought the door in a small town near Cadaqués, and the double doors had been sawn in half, resulting in four panels that were roughly the same size. These panels were secured together at the back with thin strips of wood, and were hung on a metal track, allowing them to be slid apart so pictures could be taken of the interior.

As she took her purchases to the cashier, however, she was bothered by another recollection. The components of the installation were very fragile, grass and wire and calfskin, and required their own microclimate to keep them from deteriorating further. Therefore, at some point, contrary to Duchamp's intentions, the tableau behind the doors had been protected by a glass panel.

Remembering this, she felt a renewed sense of despair. It would be all but impossible to get past the glass. Even if she managed to do it without killing herself, the noise would bring the guards within seconds.

The clerk rang up her purchases one by one. "Anything else I can help you find?"

She was about to shake her head, her thoughts elsewhere, when she noticed a package hanging on the wall behind the cash register. It was a blister pack of four porcelain spark plugs. Looking at it, she recalled a piece of lore from her delinquent adolescence. "Can I get those spark plugs, please?"

"Sure." The clerk took down the spark plugs and added them to her order. "Thirty-four dollars and eighteen cents."

She gave him two twenties, which represented all of her remaining cash. Declining a bag, she pushed the tools into the canvas tote, laying the apron on top to hide the rest, and left the store with change in hand.

Feeling adequately equipped, she headed for the museum. As she walked along the parkway, she found that she had no conception of what would happen when she was facing the installation at last. It was easy to envision the steps leading up to that moment, but when she got to the point of standing before the wooden door itself, the screen in her head went blank.

Crossing the oval, she reached the steps of the museum. As always, tourists were running up the steps and posing alongside the statue of the boxer that had been erected on the sidewalk. Maddy was feeling less than triumphant, so she merely trudged upward, the tote bag bouncing lightly against her thigh.

When she had reached the top of the steps, she paused, looking out at the museum's Greek Revival façade. Its three wings formed a bracket shape, one directly before her, the others to either side.

She stood there for a full minute, watching visitors ascend the second flight of steps that led to the main entrance. Looking around the courtyard, trying to defer the moment when she would need to pass through those doors herself, she saw that the layout of the museum was perfectly symmetrical. The east and west wings mirrored each other exactly, with a sense of balance that was rigorously enforced.

A second later, she observed that this was not precisely true. There was, it seemed, a single asymmetrical element. Off to her right, at the center of the eastern portico, a window the size of an ordinary door had been set among the pillars, looking into one of the galleries on the lowest level. When she looked at the wing to her left, she saw that there was no corresponding window on the other side.

Looking at the anomalous window more closely, she took a sharp breath. Through the opening, she saw a vertical pane of glass divided by a horizontal strut, with faint images picked out on its surface. It was *The Large Glass*. The window opened on the room devoted to Duchamp.

She continued to look through the window, which was the only one that opened onto any of the galleries, convinced there was a message here that she was supposed to see. The gallery had been placed at the exact center of the eastern portico, and for reasons that she could not begin to imagine, a window had been installed there, and only there, disrupting the symmetry of the larger museum.

In the end, she tore herself away from the window and

forced herself to mount the main steps. Passing between the pillars, she paused briefly at the entrance. In the glass of the doors, she could see her reflection outlined against the afternoon sky. Although it was hard for her to make out the features of her face, she did not think that she looked like a lunatic.

She pushed open the door and went into the foyer. Behind her, the door swung shut. For a moment, except for the distant sounds of visitors in the courtyard, the space at the top of the steps was silent.

After a calculated pause, a figure emerged from the shadow cast by one of the pillars. Sharkovsky wore a watch cap pulled down to his eyebrows, along with sunglasses he had bought from a vendor near the museum. He waited for a few seconds, wanting to be sure that the girl would not reappear unexpectedly, then opened the door and followed her inside.

56

"Thanks for meeting with us on such short notice," Wolfe said, taking a seat in the conference room. She looked across the burnished table at her interviewee. "I hope it wasn't any trouble."

"Glad to help," Reynard said. "It isn't a problem. I was in the office anyway—"

Powell pulled up a chair beside Wolfe, placing his briefcase on the table. "Do you often work on the weekends?"

Reynard smiled. Beneath his confident features, there was a hint of strain. "It's been a rough week. How can I help you?"

Wolfe took the lead. "We'd like to ask you some questions about your database."

Reynard's expression remained neutral, but Powell detected a trace of uneasiness in the fund manager's eyes. "I was under the impression that you were investigating the incident in the Hamptons."

"We are," Wolfe said. "Your provenance database falls within the scope of our investigation." From her own briefcase, she removed a sheaf of photocopies. "As you probably know, Archvadze had an extensive art collection. As part of our investigation of the heist, we've been looking into the provenance of these paintings. Purchase records provided by his lawyer indicate that most of the works were bought from an art dealer named Alexey Lermontov. Do you know him?"

"I know who he is," Reynard said. "My job obliges me to know something about all the major dealers in this city. I'm not surprised that Lermontov was the source. He has an impressive client list."

"We know." Wolfe pushed the stack of photocopies across the table. "But something else was involved. Take a look at these."

Reynard examined the papers. "Provenance records. These belonged to Archvadze?"

"That's right," Wolfe said. "His lawyer has the originals, along with the sources that were used to compile the information. Archvadze commissioned a team of historians and art consultants, mostly from the Frick, to independently research the provenance of each painting that he acquired from Lermontov."

"It isn't uncommon for collectors to conduct their own provenance research. Filling out the provenance can be an effective way to increase the value of a painting. But I don't see why this is significant."

"After I received these documents, I became curious as to how much of this information was in the public domain," Wolfe said. "The obvious place to look was your database, which is freely available to researchers. But when I consulted the database, I found that the records didn't match up. For most of these paintings, the provenance history provided by your database and the data that Archvadze compiled on his own are completely different. How do you explain that?"

Reynard's smile grew wider. "There's no mystery here. Provenance information is often unreliable. Any art historian will tell you this. We've devoted thousands of employee hours to cleaning and checking the database, but discrepancies still appear from time to time. Without further investigation, there's no way to know if Archvadze's information is any more reliable than ours."

Powell was impressed by the fund manager's aura of calm, which he took as a challenge. "You may be right about that, but you're wrong if you think that Archvadze was only trying to increase the value of his collection. He never intended to resell those paintings. He bought them because he knew that Lermontov was moving stolen art from overseas. He was willing to spend millions of dollars to build his case, but always lacked a smoking gun. Until now."

Reaching for his briefcase, Powell undid the clasps and raised the lid. Inside was the wooden stretcher. He set it on the table, faceup, so that the marks on the other side were hidden from view.

Reynard's smile vanished, replaced by a look of pointed indifference. "What's this?"

"It's the stretcher from *Study for Étant Donnés*," Powell said. "The thief who stole the painting removed the canvas. We haven't recovered the painting yet, but the stretcher has been surprisingly instructive."

Turning the stretcher over, Powell tapped his finger against the strut that ran across the center. On the wood, painted in straggling black characters, were the words ROSENBERG BORDEAUX.

"Before the painting was sold at auction, someone pasted a forged label across these words, hiding them," Powell said. "We don't know who was responsible, but we suspect that the forgery took place in Russia, which is where this painting resided in recent years. You recognize the words?"

Reynard's face was very still, like a waxen cast of its former self. "No, I don't."

"They indicate that this painting was, at one point in its history, part of the collection of Paul Rosenberg, who was one of the most important Jewish art dealers and collectors in the Paris of the thirties and forties. He represented Picasso, Braque, and Matisse, along with many other artists. At the start of World War II, he fled to the United States, leaving the bulk of his collection at a bank in Bordeaux. The following year, it was seized by the Nazis."

Powell pointed to a square of paper pasted to the stretcher, which had also been concealed by the false packing label. It bore the words DUCHAMP / ROSENBERG / NIKOLSBURG / 2.12.1941. "This label indicates that the painting was taken to Nikolsburg Castle in the Sudetenland, which was a storage facility for looted art, including works owned by collectors who died in the death camps."

Reynard examined the label, but did not visibly react. "I still don't know why you're showing this to me."

"We're getting there," Wolfe said, taking up the thread. "When the Russian army occupied Czechoslovakia near the end of the war, the castle ended up in the hands of the Soviets. The official story is that the castle was burned in the fighting, along with all the paintings inside. However, catalogs and other documents from the

Rosenberg collection have been found in an archive in Moscow, which has led historians to conclude that the art was taken secretly to Russia."

"It was state policy," Powell said. "Russia had assembled a task force of its own, the Trophy Commission, to seize art and valuables as its army smashed through Germany. They saw it as a form of retribution, reparations for twenty million dead soldiers and civilians. Some of these works were returned, but others, like this one, disappeared. Based on other hidden marks on this painting, which our art crime team is still working to identify, our best guess is that it spent the past sixty years in a vault controlled by Russian intelligence."

"In recent years, with the breakdown of more conventional methods of money laundering, these paintings have reappeared on the market as a means of financing covert operations," Wolfe said. "We believe that Archvadze learned that Lermontov, while posing as a sophisticated art dealer, was actually the leading paymaster of Russian agents in the United States. More recently, he's branched out into arms trafficking, but he built his fortune on looted art. Many of these works were owned by men and women who died in the Holocaust."

Reynard's face, although still fixed, had gone pale. "And Archvadze told you this?"

"Archvadze is dead," Powell said. "He was poisoned at his own home, on the night of the heist, with a binary weapon provided by the assassination laboratory of the Russian secret services. He was killed because he was getting too close to the truth. Or didn't you know this already?"

"You still haven't explained why you're telling me

this." Reynard's voice was very quiet, as if he did not trust himself to retain control at a higher volume. "This has nothing to do with me."

"But it does," Wolfe said. "Faking provenance was simple in the past, when sale and ownership information was opaque and easy to falsify. These days, however, most of this information is online, which makes it much more transparent. In order for the flow of stolen art to continue, Lermontov had to find a way to fake provenance in public databases. Especially yours."

A point of color appeared in each of Reynard's cheeks. "If the database contains false information, I take full responsibility. But it doesn't mean that I, or anyone else at this firm, approved the deception."

"That's hard to believe," Wolfe said. "I know something about your business model. You use algorithms to search for anomalies in the information you've gathered, both to catch bad data and to identify potential investments. Provenance history that seems inconsistent with similar works by the same artist is exactly the kind of deviation that your algorithms are designed to discover. Lermontov's fake provenances should have sounded the alarm. But they didn't."

"There's only one explanation," Powell said. "It was deliberate. Which would only be possible if someone built a back door into the system, a way to override your database's internal checks. As far as we can tell, you're the only person at this firm with the access and authority to do so."

There was a pause. Reynard's mouth was pressed in a tight line, like that of an angel on a gravestone. "What do you want from me?"

Wolfe handed him a sheet of paper with a Bureau letterhead. "We're here to offer you a deal. Immunity in exchange for your testimony against Lermontov. You'll be treated as a confidential informant, so your name will stay out of the public record. This offer expires in exactly one minute."

Reynard studied the page as if he were reading a bad balance sheet. "And if I refuse?"

"We come back with a subpoena," Powell said. "We confiscate your records, the data on your servers, and the art in your storeroom uptown. And we'll make sure that the press gets there ten minutes before we do."

The fund manager's eyes grew dangerously bright. "You don't have any evidence."

"We don't need evidence to get what we want," Wolfe said. "You're already vulnerable. Investors are wondering if you can be trusted. If we raid that storeroom, it's over. You have two options. If you cooperate, you can walk away with your reputation intact. Refuse, and we bury you. The choice is yours."

Reynard only stared at the page. Watching him, Powell reflected that the agreement conceded a great deal, but they were running out of time. If they wanted to keep the case away from counterintelligence, they had to push the art trafficking angle at their briefing with the executive assistant director, which was only a few hours away. In the end, the fund manager, though a tempting target, was secondary. It was worth giving up their case against him for a stronger position against Lermontov.

When Reynard looked up, his eyes were cold. "If I'm doing this, I want protection."

"Of course," Wolfe said. "We have an interest in keeping you alive. Anything else?"

"No. There's nothing more that you could possibly do for me." Taking a pen from his breast pocket, Reynard signed the agreement. He contemplated his own signature for a moment, then said, "I want to make one thing clear. I knew that Lermontov was moving art, but he never said where it came from. We had a deal. He would be allowed to falsify information in our database, and in exchange, he'd feed me information about private art transactions."

Powell guessed that this was less than the complete truth, but decided not to force the issue. "What else did he ask you to do?"

Reynard exhaled. "Favors. Like bidding on the painting. He was the one who told me to buy it—" He broke off. "There's another thing. Maddy is in danger. Sharkovsky has orders to kill her in Philadelphia."

Powell looked up from his notes. For a second, he was unable to process what he had just heard. "*What?*"

"She got paranoid," Reynard said, a tremor appearing in his voice for the first time. "Most of what she said was nonsense, but along the way, she figured out that some of the provenance data was fake. Sharkovsky was sent to silence her, but she got away. Instead of going to the police, she took a bus to the Philadelphia Museum of Art. I don't know why. But he's following her there."

Powell's eyes fell on the immunity agreement on the surface of the table. In his mind, he saw Maddy's face, strangely confused with that of Karina Baranova. "If she dies, the deal is off."

"I know." Reynard's voice was toneless. "It isn't what I wanted. I had no choice—"

Wolfe, looking through her notepad, pulled out her

phone and dialed a number. "We need to warn her. If she turns herself in to the police, she should be safe until we can get her into protective custody."

As Wolfe waited for Maddy to answer the phone, Reynard turned to Powell. "I'm not a monster. You don't understand the kind of pressure I'm under. My investors depend on this fund's reputation. Endowments and pensions have entrusted me with their savings. If Maddy had gone public, it would have destroyed people's lives. Everything I've built for myself would be gone—"

Powell wondered if Reynard really believed what he was saying. He thought of the woman under the boards, her head and hands missing, her identity erased. Again, for an instant, he saw Maddy's face superimposed over that of the dead girl, and imagined how it would feel to see her body in the morgue.

A second later, Wolfe closed her cell phone. "No answer. It went to voicemail."

Powell looked at Reynard. They came to the same conclusion at once, but Powell was the first to speak. "She's turned off her phone," Powell said, rising from his chair. "She's at the museum now."

57

Maddy had switched off her phone a few moments earlier, out of sheer habit, soon after passing through the museum's doors. Inside, a wall was covered with the inscribed names of donors and trustees. She turned away from the roster, oddly afraid of what she might see there, but not before glimpsing the names of two of the dead: WALTER AND LOUISE ARENSBERG.

As she had expected, there was no bag check, and security was nonexistent. After buying a ticket, she went into the great hall. A wide stone staircase ran up one side of the room, with visitors seated on each of the steps. At the top, a bronze huntress pointed an arrow toward the main doors.

She entered the galleries, clutching the strap of her tote bag. The paintings were a blur, but as she passed one doorway, her eye was caught by the image of a woman lying naked before a seascape, her pose startlingly familiar. Going closer, she found that it was a nude by Courbet.

When she saw the artist's name, she discovered that the entire museum was speaking to her. This sensation was accompanied by an equally strong conviction that she was being watched. Turning, she saw that the gallery was empty except for a teenage couple staring at another nude, their fingers interlaced. No one was watching her. The only voyeur here was herself.

She returned to the main line of galleries. Two rooms later, she passed a painting by Paul Gauguin, who had read Rosicrucian books on the beaches of Tahiti. It was a picture of a yellow hill, the grass dry, girded by a fence decorated with human skulls. A smoldering idol perched on its crest. The caption helpfully noted that the hill was a sacred enclosure where human sacrifices took place.

After entering a rotunda with an obsidian fountain, she rounded a corner into the eastern wing. The nineteenth century fell away, replaced by modern and contemporary art. Here, for instance, was a sculpture by Max Ernst, a bronze idol with two circles for eyes and a larger circle for its howling mouth. The caption said that Ernst had once taken the sculpture into a hayfield, laying it in the grass so that he could view it under the light of the moon.

A few rooms later, before she was ready for it, she entered the Duchamp wing.

On the wall beside the door, a placard read *MARION BOULTON STROUD GALLERY*. She glanced at it briefly, vaguely recognizing the name of a dead patron of the arts, but then her perspective shifted and the words disappeared, replaced by another set that had been concealed by lenticular lenses. When she saw these new words, she knew that this room, too, had been prepared for her arrival.

The hidden words, revealed as if by an act of magic, were *GALERIE RROSE SÉLAVY*.

Maddy moved farther into the gallery. Visitors drifted

between the works on display, passing through on their way to the next obligatory stop on the tour. To one side hung an early work by Duchamp, the portrait of a bearded man whose left hand glowed with an otherworldly light, as if it had been dipped in phosphorescence. The anomalous window stood nearby.

To her left, a doorway led to a small room adjacent to the main gallery. The room was dim and nondescript, with no indication of what lay inside. She did not want to go into it yet, but knew that she had no choice. Gathering the remaining shreds of her courage, she crossed the threshold.

Her initial response was one of disappointment. The room was small and shabby, like a penitent's cell. Under her feet, there was a soiled carpet, in contrast to the other galleries, which were floored with concrete. A wooden door stood to her left, taking up most of the wall. The door was weathered and worn, set into an archway of real bricks. There was nothing else.

But through a pair of tiny holes, drilled at eye level, a cool white light was visible.

Maddy looked up at the ceiling. There were no cameras. From the main gallery, it was impossible to see the wooden door, which was set perpendicular to the entrance. Reassured by her apparent solitude, she went up to the door, catching the scent of fragrant wood, and bent her face to the eyeholes.

Her first impression was that she was looking at her own corpse. For a second, it was as if a window had opened on the past, and she knew, with horrifying certainty, that she had died on the floor of Ethan's apartment, and all that followed had been nothing but a fantasy generated by her dying brain.

Then her vision cleared, and she saw that she was looking at a different body, a nude woman lying in the grass, her face concealed by the edge of a brick wall, a lamp shining in one hand. Pictures did not do justice to the persuasiveness of the illusion, the Lake Geneva landscape remarkably convincing, a waterfall sparkling in the background, an effect created by a rotating disc and a lightbulb in a biscuit tin. *While living, I made this compact copy of the universe, my grave—*

A second later, she grew convinced that someone was standing just outside the room, watching her in silence. She pulled away from the eyeholes, looking over her shoulder, but the doorway was empty.

Maddy turned back to the wooden door, her paranoia dissipating, and looked inside again. After a long moment, she knew. Whatever the answer was, she would not find it from here. Part of her wanted to pull back now, when it was still possible, but deep down, she saw that even as she boarded the bus to Philadelphia, she had known in her heart that there was no other way.

She forced herself to concentrate. Her first task was to determine if the installation was, in fact, protected by glass. Through the eyeholes, she thought that she could detect a breeze, perhaps the hum of an air conditioner. Then she saw a tiny smudge hovering a few inches from her eyes. It was a fingerprint.

"Goddamn it," Maddy whispered. Judging from the print, the glass was a good eight inches behind the door. It would not be hard to break through the wood, but the glass was another issue entirely.

Maddy left the darkened room and went back into the gallery, which was empty. Taking a seat on the bench, she unfolded a map of the museum across her lap. On the map, each of the rooms was numbered. Adjoining the room with the wooden door, however, she saw a room with no visible entrance or exit. It was the only unnumbered square in the entire museum.

She went into the next gallery, which was also deserted, with gleaming sculptures by Constantin Brâncuşi arranged in a kind of altar. If there was a way into the hidden room, it had to be here.

Sure enough, to one side of the altar, she saw a closed door with no visible markings. Sensing that it was necessary to move boldly, she went up to the door and tried it. It was a sliding door with a recessed handle below the keyhole, and it slid an eighth of an inch before catching on the latch. The door itself was thick and heavy. She stood there for a moment, hoping that she would see another way inside, but was finally compelled to accept the inevitable.

A few startled tears sprang into her eyes. Fuck the men who were trying to kill her. Fuck Ethan for leaving her alone. She had never asked for this. Her one source of consolation, in this moment of utter loneliness, was that by breaking into the installation, she was knocking the pieces from the board.

A restroom lay in the direction from which she had come. Maddy retraced her steps, ignoring the persistent sense that she was being watched. Pushing open the door of the ladies' room, she went inside.

The bathroom was empty. Maddy entered the stall farthest from the entrance and shut the door behind her. She emptied out her canvas tote, placing the tools on the floor, and used the box cutter to slice open the pack of spark plugs. When she was done, she slid the box cutter into her pocket, removed the spark plugs, and put one of them inside the empty bag.

Wrapping the canvas securely around the spark plug, she set it on the toilet seat, took the hammer, and shattered the plug with two sharp blows. The sound of porcelain breaking was muffled, but still audible in the bathroom's close confines. She set the hammer aside and opened the bag. The spark plug had fragmented into several irregular shards. Fishing around with her fingers, she chose two of the largest pieces and slipped them into her other pocket.

Maddy replaced the tools in her bag. The remaining spark plugs and blister pack went into the garbage. Then she washed her hands and emerged into the corridor, heading for the Galerie Rrose Sélavy.

58

Years ago, in Moscow, a boy of fifteen had waited in a restaurant, listening to an old man explain how to follow a person without being seen. The *vor* had revealed a mouthful of yellow teeth whenever he chewed a piece of salted fish, washing it down with vodka; the boy, who had not been offered a taste, had been young and bursting with ambition, but he had also been smart enough to listen.

"You think you're ready," the old man had said, his breath sour with pickled vegetables. "But shooting a drunk in the back of the head and following a cautious man through the city are two different things. You always want two men. If one gets picked up, the other takes over. Put yourself where he is going to be, not where he is now. And when the time is right, you gun him down."

Now, many years later, Sharkovsky thought back to that old conversation. Before the girl appeared at the museum, he retrieved a copy of the floor plan from a trash bin at the foot of the steps. The east entrance, where he was standing, was the most prominent, but another set of doors lay to the west. Even if the girl entered here, there was no guarantee that she would leave by the same way.

When the girl appeared at last, then, he silently followed

her into the museum, hanging one or more rooms behind unless there was reason to go closer. Before long, he began to guess where she was going, and was not surprised when she entered the darkened room adjacent to the main gallery. She remained there for a long time before emerging, her features intense and pale. Before heading after her, he lingered behind for a second, then slipped into the tiny room.

Inside the cramped space, he saw the wooden door, and understood immediately that there was something of value behind it. Going up to the eyeholes, he peered inside. At first, the sight made him smile, but when he considered what the girl might be planning, it stifled his amusement at once.

He turned away from the eyeholes. As he had expected, she was still in the gallery next door. Glancing inside, he saw her trying a door next to the altar, one that could only lead into the rear of the installation he had just left. It was not difficult to guess what she had in mind.

When the girl headed for the bathroom, Sharkovsky retreated into another gallery. As he waited for her to come out, his eye and jaw continued to ache. It was hard to think clearly through the fog of pain, but he forced himself to focus. If the girl broke into the installation, the guards would appear at once, taking her out of his reach forever. There would be no room for error.

After she emerged from the restroom, Sharkovsky tracked her at a distance until she returned to the gallery. From around the corner, he watched as she took a seat on a bench, looking fixedly at the upright panels of glass on display, which caught the rays of the sun through a nearby window. Reaching beneath his sweatshirt, he checked his revolver, then withdrew into the next room.

As the minutes ticked away, the girl remained on the bench, not moving, her eyes on the work of art before her. Her hands were folded in her lap, the canvas tote bag over one shoulder. Around her, other visitors drifted singly and in pairs. She ignored them, or so it seemed, as if there were nothing on her mind except the masterwork that stood a few feet away.

Maddy, for her part, was really looking at the guards, two of whom were posted in this wing. Every few minutes, one would peek into the gallery, sweep an eye across the room, and leave. It was half an hour before closing time, and the crowds had gradually diminished.

At last, she watched as one of the guards, a woman, passed through the gallery, then left through the door at the far end of the room. There was no one else in sight. For the moment, she was alone.

She forced herself to stand. The room with the installation was a few steps to her left. Moving forward, she approached the doorway, a shuddering void in her chest where her heart should have been, and went inside.

Before her stood the wooden door, light shining through its eyeholes. She reached into her bag and removed the putty knife. Approaching the installation, she inserted the knife in the vertical seam between the two halves of the door. With her hands gripping the handle tightly, she slid the blade upward, feeling it snag on the strip of wood that held the panels together.

Maddy forced the knife farther up, the wood splintering, and felt the blade break through. She withdrew the knife and let it fall to the floor. Reaching out, she took hold of the upper panels, as if opening a pair of shutters. Under her fingers, the wood was rough but fragile. When she drew the panels apart, they slid open like barn doors, guided by an unseen metal track.

Behind the panels hung a curtain of velvet with an opening cut for the eyeholes. Pulling this curtain aside as well, she was met by her reflection in the glass. When her focus shifted, she saw the chamber. A short intervening space was lined with more velvet. At the end of it, four feet away, lay a brick wall with an irregular opening through which the body in the grass was visible.

Reaching into her pocket, she removed the two shards of porcelain. She set one of the pieces on the floor, keeping it in reserve in case her first attempt failed, then weighed the other shard in her hand. It was no larger than the joint of her thumb, but she knew that it would be enough.

She remembered what she had once learned in a high school parking lot. Tempered glass was under tremendous pressure. If breached at any point with something small and sufficiently dense, it would shatter cleanly.

It was not necessary to throw it very hard. Rearing back, she concentrated on a point at the center of the glass, as if aiming for the body's hairless gash, and tossed the shard smoothly forward.

The result was astonishing. As soon as it was struck by the porcelain, the glass disintegrated, making a soft tinkle as thousands of fragments, like snow or sleet, rained down to the floor. She was amazed that it had worked so well. Only a few frosty stalactites still hung from the top of the installation. Using her bag like a cudgel, she knocked away the remaining pieces, feeling cold air on her face.

Maddy went into the chamber, her feet crunching in the glass, and found herself in a cramped space hung with black velvet, like the interior of a photographer's hood. The air was cool, with an odor of moldering cloth. Turning briefly around, she drew the sliding doors shut behind her, leaving only a narrow gap. As she approached the opening in the wall, she felt a trickle of warmth along her right arm. Looking down, she saw that she had cut her elbow.

Through the opening in the brick, the dummy lay on the table. Now that she was inside the chamber, rather than looking through the eyeholes, its careful mimesis fell apart. The trees in the background were nothing but ink and paint, with a sheet of blue plywood and some wads of cotton standing in for sky.

Up close, the figure lying in the grass, rather than a woman's naked body, seemed like a dismembered doll. It did, in fact, have a head, which was normally hidden by the bricks. The area where the face should have been was covered in a blond wig, as if the head had been twisted brutally around.

Maddy reached through the opening, which was large enough for her head and shoulders, and took the dummy in her arms. As she lifted it, twigs snapping and breaking, the body came apart in three pieces. The largest piece, the one with the torso, turned out to be a framework covered with calfskin. Another piece consisted of the hand and forearm. The last piece was the left thigh, which detached itself from its socket as she hauled it up from the table.

Beneath her hands, the dummy was brittle, carefully painted to look like human flesh. When she reached around to where the figure's back should have been, she found that the armature was hollow, like half of an industrial mold. As she raised it, the head fell backward, nearly spilling off the neck.

Maddy turned the figure over. When she saw the struts

of the underlying framework, which was lined with gray putty over a grid of wire, she was seized by a deepening horror. There was no interior, just half of a shell, with nothing to be found underneath. No secret. No message.

She ran her hands across the armature, searching frantically for something, anything, that would justify what she had done. After an endless second, her fingers found a lump at the base of the figure's neck where the spinal column would have been. Something was buried in the putty.

Maddy pulled the figure through the opening in the wall. She heard something crack as she turned it upright. Taking the box cutter from her pocket, she extended the blade and began to chop at the putty on the neck's inner surface, her elbow and forearm slick with blood.

Caught up in the work at hand, she did not notice the shadow that had fallen across the entrance to the chamber. Sharkovsky looked through the gap, seeing the girl's head outlined against the light. He felt a flicker of regret that he would not have a chance to prolong his retribution, but the feeling passed.

Raising the gun, he aimed at the back of her head and pulled the trigger. The gunshot was loud in the confined space. A hole appeared in the girl's skull, light visible through the clean aperture, and she fell forward, dead at once.

Sharkovsky lowered the gun. He was about to turn away when he realized, belatedly, that instead of the damp explosion of a bullet striking bone, he had heard a dull whump. He had shot the dummy by mistake.

He raised the gun again. As his vision adjusted to the dim light, he could see Maddy staring at him, the dummy lolling back in her arms, her eyes wide. She opened her mouth to speak.

"No last words," Sharkovsky said. He aimed, his finger tensing on the trigger—

—and then his body convulsed, an electric surge of pain traveling along the highways of his nerves. His hand spasmed, pulling the trigger, the bullet sinking harmlessly into the ceiling. The room tilted like a fairground ride, and then the floor came up to strike him on the side of the face.

Sharkovsky lay on the carpet, trying to move his arms and legs, his mind caught in useless suspension. He wondered if this was how it felt to die. With an effort that struck him as heroic, he rolled his eyes upward, taking in the shadowy figure standing above him. The shadow let the stun gun drop to the floor, then knelt and pried the *vor*'s fingers away from the revolver.

Ilya straightened up, pointing the gun at the man on the ground. Out of the corner of his eye, he saw that the girl in the chamber was staring at him. Without turning his head, Ilya asked quietly, "Are you all right?"

Maddy did not reply. A second later, she allowed the body to drop from her hands. She followed it to the floor, slumping against a curtain of velvet, blood streaming from the wound in her elbow.

Ilya turned back to Sharkovsky, gun still raised. As the old man's gaze met his own, he sensed that their long story was reaching its conclusion. Faintly, he heard footsteps and shouts.

Behind him, hands clenched, Maddy forced herself to her feet. Her face was pale, but her eyes remained fixed on his. "*Don't*—"

Ilya glanced at her, surprised, then turned back to Sharkovsky. He aimed the revolver at the *vor*'s good eye. And then he paused.

There was more than one kind of balance to consider. If he killed Sharkovsky, the full remembrance of his crimes would die along with him. Memory was a fragile thing. It did not persist beyond the lives of the men involved, which lasted for only a moment. There were other debts, too, that had yet to be paid. And as he felt the girl's eyes on his face, it occurred to him that there might be another way.

He lowered the gun. Reaching into the bag at his side, he removed a cardboard tube and placed it in the old man's arms. Sharkovsky stared up at him, a crust of froth on his lips, his eyes throwing sparks of hatred.

Ilya was turning away when he saw something on the floor. Recognizing it, he picked it up, the shard strangely heavy in his hand. He closed his fist around it. Then, eyes meeting Maddy's for one last time, he left the room.

Outside, the gallery was packed with guards and visitors. At the sight of the gun, they fell back. Looking past their startled faces, Ilya observed that both of the exits were blocked.

Without pausing, he went to the window that looked out onto the courtyard. He tossed the porcelain shard underhand, as if skipping a stone on a pond. The heavy glass clouded but did not shatter. He shot the window twice, then lunged forward, head down, and plowed through to the other side, falling to the courtyard below. Through the window, a breeze ran through the gallery for the first time in years, carrying with it the sounds of the unseen city.

59

When Maddy awoke, her first impression was that she was dreaming. She was draped in what felt like a gossamer dressing gown, loose around the shoulders, the kind that a heroine might wear in a gothic romance. Before her eyes hung a diaphanous curtain, as if she were lying in a canopy bed. A bracelet encircled her wrist. Off to one side, an unseen object glowed with an unsteady light.

A moment later, her head cleared, and she saw that what she had taken for a canopy was a translucent sheet strung along a rod next to the bed, that her gown was fastened at the back with twill tape, and that the bracelet around her wrist was a plastic identification tag.

Someone was seated nearby. It was Powell. He was leaning back in an armless chair, reading a hardcover book. Without the slightest sense of surprise, she saw that it was a biography of Duchamp.

Maddy sat halfway up, the sheets sliding smoothly beneath her body. The glow to her left turned out to be a rack of medical monitors. A pulse oximeter was clipped to her finger. "Am I under arrest?"

Powell looked up. "Because of certain extenuating

circumstances, the museum won't be pressing charges. How do you feel?"

"I'm fine," Maddy said automatically. A second later, she realized that this statement was true. Her elbow warmly throbbed. Looking down, she saw that the gash in her arm had been sutured and bandaged. At first, she was unable to remember how she had cut herself, and then the memory of what she had done came rushing back. She sank back against her pillow. "Fuck."

"Try not to move too much," Powell said. "You lost consciousness at the museum, partly from shock and blood loss, but also because of some other issues. We need to keep you under observation for a few days."

Maddy pressed the heel of her hand against her forehead. "The man who came after me—"

"Sharkovsky, you mean? He's in federal custody. You don't need to worry about him. The man who saved your life incapacitated him before he escaped. He returned the painting, too. We're not sure why. As far as we can tell, it's undamaged. Unlike the installation."

The memory of the man at the installation reminded her of why she had broken into it in the first place. "You need to listen to me," Maddy said, trying to express her thoughts in a manner that would not seem insane. "I'm not safe here. They're going to come after me. The Rosicrucians—"

"They don't exist," Powell said gently. "At least not in the way you believed. There was a conspiracy, yes, but nothing occult was involved, only secrecy and greed. Lermontov and Reynard were trafficking in stolen art. When Ethan found out, Lermontov killed him. I'm sorry."

Maddy looked down at the rumpled bedsheet. When she searched herself for anger or shock, she found that she had been hollowed out, leaving only an armature behind. "Tell me what happened."

As she lay back, feeling the pillow press against the nape of her neck, Powell told her what he knew. When he was done, Maddy stared up at the acoustic tiles of the ceiling. "What about Reynard?"

"He cut a deal," Powell said. "Immunity in exchange for his testimony. We're keeping him in protective custody until we figure out what to do with him. Lermontov is missing. We don't know if he'll come after you, but you need to be careful. And if I were you, I'd start looking for another job."

Maddy managed to smile at this, but then, to her astonishment, the room around her dissolved, and she began to cry. When she turned back to Powell, she saw that he was holding out a tissue. Accepting it, she blew her nose. "Tell me about the oligarch. What was he really doing?"

"I suppose you deserve an explanation." Powell picked up his book again, toying with the dust jacket. "Archvadze spent much of his life trying to undermine Russian policy in Georgia. Lately, he'd stepped up his activities in response to the unrest in South Ossetia. A year ago, he learned that state intelligence, with the help of the mob, was financing its activities with stolen art, and resolved to turn this knowledge into a weapon. After determining that the art was moving through one particular gallery, he began using intermediaries to buy paintings from Lermontov. He accumulated an impressive array of evidence, but what he needed was tangible proof."

Drying her eyes, Maddy remembered the bad paintings on the oligarch's walls, and realized that they had been deliberate distractions. "And he thought that this painting was the proof he needed?"

"He made sure of it. One of his contacts told him that a particularly valuable work from the Rosenberg collection would be smuggled out soon. Normally, all traces of the painting's source and provenance would have been erased, but his contact arranged for the marks to be covered up instead. Archvadze planned to let Lermontov take delivery, then buy it on the other end, giving him an airtight case. But he made a mistake. He arranged to meet the courier in Budapest to verify that the marks were still there, but someone tipped off the mob first. The courier was killed and the painting vanished, until it reappeared at auction."

All at once, Maddy understood. "Lermontov told Reynard to bid on the painting."

"That's right. That night, he was watching from the skybox. Afterward, Reynard was going to give the painting to Lermontov, who would erase the provenance marks and return it to the fund. Reynard wasn't aware of the painting's true significance, at least not then. Archvadze, of course, knew exactly what it was, so he sent Kostava, his assistant, to bid on his behalf. What he didn't know was that the mob had once crossed paths with the very man he sent to the auction. And as soon as the bidder's face appeared in the press, the *mafiya* knew where the painting was."

"But if they knew this already, why did Reynard ask me to track down the buyer?"

"He wasn't told the buyer's name until afterward.

Once he found out who it was, he couldn't cancel the assignment without arousing suspicion. Later, when he found out that you had been at the party, he was afraid that you were there to tip off Archvadze. That's why you were put under surveillance."

"What about Lermontov? Why did he spin that story about the Rosicrucians?"

"He took a professional interest in secret societies. The secret of the Rosicrucians is that there *is* no secret. Power lies in the act of secrecy itself. In a sense, then, every intelligence agent is a Rosicrucian. Lermontov was a student of history, and he had thought deeply about his predecessors. When you came to him, he used the Rosicrucians to put you on the wrong track, knowing that it would only take you in circles. In the end, though, your paranoia led you to the truth. This was his fault as well. Did you touch anything at the mansion?"

The question took her by surprise. "A cell phone. We looked at the list of contacts."

"You both touched it?" Powell seemed satisfied by this. "I thought as much. You see, Archvadze was killed by a binary poison. One of the substances was sprayed on the target directly. The other was brushed on his phone."

Maddy remembered how Ethan had plucked the phone out of her hand. "What did it do to us?"

"From what I understand, paranoia is a known side effect of certain drugs that can cause toxic epidermal necrolysis. When you were exposed to half the weapon, you didn't develop the disease, but you did suffer psychological consequences. Paranoia, fixation, obsessive behavior. And because you were better at processing information than any sane person has a right to be, the paranoia that fed your delusions also allowed you to discover something real."

Maddy weighed this in silence. If she had resisted the temptation to look at the phone, she thought, Ethan might still be alive. "But I broke into the installation. I smashed the glass and tore it apart. I destroyed a masterpiece because I thought something was inside. Don't tell me that this wasn't insane—"

"Christ, I almost forgot to tell you." Powell withdrew a plastic bag from his pocket. "There was something there after all. The paramedics found it in the gurney. It looks like it was clutched in your fist."

He gave her the bag, which contained something tan and conical. She unsealed it and tipped it over the palm of her hand, allowing the small but heavy object to fall out. It was a chess pawn.

"You must have found it inside the dummy," Powell said. "As far as I know, the museum doesn't know about it yet. According to the book I've been reading, though, it looks like part of a chess set that Duchamp made for himself when he was living in Buenos Aires."

Maddy listened, but did not look away from the pawn. "So what does it mean?"

"Damned if I know. Duchamp was interested in chess, wasn't he? Well, I don't know much about chess, but I do know that a pawn that makes it all the way across the board becomes a queen."

Powell glanced at his watch. "I should probably give my father a call. And I'll let the doctor know you're awake. Be careful with that pawn. Who knows? It might even be worth something."

Maddy did not reply. As Powell left the room, she

kept her eyes on the pawn, which lay curled up in her hand like a chrysalis.

A sentence entered her mind without warning. Duchamp, in his will, had requested that no funeral be held after his death. He had been cremated, his ashes buried alongside those of his brothers, and his epitaph, which he had written himself, had been inscribed on a flat headstone. As she remembered it now, Maddy closed her hand over the pawn and squeezed it tightly:

D'AILLEURS, C'EST TOUJOURS LES AUTRES QUI MEURENT.
BESIDES, IT'S ALWAYS THE OTHER ONES WHO DIE.

EPILOGUE

Nobody knows what I lived on. This question, truly, does not have an exact answer . . . Life is more a question of expenses than of profits. It's a question of knowing what one wants to live with.

—Marcel Duchamp

The murdered man lay dead in his bath, the water tinged with blood, the abrupt gash of a knife visible below his collarbone. On the floor lay the knife itself, next to his dangling hand, in which a quill pen was grasped. His other hand clutched a letter, a bloody thumbprint staining the page.

"You know the story?" Lermontov asked. "He was in the bath, reading the note from Corday, when she stabbed him with the kitchen knife. He died at once, slumping over as you see him here, pen in one hand, letter in the other. But look. There is a bloody fingerprint on the page, but the hand with the letter is clean. So where did the fingerprint come from?"

Vasylenko studied the painting, which was on loan from the Royal Museum in Brussels. "When he raises his hand to defend himself, he gets blood on the note. Then, as he dies, his grip changes."

"But if that were true, wouldn't the note be spattered with blood? And wouldn't his fingers be bloody? No. The truth is altogether different. The prints belong to Charlotte Corday. She stabbed Marat, then put the letter in his hand, so that everyone else would see it."

They regarded the painting for another moment, waiting for the onlookers to disperse. Once they were alone, Vasylenko spoke in a low voice, his eyes still on the canvas. "It will be a few days. A week at most."

"You've told me that before," Lermontov said. "I've been waiting for a long time."

"I know. It has been a difficult year. But final preparations are under way. We'll be in touch with you soon." Detaching himself from the crowd, Vasylenko turned and disappeared into an adjoining gallery. Lermontov lingered for a minute longer, then left the museum as well.

His car was parked a block away. On the backseat, a newspaper had been turned to an article about a Sotheby's auction that had generated less than half of its presale estimate. As his driver pulled into the street, Lermontov glanced at the headline. It had been a good time to get out of the art game. He almost felt sorry for Reynard, who had thought himself so clever by cutting his little deal, when he would have been better off liquidating the fund then and there.

Tossing the paper aside, he looked out the window. With each passing day, London felt more like Reykjavik. Vasylenko's face, which seemed to grow more careworn whenever Lermontov saw it, told the whole dismal story. Russia, for its part, was having problems of its own, which had delayed his return. In the meantime, he had been obliged to occupy himself as best as he could.

They arrived at his rented home, an elegant deconversion in Fulham. The car pulled up to the curb, dropping off its solitary passenger, then drove around to the coach house at the rear. Lermontov mounted the steps, his head lowered against the damp, passing between the alabaster lions. Then he paused.

On the door of the house, at the level of his eyes, had been painted a single red cross.

He turned around at once. A row of gray houses stood across the road, their windows vacant and dead. He stood there for a long moment, warily scanning the deserted street, then unlocked the door and went inside.

Entering the foyer, he closed the door quietly. In the darkness, he could make out the outlines of the sitting room, which was nearly bare. On his arrival, he had not anticipated how long he would be stranded here, so he had not bothered to furnish the house in the style to which he was accustomed.

Pulling aside a leather curtain, he passed into the drawing room, going immediately to an unusual frame that was hanging from one of the walls. It was a double frame with a sliding panel, now closed, made of burnished pine. Inserting his fingers into a hidden recess, he drew the panel open.

Before he could properly regard the canvas on the other side, something made him turn sharply around. A man was seated in the shadows at the far end of the room, a gun in one gloved hand.

"Hello, Lermontov," Ilya said softly. He held up the revolver. "You recognize it?"

Lermontov said nothing. There was a pistol in the drawer of his desk. Before he could move, however, Ilya switched on the lamp beside him, revealing the end table next to the armchair. On the table, in the opalescent circle cast by the lamp, lay the pistol, wrapped in a white handkerchief.

Lowering his hands to his sides, Lermontov took in the Scythian. He was thinner than in his most recent photos, his face pale and tense. The hand that held the gun was steady, however, and when Lermontov searched for signs of weakness, he saw none. "How did you find me?"

Ilya gestured toward the painting on the wall. "*The Origin of the World*. It was the only painting that you took with you, and we both know that it has always been displayed behind a panel or screen. When I heard that a double frame of the proper dimensions had been commissioned from the House of Heydenryk, it wasn't hard to determine where you were."

Lermontov almost smiled at this. "Affectations can be dangerous. And Vasylenko?"

"They're raiding his club now. He'll be tried and convicted, as he should be." Ilya's tone was detached, as if he were describing an event that had nothing to do with either of them. "Such a man doesn't deserve a *vor*'s death. That's why I'm content to leave him to the police."

Ilya leveled his gun at Lermontov. "But your case is different. Relations with Russia are delicate these days. A trial would be an embarrassment for all concerned, so it's likely that a deal will be made. You're still a useful man to the Chekists. There's plenty of art in their coffers that could finance their activities, given your expertise. The cycle of murder will continue. And that's something I can't allow."

There was a long pause. Lermontov saw that the man in the shadows showed no sign of wavering. At last, he sighed. "I see. You're right, of course. There's no other way." He indicated the room around them. "Here?"

In response, Ilya only stood. Lermontov turned to face the wall, then lowered himself slowly to his knees, his eye on the painting. His pulse was steady. Behind him, he heard footsteps as Ilya came closer.

"The double frame," Lermontov said abruptly. "That wasn't your own idea, was it?"

"No," Ilya said. There was a rustle as he withdrew a piece of paper from his pocket. Then, standing over the gallerist's shoulder, he held the page before Lermontov. The note was only a few lines, written in a feminine hand. As he read the signature, Lermontov felt a smile cross his face. Then he closed his eyes.

Outside, from across the street, the house was peaceful and still. After a minute, the front door opened, revealing Ilya standing just inside. He shut the door, not bothering to lock it, then descended the steps of the porch.

A woman in a long dark coat was standing at the opposite curb. "Is it done?"

"Yes," Ilya said. Before reaching her, he halted, so that they stood a few feet apart. "You'll take care of the rest?"

She nodded. "I'll text the police with the address. It won't be traced back to us."

"Good," Ilya said. He found himself studying her face, which had changed since the night at the mansion. It was harder, sadder, with something unreadable in her eyes. That quality, which he had glimpsed briefly at the museum, was what had inspired him to contact her again. And yet, for all their hardness, they were not the eyes of a Scythian. "Is it what you hoped it would be?"

"No." She turned to face the house, which stood silently across the road. "It isn't."

Following her gaze, Ilya became aware of something heavy in his coat pocket. "You should be glad of that."

Maddy did not reply. Ilya was tempted to say something more, but instead, he headed up the block, alone. When he reached the corner, he looked back. She was standing at the curb, facing away from him. As she pulled the phone from her purse, he caught a glimpse of her profile, but only for a moment. Then he turned away again.

A short underground ride took him to the Thames. As he walked along the river, the wind pushing the hair back from his face, he stuffed his fists into his pockets and plowed onward, head bowed against the breeze. He had not been aware that he had a particular destination in mind, but as he pressed on, it gradually became clear to him where he was going.

In time, he reached the silvered arc of the bridge. When it first opened, he recalled, it had swayed alarmingly underfoot, contrary to all engineering calculations. What the designers had failed to anticipate was that when the bridge oscillated with foot traffic, the pedestrians, feeling the movement created by their own presence, would naturally sway in step, unconsciously worsening the resonance.

Today, the crowd on the bridge was minimal, with only a handful of tourists taking in the view. At the halfway point, when no one else was watching, Ilya slid the gun from his pocket and dropped it over the edge. It fell for a second, suspended in midair, then left a minor splash on the river's combed surface, which erased the ripples at once. Then he turned back the way he had come, walking out of step with the others, and headed alone into the city.

GLOSSARY OF FOREIGN WORDS

Blatnie pesni: A genre of music, associated with the Russian underworld, that chronicles the lives of criminals and thieves.

Bratva: Russian slang for "brotherhood." An alternative term for the Russian *mafiya*.

Chekist: An agent of Russian state security. The term originally referred to members of the Cheka, the Bolshevik secret police, but has since been extended to the KGB and its successors.

Keelyer: Russian slang for a professional assassin, derived from the English word *killer*.

Kukly: Russian, "puppets" or "dolls." Slang for bankrolls with real bills covering slips of blank paper.

Obshchak: A central monetary fund, to which all members of the *mafiya* contribute, used for financing criminal operations, paying bribes, and supporting imprisoned thieves and their families.

Suka: Russian, "bitch." A derogatory term that can refer to both males and females. In particular, a traitor or informant.

Tzaddik, pl. *tzaddikim*: Hebrew, "righteous one." According to the Talmud, one of thirty-six honorable men and women for whose sake God refrains from destroying the world.

Udachi: Russian, "Good luck."

Vor: Russian, "thief." A member of the *vory v zakone*, or brotherhood of thieves, a circle of powerful criminals within the Russian underworld.

Zhid: A derogatory term, equivalent to the English "yid," for a person of Jewish descent.

ACKNOWLEDGMENTS

Many thanks to David Halpern, my agent; to everyone at the Robbins Office, especially Kathy Robbins, Louise Quayle, and, above all, Ian King; to Jon Cassir and Matthew Snyder at CAA; to Mark Chait, Kara Welsh, and the rest of the team at New American Library; and to Azam Ahmed, Charles Ardai, John DeStefano, Alla Karagodin Holmes, Brian Kinyon, Katy Lederer, Kavitha Rajaram, Stanley Schmidt, and Stephanie Wu. Thanks as well to my entire family, especially my parents and brother; to all the Wongs; and to Wailin.

Turn the page for a special preview
of Alec Nevala-Lee's next novel,

CITY OF EXILES

Coming from Signet in December 2012.

Manuel was watching the man with the books. For most of the past week, he had waited outside this man's home and office, studying his habits and quiet routine, and by now, he thought, he had come to know him rather well. All the same, he still had trouble believing that this was the person he was supposed to kill.

Tonight, his target was dining at a restaurant near La Plaza de los Naranjos. Watching from the van across the street, Manuel could see the man in question, whom he generally thought of as the translator, seated at a table with his books and a glass of red wine. Next to him sat an attractive young woman, her head bowed over a book of her own, following along intently as the translator pointed to the page.

The van was parked before a whitewashed hotel. Behind the wheel, looking out at the restaurant, sat a pale, thin man in his twenties. Manuel did not know his name. "It would be easier to do it here."

Manuel shook his head. "No. Your employers may not have to live with these people, but I do. Are we clear?"

The pale man lifted the flap of his jacket, revealing the grip of a pistol. "We're clear."

"Good. And don't forget this." Opening the bag at his feet, Manuel pulled out a sawn-off shotgun, uncovering it just enough for the younger man to see. "Bring this to the Calle Lobatas. And when you get there—"

A few minutes later, the translator left the restaurant. Every night, as the other tables cleared, he spent an hour tutoring this girl, a waitress, in English. When the lesson was over, he accompanied her to the door, where they parted ways with a smile. As the translator headed off, the girl looked after him for a moment, then turned aside. Reading her dark eyes with ease, Manuel reflected that if he had been in the translator's place, he long since would have taken to walking her home.

From the glove compartment, Manuel removed a pint of rum in a paper bag, which he slid into his pocket as he climbed out of the van. Closing the door behind him, he waited as the pale man started the engine and pulled away. Once the van had rounded the corner, Manuel headed after the translator on foot. Under his coat, resting against the bottle, was his gun.

Manuel followed the translator into the labyrinth of streets to the north of the plaza, careful to keep well back. He was good at this sort of work, if somewhat slower than in his prime. As a young man, he had survived many bloody years in Marbella, but now he was almost fifty, the world had changed, and he was taking orders from a stranger less than half his age.

Beyond the plaza, the winding streets grew narrow, the balconies to either side heavy with flowers. Up ahead, the translator moved quickly along the sidewalk, little more than a shadow in the darkness. He was a slender man of medium height, his age hard to determine. As usual, he was neatly but unremarkably dressed, his brown suit simply cut, a leather satchel slung across one shoulder. His face was intelligent but nondescript, the kind that was easy to forget.

And then there were his books. Manuel knew that he worked as a translator for a firm on the Calle de Ricardo Solano, and could often be seen with books in both English and Spanish, as well as a third, unfamiliar language, perhaps Hebrew. Yet for all his close observation of the translator's unassuming life, he still had no idea why anyone would want this man dead.

Caught up in these thoughts, Manuel belatedly noticed that the translator had turned onto a different street than usual. He quickened his pace. If the target was taking another route home, it would upset his plans. For a second, he considered calling his partner, then decided to wait and see where the other man was going. From his pocket, he withdrew the rum, which would allow him to pose as a drunk, if necessary. Taking a careful swig, he spat it out, then continued into the night.

A short time later, some distance away, the pale man was waiting on the Calle Lobatas, in a doorway across from the villa where the translator lived. In his right hand, well out of sight, he held his pistol, and he stashed the shotgun nearby, tucking it into one of the heavy planters that lined the sidewalk.

As he lurked in the shadows, waiting for the translator to appear, he was startled by a noise at his side. His cell phone was ringing. Cursing softly, he pulled the phone from his pocket and checked the display. It was Manuel. Turning away from the street, he answered. "What is it?"

There was no response. He was about to speak again

when he felt something cold and hard press against his back. A voice came in his ear: "You should always turn the volume down."

The pale man did not move. Out of the corner of his eye, he saw the man behind him close the phone he was holding, put it away, and take something else from his pocket. It was Manuel's pint of rum. He tossed the bottle to the ground, where it shattered to pieces on the curb.

As the pale man closed his eyes, the other man took away his pistol and phone, then checked him for weapons. At last, he withdrew the gun. "Take a step forward and turn around."

The pale man obeyed. When he turned, he found himself facing the translator, who was holding Manuel's pistol. He had removed his shoes, and was standing in stocking feet. In his other hand, he held the phone. "If I were to check the call history, what would I find?"

"Nada," the pale man said. "We wouldn't be stupid enough to carry our real phones."

The translator seemed to grant this point. He slid the phone into his pocket. "Where are you from?"

"London," the pale man said. "But it doesn't matter. I could be from anywhere."

"I know." The translator raised the gun. "You were in a red van. Where is it?"

"Around the corner." The pale man jerked his head. "If you want it, it's yours."

"First, we're going for a ride." As he spoke, the translator reached over with his free hand and undid the flap of his satchel. The pale man watched with interest as the translator slid the pistol into the bag, still holding it, then motioned for him to go first. "Hands away from your body."

The pale man turned obligingly, his hands raised, then stepped onto the pavement, his eyes scanning the deserted street. Across from him stood the villa. The van was parked around the corner, just out of sight.

And up ahead, a few steps in the same direction, was the planter with the gun inside.

He went slowly forward. The planter was directly in front of him. As he walked on, straining to hear the translator's faint footsteps, his eyes remained fixed on that cluster of flowers. A single quick movement forward and down, and the gun would be in his hands. It would be easy.

Another step. Now the planter was within reach. It seemed to fill his entire field of vision. And he was just about to walk past it when, from overhead, there came the sound of a shutter being drawn back.

Behind him, the translator looked up at the woman who had appeared at the window of the villa. The pale man saw his chance. Falling to his knees, as if he had stumbled at the curb, he found himself eye to eye with the planter. His hand plunged into the flowers and closed at once on the shotgun's grip.

The translator had no time to draw his own gun. As the pale man brought the shotgun around in a flurry of leaves, shouting, the translator simply raised the hand in his satchel and fired, blowing a hole in the bottom of the bag.

Silence. The pale man looked down at the wound in

his chest, the gun tumbling from his fingers. For a second, he seemed inclined to retrieve it, but evidently decided that it wasn't worth the effort, and fell back against the whitewashed wall. Then he slid to the ground.

Coming forward, the translator kicked the shotgun away, then reached down and tore open the dying man's shirt, revealing a gout of arterial blood, which came in waves with each slowing heartbeat.

He looked into the pale man's face. His voice was a whisper. "Tell me who sent you."

The pale man only stared back. A moment later, the flow of blood slackened, then ceased altogether.

From above, voices were rising. Ignoring them, the translator checked the dead man's pockets, finding nothing but a set of keys, which he took. Then he parted the man's shirt more carefully. On the pale chest, through the blood, he could make out a tattoo. It had been etched in white ink, the lines translucent and raised, and depicted a bird, perhaps an eagle, with a pair of outstretched wings.

The translator studied the tattoo, memorizing it, then pulled the shirt shut again. From overhead, he heard more voices. He pocketed the keys, then headed up the block, leaving the pale man lying among the flowers.

Rounding the corner, the translator, whose name in another life had been Ilya Severin, and in darker times the Scythian, moved quickly through the shadows. He was angry with himself. At first, Marbella had seemed safe, but he should have known that it was still too close to home. He had grown careless. And it would not be enough to simply vanish once more.

He looked back over his shoulder at the villa, thinking

of the shelves of books he had collected over the past two years. It was a shame to leave them behind. The books were a part of him, in ways that few others would ever understand, and now he would never see them again.

But even as he disappeared into the darkness, he knew that there would be others.